Everything IS FINE

GILLIAN HARVEY

ORION

An Orion paperback

First published in Great Britain in 2020
by Orion Fiction
an imprint of The Orion Publishing Group Ltd
Carmelite House, 50 Victoria Embankment
London EC4Y 0DZ

An Hachette UK Company

1 3 5 7 9 10 8 6 4 2

A CIP catalogue record for this book is
available from the British Library.

ISBN (Mass Market Paperback) 978 1 4091 9186 5
ISBN (eBook) 978 1 4091 9187 2

Typeset at The Spartan Press Ltd,
Lymington, Hants

Printed and bound in Great Britain by Clays Ltd,
Elcograf S.p.A.

www.orionbooks.co.uk

For Ray, for everything

Chapter One

#bestmealoftheday
#protein
#healthyfats

The morning hadn't begun well.

For a start, the picture of poached eggs with salmon Jessica had posted on Instagram – #breakfastgoals – had drawn thirty-seven negative comments from an online fitness forum whose members had criticised both her choice of eggs (free range, but not organic) and the fact that she was eating salmon at all (#fishhavefeelings).

She hadn't the heart to tell her trolls that actually she wasn't eating *any* of it – in fact, she'd literally cooked it up so she could photograph it on her new mock-vintage plates and pretend she was living the life of Riley (if Riley was, as one of her trolls had termed her, 'cruel and thoughtless').

It had been fun at first when she'd started the diet and fitness blog and begun tweeting and posting snaps on Instagram. Being answerable to the ten or so followers she'd used to have (at least two of whom were her parents) had been a way to keep herself motivated.

Then, a year ago, when she'd met the muscle-bound gym-loving Dave, everything had changed. One picture of his ripped torso on Twitter and suddenly her blog had had more hits than Taylor Swift.

Dave was one of those people whose passions were infectious (he'd also given her chlamydia in the first month, but they were over that now) and she'd suddenly found herself pumping iron and posting the kind of selfies usually only taken by millionaires with buttock implants. The clicks on her blog had gone through the roof, and she'd even had a post-workout picture of her sweaty cleavage go viral.

But who can keep that level of commitment up long-term? she thought. After all, she was only human, and had eaten so many eggs in various guises recently that she'd forgotten what it was like to do a normal poo.

Scraping the poor, murdered salmon into the bin, she guiltily poured herself a generous bowl of her daughter Anna's choccy snap-snaps in its stead and sighed like an addict shooting up as the forbidden sugar hit her taste buds.

At first, this popularity thing had been great: thousands of people seemingly fascinated by the size of her bottom, or the fact that she had abs in a certain light. But what Twitter giveth, Twitter can also taketh away, she'd soon found. Hardcore fitness fans could be mean and would unfollow at the first sign of cellulite or minor menu mishap.

It wasn't as if she'd been *fat* in the first place. She'd lost the seven pounds she'd set out to shed when she'd started her blog and had already been back in a size 10 by the time Mr Sexy had swanned into her life. She'd intended to wind up the blog after meeting her goal. But once Dave had arrived on the scene, she'd found she couldn't – she was addicted.

Not addicted to the gym; she'd happily cosy up in her PJs most evenings, and felt a sense of rising panic when she woke on workout days. And definitely not to the clean-eating-inspired, protein-fuelled diet plan that she and Dave had come up with over a cup of decaf, bean-free coffee. But addicted to having the perfect man on her arm and feeling – for the first time in her life – popular.

She hadn't exactly been an ugly duckling as a kid, but her painful teenage shyness had placed her firmly in the unpopular category. At school, the only boy who'd ever shown an interest had had buck-teeth and a propensity to grind them against her own when they kissed. (Yes, kissed. When you're that low down in the social pecking-order, you take what you can get).

Even at uni, she'd never felt she fit in – perhaps one of the reasons she'd dropped out after two years. She could talk a good talk in a seminar, but when it came to social stuff, she was right back in the school playground. Sure, she'd had a boyfriend or two, but she'd never been brave enough to approach anyone popular or ostensibly good-looking. Instead, she'd tended to date misfits – the perfect face, finished off with enough teeth to furnish a whole village; a stonking great hooked nose; or a laugh that sounded like a donkey on speed.

Now she had Dave and a whole new body, she'd (accidentally) become an 'influencer' (as one monthly women's mag for the over-thirties had recently termed her). And the likes, retweets and followers she'd gained had given her the confidence boost she'd needed all her life.

What's more, her little business – a public relations enterprise that had been ticking on well enough with its four clients – had suddenly had a raft of enquiries from people who felt sure she could get them in the *Daily News*. She'd even taken on staff! Two people whose income and her abs were interlinked.

'Jessica Bradley seems to live a charmed life,' a journo had enthused in a recent write-up. 'Perfect body, successful business, charming home and dream boyfriend . . .'

'That's just it,' her best friend Bea had told her when Jessica had laughed at the article in disbelief. 'You're great at seeing the best in everyone, except when it comes to yourself.'

Problem was, Jessica thought, pouring a second helping into the bowl, living through her online image meant she could never relax, never let her guard down. Maintaining her following meant a lifetime of eating millet when she really wanted Maltesers; creating free-from recipes and posting them as #foodporn; and snapping inspirational workout pics to post on Instagram. Most of the time, it was worth it. But recently she'd felt as if she'd sell her soul for a Big Mac.

'I don't know why you bother,' her mum had said recently, sniffing at her date-sweetened, non-chocolate, low-fat brownie crispbreads. 'When I was your age, I was too busy bringing you up to plaster pictures of my supper all over the neighbourhood. And since when was sugar bad for you? It never did your father any harm.'

'It doesn't matter!' her brother had laughed when she'd recently confessed to him that she'd set the bar too high for herself. 'Just enjoy it! It's not as if anyone knows you properly anyway. You don't have to stick to all the fitness stuff in real life.'

'That's just it, Stu,' she'd groaned. 'People come to me expecting to meet *the* Jessica Bradley! I can't exactly sit there in a string vest covered in chip fat and let it all hang out.'

'Thanks for that image.'

'I can't even talk to Mum about it – she's started commenting on my blog now!'

'Take it down then!'

It was easy for him, though, wasn't it? Mum and Dad's first-born and firm favourite. Straight As at A level, university degree, well-paid job and barely a tweet in sight. Whereas she'd been a dropout with a kitchen-table start-up until her bone-broth and date doughnuts, teamed with candid shots of Dave's bod, had caught the eye of the masses. Now her firm was turning over five times the revenue it had a year ago and it all pivoted on her accidental fake lifestyle.

'Hi, Mum.' Anna sloped sleepily into the room, eyes half shut. 'Hey!' she added, suddenly animated with indignation at the sight of Jessica shovelling down the choccy snap-snaps. 'They're mine!'

'Don't worry, there's loads left.' Jessica slid another bowl across the table.

'It's not the point! If you keep eating them, what am I meant to have for breakfast? The one thing that's meant to be just for me!'

'Sorry – look. Here you go.'

'Nah, thought I'd have toast today,' came the response.

As Jessica watched her daughter cut two wedges of bread and squash them into the toaster, it occurred to her that this little girl – on the cusp of her teenage years – was one of only two people in the world who knew that whilst Jessica might still retain the accolade of being 'one of the most influential fitness bloggers on WordPress' she had, in reality, morphed into a middle-aged fraud with a penchant for sugary children's cereals.

The other person in the know was Dave, who'd noticed the fact that the woman who'd once been huffing and puffing next to him on the treadmill six nights a week had gradually cut back on her activity levels. He'd also caught her a couple of times recently at the biscuit tin when she'd thought he was out and looked at her with such horror that she'd felt as if he'd seen her shooting up heroin.

'Carry on with the blog,' he'd told her, his brow furrowed with concern as he'd gently removed half a biscuit from her hand. 'But for God's sake, don't tell anyone about the Hob-Nobs. This can be our secret. And don't worry,' he'd added, like a sponsor soothing an off-the-wagon alcoholic. 'We'll get you back on track.'

What he didn't realise was the 'blip' he'd described her as having was actually not a blip at all. It was the original, slightly softer-edged, chocolate-loving, more relaxed Jessica Bradley re-emerging, like a chubby butterfly from a size-8 chrysalis.

But before she'd had a chance tell him that she actually quite liked the other, slightly less intense track that she'd slipped onto (after all, the food was better along this route), she'd had a big PR client approach her – Little Accidents, a feminine hygiene product. Suddenly her potential revenues had skyrocketed.

'We wanted someone with a great social-media presence,' Linda, the account manager had gushed. 'It's all about getting out there, don't you think? Getting the message out that if you're incontinent, then that's really OK. Even sexy!'

And as Jess had nodded her way to signing the biggest contract of her life, she'd realised that it wasn't Jessica Bradley PR they were signing with at all – it was Jessica Bradley, brand ambassador, retweeter extraordinaire, #fitspo, toned-stomached, Instagram queen. She was signing up to a life of tweeting pictures of her low-fat, low-calorie, low-sugar, low-flavour, mock-chocolate cake and having to eat the damn stuff too.

'I love your blog,' Linda had added as they'd shaken hands. 'Honestly, I don't know how you do it all!'

So here she was. Caught between two diets.

'Mum, is Dave taking me this morning?' Anna said as she sat down with her barely browned, butter-coated toast. Her light brown hair hung neatly against her shoulders;

she'd clearly got up early this morning to curl the ends. Jessica wondered, again, where her daughter had inherited her lovely hair – it certainly wasn't from her. Jessica's hair looked reasonable after a wash and blow-dry, but any style it was forced into would soon break down over the course of a day.

Anna's hair must be from her dad's side of the family, she thought, although it was hard to remember what Grahame's hair had been like before it had started to drop out.

'Not sure. Why?' she said.

'It's just, well, can he drop me round the corner from school this time? He's so *embarrassing*.'

'Anna! He is not embarrassing.' Although Jessica knew what her daughter meant. Recently, Dave had taken to wearing his gym gear outside of his circuit training classes. And she didn't want to be disingenuous – he had, after all, got a great body. But you had to be a special kind of bloke to get away with the bright yellow, budgie-smuggling Lycra leggings he'd started to favour. She'd even come home the other day to find a skintight onesie in a plastic bag on the bed.

The man didn't even own a bike.

'He is! He's totally embarrassing. He always wants to walk me right to the gate. Like I'm, what? Eleven or something!' Anna's face screwed up with distaste. After all, she hadn't been eleven for, like, nine months.

'OK,' Jess nodded, relieved Dave's apparent crime was just babying Anna rather than parading in his new 'ergonomic leggings' in front of her friends.

Where was he, anyway? He'd need to get a wriggle on if he wanted to get to the gym between the school run and work.

'Am I at Dad's this weekend?' Anna asked.

'Yeah, that OK?'

7

Anna nodded. 'Yeah, it's good.'

Jess struggled to keep the questions inside – did good mean better? Was Anna enjoying sipping vegan hot chocolate and wearing her hand-knitted slippers around Mr and Mrs Perfect's house? Playing with Forest and River, their adorable twins? It had been ten years since she and Grahame had broken up and she did wish him all the best – of course she did! She'd even forgiven Tabitha, his new wife, for her part in their split. But it would be nice if he could stop living such a perfect life. Nice if he screwed up occasionally. Just in a minor way. Just to make her feel a little bit better – the odd shameful skid mark on the otherwise unsullied Y-fronts of his perfect life.

'Good,' she said at last. Christ, was that the time? Where was Dave? 'Isn't it time to get going?' she added. 'Or at least get dressed? Dave will want to leave in a minute.'

'Oh, is he back?'

'What?'

'He popped out, so I thought, well, I don't exactly have to rush do I?'

'Popped out?'

'Yeah. I saw his car going this morning.' Anna said, taking a bite out of her toast.

'Oh.' Perhaps he'd popped out for milk. But they had plenty of milk. Jessica mentally checked: soya – yes, goat's – yes, oat – yes. They even had coconut water and something called 'nectar of wheat'.

Then she saw it. The note propped against the porridge oats on the kitchen counter. She walked over and casually picked it up, as if she'd always known it was there.

'What's that?' Anna asked, crunching her toast.

Jessica felt the same sensation in her stomach that she had

8

when she went too fast over a speed bump, or woke up the day after eating too much bran.

I'M SORRY, it said. IT'S OVER.

Shit.

'What is it, Mum?' asked Anna again.

'Oh, nothing,' she said, her mind whirring. Surely things hadn't been going badly? She'd have known, wouldn't she? Her eyes darted to the slight muffin top that had developed over the top of her skinniest jeans. Was it the weight? The fact that she'd been in top condition and now occasionally skipped her nightly sit-ups in favour of a Prosecco and *Poldark*?

She felt hot, salty tears welling in her eyes. Surely it couldn't be just down to her gym-dodging? Maybe he'd found someone else? Maybe those evenings she'd skipped the gym had opened up a window for a perfectly honed, freakishly fit gymbo to take her place; proving both her paranoia and – oddly – the evolutionary theories of Darwin right in the process.

Slipping out of the kitchen and into the loo, she washed her face and looked at her flushed complexion in the mirror.

'No,' she said. She wasn't going to let this happen.

Dave was the best thing in her life right now, and he couldn't just leave her! She'd just signed with Little Accidents. The phone was ringing off the hook. She was gaining about a hundred followers a day. Instagram – while a bit abusive – was raising her profile. And Dave with his bulging biceps was part of the deal. His muscly good looks; his dark, brooding eyes; his revealing mirror selfies from the gym changing room. It all helped. And, well, the sex wasn't bad either.

Plus, she loved him. Of course.

He was part of the structure of Jess Bradley enterprises, integral to her blog.

Gone.

She needed to fix it fast. And one thing was sure.

Nobody could know.

Chapter Two

'Mum, we're going to be late!' Anna moaned as they reversed out of the drive. 'And do you have to wear those giant sunglasses?'

'Yes, I do, actually,' Jessica snapped. She'd done the mum thing of swallowing her emotions and pasting on a smile, but she knew her eyes would be a giveaway. She couldn't turn up tearful on the school run or she'd attract nosy mums like a magnet. 'I've . . . my hay fever's flared up again.'

A decade ago, when Anna's dad Grahame had ditched Jessica for someone 'more on his level' (which had turned out to mean someone with a 36DD bust), Anna had been a toddler. Meaning Jessica could palm her off on the grandparents and wallow under her duvet (until her best mate Bea had used a mixture of coaxing and bullying to get her out of bed).

When the two-year-old Anna had noticed Jessica's red eyes on her return each day, she'd been interested rather than worried, poking her fat little fingers into them with fascination and peeling the lids open.

Jessica missed the days of probing fingers, however sticky. Much easier to deal with than probing questions.

'OK. Well, can you drop me—'

11

'Anna Bradley, I will drop you by the gate and watch you walk in. And when you're a mum, you will understand why!'

'But Mummmm! I'm twelve! Half my friends walk to school.'

This was, actually, true. Was she babying Anna too much? She'd wanted another baby after Anna was born, but then Grahame had said he couldn't commit to a second child right then because of a "work project" (which had turned out to be less of a business affair and more of a romantic one). He'd left shortly afterwards to set up a new life with a younger, more organic model. Now, due to her dodgy genetics, Jessica's ovaries were probably shrivelled up like raisins.

Mum was fond of graphically recounting how she'd gone through the menopause before forty, so Jessica was probably right on the cusp. 'One day I was having my monthlies, the next I'd dried up like a desert lagoon,' she'd told them over Christmas dinner one year. 'It was like someone had turned off the taps! Cranberry sauce, anyone?'

Unless Jessica was gifted a newborn by a kindly stork, Anna was destined to be babied for a good few years yet.

'Sorry,' Jessica said, in an uncharacteristic fit of honesty. 'I don't seem to be able to help it.'

Her daughter softened then. 'S'OK,' she said. 'I hate walking anyway.'

Jessica pulled up outside the school behind a triangular-looking Smart car and something that looked like a Land Rover but wasn't.

'Bye, then.' Anna grabbed her bag and gave her mother's arm a little rub.

'Hang on,' said Jessica, leaning over and giving her daughter a proper hug.

Anna squirmed a little in her embrace. 'Mummm!' she protested. 'People will see.'

12

'Sorry,' she said, with a *what can you do?* shrug as Anna got out of the car, red-faced.

She was just about to rev up and get the hell out of there before the last-minuters arrived and hemmed her in, when a cascade of glossy hair tumbled through the window. A woman, her horsey face perfectly made up, leaned in.

Jessica self-consciously tucked her dark-blonde hair behind her ears. She'd given it a cursory brush before setting off, but hadn't bothered with the straighteners. Being confronted with a barnet fit for a shampoo ad made her even more conscious that she wasn't looking her best. She had a beauty appointment before work, too, so hadn't bothered with make-up.

'Jessica!' the woman/horse said, in the kind of breathy, excited tone that people use when they've found a long-lost relative, or been given the gift of a lifetime. 'I thought it was you! Wow! Love the sunglasses! I didn't realise those giant frames were back in vogue!'

'Thanks.'

A manicured hoof thrust its way towards her and Jessica shook it briefly.

'I'm Liz – you know, Jasper's mum?'

Jasper was a malnourished-looking boy in Anna's class. He and Anna had played together briefly as toddlers.

'Oh, yes. How are you?' Jessica smiled, painfully aware that she was due at a salon to trial one of the latest trends in facials for an on-blog advertorial.

'Yes, yes. Fine.' Liz waved her hand dismissively as if she was never anything else. 'I just wanted to say, it's been *ages* since we caught up.'

'Yes.' *Because we developed an intense dislike for one another after you told me that Anna was a bad influence.*

It had almost been a decade ago, but Jessica had never

13

quite forgiven Liz for suggesting that Jasper's new-found love of the word *boobies* must have come from the then three-year-old Anna. It had been true, mind . . . but still.

'Anyway, I'm organising another of these quiz nights,' the hand waved again. 'You know, raising funds for the school, blah blah blah. And then I thought – why am I writing these questions when I know a professional *writer*. I've read your blog, of course. And I thought, who better to write the questions and – um – maybe get a bit more *interest* in it all, you know, than the famous Jessica Bradley! As featured in *Fit Woman* magazine,' she whinnied, using her fingers to make virtual quotation marks.

'Well . . .' The last thing Jessica wanted to do was add something else to her workload.

'Of course, if you're too busy . . . It's just that, we're so hoping for the new minibus this year . . .'

Jessica felt a sudden rush of guilt. Would it really hurt her to write a few questions for a quiz? She could probably do it in her sleep. And this was Anna's school; potentially Anna's minibus. Anna was always moaning that Jessica never turned up for anything except parents' evening (which apparently 'doesn't count').

The main drawback was that it would mean working with Liz – one of those perfect mothers whose involvement in everything and seemingly endless enthusiasm left Jessica feeling like a complete parental failure.

'Of course. Of course. I mean, I can't stop now. I'm . . . uh, having a facial. But I'll give you my number,' Jessica found herself saying. Perhaps she ought to offer Liz a job. When she failed to raise a client's profile, Liz could gallop in and make potential customers feel guilty enough to buy anything.

'No need. Got your email,' Liz winked conspiratorially. '*Website*,' she mouthed.

A car beeped behind. In the rear-view mirror of her Citroën, Jess could see a vehicle that was either a minibus or a small lorry. Either way, she was quite grateful for the excuse to get away. 'Well, speak soon!' she said revving the engine slightly.

Liz straightened herself and shook her glossy mane into place. 'Yes, looking forward to it!'

Jessica put the car into first and started towards the city centre.

'One of the benefits of blogging,' she'd said to her new PA, Candice, last week when the email had arrived offering her the treatment, 'is the freebies.' A salon, a new ultra-modern place and part of a national chain, had offered her a trial of their new skin-rejuvenating 'LifeForce' facial in return for an 'honest' online review.

Since the Dave-effect had netted her a fantastic following, Jessica had been gifted everything from gym shoes to bleach-your-own-bumhole kits. People were approaching her with offers of paid-for posts, and she was showered with freebies every morning in the mail.

Some opportunities she'd turned down – the DIY dentistry kit; the puréed fish eye plan; a build-your-own luxury coffin workshop. Others, she'd taken up either because the product was desirable or, like this one, because it would drive a lot of traffic to her site. And traffic, as she now knew, was more important than all her training, experience and bulging contacts book combined.

'Their website gets over a hundred thousand hits per month,' Candice had trilled across the room. 'First page of Google. Could be good for business.'

Good for business. Candice had only been at the firm for a

week and a half, and was barely into her twenties. But that meant, of course, that she was representative of the younger generation; she had a finger on the pulse.

When Jessica was younger there had been a natural progression to most people's careers. You'd start at a lowly position and work your way up, gaining experience and expertise. Younger staff would look at those more senior as mentors and educators. Now, women of her generation were getting out of date – like a forgotten pack of ham at the back of the fridge. You missed an online trend and it was over.

Rather than hide in the shadows, she'd taken some steps to raise her own profile – pimping up her Twitter account and linking it to her public relations page. 'The more followers you can get personally, the better,' one of her peers had confided at a training day. 'People like to know who they're dealing with. Start a blog, maybe? Get yourself on Instagram with some cute pictures.'

Social media meant that clients expected a lot more from her too: local, tinpot firms wanted to be featured in *Vogue*; the pig farmer around the corner had asked her if she could get him into the *Telegraph*. The internet had increased reach, but also increased expectations. People wanted everyone to know about their business and to create the right image, the right brand. The bubble continued to inflate with no sign of bursting.

As she pulled into the car park, she saw her face briefly reflected in the salon's mirrored window. A little white disc, her eyebags visible even from this distance. Since employing Candice, Jessica had become painfully aware that she didn't look quite as young as she'd optimistically convinced herself she did. It was hard not to notice the cracks and crevices in her skin when confronted with her employee's annoyingly smooth complexion every morning.

'Anti-ageing,' she said quietly to herself, remembering some of the claims for the facial. At least this afternoon she was going to look hot. She tried to forget about Dave and think instead of how fabulous she'd feel when the promised ten years had been knocked off.

She took the obligatory (heavily-filtered) selfie outside the salon, making sure the signage was clearly displayed, and quickly popped it onto her social-media feed – #beautytreatment #antiageing #thisisthelife #soexcited – then stepped inside.

'Hello, it's Jessica, right?' a perky, red-haired woman smiled at her from reception as she entered. 'Let me just get Lucy to pop down and show you where to go.'

'Thank you.' Jessica perched herself on one of the salon's waiting chairs and eyed the pile of magazines and brochures scattered on a nearby table. One showed a woman, completely naked, but sitting in a kind of half-Buddha style that meant all the rude bits were hidden in a complicated tangle of hair-free arms and legs.

Jessica remembered a time when women were allowed to have body hair. When pubes were only frowned upon if they escaped round the edge of your bikini bottoms like curious infants peeking from behind their mother's skirt. It had been a simpler time.

Hairier, but simpler.

These days, instead of pubic hair, most women's nether regions went through a wax-and-growth cycle that Shakespeare – had he been around – might have termed the Seven Stages of Fan: just-waxed rash, post-wax vag-pox, smooth and nude, sandpaper prickles, designer stubble, soft and fluffy, and, finally, rampant overgrowth. And round the cycle went. Perhaps, Jessica thought as she studied the the price list on the wall, that's what people meant by the circular economy.

Before she even had time to pick up a magazine, a door opened and a young woman with cropped blonde hair, wearing what appeared to be a lab coat stepped through it.

'Hi, Jessica!' she gushed, shaking Jessica's hand enthusiastically. 'I'm Lucy. Lovely to meet you at last! Love the blog – so honest!'

'Thank you.'

'If you just want to come through,' she said, gesturing to a door on their left. Inside the room, everything was light, bright and brand new. A leather treatment table sat in the corner, and the air was heavy with the scent of lavender oil.

Jessica felt herself begin to relax. This was just what she needed.

After settling her into the chair, Lucy began to apply a cool liquid to Jessica's face. 'You know, not many people wanted to come and try this facial,' she said, her fingers working the liquid into Jessica's skin quite forcefully. 'But it really does have amazing results.'

'Really?' Jessica closed her eyes and began to enjoy the sensation of Lucy's fingers working into her skin with quick, firm movements. The serum had a familiar smell – odd, but not unpleasant.

'Yeah. I suppose they just thought it was a bit gross,' Lucy continued, pouring a generous measure of the serum into her palm, before rubbing her hands together. 'Whoops. Sorry. Dripped a bit on you there,' she said, reaching for a tissue and dabbing Jessica's jumper.

'That's OK.' Jessica relaxed as Lucy began again on the serum. 'They thought it was gross, you say? Why?' It certainly seemed a fairly normal facial so far. Was she going to be required to strip naked and have the serum rubbed over the rest of her body? Or was there a horrible product to apply afterwards?

'Yeah, you know. The semen.'

'The serum?'

'No, semen. Bull semen.'

'Bull, what?'

Lucy slapped her palms together again. 'Yeah, it's meant to be rejuvenating. It's all organic and that.'

'Bull semen?'

'Oh, shit, sorry. Got some in your hair.' Out came the tissue again.

'Sorry. This is bull semen?'

'Yeah. It's great for the skin. Some women use their own partner's, but apparently bull semen has more antioxidants.'

Jessica closed her lips as some of the serum ran across her mouth. 'Mm hmmm,' she said. Then 'I just didn't realise . . . ?'

'Oh, sorry. That's probably why you said yes, right?' Lucy smiled. 'But honestly, it's worth it.'

'Right, good.'

'And it's all hand-sourced – from field to face.'

'Great.'

'And we refrigerate it, so like it's fresh and everything.'

'Right.' Because what else could you say?

'OK, that's you done,' smiled Lucy. 'I'll just leave it on for a few minutes to let your skin really absorb the nutrients.'

And she left the room, leaving Jessica to relax to a CD of natural countryside sounds before returning, rubbing off the excess with a warm facecloth and posing with Jessica for a thumbs-up after-shot.

Loved my #LifeForce Facial! #rejuvenating #natural #farmfresh #cuttingedge #freerange #odourfree

Four face-scrubs later, Jessica could still smell a faint whiff of bull jizz on her skin.

Driving back, she called the office from her hands-free, hoping to get her mind off it.

'Star PR, Candice speaking!'

'Hi, Candice, it's Jessica.'

'Oh hiya! How's it going?'

'Erm, fine thanks. On my way back. Just wanted to know if there were any messages.'

'One from Hugo. He said he'd try your mobile.'

'OK.'

'Yeah, it was weird. He rang back twice after that, but hung up both times when I answered.'

'I put my phone on divert to the office while I was in the salon. Sorry, should have said.' Jessica imagined Hugo – not the most technically minded of clients – repeatedly dialling her mobile and finding her office at the end of the line. 'Look, I'll be there in ten minutes. If he calls again tell him I'll ring him right back,' she said, although in all honesty she wasn't sure if she was up to a dose of Hugo.

'OK, see you then! Oh, and Jessica?'

'Yes?'

'How was the appointment?'

Did Jessica detect a hint of a giggle there? 'Oh, fine,' she breezed.

'Skin looking good?'

Jessica glanced briefly in the rear-view mirror. Her reddened face looked back at her.

'Well, very, er, clean.'

'Right.'

'Candice?'

'Yeah?'

'Did you know what a LifeForce Facial involved when you booked me in?'

There was a silence. 'Line's breaking up' Candice replied after a suspicious pause. 'Sorry – what did you say?'

'OK, well, see you in a minute.'

'OK. I'll get you a coffee, shall I?' Evidently, the technical problem had resolved itself.

'Oh, OK.' This was a new level of efficiency for Candice. 'Do you want . . . want some milk in it?'

Chapter Three

Jessica applied a little powder to her rather inflamed skin before leaving the car, then adopted the kind of poise she imagined a CEO ought to have. *Head high, Jessica*, as her mum used to say whenever she'd got nervous as a child.

When she entered the office, Candice was sitting at her desk, typing furiously; Natalie was finishing a phone call, her face animated.

'Hi, ladies!' Jessica said, in greeting, trying to keep her voice upbeat. 'Got a couple of goody bags for you!' She placed the bags handed to her by the salon (no sperm included) by the coat stand before hot footing it to her desk and sliding her sunglasses off.

'Hi, Jessica!' breezed Natalie, her assistant, hanging up her phone and giving her a wave. 'Thanks for that! And love your sunglasses! So retro!' She stopped, and screwed her eyes up slightly. 'Oh! Have you been crying?'

The answer, of course, was yes, that she'd bawled her eyes out earlier when her boyfriend had dumped her by Post-it. But that was unlikely to be the reason for her now red skin.

'No, just had a facial,' she said, trying to smile but feeling her skin ache.

'Ooh, you do look ... *fresh* ...' Natalie's smile froze slightly as she looked more closely at her boss's skin. 'Was it one of those vampire ones?'

'Vampire?' It seemed the world of beauty was getting a whole lot more dangerous.

'Yeah, you know. They scratch up your face and then inject some serum made from your blood . . .'

'Ooh, no!' Jessica screwed up her face (at great personal cost) and shook her head. 'No, I don't fancy that at all – too squeamish.'

'Oh. Great for ageing, though. I read an article that called vampires "the secret to eternal youth",' Natalie added, helpfully. 'So what did ya get? Microdermabrasion?'

'No, it was a . . . LifeForce facial.'

'Oh. So what's one of those?'

'Just some sort of, erm. Serum stuff. You know.'

'Right.' Natalie's attention turned back to her phone. 'Oh, I'd better take this – but you look great!' she lied, giving her boss the thumbs-up. She pressed the phone to her ear – no mean feat with her erratic curls.

'Serum, eh,' said Candice, plonking down a black double-decaf, root-roasted clean non-coffee coffee onto Jessica's Michael Bublé coaster. 'Never heard it called that before!'

'So you did know . . . um, about the *special ingredient*?'

'The sperm? Well, yeah. I read up on it. But I'd already said yes and, like, I thought . . .' Candice trailed off, her cheeks flushing.

Jessica was being ridiculous, she realised. It wasn't as if she'd been assaulted in a farmyard. This was, after all, a Genuine Beauty Phenomenon.

'Oh, don't worry. I'm all for trying new things!' she tried to breeze.

'Yeah,' replied Candice, obviously relieved. She looked at Jessica, her blue eyes as innocent and wide as a Disney character's. 'Plus they did say it was the elixir of youth,' she added, with an apologetic smile.

Elixir of youth? Elixir of hoof, more like.

She'd have to find a way to make it seem palatable, though, in the write-up. She looked at her face, still clearly red even when reflected in her computer screen. Good thing she'd taken an 'after' shot before she'd gone to town with a Brillo pad. Because it would have to be a positive review if she wanted the freebies to keep rolling in.

'So you said Hugo had called?' she ventured, changing the subject.

Hugh was a designer and artist who'd looked so promising when she'd taken him on a few years ago, but had promptly turned from an upbeat watercolour painter and model-maker into a brooding sculptor creating classics such as *Death in a Restaurant* and *Dead Man in Street* – a far cry from the delicate models and gentle watercolours he'd been producing when she'd seen his initial promise.

Jessica knew that she probably ought to ditch him as a client if she no longer believed in his work, but something made her hang on. Thoughts of his initial promise, perhaps? Or some sort of loyalty that he'd been prepared to let her represent him when she was a one-woman band with barely any experience?

With a heavy heart, and a fishy smell wafting towards her nostrils whenever she moved, Jessica dialled.

'Hugo speaking.'

'Hi, Hugo, it's Jess,'

'Hi, Jess!' he cried, with uncharacteristic cheerfulness. 'I'm so glad you've called . . .'

'OK . . .' She braced herself for what was coming next. The only time Hugo sounded upbeat in the last six months had been when he'd called her mobile – blind drunk – at 3 a.m. to tell her he'd had a breakthrough. 'Empty toilet rolls!' he'd exclaimed. 'Just think: an everyday item, but I think (and don't tell anyone) they could be used to make models! Jessica, it's a revolution!'

'I wanted to ask if we can meet up next week sometime? I'd like to discuss my work.'

'Right, no problem. In what way?'

'Sorry?'

'I mean, what thoughts did you have?' she said.

'Well, to be honest, I've moved the work in a different direction. I think my dark phase is drawing to an end. Jess,' he paused dramatically, 'I've had an epiphany!'

'You have?'

'Yes! Oil paints! I've never realised before how, well, how versatile they are. I mean, the other day I, well, I won't go on. But I really do feel excited about my latest work. You know the competition – the Independent Artists' Award?'

Jessica had emailed Hugo a link about a competition recently. It was a small award with a bursary and some gallery space awarded to the winning artist. 'Yes, you were thinking of entering *Drowning Man on Fire*, weren't you?'

She remembered the day when he'd called her over to see his new work two years ago. She'd been quite excited. She'd always loved his soft watercolours, simple charcoal sketches and occasional sculptures of birds.

But when he'd whipped off the black cloth covering his new work, what had confronted her was the head of a man fashioned from clay, his tongue lolling and some sort of rubber 'water' dripping from his hair. The rest of the man's figure had been engulfed in copper flames, leaving only the ghastly head visible.

When Hugo asked if she approved, she'd been so shocked that she'd said yes. (Although she had enquired later whether – in an unconnected way – he'd had any hard knocks to the head recently.)

'I'm so glad,' he'd said, grabbing her hand in his and tearing up slightly. 'I am so, so glad.'

Another lie she was trapped in, she realised.

'Anyway, Mathilda, you know, the woman from next door?' Hugo continued. 'Well, she came over and gave me some oil paints – someone had given them to her as a gift and she didn't want them. So I thanked her . . . but didn't think anything of it. I mean, I always thought oil was such an *old-fashioned* medium – far too clunky for anything truly beautiful.'

'Yes?'

'But in the middle of the night . . . Jessica, I was inspired! I leapt up and began sketching, naked as a baby. And, well, the result is just . . .' he trailed off, too dazzled by his own talent to finish the sentence.

'That sounds great.'

'Anyway, I rejigged the entry form and dropped it off this morning.'

'You have?' Jessica felt her heart sink. 'Already?'

'Yes! And I really feel that this could be an exciting time for us all!'

'Well, that's great.'

It was hard not to be a little infected by his enthusiasm.

Just spoke to @ArtyHugo #HugoHenderson about his new direction. #sotalented @IndependentArtists

'Was that really Hugo?' Candice said, turning around from her screen, brow furrowed.

'Yes.'

'But . . . you're smiling!'

'Yes. He seemed, well, happy!'

'Has he finally finished *Death in an Office*?'

26

'No, apparently, he's moving into a more colourful phase now: oil paintings.'

'Oh, that's good. I mean, well, I know how enthusiastic you were about his sculptures, but art's so, so . . . individual, isn't it, when it comes to taste?'

'Yep.'

'Just when you think you know someone, eh. You just never know what's going to happen next!'

'Yes,' replied Jess, more flatly now, thinking of Dave's note. 'People are full of surprises.'

She'd call him, she thought. She needed him home.

Fit at 30

REVIEW:
Style and Style, LifeForce Facial

If there is ever an elixir of youth, it makes sense that it comes from a life-giving product. So when I heard that the LifeForce facial used bull sperm (hand-sourced) to enrich the skin and stimulate repair and rejuvenation, I thought I'd give it a try.

The semen was cool and rather refreshing, and after a facial massage, I was left to absorb all the nutrients from this rather unusual beauty product for twenty minutes.

At the end of the process, the remaining semen was removed with a damp cloth, but my therapist Lucy told me that it was better not to wash the skin for twenty-four hours to benefit from the full results.

As the semen is refrigerated, there is no smell. And two days later, I must admit my skin feels fresh, taut and more youthful than it did before.

I'd thoroughly recommend it! 10/10

COMMENTS

Anonymous:
Thanks for this review. It's really great to read that the treatment doesn't smell – I was worried about that. I've booked myself in for next week – wish me luck! Steph.

Mrs B.

I usually love reading your online diary, Jessica. But this is in rather poor taste. Is it appropriate to be writing about such private things on the internet? Anyway, I thought I'd ask about next week – is it OK to bring profiteroles? Or are you going to make one of your special desserts? Your father wanted me to ask whether you'd mind avoiding prunes this time – they do tend to make him a little gassy I'm afraid. Let me know. Mum.

Gail

Hi Jess! Just found the blog and love the tips on healthy living! Am going to try the vegan brownies recipe. Not sure about the above though 😬 Maybe one day!!!! Lol.

Chapter Four

'I'm home!' she cried, as she walked through the door. Before she remembered that there was no one there to hear her.

Grabbing her phone from her pocket, she dialled Dave's number again. And was rewarded – again – with the sound of his answerphone. 'Hi, it's Dave. If you can't get me, I'm probably at the gym.'

'Hi, Dave,' she said, trying not to sound annoyed. 'Can you call me when you get this? About, well, obviously, it's about the note. I . . .' she caught a glimpse of herself in the mirror – dirty hair, hastily pinned back with strands escaping and framing her still-red face like spider legs. 'I think we need to talk about it, don't you?'

She checked Dave's social media but there was nothing unusual there. Earlier, he'd uploaded a mirror selfie from the changing room wearing his favourite, red workout thong, leg up on a bench. Nothing out of the ordinary. #gluteousmaximus

She automatically flicked on the coffee maker (bean to cup, with milk frother) and made a half-hearted, low-fat, soy cappuccino with cinnamon top. And a black de-beaned coffee, for good measure. Placing the pair on the table, she took a quick slurp of the cappuccino, then rummaged in the cupboard for a couple of cookies, one of which she crumbled artistically onto the saucers. Then she whipped out her phone to take a snap. 'Chilling with OH over a caffeine-free fix, with home-made, non-sugar oat-cookies,' she typed. '#goodtimes #soymilk #beantocup #fitness #relaxation.'

It hit her then how much had changed: yesterday she'd have written at least six more hashtags. But today she was really struggling.

And she might have even baked the cookies rather than faking out with a pack of Anna's favourites – full of sugar and not an oat in sight.

#heartbroken

'Loving my new bean-to-cup coffee machine,' she tweeted for good measure. 'First one I've found that froths #soymilk properly.'

The machine had been a blogging perk – she got to keep it, provided she waxed lyrical about it on social media from time to time.

Just as she finished the hashtag, the phone rang and her screen was flooded with a picture of Dave – one she'd taken on their holiday last year, lying on the beach in tiny trunks. Those tight little swimming pants had driven her almost mad with desire at the time. 'They're a specialist brand,' he'd told her, 'designed to *lift and sculpt* the glutes.' What he'd failed to mention was the significant amount of padding around the crotch area, which she'd noticed when she'd hung them on the line. (Although it had explained why, when someone's frisbee had hit him in the groin earlier that day and bounced into the sea, he'd barely broken his stride).

'Hello?' she said, feeling nervous.

'Jess,' he said. 'You called?'

As if he had no idea what it was about! 'Yes, about your note.' Tears pricked her eyes and she blinked, annoyed with herself.

'I tried to tell you, you know? But you always had your head in the computer.'

'What? Tell me what?'

'Come on, you can't seriously think it's been going well?'

'It was going . . . OK . . .' she trailed off.

'Face it, Jess. You're not interested in me any more.'

'I . . .'

'You used me as a personal trainer . . . a . . . a . . . *gym gigolo!* Now you're off exercise, it's like we never spend any time together. I mean, when's the last time you asked me something when you didn't need the answer for your blog?'

'But the blog is—'

'I tried to get your attention. I bought sexy new outfits. But nothing! You've changed! You're comfort eating – tempting . . . tempting me with carbs. Do you know,' his voice went slightly squeaky and she realised he must be close to tears. 'Do you know how *hard* it is for me to have mashed potato paraded in front of my face after everything I've been through?'

'I didn't exactly—'

'And *bread!*' he squeaked. '*Bread, Jessica, BREAD!*'

'I'm . . . sorry.'

'What has happened? Where has my gym Jessica gone?'

'Hey! I'm still me!' She wasn't exactly a couch potato, let alone a mashed one. She still tried to keep as healthy as possible. And surely there was more to their relationship than comparing biceps and urging each other on. 'Just come home and we can sort it out!' She heard her voice – and it wasn't the voice of a *'successful businesswoman on an upward curve'*.

'I can't, Jess. I guess I'm on a journey and it's like you're no longer part of it.'

'But—'

'And, you know. It's not like we fit together, is it?'

'What?'

'Well, I didn't want to say anything, but you know . . . You're looking a bit . . .'

'What?' Her tone was harder, daring him to say it.

'You've got a bit, you know. Fat.'

His face disappeared from the screen as she hung up.

Before she put the phone down she noticed a new glut of notifications on her Instagram icon. Twenty-four new followers since lunchtime.

Once that would have made her happy.

Fat? She looked at her midriff feeling horrified. She'd noticed some of her outfits getting a little bit tighter, but she was still in her size 10s.

Her midriff looked back at her accusingly. *You've neglected me!* it seemed to say. Perhaps Dave was right? He made all the effort and she'd done nothing to keep him interested.

Before Jessica could decide how to react, the sound of Anna's key in the lock sent her scampering to sweep up the forbidden crumbs before she was exposed as a biscuit snaffler.

Fat, she thought again, this time a bit more defensively as Anna busied herself in the hallway. She'd put on half a stone at most. If that was really enough to put him off, then she was better off without him. Wasn't she?

Grahame had at least had the common decency to ditch her for someone else. Being dumped was hard enough, but having a partner who'd had his head turned by someone with a 'large intellect' (as he'd put it) was one thing. How was she meant to feel when someone left her for no one? When someone was literally saying that she wasn't even better than nothing?

Plus, at least Grahame had had the guts to tell her to her face. Cooking her a meal for when she got home from work, and even waiting until Anna was snoozing to drop the bombshell and zoom off in his Audi. 'It's just not working,' he'd said. 'And, Jess, I've met someone else.'

The rest of the evening was a bit of a blur. Her lasting memory was of him ducking out of the front door, covered in spag bol.

She picked up the phone to ring Bea but put it down again. Her best friend hadn't been very happy with her last time they'd spoken. 'You never ring me any more!' she'd complained. 'You're on Facebook all the time, but you never seem to get my messages.'

Jessica and Bea had been friends since the age of eight and had always shared everything. But she could see now how much she'd allowed herself to drift away a bit in recent months – what with the gym, her business and Dave, there hadn't been much time.

She could hardly contact her now, could she?

By the time Anna entered the kitchen, Jessica was sitting at the table, innocently sipping her (pretty disgusting) cinnamon-topped drink, slightly flushed from a mixture of guilt and exertion after her rushed cookie crumb-cleaning attempt (the way she'd probably looked as a teenager when Mum burst in her bedroom and Jack – her then boyfriend – had just dived into the wardrobe).

'Hi, love,' she said, trying to look normal.

'Hi.' Anna narrowed her eyes suspiciously. 'What's going on?'

'What do you mean?' Did she look upset after the phone call? She'd teared up a bit, but was pretty sure her mascara was in place.

'For starters, you didn't ask me how I got home.'

'I know how you got home!' she said defensively. 'Jenny's mum – I organised it earlier?' Jenny was Anna's sometime best friend – they'd stay behind for drama club and their mums would alternate lifts.

'No. I walked – Jenny's mum couldn't take us after all. And Jenny's *allowed*!'

Suddenly, Jessica felt indignantly alert. 'Why didn't you call me?'

'I didn't have my phone, remember? You said I couldn't take it to school.'

It was true. So many teenagers getting addicted to social media these days. 'But you should have asked the office or something.'

'Anyway, you're always busy,' Anna sniffed.

It was true. She'd probably have been bogged down on Instagram. 'That's not the point, Anna. You know how I feel about you walking home.'

Anna's lip trembled slightly – a younger, more fragile child breaking through for a moment. 'Yeah, well, you don't care about me,' she said.

'Oh, of course—'

'Hang on, have you been eating my cookies?' her daughter interrupted, back in surly mode almost instantly.

'What do you mean?'

'Those crumbs,' she said, pointing to a pile that Jessica had missed. 'Are they my chocolate cookies?'

'Oh these! Well, yes – sorry.'

'Mum!' Anna rushed to the crumpled, empty packet like a mother to an injured child. 'They were the last ones! You know I always need chocolate after double maths!'

A couple of months ago, mid-diet, Jessica would have questioned the word 'need'. *Nobody 'needs' sugar, Anna. You'd be better off with a rice cake.* But after the day she'd had, her stomach grumbled in sympathy. 'Sorry,' she shrugged, trying to look nonchalant. She daren't tell her daughter that the biscuits had been crumbled, for photographic, fake lifestyle, clickbait Insta-snaps, and were now in the bin.

'Well, why didn't you have one of your millet things? You're always telling me that they give you more *good energy* or whatever.'

'Well . . . it's just—'

'I hate you! You pretend to be all fit and good and everything and you just nick all my stuff!'

'Hey. It was only two biscuits . . . and . . . and anyway,' said Jessica, seizing on an idea, 'it wasn't me; it was Dave!'

'Dave?'

'Yes.'

'And where's—'

'Gym.' At least that was probably true. 'He wanted to work off the calories.' The lies flowed more easily than they probably should have between mother and child.

'Why didn't you say anything to him?'

'I . . .' In for a penny, in for a pound, she thought. 'I came in and he was already munching them. Look at all those crumbs!' Jessica shook her head, feeling almost indignant. An hour and a half firming his buttocks every morning, and the man couldn't take five minutes to put his cookies on a plate.

She got up and went to the cupboard. 'Look, I've still got some of . . .' her hand hovered over a packet of date thins. #wholesome #guthealth #magicfibre

'No thanks.' Anna cocked her head to one side. 'Mum, are you sick or something?'

'No? Why?' Did she look sick? It was probably time for a spray tan – she'd been avoiding going back to her usual salon after a recent paper-knicker-tearing-while-bending-over incident – something she and Bea referred to as 'crackgate'.

'It just smells like you might have thrown up or, I dunno, eaten something fishy?'

'Oh, that. No, just – I just, um, spilled something.' Jessica rubbed the crispy white stain on her jumper self-consciously with her sleeve.

'Right. What's for tea?'

'Not sure. Takeaway?' she said, feeling suddenly simultaneously ravenous and reckless.

'Really? But you never eat takeaway!'

'Look,' Jessica said, slipping her arm around her daughter's back. 'I won't tell anyone if you don't.'

Before they left, she Instagrammed a picture of a salad she'd taken two weeks ago. 'Gotta love feta!' #healthychoice #fiveminnutemeal #spinach

Fuck Dave. Fuck that man and his stupid padded swimming trunks . . .

And his gym-honed biceps. And his ripped stomach. And his impossibly peach-like derrière. And his eyes, like pools of dark chocolate just waiting to be dived into . . . And his Twitter stat-boosting selfies . . . And his 2.1 million followers . . .

Second thoughts, she'd call him tomorrow.

Chapter Five

#freshlemonandginger #morningcleanse #fitnessfirst

Morning! For a great start to the day, squeeze quarter of a lemon into some hot water, and for an extra kick, add a little fresh ginger. Great for stimulating the senses and helping you get ready for anything!

Jessica snapped a quick picture of her barely tasted lemon and ginger and sighed. Opening up her laptop she saw her reflection hover briefly before the Windows logo kicked in and the machine booted itself into life. If only there were filters for reflections as well as photos, she thought, noticing a new depth to her eyebags, then she'd never have to face reality.

Before she could open her emails, there was a knock at the front door. She heard Anna's footsteps running down the stairs – the only time she ever ran – then the door being opened and the low tones of a delivery driver. Pulling her dressing gown more tightly around her waist, Jessica walked into the hall to see what had arrived.

Anna handed her a package. 'What is it, Mum?' she said.

'Not one for you, I'm afraid.' Jessica was often sent free samples and tester kits, and when she could she passed them on to Anna. Little eyeshadow pallets, hairbrush sets, perfume samples – Anna had a whole box of them in her room that she'd try out whenever a friend came over.

But this box was marked 'Bronzed Beautiful' – a sample set of a home-tanning kit Jessica had promised to review. Opening up the box, she found a bottle of 'deep mahogany', together with a sponge and a body brush. The bottle of lotion, when opened, smelled a little like shoe polish.

'Are you going to try it?' Anna asked. 'Can I have a go?'

'I'm going to try it, but it's not for you, love. Maybe when you're a bit older.'

She set the box down on the hall table and glanced up into the mirror. She was looking pretty pasty – the tanning kit had come at the right moment. Sadly, there wasn't time to put it on before work.

Padding back through to the kitchen, she took a slug of coffee before turning her attention back to her inbox.

To: jess@StarPR.com
From: rob@easymail.com
Subject: PR enquiry

Dear Jess,

Not sure if you'll remember me – we met briefly at Jeff Conby's book launch (*100 Most Interesting Facts About Corduroy: 2*) and you mentioned you did his PR?

At the time, I was working on a book (*Remembering Rainbows*) and I'm really excited to say that MindHack Publications made me an offer – the book's out next week!

Anyway, as you probably realise, there is very little budget behind the launch, so – as I want to get the book out there as much as I can – I've decided to fund some personal PR. I wonder whether we could meet up to discuss the kind of thing you do (and the cost!).

I've attached an info sheet to give you an idea.

Thanks very much.

Robert Haydn

PS: started reading your blog. Very inspiring!

Book Info:
REMEMBERING RAINBOWS

Remember the feeling of seeing your first ever rainbow? That sense of childish delight and wonder? How long has it been since you felt pure excitement and joy?

For most of us, the answer is 'not for a long time'.

So how can we recapture those simpler, more authentic feelings?

Robert Haydn, psychologist and father of two, is a man on a mission to help you find your inner child once again! Through a series of tutorials, he will help you to embrace the simpler side of yourself, and find true happiness!

To: rob@easymail.com
From: jess@StarPR.com
Subject: PR enquiry

Dear Rob,

Thanks for your enquiry – yes, I remember meeting you and hearing all about your book. Well done for getting a publication deal!

I'd be more than happy to meet up to discuss strategies.

If you could call me on the number below perhaps we can arrange a suitable time.

Best wishes,
Jessica Bradley
CEO Star PR

Loving my new laptop! @PCLife #techsavvy #multitasking #winning

Pressing send, Jessica flicked onto Google and typed 'Robert Haydn' into the search box. After a few false starts, she found the right website and studied his picture. Dark hair with a slight curl, light green eyes, glasses and a slightly lopsided grin.

Had she met him? The book launch he'd mentioned had been two years ago – all she remembered was rushing about trying to make sure she spoke to everyone and getting Jeff to sign any copies requested. She'd talked to a lot of people.

She looked more closely. In the picture, he looked about forty-five. He was wearing a white shirt, which with his pale colouring didn't do him any favours. Teeth a little too white, but maybe that was Photoshop?

She'd had her own teeth whitened to a natural cream colour a couple of months ago but had stopped short of traffic-stopping, showbiz brilliance. 'Don't want to scare off the clients,' she'd joked to Bea when she'd chosen from the shade chart. 'I want to dazzle them with my PR, not my gnashers.'

Mum had taken Jess having her teeth whitened as an insult to her parenting skills, of course. 'I don't see why you need your teeth to be any lighter,' she'd sniffed when Jessica had told her. 'They look perfectly fine to me!'

'Thanks, it's just—'

'Your brother's never seen the need to have *his* teeth whitened.'

'It's not that, it's—'

'And I suppose you're going to say that I should have stood over you every night when you cleaned your teeth! Well, I'm sorry, but I did my best!'

'Honestly, Mum, it's not that. You did a great job. It's all the . . . coffee and red wine,' Jess had desperately searched her limited knowledge of the culprits behind teeth staining. 'I'm not—'

'Red wine? How much wine are you drinking exactly?' Her mother had charged down the conversational rabbit hole like a whippet. 'Your father likes a glass, and his teeth are fine – at sixty-six! Except for the one that's gone grey. But that was due to that incident with the garden rake. Silly man. I told him to put his tools away – but would he listen? You don't think you might have a drink problem, dear?'

Two weeks later, her mother had had her own teeth whitened. Significantly whitened.

'Did I say that?' she'd replied when Jess called her on it. 'I'm sure we've never spoken about whitening. Carmella – you know, that lovely girl at the club? – she says it's all the rage!' She'd leaned a little closer. 'You know, perhaps you should get your own done? They're looking a little dull.'

Jessica looked again at the write-up of *Remembering Rainbows*. It sounded like reading the book might do her some good. If embracing her inner child meant happiness, she was all for it.

Chapter Six

Jessica hadn't been to this particular café before. Tucked at the end of the high street, its small window revealed a couple of metal chairs and glass-topped tables, a counter displaying a selection of cakes, and a fridge stacked with spring water and fruit juice.

She pushed open the door and stepped inside. Almost immediately, she was bombarded with a plethora of delicious smells: freshly brewed coffee, cakes, and something else she couldn't put her finger on. A jazz compilation – the sort she always felt she should play but never quite got around to streaming – hummed softly in the background.

Robert hadn't yet arrived, so Jessica took a seat and looked idly at the menu. It was 10am and the café was surprisingly quiet for a Saturday – debris on the tables suggested the breakfast shift had just ended, and it was probably too early for mid-morning coffee and cake. She shared the space with an elderly woman reading a novel and a couple of young mums whose children sat in highchairs nibbling messily on chocolate cookies.

Jessica tried to think of the last time she'd taken Anna out to a café for a treat. It had been quite a while. Avoiding temptation had been one of the challenges of her health and fitness regime, and the sights and smells of cafés or bakeries would have been too hard to bear. But did that mean she'd deprived Anna? Not of the cakes or the carbs, but simply of the time together; the uninterrupted pleasure of sitting and talking? And here she was, on a Saturday, meeting a client while Grahame was probably taking time to treat Anna and have fun.

Before she could finish her train of thought, the door opened and a man she recognised as Robert entered, carrying a small plastic bag and holding a book in his hand. He was slightly better-looking in the flesh than in his picture. One of those unlucky people for whom photos do no favours, because his crooked smile and the crinkling around his eyes that had aged him in the pics were somehow charming in reality. She'd assumed he was about forty-five, but now he seemed closer to forty, maybe even late thirties.

He was wearing a checked shirt in blue and white with a pair of chinos and had completed the look with some battered trainers that the mum in her longed to rip from his feet and wash or replace.

He glanced around, saw her and walked towards her with a grin.

'Hi, Robert,' she said, sticking out her hand. He gripped it in a brief handshake.

'Hi. Call me Rob,' he smiled, taking off his glasses, setting them on the table, and running his hands through his hair. It reminded Jessica of one of those movie-moments where the nerdy girl takes her specs off to reveal she's actually both sassy and sexy.

Why, Dr Haydn! You're beautiful!

Actually, though, he was quite cute once his glasses were removed and she could see his eyes – greener than they'd appeared online. His hair sprang out from his head in dark curls. She reached up instinctively towards a particular curl that had fallen across his forehead, then snatched her hand back just in time. What was she doing?

A slight girl, dressed in a black polo-shirt and black trousers approached, notebook in hand. 'What can I get you?' she asked.

'Just a green tea for me, please,' Jessica smiled.

'Same,' said Robert, sitting down with a sigh.

The girl nodded and disappeared behind the counter.

'So, thanks for meeting me here,' Rob started. 'I know you wanted me to pop into the office but I really wanted you to see this place.'

'You did?' she asked, glancing around.

'Yeah.' He blushed slightly. 'This was the place where I came up for the idea for *Remembering Rainbows*.'

'Oh?'

'Yeah. I mean, it's not the café as such – I mean, it's a nice café; good music. But it was a day when I was feeling really depressed. Jane, that's my ex-wife . . . well, we'd just decided to get divorced. I'd gone for a walk and I popped in here because it had started to rain a bit, you know?'

Jessica nodded. Divorced, she thought. A fellow relationship fucker-upper.

'And I hadn't expected it to be so relaxing. It was the music, I think. And the staff being so friendly. I ordered myself a slice of their carrot cake – which I recommend, by the way – and sat here for about an hour. And it occurred to me that I'd never usually have stopped and treated myself to anything. And how that little bit of cake made me feel so much better.'

Jessica nodded, hoping that there was more of a message to *Remembering Rainbows* than simply the idea that 'cake makes you feel better'. She'd known that since she was two years old.

'The cake wasn't anything special, not really. It was the idea of treating myself. A nod to my inner child.' He twirled his glasses nervously in his hand.

'So tell me about the book – what kind of advice do you offer?' she prompted.

He reached into a small leather bag propped against the table leg and slid out a copy of a white book. On the front, it had a woman's face gazing in wonder at an enormous rainbow, with tiny children dancing along it.

'Rather than simply giving advice, it's more of a programme of embracing your inner child,' he said, passing her the copy, his eyes lit up with inspiration. 'You know. That very primitive part of yourself. Doing all the things you liked to when you were a kid.'

'Uh huh?' Jessica flicked open the cover to reveal a picture of Robert walking through a park with a Labrador.

'So, there's a chapter on playgrounds – how if we pass one in a park, there's no harm in having a quick go on the swings or the roundabout,' he continued, gesticulating enthusiastically. 'Although my kids aren't too keen if I do it when I'm out with them. They're twelve and fourteen – just at that age where they think pretty much everything I do is embarrassing.'

'I've got one like that at home!' Jessica smiled. She caught his eye and he grinned back.

'Anyway, it's doing that – giving in to your inner child. Dancing madly to music rather than just stepping a bit to the beat. Drawing pictures, even if they're rubbish. Making paper planes. Singing at the top of your voice.'

'OK,' Jessica nodded, thinking of Anna's pleasure years ago whenever she'd got the paints out.

'Because for me, remembering those parts of myself – the parts when I just did what I felt like and didn't even consider what anyone would think – were the ones that kind of contained my happiness, you know?

Jessica hadn't expected to particularly warm to the idea of Robert's book. But something about this idea appealed to her. And *he* was appealing too, she realised. Intelligent, passionate, caring; if she could get him some airtime on radio or even TV, he'd go down a storm. Plus it was nice, she thought, to talk to someone about happiness rather than comparing muscle-to-fat ratios or arguing over whether carbs are naughty or irredeemably evil.

'It sounds good.'

'Oh, do you really think so?' His uncertainty was quite charming.

'Yes, yes I do. And more importantly,' she leaned forward, 'I think it might really appeal to readers.'

He blushed then, as if he'd never considered that someone might actually *read* his book. She started to form a press release in her head – the magazine editors she could send it to, perhaps something on TV. Celebrity endorsement?

'Yes. I definitely think I can help with this,' she said, reaching into her bag for a contract.

As he put out his hand to grab it, their fingers touched and she felt a sudden rush of heat to her cheeks. Talk about embracing your inner child, she thought wryly. I'm embracing all the worst elements of teenage embarrassment.

'Sorry,' he said, for no reason at all.

Why the blush? Sure, he was a good-looking bloke but it wasn't as if he'd made a move. And she wasn't on the market for anyone. Not when there was a chance of winning Dave back. Plus, she found herself thinking, Robert wasn't boyfriend material – not really photogenic enough to go on the blog.

'Are you OK?' Robert's voice interrupted her thoughts. 'You look a bit, well . . . red.'

'Yeah. Yeah.' She straightened in her chair and tried to smile. 'Miles away for a minute . . . Thinking of strategies, how to get you *out there* – you know!'

'God, I don't know how you do all that.'

'All what?'

'That social-media stuff. I mean I get how it works – I've put pictures online, tweets – that kind of thing. But getting things noticed – going viral, or whatever – I wouldn't know where to start.'

'Well, I . . .'

'That's why I chose you.'

'What do you mean?'

'Well, it was your blog I came across first when I googled "PR in St Albans". Imagine that – all those PR agencies touting for business online, and probably paying for a better place on the Google rankings or however it works, and your blog beat them all. So, I thought you must know what you're doing when it comes to online promotion.'

'Oh. Yes.' The blog's ranking had been a recent boon, based on the fact she'd had several mentions in the press lately with backlinks to her site. (Plus, the fact she now put so many keywords and hashtags in her blog posts they sounded as if they'd been written by a SEO bot).

'Anyway, so I started to read the blog – it's hard not to sometimes, isn't it, when you come across something interesting. And it was great. I really admire all that "healthy eating" stuff.' He patted his barely existent belly. 'Hence the green tea today – I'm usually a builder's tea with milk and two lumps,' he grinned, self-consciously.

'Well . . .' she was going to tell him that, actually, she quite often indulged in a nice strong cuppa herself these days but something made her stop.

'And that's what I want. Discipline, commitment. Your blog really sold you to me, and so I looked up your agency and bingo! Here we are!'

So it was the blog again, she thought grimly. Commitment. The fact she looked as if she had all the answers when online. She held her stomach in, aware that it had started to droop slightly. Bloody gravity.

'Thanks,' she said. 'Well, I'm really pleased that you found me. And really sure I can do a good job for you. If you could take a look at the contract and sign it if everything looks OK, then we can get moving.'

'OK – and I'll keep reading that blog of yours,' he said, reaching out his hand for another shake as she got to her feet. 'Cheering you on at the gym and all that.' He slipped his glasses back on and smiled – Clark Kent once more.

'Great. That's . . . great.'

'Say hi to Dave for me!'

As their hands connected again, she felt herself shiver. 'I will. I'll see him later, you know. At the gym,' she added, unnecessarily, pulling her cardigan a little more tightly around her.

And that was it. The web of her deceit tightened a little more. Because she'd sold a false persona to this man and he'd employed her on the back of it. And she'd blown her chance to come clean.

Chapter Seven

She'd barely poured her first coffee of the morning when the phone rang and her mum's number flashed up.

'Hi, Mum.' Jessica tried to smile. Mum could always tell when she wasn't smiling.

'So, I just wanted to ring quickly to ask whether you want me to bring anything on Saturday?'

'Saturday?'

'Yes, you know. For dinner. And what's the matter, dear, you sound absolutely miserable!'

The dinner party had been arranged weeks ago at a time when she'd been confident her life was on a settled track.

'No, Mum. I'm fine. But . . .' Jessica stretched her lips into a wider grimace, hoping it would make her voice sound more upbeat.

'Lovely. I'll just bring along a few profiteroles, shall I?'

'No, honestly, Mum. I can manage, but I need to—'

'Oh, of course. I *know* you're going to do some lovely ice-cream. And, well, one of your delicious sugar-free recipes that we're all just so enthusiastic about. But your father really enjoys profiteroles at the moment. And I've found a *lovely* recipe . . . And you know,' her mum lowered her voice as if revealing a state secret, 'desserts aren't really your *strong* point, are they. Remember the plum crumble?'

Jessica wondered briefly if there was a statute of limitations on pointed anecdotes. She'd made that crumble when she was seventeen. Yes, it had been burnt. Yes, the plum filling had been a little dry. But surely, twenty years later, it was time to move on. 'Well, I was going to . . .' She thought about the cooking she'd been planning and suddenly felt drained.

Worse, of course, there was the issue of the elephant in the room, or in this case, the tight-pants-wearing, muscle-bound, slightly deluded Adonis who would most definitely *not* be in the room. Or even the house.

Mum was the last person she'd want to find out. Before Dave had come along, she'd been so desperate for Jessica to get herself 'off the shelf' that she'd spent half her time arranging blind dates for her. Post Dave, she'd backed off and given her some breathing space. (OK, now she mentioned marriage, engagements or babies at least once a week, but this was far preferable to pimping her out to her friends' eligible sons.)

'Actually, Mum—'

'And shall we bring a bottle? Red or white?'

'Honestly, we've got lots of wine, Mum!'

'Oh, of course! And you do *so well*, don't you, to find such *bargains* at the supermarket. It's just, well, me and your father, we're a bit set in our ways. We prefer more traditional wine, I suppose. Silly really.' Her mother tittered.

'Actually, we won't be able to do this weekend,' Jessica interjected – quick and to the point – ripping off the plaster to expose the wound.

There was a silence in which Jessica could imagine her mother's hurt expression. She could just make out the sound of her mum's indignant, huffy breath on the line.

She guiltily scrabbled around for a suitable excuse that didn't involve admitting she was now, to all intents and purposes, single. 'It's just we've been a bit poorly this week and I think . . . I think Dave is probably coming down with it. You know, a tummy bug.'

'Really? Poor Dave. You know, I wouldn't be surprised if it's all that protein stuff he's drinking. Protein! Whatever next? We never had protein in my day, I'm sure.'

'Well, no, It's—'

'I told your father. If that man keeps drinking all those funny milkshakes, he'll give himself a runny tummy. And now look!' her mother paused dramatically, ostensibly to give Jessica the chance to imagine Dave sitting on the lav. 'It doesn't do to drink all that rubbish, I'm sure.'

'Well, maybe not.' Actually, Jessica agreed. She'd never been convinced about the Man Up! Powershakes Dave seemed addicted to. And wasn't particularly keen on the idea of sticking up for him now.

'Tell him,' her mother lowered her voice conspiratorially, 'tell him to drink some mint tea.'

'I would, but—'

'Yes, I know, I know!' her mother put on a voice, clearly meant to be an imitation of her daughter. 'It's a bit "new age" – but Carmella – you know, that lovely girl that helps out at the club? – swears by it. And I thought, well, why not! Although your dad won't go anywhere near it. He says—'

'Mum!'

The silence was almost tangible.

'Mum,' Jessica continued, more quietly. 'I really don't think it's the protein shakes. There's a lot of it going about. Tons of kids off in Anna's class.'

'In that case, it's even more important that we come!'

'Oh?'

'Yes, you'll be exhausted looking after Dave. Besides, I'm sure he'll be right as rain by Saturday night – big strong boy like that.'

'I just thought that – you know. Germs.' Jessica played her trump card. Mum was terrified of picking up a bug.

'Oh, don't worry. Your father and I have been taking some special vitamins.' Jessica heard the rattle of a pill bottle being picked up. ' "Supports a healthy immune system." There, you see! We'll be fine.'

'I don't think—'

'Perhaps I should bring a few over for Dave? I thought he was looking a bit peaky in his last photo.'

Has Mum joined Instagram now? Jess shuddered at the thought of her mother seeing the thong. 'I guess—'

'So, that's settled then. Shall we say seven?'

'Well—'

Her mother hung up without waiting for a reply.

Would it have been so difficult to tell the truth?

But it wasn't telling the truth that would have been disastrous. It was what would happen afterwards. Now that Jessica was, according to her mother, on the highway to menopause ('it's a slippery slope after thirty-five, Jessica!') her constant desire to fix her broken daughter's life would go into overdrive if she found out about the split.

And the (slightly stagnant) pool of young men that Mum had rounded up in hope of sourcing herself a future son-in-law had already been fished dry.

Before Jessica could work out what to do, the phone rang again and a hunk in trunks appeared on the screen. All thoughts of looming dinner disasters vanished.

Dave.

'What are you doing?' he asked as soon as she answered.

'What?'

'That photo thing online. What are you trying to say?'

She'd forgotten about the coffee/crumbs. But where was the harm? 'I just thought . . . I mean – you know, the blog.'

'But what about me? My life?'

'Your life? How could a picture of a cup of coffee affect your life?'

'The crumbs,' he said simply. 'I have an image to maintain, you know? Biscuits! I haven't eaten a biscuit since 2012.'

'That's what you're worried about?'

'Yeah. You're not the only one with followers!'

'Oh. But you were the one who said to keep things going online. That it was OK to fake things a bit . . . until . . . until . . .' she felt almost teary. Was this really happening?

'Well, yes. But that was when . . . when you first began to . . . When you stopped going to the gym, you know? Not when I . . . when we . . .'

'When you left, you mean?'

'Now, that's not quite—'

'When you left and dumped me by Post-it? Should I write about that?' she half sobbed.

He softened a bit. 'It's not . . . I mean, I understand . . . it's just, couldn't you have used like something healthy? At the very least avoided carbs!'

'I . . . I suppose . . .'

'And, you know. Well, you're going to have to say something about us eventually.'

'Can't we . . . don't you think we could talk about it? I mean properly?'

He was silent for a minute. 'Maybe. Maybe. But, I don't like lying to everyone.'

'Well, *I* have to lie about everything!' Jessica felt self-pitying tears prick at her eyes and wiped them crossly away. 'My food . . . our . . . our relationship! Semen stains!'

He was quiet for a moment.

'OK,' he said, at last.

'OK?'

'OK, say what you want. For a little while,' his voice was softer.

I miss him, she thought suddenly. 'And you really can't come home?!'

But he had already hung up.

#WinningatLife #LovemyBoyfriend #TrueLove

Feeling the need for a happiness boost, she placed the phone back in her handbag, picked up *Remembering Rainbows* and started to read.

REMEMBERING RAINBOWS

Are you smiling yet? If you've decided to read this book, chances are you will be soon! By purchasing *Remembering Rainbows* you've opened a gateway back to a happier, simpler time.

With the guidance of top psychologist Robert Haydn, *Remembering Rainbows* will take you through a programme of activities designed to help you embrace your inner child – that little boy or girl whose happiness is still entwined with your own.

And, by remembering the colour and excitement of childhood, you will find a more authentic, more personal route to happiness.

So what are you waiting for?

Chapter Eight

#MondayMotivation How do you spend your time when locked out of your own office? #buttcrunches @Fitat30 #fitnesscrazy

'Seven, six, two, four,' Jessica punched the numbers into the entrance keypad and waited for the door to buzz her in. It didn't.

'Seven, six, four, two?'

No response.

'Six, seven, two four?'

Nothing.

The building was dark; half eight and nobody had arrived yet. Which was annoying in a way she'd got no comeback on at all. No one was contracted to start before nine. But still, what happened to enthusiasm? she thought, as she brushed some mud from the front step and sat down to wait. She pulled Robert's book from her bag – at least she could use the time productively.

REMEMBERING RAINBOWS

A guarantee from the heart.

It's so easy to let happiness pass us by. Or to chase dreams that we think will make us happy, only to find out that they don't. But happiness isn't something that we should have to chase. It's something we already have – we just have to learn how to tap into it.

You were happy once; and you will be again.

That's my promise to you.

Dr Robert Haydn

It was quite a promise to have on the opening page. She only hoped the activities and advice in the actual book lived up to it.

'Sorry.' Candice looked chastened, like a forlorn puppy when she finally turned up to work and let her boss into the office. 'I just didn't think; I'm so stupid. I just feel as if everyone knows that date.'

Which meant that Jessica had felt obliged to say that it didn't matter; that it was no big deal. That it was by no means stupid to change the entry code to your birthday and forget to tell anyone else. 'Don't worry,' she smiled. 'We've all done things like that.'

She'd become preoccupied with lying recently. How truthful were other people? Not just on social media, where most people play a subtle passive-aggressive game of one-upmanship by posting carefully selected pictures and deleting anything off-message; but generally. How much lying is normal?

She could have hardly told Candice the truth – that being locked out of the office had meant she'd had to sit on the work steps for over half an hour, which would mean racing around for the morning to try to catch up.

She felt guilty already after lying to Anna this morning when she'd asked why Dave hadn't come back from the gym last night. She'd made something up about his being called into work.

Who on earth calls a sales team leader into work urgently?

'Emergency, extra-large order coming in.'

'But sir, we'll never make it in time!'

'Don't worry, I've got Dave on call.'

It was a little like the time Anna had started asking questions about Santa. 'Will Santa die?' 'How old is Santa?' 'Can Santa see me in the bath?' 'Is Santa watching us right now?'

When does a bit of Christmas magic move from harmless fun to tangled deception?

After drinking a few sips of the herbal tea Candice had made as 'a peace-offering' (despite the fact that it was part of her job to make everyone in the office tea), Jessica logged into her emails.

To: jess@StarPR.com
From: hugo@freemail.com
Subject: Sculptures

Dear Jess,

I've been thinking about my change of direction, artistically speaking, and wondered if you could cancel my sculpture exhibition? I want to portray something softer in my work now, and the thought of *Drowning Man on Fire* or *Proud Man* being on public display seems wrong somehow. They are such raw pieces – so moving. And – to be honest – I'm not sure the public are ready.

Hope your Monday is proving inspirational!

Hugo

To: hugo@freemail.com
From: jess@StarPR.com
Subject: re: Drowning man on fire

Dear Hugo,

Thanks for your email. I'll try to get the pieces taken down, although it might take a few days.

Best wishes
Jessica Bradley
CEO Star PR

To: vicar@hatfieldchurch.com
From: jess@StarPR.com
Re: Hugo Henderson

Dear Pete,

I'm really sorry to do this at the last minute, but Hugo Henderson's exhibition in the entrance of the church hall is going to have to be cancelled I'm afraid.

Apologies for messing you about.
Kind regards,
Jessica Bradley
CEO Star PR

To: jess@StarPR.com
From: vicar@hatfieldchurch.com
Re: re: Hugo Henderson

Dear Jessica,

I was very surprised to read your email, especially after you explained your struggle to get this particular artwork displayed. However, I must say, it's rather a relief not to have to tackle the committee again about the piece.

Thanks for letting me know.

And thank you for the donation towards church funds, which I assume still stands?

Peace be with you.
Pete White, Vicar
Hatfield Church

To: curator@albanhall.com
From: jess@StarPR.com
Re: Hugo Henderson

Dear Sally,

Thanks for your agreement to display Hugo's Henderson's *Proud Man* sculpture in the foyer of the library building. I'm so sorry, but Hugo has had a change of heart and would like to have the work removed.

I realise it has only recently gone on display and hate to put you to any trouble.

Apologies.
Best wishes,
Jessica
CEO Star PR

To: jessica@StarPR.com
From: curator@albanhall.com
Re: Hugo Henderson

Dear Jessica
Thanks for your email!

I'm really sorry, but it's going to take a few days to get the work removed. I'll have to raise it at the management meeting next week. Hopefully we can sort something out. On a personal level, I'm quite disappointed as the work is a real favourite of mine.

Best wishes,
Sally

Jessica switched her computer off and sat for a minute, looking at her vague reflection in its black screen. A far cry away from the smiling, pouting selfies of her blog, her face looked resigned; tired and slightly chubbier than she would have liked.

'You look like you need another cup of tea!' Natalie said, passing, cup in hand. 'Do you want me to make you one?'

'Oh God, do you mind? It's been one of those mornings.'

'Not at all. In fact, why don't you have this one? I haven't touched it. Changed my mind – and it's your favourite!'

She plonked down a white cup filled with a murky liquid that smelt slightly of grass on Jess's coaster.

'I know you recommended this rooibos stuff on your blog, but I just can't get used to it.'

'No? Well, thanks.' Jessica had lifted the cup to her lips and tried not to gag. 'Great. Mmm. I'll drink it in a bit when it's cooled,' she lied. She'd wait until Nat was at her desk and subtly tip it down the sink.

'Honestly, I wish I liked it as much as you do. It just tastes like peppery pee to me.'

'Oh no, it's delicious!' Jessica lied. 'I'll be downing the whole lot in a sec!'

'Great, well, I'll grab my latte and we can drink them together while we have that meeting.'

Jess had wondered whether this was what was meant by putting her foot in her mouth.

It certainly tasted that way.

Chapter Nine

@BronzedBeautiful #soexcited to be using your #selftan kit before hitting the pub! @StarPR

Standing in the shower, having dried her skin until it was only 'moist', as required by the tanning kit, Jessica began to brush her body in 'a slow, circular motion' as stated in the Bronzed Beautiful instructions. The brush was wiry and her skin soon began to flare up in protest. She'd always had the kind of skin that marked very easily, so the redness didn't bother her – it would soon fade.

It reminded her a little of sanding down a piece of wood before painting it. 'Exposing the grain,' Grahame had used to say when they were trying to do up their bedroom. She'd never been much good at DIY. 'Make us a tea,' he'd said in the end, taking the sander from her and giving her a kiss. 'You're great at making tea.'

She'd laughed. They'd probably only been together a couple of years at that point. She'd forgotten the way they used to laugh together.

Her body now red from top to toe, Jessica gratefully put down the brush and picked up the bottle of bronzer. 'Apply with care!' the bottle warned. 'Using the gloves provided, apply lotion to prepared skin and gently rub in. Wait ten minutes before showering.'

The cream tingled a little as she applied it to her skin,

but the sensation wasn't unpleasant. Then came the waiting. Ten minutes doesn't seem long when you were watching TV, or driving to work. Sitting in the bathroom, feeling damp, tingly and a little bit cold, the minutes stretched ahead like hours. She spent some of the time cleaning out the underneath of her nails with a pair of tweezers, and the rest staring at her rather alarming reflection in the mirror. The cream was very, very brown, but she knew from experience that – when washed off – it should make her skin just a couple of shades darker, as promised by the leaflet. When she'd read 'dark mahogany' she'd been a little concerned, but the saleswoman had been very reassuring when she'd phoned to double-check. 'It's just a deep, summer tan,' she'd said. 'Quite natural-looking!'

Finally, the time was up and she stepped into the shower and gratefully turned on the warm water. Washing herself down, she watched the orange liquid running from her body in little rivers. Her skin underneath showed up a golden tan colour – perhaps a little darker than she'd hoped, but absolutely fine.

It was only when she stepped out of the shower, towelled herself down and looked in the mirror that she realised it wasn't exactly the ideal Hollywood glow. Her body was evenly covered, even her face was a pleasant golden colour. Except around one eye, and – bizarrely – on the knuckles of each hand. Whether she'd had a little dry skin in those places or not she wasn't sure, but each had turned two or three shades darker.

'Shit,' she said, running her hands under the tap in the hope that she could remove some of the colour. She'd wanted to look as if she was ready for a night out, not as if she'd been brawling outside the bar.

She looked at her watch. She was meeting Bea in an hour, and she couldn't cancel again.

'Mum!' shouted Anna from outside. 'Have you finished?! I need to pee!'

Wrapping herself in her dressing gown, and shoving the empty bottle, sponge and body brush into the bin, Jessica left the bathroom, face firmly turned towards the floor like a guilty teenager.

Back in her room, she took a passable selfie using a filter and with the slightly dodgy eye the furthest from the camera. The tan looked OK in the pic – which was the most important thing. And perhaps tomorrow morning she'd look slightly less battered and bruised in real life

She rough-dried her hair then heated up the straighteners and forced her reluctant, kinky barnet into a sleeker style. Applying a bit of mascara and eyeliner to highlight her green eyes – and hopefully draw attention away from her dodgy eye stain – she then added a slick of neutral lipstick. She evaluated the result. Not too bad at all, if she kept her left eye in the shadows.

And it didn't really matter that much, she thought to herself. It wasn't as if she was getting glammed up for a blog-shoot or meeting a client. Bea wouldn't care what she looked like at all.

Fit at 30

Bronzed Beautiful – Self-Tanning Kit

I'd been feeling a bit pasty recently, so decided to try out some home tanning. I've often been put off home tans with tales of an uneven appearance, or been worried that I'll do something wrong. So I was reassured at the clear instructions on the pack, and the fact that Bronzed Beautiful offer tips for preparing your skin to avoid potential problems.

The cream went on smoothly, with a pleasant, tingling sensation, and in ten short minutes I looked as if I'd been sunning myself on a Mediterranean beach (and who has time for that?!).

I'd thoroughly recommend this tanning kit – it's worked wonders for me!

#bronzedbeautiful #lookinggood #selftanning

COMMENTS

Jill
Thanks, I'm off to get myself a bottle!

LM
Natural is best – embracing who you *really* are. For thoughts on this, visit www.naturalisbest.org

UJ

Hello dear. You don't know me, but I am the son of His Honourable Prince Alid of Mozambique. I read your website and wish to make contact to discuss a financial transaction that may prove very exciting for you. Please send your account details to roy78w78@hotmail.com and my business associate will be in touch.

Chapter Ten

Old friends – good times. @thecockinn

Sitting in the pub waiting for Bea, Jess felt like she was waiting for a blind date. Her stomach fluttered with nerves and she realised in that moment how much she'd missed her friend. It had been so easy to get caught up with her new life, and it was only now the chips were down (or actually back on the menu) that she'd bothered to make a date.

She'd been quite surprised, actually, that Bea had agreed to meet her at all. Last time they'd met up Bea had cooked dinner for them both at her place, and Jess had refused to eat most of it as it didn't conform to her new dietary plan.

It had been a couple of months ago, and Jessica had just managed to meet her weight-loss goal, plus had found that her Instagram had gained a lot of #cleaneating followers. 'I just can't eat dumplings,' she'd said, after Bea had dished out a plate of hearty stew. 'And red meat's a big no-no.'

Had she really been so selfish?

Had she really said 'no-no'?

Sipping her Diet Coke, Jessica felt her cheeks redden.

She hoped her friend would turn up; Bea was often late after work and sometimes had to stay unexpectedly for a couple of hours of unpaid overtime. Jessica had promised Anna she wouldn't leave her with her grandparents for too long. 'Mumm!' she'd protested when Jessica had told her where she was headed for the evening. 'I wanted to watch *Hollyoaks*! Granddad'll be watching some sort of sport thing.'

'You'll be fine.'

'Can't I come to the pub?'

'Not this time.'

'What about Uncle Stu?'

'Busy. Besides, Granny's already cooked macaroni cheese.'

Anna had given her a dark look and that had been the end of it. She might not enjoy everything about visiting her grandparents, but even she couldn't resist one of Gran's *special recipe* mac n' cheese dishes. 'I add extra cheese,' Jessica's mother had told her once, with a conspiratorial tap on the side of her nose. 'It makes it more . . . cheesy.'

When they'd let themselves in, Anna had rushed into the kitchen to give her Gran a hug and Jess had popped in to see her dad. As predicted, he was watching the snooker. The lowest rung of the sporting TV ladder. 'Hi, Dad,' she'd said, leaning down and giving him a kiss on the cheek. His skin was prickly and smelt of Manly Man aftershave.

'Hi, love,' he'd smiled, pausing the snooker in case he missed any of the action.

'Just off to the pub then,' she'd said.

'Have fun,' he'd said. 'Say hi to Bea for me.'

'Thanks. And Dad?'

'Yes?'

'Any chance you could do me a favour and let Anna watch *Hollyoaks* in a bit?'

'*Hollyoaks* you say? OK, OK, why not?' he said. 'What's it about?'

'Oh, just, well, people.'

'What sort of people?'

'Well, young . . . good-looking . . . troubled. Blond, mostly.'

'Right. Doing what?'

'Arguing, making up, struggling with everyday life, having relationships, affairs, dying in car crashes, stalking each other, finding lost babies.'

'Are you sure it's suitable?'

She'd never really thought about it. 'Yeah, I think so. Her friends watch it, so . . . and it's just real-life, everyday stuff.'

'Right. Like the lost babies your mum and I are always finding.'

'Ha. You know what I mean!' She'd smiled fondly at her old man.

'Actually, love,' he'd said. 'I wanted to ask if you're OK? Stu mentioned that you're a bit stressed at the moment.'

'Just, you know. Work stuff,' she'd said, shrugging.

'Well,' he'd said, putting a hand on her arm. 'Make sure you take care of yourself.'

'Thanks, Dad.'

Now, sitting at the table in the pub, Jessica smiled; the other men in her life might let her down sometimes, but she'd definitely lucked out when it came to her dad and Stu.

Just then, Bea walked in, her short, dark hair tousled and her round-framed glasses – her 'Harry Potter' specs – reflecting the light from the bar. She glanced around, saw Jess and gave a small smile.

'Hello,' she said, sitting at the table and dumping her bag on the floor. 'I'm going to get a drink – want another?'

'No, I'm fine, thanks,' Jessica smiled, sipping at her Diet Coke. Then, 'Actually, I could go for a small glass of white.'

Bea's eyebrows raised slightly, but she said nothing. Returning to the table a couple of minutes later, she plonked two mismatched glasses down. Hers an enormous red; Jessica's a tiny 125ml white. 'It looks pathetic,' Bea said, nodding at the glass. 'Sorry – I'll happily get you a bigger one.'

'No, no, it's fine,' Jessica smiled, taking a sip and feeling the slightly vinegary taste hit the back of her throat. 'So, how are you?'

'I'm OK.' Bea looked at her then, her expression guarded. 'So what's up?'

'What do you mean?'

'Oh, come on, Jessica,' Bea said, although her tone was even and reasonably warm, 'you don't speak to me properly for weeks, then suddenly you want to meet up. And on a gym night too!' she added, with mock horror.

Jessica set her wine down on the table. 'Have I really been that bad?'

'Oh *Bea*!' Bea said in a mocking tone. 'I'd love to come, but I don't want to lose *mo-men-tum*.' She pronounced momentum as if it was a strange, foreign word.

For some reason, Jessica couldn't help laughing along. 'Hey, there's nothing wrong with going to the gym!'

'Oh I know *that*!' Bea said, her hand hovering over her midriff. 'I know I should be going, and blah blah blah. It wasn't the fact you were going to the gym or anything; it was the fact you seemed completely obsessed with it!'

'I wasn't completely—'

'You were, Jess. And it just didn't seem like *you*. Being fit, working out – that's great. But I'd rather have a squishier version of Jessica who's still got a sense of humour and time to see me once in a while than a gym-honed stranger.'

Squishier? 'Sorry, I suppose . . . I suppose I've been a bit selfish.'

'Just a bit.' But Bea was grinning. 'Do you know, the last two times we spoke, apart from a quick "how are you?", you didn't ask me a single question about myself?'

'I didn't?'

'No. I counted. Not one. You didn't ask how things were

70

with Mark. You didn't ask about Lucas or Lewis. And you didn't ask me about work. The only time you discussed me was when you suggested I come down to the gym for a taster session, so that Dave could earn himself a free "man wax".'

'Oh.' Jessica's resolve to confide in her best friend began to drain away. 'Well, I do want to know. I *am* interested!' she said.

'Really?'

'Yeah. And I'm sorry, you know?' Jessica saw Bea's face soften and seized her advantage. 'In fact,' she said, 'that's why I wanted to meet you. I realised that I'd been a complete bitch and wanted to have a proper catch up,' she lied. Thoughts of telling Bea about the situation with Dave faded into insignificance. Not yet. Not this time.

'Well, if you must know, things have been awful at work.'

'Oh Bea! Have they?'

Bea worked as a midwife at the local maternity unit. Always a stressful profession, things had been getting worse recently – lack of funding, lack of staff.

'Yeah. We're all racing around, trying to make sure we look after everyone properly, but it doesn't feel like you can ever give enough. And I know . . .' Bea pushed her glasses back up the bridge of her nose. 'Jess, I just know that something's going to go wrong eventually. We go and go and go, and you just feel like something's got to give.'

'Oh Bea.' Jess reached over and covered her friend's hand with her own. 'Isn't there anything you can do about it?'

Her friend shrugged. 'I don't know,' she said. 'Quit?'

'Would you really?' Jessica was fascinated at the idea of being able to walk out of a job and go somewhere else to start again. That was where qualifications got you, she supposed. If you were a qualified *something*, rather than someone just making it up as you went along, you had proper choices. Not for the first time, she wished she'd followed Stuart's lead and finished her university course.

'Probably not.' Bea took a slug of her wine and raised her eyebrows. 'So, go on then. How are things on Planet Jessica?'

'Oh, they're OK.'

'Just OK?'

'They're great. I mean, I've neglected the workout a little lately,' she folded her arm self-consciously over her barely there belly bulge and smiled at her friend. 'Which I suppose might be a good thing.'

'Oh, I'm not saying that. I know I've been a bit off about it all, but I mean it's great what you're doing. I suppose I just feel a bit guilty that I don't have the energy to do it myself. There's . . . there's been a lot going on.'

'Oh?'

'And the fad diet thing is absolute bollocks of course.'

Jessica let that one slide.

'Anyway, how's the lovely Dave?' her friend continued, changing the subject. 'I mean, I know how his abs are doing from the web, of course. And a bit too much about his gluteus maximus, but how is he doing, you know – as a *person*, rather than a mannequin?'

'He's . . .' began Jessica. But she didn't have time to finish. Bea suddenly cocked her head to one side, and regarded her friend closely.

'Hang on, Jess. Are you OK? Is that a black eye?'

Jessica's hand went instinctively to her slightly too dark left eye socket. 'No. No, it's . . . just a bit of a home beauty mishap!'

'And your hand!' Bea reached across the table and grabbed Jessica's hand. 'Look, I know I had a go and all that, but if something's going on . . . I'm here for you, OK?'

'Seriously, it was just a mistake with some home-tanning stuff.'

'If you say so.' Bea's brow remain furrowed.

'Anyway, Dave's great,' Jessica said in an attempt to get the conversation away from the fact that she looked like she'd done a few rounds in the boxing ring. 'Happy. Doing well at work. You know.'

'And the lovely Anna?'

'Growing up fast!' Now, at least they were on common ground. Bea's twins were a year younger than Anna.

'Tell me about it! The boys are actually up to my eye level now. I'm either going to have to start wearing higher heels or accept that I'm going to be the smallest person in the family pretty soon.'

The conversation drifted from kids to work, to a random conversation about their obsession with Take That in the nineties. And when Jessica left the bar (after the requisite selfie) she felt that, even though she'd got no closer to working out what to do about Dave, she'd mended some bridges with her friend.

The only problem was, she'd done it by lying.

Loved meeting @MW_Bea at @TheCockInn! #catchingup #goodtimes

Lemon juice on ice – great for the #complexion

Chapter Eleven

Jessica took a quick snap of her trainers, crossed in front of her on the kitchen counter, making sure she tugged up the telltale floral material of her pyjama bottoms before she did so. It wasn't lying, exactly, if you intended to get the run done, say, in the next week or so, was it? She'd just been so tired since Dave had left. Well, before that really.

And did anyone really like running in the morning?

#earlyrun #morningburn #vitamind #NewShoe
#runningsystem #Tuesdaythoughts

Her laptop was sitting on the kitchen table in sleep mode and she booted it up. Her office, upstairs next to her bedroom, sat empty — as it often did. She'd created a home office in the box room — complete with the obligatory prints of inspirational sayings, modern glass desk and swivel chair — about a year ago. But somehow she always found herself migrating to the kitchen or the sofa when she wanted to work from home. More comfy, maybe. Or just a little nearer the front door and the street, closer to life.

Without meaning to, she clicked onto Dave's Instagram, just for a second. There was a freshly posted shot of him in downward dog, wearing only his tiny, tight shorts, in front of a mirror. It had already received 1,245 likes. She stroked the screen idly with her finger and felt some unwanted tears well.

He'd be back, right? Dogs were loyal creatures.

She dabbed at the corners of her eyes with a tissue and shook her head like a Magic 8-Ball to change the subject. *Outlook not so good.*

Opening her online diary she noticed a little heart marked next to the date. Bollocks. Today would have been the anniversary of their first date. The last thing she needed.

Dave had been the result of Jessica's first foray into internet dating – before him, she'd stuck to what Bea had termed the 'dinosaur method' (or going from bar to bar hoping to find someone worth taking home). 'For God's sake, Jess!' Bea had told her. 'Why do you think the dinosaurs are extinct?'

'Lack of Tinder?'

'Lack of Tinder,' her friend had said, decisively, passing over her phone with a profile all ready to upload.

After three swipes Dave had appeared on her screen – black hair smoothed back, shiny deep-brown eyes and the bright flash of a smile. 'Wow,' she'd said, showing the phone to Bea. 'What do you think?'

'Fine, if you're looking for the Ken to your Barbie.'

Jessica hadn't known whether or not that had been a compliment.

Like many a dinosaur in prehistoric times, Jessica had gone to the date armed with thousands of escape plans, but Dave hadn't been the sexual predator or desperate forty-year-old virgin that she'd feared. Just a cute guy with nice eyes who actually wanted to listen to what she had to say. And, well, his body wasn't bad either.

Admittedly, relief and some sort of misguided awe harking back to her school days had been part of the attraction.

She'd never have snagged a guy like that back then. (Not exactly the kind of romantic sentiment you read about in Jane Austen, or the kind of thing you'd write into your wedding vows: 'I promise to always be relieved that you weren't a sexual predator, misogynist or bigamist ... To ensure that I always make my friends jealous by posting pictures of you on my blog'.)

Things had been simpler in lower-tech times when she'd met Grahame. Internet dating had been in its infancy, and still pretty much considered to be something you should never, ever tell anyone you'd done.

'Damn,' she said. Because the anniversary would flag up on her blog. She'd have to acknowledge it.

Closing her laptop for a moment, she picked up her copy of *Remembering Rainbows*. She'd hardly got past the first chapter – not because it wasn't well written. But she just seemed to be so preoccupied with everything else.

REMEMBERING RAINBOWS

ACTIVITY ONE
Free range art

Ask yourself when you last lifted a paintbrush. Unless you're a regular painter, chances are you haven't tried your hand at a bit of art since school. And why not?

Most of us will argue that we don't have the talent, that we don't like the pictures we produce. That we aren't 'any good'.

Think about the pictures created by small children; they are uninhibited by the fact their painting might not be photographically accurate. They are also quick to cast last week's painting aside in favour of their latest artwork.

This is because it is the *process* of painting that brings

us joy. As school pupils and adults we believe that art is all about the end product – and if what we produce isn't deemed as good as that of others, then we shouldn't bother.

Almost every child likes to paint – and that's because they don't have our inhibitions. In fact, they've got it right –art is not necessarily about the destination, but about the journey.

Next time you're in town, visit an art supplies shop. Buy yourself some materials – perhaps some clay, some coloured pencils or some paint. Whatever takes your fancy – and don't worry about not having used it before.

Give yourself a morning or afternoon to explore art the way you used to. Cover several pages, or spend hours working on the same one. Make a clay replica of an animal, or simply enjoy working with the material. Whatever you end up with – whether it's gallery-ready, or something you want to hide away – you will look back and realise those hours spent shaping materials to your will have been happy ones.

'Can I borrow some of your muesli?' A little voice cut through her reverie and she jumped.

'God! Anna! Sorry, I didn't see you there!'

'Well?' her dishevelled daughter, still in her pyjamas, asked somewhat defensively. 'Is it OK if I have some?'

'Of course. In fact, don't just borrow some – I'll let you keep a bit!'

'Very funny.'

'I thought you didn't like muesli? You said it looks like cat litter.'

'I know, but . . .'

'And tastes like sawdust.'

'Yeah.' Anna plonked a bowl down on the table. 'But it's healthy, isn't it?'

'Well, yes.'

'So that's good, right?'

'Yes. Yes, it is.'

Then, 'Anna?' she said.

'Yes?'

'Do you fancy doing some art together or something?'

'Art?'

'Yes. I'm reading this book, and . . . it recommends it. Going to have a go for work.'

Anna shrugged. 'Can do,' she said, disinterestedly.

Jessica had told Anna the night before that Dave – the only sales leader to be in demand morning, noon and night – had had to go away to a conference for a few days. Which had felt awful, but had given her some thinking time.

She consoled herself that if Dave came back and told her that leaving had all been a ghastly mistake, she'd have avoided upsetting Anna altogether.

An hour later, returning from a school run on which she narrowly avoided Liz, Jessica sat down at the laptop and flicked on her emails and blog.

To: contact@StarPR.com
From: jess@mymail.com
Subject: Today

Hi Candice,

I'm going to work on the blog from home for a bit before coming into the office. Can you take messages, but send through anything urgent?

Thanks,
Jessica

She'd write the blog away from prying eyes, just in case anyone saw her face and somehow realised what she was up to.

Fit at 30

A year of head over heels

I can't believe it's been a year since I met the love of my life.

It was my first time arranging a date through Tinder, and I was as nervous as it's possible to be when I walked into the pub that night and saw Dave for the first time. But I needn't have been. This man's become my soulmate, my gym-buddy and friend.

When I saw him sitting there with his fizzy water, my heart somersaulted and I knew that this was going to be something special. Now we're living together and happier than ever.

Tonight he has promised to both (organic alcohol-free) wine and dine me at our favourite restaurant, and after we'll snuggle up at home to watch his favourite DVD, *Rocky*.

So to my hunky chunk of Italian man – lots of love and see you tonight.

COMMENTS:

Dina
Congrats! You give me hope that there is someone out there for me! Have a lovely evening.

Mrs B

Glad to read that Dave's sickness bug has cleared up; I forgot to ask whether it started with flatulence, as your father seems to have quite a lot of trapped wind at the moment. He says it's just the spicy tortilla chips he ate after squash, but – if you'll forgive me – they have a rather pungent quality to them. Hopefully it won't be the same bug as Dave.

Stu

Congrats.

Anonymous

You're so lucky! The last time I met someone on the internet he turned out to be older than my dad – didn't even have his own teeth. Although, admittedly, that did have its advantages...

RT

Love your blog.

Chapter Twelve

Jessica was just about to set off to work that afternoon when her phone rang. The number was unknown.

'Hello? Star PR?'

'Oh, sorry, have I come through to the wrong number?'

'Who are you after?'

'Jessica Bradley, Mrs Bradley – Anna's mum?'

Jess felt the frisson of fear that came when any caller addressed her as 'Anna's mum'. Had something happened? 'Yes, that's me.'

'Oh, hi, Jess. Sorry, I didn't know you'd answer the phone sounding so official!' tinkled a suddenly familiar voice. 'It's Liz – you know, from the PTA at Anna's school?'

'Oh, hi!' Jessica tried to make herself sound enthusiastic.

'Hi – hope you're not too busy?'

'No, no it's fine.'

'Great. Great. Well, I wondered whether you'd given any thought to the quiz questions?'

'Um, well, a little . . .' Jessica was loath to say that she hadn't really given the subject any thought whatsoever.

'Great!' replied Liz, her tone suggesting that Jessica had done her a tremendous favour. 'So the next step is to get together and go through them, if you're OK with that? And . . .' she paused for a second as if to prepare herself for a difficult conversation. 'And I don't suppose . . . Well, I've been reading your blog – and super congratulations by the way! – but I noticed that you hadn't mentioned the quiz at all.'

'Well, the thing is—'

'Oh, I realise it's just a school thing. But what a wonderful way to raise interest in the school! Just think, if we can drive up those donations a bit, and—'

'I do understand . . . but—'

'Oh good! I'm so glad. So, I'll keep my eye out for a mention then, shall I?' Liz ploughed on, either blissfully unaware that she'd misunderstood or employing the kind of manipulation skills usually used by the people with clipboards who made a beeline for Jessica outside shopping centres.

'Well, anyway . . .'

'Yes, yes. Of course, you need to get back to your business . . . I'm off too – all work, no play, eh!'

'Huh . . .'

'Goodbye!' The phone abruptly clicked off and Jessica was left feeling as if she'd been accosted by an enthusiastic charity pusher and signed away her life savings to a dubious cause.

She was sitting in the car, about to fire it up and get to the office, when it rang again with an unknown number. This time, she ignored it. Constant bombardment: people wanting things, after her for her status rather than her friendship. This must be how Kim Kardashian feels.

She started her car, but instead of turning right to the office, she headed into the town centre.

Chapter Thirteen

'Can I help you?' the woman asked, as Jessica pored over the different paint sets in the art section of the local craft shop. 'Are you looking for anything in particular?'

'Not sure,' Jessica replied, blushing slightly. 'Just . . . just having a look really.'

Why did she feel embarrassed at buying art materials? It was hardly as if she'd decided she was Van Gogh – she was just trying out some of the *Remembering Rainbows* activities, not aiming to paint a masterpiece or planning to hack off her ear and pop it in the post. Surely to promote Robert's book, she needed to understand it. This was a sensible thing to do.

She remembered her art classes at school – she hadn't been too bad. B at GCSE; one particular painting of a rabbit her mum still had on the wall in the downstairs loo.

But she hadn't picked up a paintbrush – other than to emulsion a wall – in years. The last time had probably been when she'd sat with a five-year-old Anna and tried a bit of half-hearted potato printing. After a while, she'd just let Anna get on with it, while she tapped away at her laptop instead. It had seemed like a waste of time – and time was something she had very little of.

She grabbed a couple of packs of air-drying clay and a few tools with which to shape it and went to the till.

'Decided then?' the woman said, smiling.

'Yeah,' Jessica shrugged. 'They're for my daughter,' she lied, for no reason at all.

'Lovely,' said the woman, taking her credit card and putting the receipt in the till.

'Sorry,' said Jessica. 'Have you got a bag?'

'Oh, I'm afraid not,' the woman said, seeming anything but afraid. 'Store policy – it's a plastic-free enterprise.'

'But the clay is . . . ?' Jessica pointed to the plastic wrap the clay rectangles were covered in.

'Biodegradable veggie plastic.'

'Oh. No paper bags then?'

'Sorry.'

Jessica opened her handbag and shoved the clay and tools inside – they just about fitted among the debris of receipts, crumbs and keys that she carried with her every day (just in case she wanted to return a can of baked beans she'd bought in 2018, or feed birds with crumbs from a forbidden KitKat she'd abandoned half-chewed a week ago).

'Well, thanks,' she said as she walked through the door.

'Bye! Have fun!' chirped the woman, turning to the next customer.

'They're for my—'

But the door closed behind her.

The bag strap cut into her shoulder as she walked back to the car; it was a designer one, bought for its look rather than practicality, and completely unsuited to lugging a kilo of clay back from the shops (unlike normal handbags, many of which have special pockets for random art materials.)

Before driving home, she popped into the office to show her face and make sure there'd been no disasters or calls from Hugo. Then she left, citing 'research'. She'd have the house to herself, as Anna had her after-school netball club on Mondays.

Which would have been fine, she'd realised when she stepped in the door and heard music coming from her daughter's room, if it hadn't been Tuesday.

'Anna?' she called. 'Everything all right?'

'Yeah, Jenny's mum said could you ring her about next week.'

'Sure – did you have a good day?

Silence.

Jessica trotted through to the kitchen and emptied her bag onto the table. The two lumps of clay fell out heavily, followed by her purse, her phone and a variety of handbag shrapnel. She swept the debris away and returned her phone and purse to the bag, before hanging it on the back of a chair.

She looked at the clay.

The clay looked back, menacingly.

Why had she chosen clay? It wasn't as if she was particularly talented in any artistic field, but surely paints would have been a more sensible choice?

She unwrapped one of the rectangles and felt the clay, cold and reluctant, against her skin. Tearing off a lump, she began to work it, feeling the texture change from stiff to pliant, the temperature from cold to warm.

She began to roll a length, then used one of her cutting implements to slice it into smaller pieces. Her fingers were grey, and each nail had a tiny black lump of glorified mud underneath.

Twenty minutes later, Anna came into the kitchen and stopped short. 'Mum!' she said. 'What is *that*?'

'I'm not sure,' Jessica said, looking at the strange, half-tree, half-human shape she'd created. 'I think we can safely say that I'm not about to become a sculptor any time soon.'

'You know you're mad, right?' Anna said, looking at Jessica quizzically.

'I'm beginning to wonder . . .'

'Can . . . can I have a bit?' Anna asked.

'Of course you can!' Jessica tossed her the rest of the block.

'Oh my God, this is harder than it looks,' Anna said ten minutes later when she held up a soggy piece of clay that was clearly fashioned to be like a cup. 'How come when they do this on the TV it looks so easy?'

'I don't know,' Jessica said, holding up her own, half-squashed sculpture.

'That looks well . . . a bit rude,' Anna said, blushing slightly.

'Anna!'

But she was right.

'It's meant to be a figure – look,' Jessica said, moving the clay so that Anna could see the area that she'd moulded to be a face.

Their eyes met and they both started to giggle. 'Actually, it looks a bit like Granny's head on a . . . on a . . . you know, from this angle,' Anna said.

Suddenly, Jessica could see it too. 'Maybe I should give it to her for her birthday!' she joked.

'Mum!'

Then they were both laughing, in a way they hadn't laughed together for ages. When had things got so serious? Jessica wondered.

'You know Jenny's mum was late today,' Anna said suddenly. 'We were standing outside for ten minutes.'

'Oh, no I didn't realise!'

'When is Dave going to start giving me lifts again? At least he was on time.'

'I'm, well, I'm not sure. Oh. Look, sweetheart,' Jessica continued. 'Perhaps you'd better start taking your phone. Things are . . . a bit hectic with Dave away. I'm settling into a new routine until he's – um – back. As long as you keep it switched off during lessons.'

Anna was so disproportionately delighted with the idea that she forgot to ask any more awkward questions. She flung her arms around her mother's neck. 'Thank you, Mum!' she said. 'Thank you!'

'It's OK,' Jessica replied, wrapping her arms around her daughter and giving her a squeeze. It had been a while since she'd been properly hugged, so she made the most of it. Perhaps she ought to also let Anna start smoking and knocking back cocktails if being a permissive mum was this rewarding.

'And Mum,' Anna added, sensing an advantage. 'Can I join WhatsApp? There's a group in my class—'

'No, Anna.'

'Why not?'

'Look, you've got the numbers of your friends. And if people aren't friends I don't want them to be able to contact you. People in your class, well, anyone could say anything.'

Jessica didn't mention how when she was at school she'd had problems with a gang of girls from her class who'd decided to pick on her for no apparent reason. She wasn't going to let that kind of nastiness into her house via Anna's phone.

'Oh, Mum!' Anna began.

'You'll thank me one day.'

'Whatever.' Anna rolled her eyes but seemed to accept she'd gained all the ground she was going to.

Jessica began to gather up the clay from the table,

sweeping the wasted portions in her hand and putting them in the bin.

Then she picked up the unused pieces and went to dispose of them too.

'Hang on,' Anna said. 'Can I have that?'

'Course you can.'

'Brilliant,' said Anna. 'I know I'm no good at it, but it was fun, wasn't it?'

'It really was.'

Before putting her 'creation' away, Jessica took a quick snap on her Smartphone. Not for her Instagram, this one – she didn't want to go off message. But she'd keep it anyway. Whether it was a figurine of her mother, or something a little more disturbing she wasn't sure – but whatever it was, it had definitely made her smile.

Chapter Fourteen

To: Stu1981@internet.com
From: jess@StarPR.com
Re: Help!

Hi Stu,

I don't suppose you'd be up for doing me a favour at all?

Mum and Dad are coming over for dinner on Saturday and I need to cancel it but can't seem to get out of it. I told them Dave is ill, but they brushed that aside – and now I can't come up with another excuse or it'll look obvious.

You couldn't ask them to come and babysit or something, could you? Then I can bow out gracefully...

J x

To: jess@StarPR.com
From: Stu1981@internet.com
Re: Help!

Hi Jess,

Why not just be straight with Mum? Tell her that you'd rather lick a tarantula than have her and Dad over for dinner?

Anyway, would love to help you out, but if Mum actually said yes I'd be a bit stuck as Erica's taken Josh to her mum's for a few days. I think it's a subtle way of giving me the weekend to crack on with the new kitchen units...

X

To: Stu1981@internet.com
From: jess@StarPR.com
Re: Help!

Hi Stu,

Oh no! What am I going to do!

I really can't do the thing on Saturday. Dave is, well, he's kind of booked up. And I've told them he'll be there!

Can't you ask Dad for some advice on the kitchen units or something? Some sort of DIY emergency?'

To: jess@StarPR.com
From: Stu1981@internet.com
Re: Help!

Sorry, sis, you're on your own. If there's anything that's going to make them suspicious then it's going to be (a) me doing DIY and (b) me asking Dad for DIY advice.

Just tell them that Dave's busy.

Come over for a coffee soon? I'll need a break from these cabinets. Or an excuse not to start. And, you're still OK to babysit Josh in a couple of weeks, despite me being such a rubbish brother?

Love to Anna.

S.

To: Stu1981@internet.com
From: jess@StarPR.com
Re: Help!

Course, don't be silly!

xx

In actual fact, Jessica adored babysitting her little nephew. After Anna, when she'd thought Grahame would agree to another one eventually, she'd imagined a boy; the perfect pair of children. Not knowing that Grahame had his eye on another kind of perfect pair.

Thankfully, when Erica and Stu had had Josh two years ago, Jessica hadn't been jealous, as she'd worried she might. Holding him in the hospital, she'd breathed in his tiny baby scent and felt a rush of love almost as strong as that she'd felt when the midwife first handed her the tiny, newborn Anna.

He might now be a sturdy two-year-old fascinated with toy cars, but he wasn't averse to cuddling Aunty Jessica on the sofa when she came around to visit. With Dave off the scene and Anna a little more reluctant these days, it was nice to have someone in her life who seemed to love snuggles as much as she did.

After signing out of her emails, Jessica put her head in her hands. Her last lifeline had been severed. What was more, she had lied – sort of – to Stu. Her brother who already knew a bit about her lifestyle/blog conflict; who would probably have tried a little harder to help her had she actually told him what was really going on.

It wasn't so much a move to deceive him, she thought; she'd actually been telling lies to so many people that she'd almost forgotten her own the reality.

Now, just days away, the dinner party was a hurdle she'd have to somehow jump alone.

Fit at 30

Don't forget to stretch!

As you know, I'm a great fan of the gym, of pushing cardio and feeling the burn. But it's important to stretch, too. And what better way to do that than Hatha yoga? I've been carrying out some yoga poses each morning recently, and I can already feel the difference! Muscles can get tight when you're constantly working the weights, so finding a way of softening and elongating is essential.

For a great start to the morning, stretch out into a *downward dog*, and do a round of *sun salutations* and to give yourself a boost both mentally and physically, finish with *warrior pose* – a great way to start the day!

#yoga #stretching #feelinggood #thebeststart #fitness-goals

COMMENTS

Jon
Downward dog's a bit tricky – pulled a muscle in my arse. Love the blog though.

JK
Did you get my email about Jenni's Flavas – nutritious

snacks for women on the move? Get in touch for a free sample!

D
Yoga doesn't burn enough calories for my liking.

Chapter Fifteen

#TeamBuilding

'So, where are we at?' Jessica looked around at her 'team' (she still got a rush of pride in realising that she was employing two actual humans now) and smiled.

'Hugo's been ringing again asking if you can go and see his new work,' said Natalie, reaching towards the plate of vegan brownies Jessica had provided for the meeting. 'I told him you'd be over soon. Mmm, these are delicious!'

Seconds later, she raised her napkin to her lips and discreetly spat out the brown, half-chewed gunge, squirrelling it away in her pocket.

'We've sent out the press release for Debbie's Delights, and I had a call from a small cancer support charity who might be interested in a bit of promotion. I thought maybe we could do something with the rates?' Candice said.

'Definitely,' nodded Jess.

'And we've been offered two passes for a spa day at The Grange in return for a review,' Natalie continued. 'Do you want me to accept them?'

'Sure! And why don't you two go?'

Candice and Natalie looked at each other briefly. 'Only thing,' said Candice. 'It's on a Friday.'

'That's OK. Book it,' Jessica smiled. After all, she shouldn't be the only one to benefit from the raft of treats that seemed to be coming their way at the moment.

Plus she'd developed an irrational fear of beauty treatments, for some reason.

'Wow, thanks!' They said almost in unison and Jess felt briefly like boss of the year. Karen Brady eat your heart out, she thought, imagining herself gracing the cover of *Careers* magazine, or being awarded a prize at some glamorous awards event for entrepreneurs.

'I've been writing down ideas for the blog, like you asked,' added Candice. 'And we were thinking maybe a listicle – you know, the top ten things about . . . One of those.'

'OK . . .' Jess nodded.

'Anyway, I thought maybe the ten best things about being in a relationship; or how to build a perfect relationship, or something? You know, to follow on from the anniversary post.'

'Oh, I don't know. I don't know whether I ought to keep . . .'

'Oh you should really! You get a lot more clicks when it's something about you and Dave together, rather than just, you know, *you*,' said Candice, turning her laptop around to show a spreadsheet headed 'website analytics'.

The little chart of clicks and likes showed that whenever Jessica mentioned Dave, she got 10 per cent more attention. And when there was a picture of him, the numbers soared.

It wasn't exactly confidence-boosting to find out she wasn't the most popular person in her own virtual life.

'OK, I'll do it,' she said with a forced smile and the kind of sinking feeling you get in your stomach when you realise that the mud you've been happily stomping in is actually a pile of festering dog shit.

'Anyway, I thought I'd give you a bit more info on Robert

Haydn; you know, the author of *Remembering Rainbows* I briefed you on?' Jessica continued, giving Candice and Natalie a press release with Robert's face and a picture of his book cover on it. 'He's written what seems to be a really "on-trend" book, but the issue is going to be getting it out there, making it stand out from all the other self-help books on the market.'

Natalie looked at the details on the press release. ' "Embracing our inner child",' she said. 'Sounds interesting – but it's been done, right?'

'I don't think so, not in this way,' Jessica replied, explaining about the activities the book recommended to help readers reconnect with their more organic selves.

'Oh, OK,' Natalie replied, nodding. 'Sounds good. And he's pretty hot, right, which doesn't hurt?!'

'You think?' Jessica said, remembering the green eyes again. Then she thought of Dave – his stocky, gym-honed body, perfect skin, hair that took thirty minutes to perfect. Robert had that ruffled, academic cuteness about him, but in the Instagram age, it wasn't what people were looking for.

'Definitely! I will if you don't!' Natalie joked, before blushing. 'Sorry,' she said. 'Too much.'

'It's fine,' Jessica said, grinning. 'I know what you mean. Anyway, I'm thinking of offering him as an expert psychologist to journalists as a starting point. Candice, if you get the press release sent to the usual suspects, and I'll put something together for TV.'

'Oh, also,' Natalie began, flicking a strand of light-brown hair that had escaped from her tight ponytail, 'we've had a bit of a problem with Hugo. Well, his art installation. You know, at the library?'

Jess nodded.

'Well,' Natalie glanced at Candice briefly. 'Well, we've had a call from them. Apparently a guy fitting Hugo's description, wearing a large hat, went into the library and tried to take the sculpture away. One of the staff tried to stop him, and unfortunately the piece was broken. They didn't recognise him, see. Thought he was some opportunist thief.'

God, why hadn't Hugo spoken to her? Jessica wondered. The installation was due to be removed in a couple of days.

'Anyway, it made it to a local news site.'

'Great.' That was all she needed. Prospective winner of an art award, looking idiotic in the local news.

'And . . .'

There was more?

'And, you're not going to like this, but the story got picked up by the *News*.'

'What the *Hatfield News*?' Jessica asked, thinking of the larger of the two local papers.

'No, the *Daily News* online.' Natalie grimaced.

Jessica felt a surge of panic. All this time spent trying to get Hugo recognised, and now he was getting coverage in the national press for appearing like a thief – or a lunatic – and snatching parts of sculptures from public buildings. She'd never get him an exhibition slot again! As it was, just getting his work in the public eye had cost Star PR over £200 in 'donations'.

'But why . . . I mean, why would they be interested in an attempted theft in a local library? It was hardly as if he was stealing the crown jewels or something.'

'No . . . yeah. I get it. It's . . . it's the picture and the mobile phone footage some idiot recorded that captured their attention. You see, the sculpture he was trying to take back was *Proud Man*.'

Jessica didn't have a comprehensive knowledge of the titles of all Hugo's work, but *Proud Man* – a metre-high model of a man upon which Hugo had fashioned the largest penis imaginable – was one that had stuck in her head (figuratively speaking).

'You see, men are objectified for one attribute and one only,' he'd said sadly to Jessica when he first showed her the sculpture. 'In order to feel pride, we need to feel we are the biggest . . . we have the biggest penises . . .' he'd paused and shaken his head mournfully. 'Metaphorically, of course,' he'd added, tapping the side of his nose as if imparting a secret.

Jessica had tried to find something diplomatic to say and failed. She had no idea what he'd meant about a metaphorical penis. And the fully erect specimen on the sculpture was about as literal as a penis could be.

'Oh, I don't expect *women* to understand the sculpture fully,' Hugo had added generously. 'I mean, women just don't have the same experiences of being objectified, body-shamed – the whole penis envy thing, Jessica, it's soul-destroying!'

'Uh huh.'

While Jessica was reminiscing, Natalie pushed her tablet across the table. On it was a picture of Hugo, in an enormous trilby hat, running through a library foyer, carrying a three-metre penis made of papier-mâché.

'It's trending too,' Natalie added, as Jessica stared aghast at the screen. 'On Twitter.'

'Trending?' After an initial near-gag of horror, Jess felt a little flicker of hope. When people got their names out there, for whatever reason, the light of the media would rest on them for a while. Penis or no penis, could it be a chance to promote Hugo's genuine artwork? She could use the hashtag to direct traffic to his website, perhaps. Get some of his better work noticed, and who knew what might happen next?

'Yeah.'

Jessica picked up her phone and swiped onto her Twitter

account. And there, trending with over 5,000 mentions, wasn't 'Hugo Henderson' but #penisguy

Penis guy.

> Can't believe he can run with a penis that size! #penisguy
> That's nothing, you should see mine! #penisguy
> Look out, ladies! #penisguy
> Proof that men are obsessed #penisguy
> I'll show you mine if you show me yours! #penisguy

The last one had been retweeted over 3,000 times, including by a couple of minor celebrities and rent-a-gobs.

Excellent.

It was with a heavy heart that she drove to the gym after work for the first time in an age. At one time she'd got into a bit of a routine, and even begun to enjoy spending time working out. But the urge to lift weights and run on an artificial surface had faded away and now she viewed the harshly lit room with its wall-length mirrors with the kind of dread she'd used to reserve for the dentist.

Where had it gone, her desire to work out? She'd felt, at one stage – a few months ago maybe – that she had adopted a whole new lifestyle, become a new person. But one session missed here, one there, and gradually her body had got used to a cuppa on the sofa in front of the news, rather than headphones and pounding at the gym. Like a gym membership cliché, she'd slipped back into her old habits.

She envied the ordinary people for whom quitting the gym would be met by understanding – for her, posting gym updates and mirror selfies was part of the 'package'. It wasn't as if she'd started smoking crack or developed a gambling problem. But admitting she'd fallen off the treadmill would be blogicide.

To keep up appearances recently she'd kept her Instagram updated by recycling old shots or taking pictures of scenic views from the car, claiming country walks or street runs; she hadn't hit the gym for longer than she'd care to remember.

But now, having lied to her newest client, she thought she ought at least to get a selfie there. More ambitiously, she was going to try to get Dave to appear in the shot.

She pulled into the gym's small car park and grabbed her bag from the back seat, where it had been since her last visit a few weeks ago. A time when she'd felt – if not completely satisfied – at least secure in her relationship with Dave. Because they were living together, things had seemed permanent. They'd never officially talked about it, but he'd stopped over one night a few months in and never really left. She'd assumed that was a commitment.

That was the problem, she supposed. The assumption of it. That his moving in meant they'd moved into a different category of relationship. Probably he'd liked living with her because it was closer to the town centre, or more convenient for work.

But it was hard, wasn't it? To actually ask those questions. To risk coming on too strong and scaring someone off. So many single men in their forties seemed to be obsessed with *Doctor Who* or *Star Wars*, or were frighteningly close to their mothers, or – if they were relatively normal – commitment-phobic.

Prior to meeting Dave, she'd gone on a blind date with one guy – a doctor from the hospital where Bea worked – who'd told her he was looking for a serious relationship, then dumped her after their first night together. Another had taken her out four times before admitting he was married, and had another girlfriend to boot.

The date that finally broke her – and left her more open to trying something online – had been with a bloke who'd seemed completely normal when she'd met him in the pub. But when he'd turned up on her doorstep the next day, he'd been wearing a tin-foil hat. 'You live close to a mast,' he'd explained, as if it was completely normal to fashion headwear out of kitchen paraphernalia. 'Can't be too careful.'

Compared to them, Dave had been a real catch – she'd been scared to put a foot wrong.

She slipped into the changing rooms unnoticed, using her swipe card to get through the revolving gate. Then she changed into her – slightly tighter, she noticed – gym kit and wandered into the main workout space, trying to look casual, but scanning the room for Dave.

He was there, as usual, sitting on a bench in front of a mirror, lifting an enormous-looking weight and staring at the rise of his muscle as he performed a bicep curl. Immediately she was filled with so much longing, it was all she could do to stop herself flying across the room and wrapping herself around his legs like a toddler.

She reached for the phone in her pocket, but before she could take a snap, their eyes locked in the mirror. He put the weight down and stood up.

'What are you doing?'

'Nothing. You know, just taking a quick picture.'

'Of me?'

'Yeah. You know,' she tried to play to his male pride. 'Your biceps are looking amazing.'

He didn't bite. 'I know. But why a picture? For your blog? We talked about this.'

'Yes, but . . .' she said, feeling unexpected tears prick at her eyes. 'But you said ... and it's just, well, I'm not ready to tell people yet. About us. I haven't even told Anna.' This was true, at least.

He softened then. 'OK,' he said putting the weight down and walking over to her. 'I know. I mean. Shit. I'm sorry, Jess.' He sat down heavily on a leather bench. 'I've been a bit crap, I suppose.'

'No!' she said, although that was true, wasn't it? What sort of person leaves a year-old relationship with a live-in partner and a sort of surrogate daughter, with a four-word Post-it note! Not even a text, she thought to herself. Not even an email.

'Look, Dave,' she continued, biting the bullet. 'I know things haven't been great, I know ...' she gestured silently at her barely there belly bulge, 'but surely it's not all about ...' her eye rested on his enormous calf muscle and she lost her train of thought for a moment. 'You know ... not just, erm ...'

'Not just about looks?' he said, helpfully, his chocolate eyes focusing on her face. 'Not just about the sex.' He gave a subconscious, slight pelvic thrust at the word.

'Exactly,' she said, feeling slightly flustered, and self-conscious that she hadn't reapplied her foundation before leaving the changing room. 'It's ... we're more than that, surely?'

'What, more than just sexual partners? Lovers?'

'Um ...'

'More than just two people consumed by lust? Sexually connected by desire? Drawn to each other's naked bodies?'

'Well ...'

'Of course, there was more to our relationship than sex, than making love, than the act of physical affection,' he said, still subconsciously gyrating. 'Sex ... Well, sex is great. Our

103

sex – the sex between you and me – the sexual attraction, physical desire was amazing. But sex isn't everything.'

'No . . .' How many times did he have to say sex?

'Sex,' he said, for no reason at all.

'Right.'

'I, well, it's complicated,' he said. 'Maybe . . . Can we talk about something else? I know! How about a couple of pics for that blog of yours?!'

It was classic subject-changing – exercised with the same level of subtlety she'd had to use when distracting a three-year-old Anna with cartoons. 'Oh look! It's Peppa Pig! That's right; forget about the chocolate.' But she grabbed the opportunity. Turning and raising her phone, she took a couple of selfies of them together – just like old times.

Later, once Anna had gone to bed, and Jessica was uploading the snaps to her social media, she had to fight unexpected tears again. Because in the picture, she looked as if she had it all. Grinning with her burly boyfriend, working out at the gym, everything going well.

Whereas in reality, she'd ducked out of the gym with barely a leg lift, cried in the shower and picked up a pathetic half-cucumber and diced lettuce from the Co-op on the way home. Anna hated cucumber. And Jessica would never get through a whole one herself.

The cashier had been friendly, but they'd both known what half a cucumber really meant.

She'd never felt so alone.

STOP! PENIS!

A petty thief has taken the internet by storm due to the nature of his haul. Hugo Henderson, 42, from St Albans, who describes himself as an artist, was caught stealing a giant replica penis from a sculpture at the city library this morning.

Henderson, who claimed that the sculpture belonged to him, was confronted by a member of staff, who attempted to restrain him. However, the would-be art thief grappled with the surprised employee, wrenching the three-metre penis from the sculpture in the process.

Henderson – who had disguised himself with a large hat – then ran through the library foyer, complete with three metre penis, in an attempt to get away with the stolen item.

John Foster, 22, library assistant, said: The first thing I knew, there was this guy acting suspiciously by the penis statue. Then, he picked it up off the stand and started to walk off! I asked him to stop, and placed a hand on him to restrain him, but he went mad. He said something about his art and how he had his mind on bigger things. Then he ran off with the penis.'

The sculpture *Proud Man*, which was eventually discovered to be the work of Henderson himself, had been a controversial exhibit in the library foyer for two weeks, receiving a number of complaints from parents, as well as the pressure group 'One Size Fits All', who campaign against the objectification of men.

Doris Halliday, 87, was in the foyer when the scuffle took place. She told reporters, 'All that fuss over a sculpture! I've always thought they were overrated, myself.'

The remainder of the statue has now been removed from the exhibition stand and will shortly be replaced with a rather less controversial exhibition of local pottery.

Sally Jones, 56, who is in charge of arranging exhibitions for the library and surrounding municipal buildings, defended her choice of exhibit. 'True art should challenge our perception of the world,' she claimed. '*Proud Man* is a powerful work of art, which appeals to me on a very personal level.'

Hugo Henderson refused to comment on the incident.

Police have issued a caution for public disturbance, but no other charges will be entered.

Chapter Sixteen

#WalnutSalad for tonight's dinner – check out the recipe
here. And finally catching up with BFF @MW_Bea
#LifeisGood #Winning #Protein

It was great to hear Bea's voice on the phone; once again she
was reminded how much more personal it felt than emailing.
And Bea wasn't a fan of online chats – probably one of the
reasons Jessica often forgot to get in touch.

'Hang on, so you're telling me that penis guy is one of
your clients? I saw him in the *News*!' Bea laughed down
the line.

'His name's Hugo, and yes, he's probably my longest-
standing client.'

'Longest-standing . . . in what way?'

'Bea!' but Jessica couldn't help but smile. '*Proud Man* is a
serious piece of artwork!'

'Oh yes, I wasn't suggesting . . .' Bea giggled. 'I mean, it's
certainly a seriously big . . .'

'Stop it! Anyway, it's a complete nightmare. I've spent
years trying to get Hugo some proper attention in the press,
and now he's everywhere, but for all the wrong reasons.'

'No publicity is bad publicity, so they say.'

'Yes.' Jessica wondered who 'they' were. And whether
they'd ever heard of Twitter or the *Daily News*. Because
when it came to this sort of thing, there was definitely such

a thing as bad publicity. Hugo might well be offered a place on the next reality series going, but a space in a serious broadsheet weekend section or inclusion in a well-known gallery now seemed like a distant dream.

'Sorry, Jess. I know it's a nightmare.'

'Yep. Never mind. Are your lot OK?'

'Yeah, you know. Same old, same old.'

'No giant penis thefts I should know about?'

'Not a giant penis in sight.'

'Well, think yourself lucky.'

As Jessica hung up the phone she wondered why she didn't spend more time speaking to Bea. Somehow she always managed to put the world to rights.

Although she'd still wimped out of telling her about Dave.

Sighing, she turned back to her PC.

Having uploaded the gym picture, Jessica switched on to social media and began the usual round of tweets.

Check out my new blog! #fitat30 #lowcarb #fitnessgoals

She'd deal with Hugo and his penis tomorrow.

Fit at 30

Loving the gym

Those of you who read regularly will know that I try to add a little variety into my workouts – taking a new exercise class or hiking in the country are great ways to shake up your regime. So recently I've been trying fitness DVDs in my living room, and running up and down the stairs at work during my lunchtime. I've even bought myself a hula hoop (more later)!

But having gone to the gym last night, I realised that while variety is great, gyms are truly wonderful places if you want to get yourself in shape. They're packed with inspirational people (like my wonderful Dave) and as well as having a fantastic calorie burn, you can also make friends and have a great time.

Last night, I started off with a twenty-minute fast-paced warm-up walk on the treadmill, before doing thirty minutes on the ski machine and ten on the rower (the only machine that gives you a full-body workout). Then I did my usual floor routine, leg raises and free weights, before cooling down on the treadmill again.

Yes, the whole workout took nearly two hours, but now I've reached my fitness goal, I feel as if I'm more energised than I've ever been! And the diet is helping too – I've upped the lean protein and am trying to eat an extra few calories a day (that's right – MORE calories, as long as they're the right ones).

So if anyone's going through a bit of a slump with their exercise, take it from me – it's worth persevering.

Love, Jess

COMMENTS

Bob
Good for you – although remember to get outside too for your vitamin D! Coach Bob

Stu
Oh stop it, you're making me feel lazy.

D
???

Helen's Hulas
Hula hooping is the new sit-up! Visit www.helenshulas.com to try out our latest fat-blasting heated rings!

Chapter Seventeen

LITTLE ACCIDENTS – Press Release

We've all been there. A random cough, an unexpected sneeze and – oop! An accident. If you've experienced urinary incontinence you might feel embarrassed, might not want people to know.

Little Accidents are here to change your life! Our discreet 'safety net' range of products will keep you as dry as a newborn baby. Better still, they come in a range of sexy styles – from sequinned goddess to our fun 'umbrella motif' range.

Once you get used to Little Accidents, you'll wonder how you managed without them!

Goodbye knicker washing! Goodbye underwear shopping! And goodbye frumpy panty liners!

Hello to a glittering undercarriage and the confidence that you're safe – no matter how much you laugh.

Have a Little Accident every day!

Tamzin Peters (star of hot reality show *Dagenham and Diamante*) swears by Little Accidents.

'Before finding out about Little Accidents I felt awful about my bladder weakness. But now I feel blessed! Without my condition, I'd never have this fabulous range of underwear

alternatives to choose from each morning! Slim-fitting,
with only the smallest of bulges, Little Accidents not only
keep me comfortable, they give me a Kardashian-style
bottom boost!

'Incontinence has been a blessing.'

Jessica looked at the press release one last time. Sure, she was fine with helping to promote products, provided they didn't hurt anyone. And this range could be a godsend for women who were suffering. But she hated the normalisation of bladder weakness, when there was so much that could be done to ease the suffering.

She'd suffered a bit herself post-Anna, but Grahame had read up about biofeedback and encouraged her to go to a physio. While his skill as a husband had left a lot to be desired, he'd at least ensured she had a pelvic floor worthy of shooting ping-pong balls, should she choose to indulge.

'Incontinence has been a blessing', she read aloud to herself.

'Sorry? What was that?' Candice peered around her computer. 'Incompetence?'

'Incontinence.'

'Oh, I'm sorry!'

'Not me!' Jess said. 'It's just Little Accidents.'

'Yeah, my mum has those,' Candice acknowledged with a sympathetic grimace.

'No, this campaign,' Jessica waved the printout at Candice, but she'd turned back to her screen and begun furiously typing once more.

With a heavy heart, Jessica pulled up her list of contacts and began to send the press release to anyone she thought might be interested in featuring the product, together with its celebrity endorsement.

To: linda@littleaccidents.com
From: jess@StarPR.com
Re: Press Release

Dear Linda,

How are you?

Just a quick note to say that I've put some feelers out for Little Accidents. I'll let you know if there's any feedback, and do a chaser in a couple of days' time.

I hope all is going well your end.

Kind regards,
Jessica Bradley
CEO Star PR

To: jess@StarPR.com
From: linda@littleaccidents.com
Re: Re: Press Release

Oh hi, Jessica! Fab news about the press release!

I wanted to ask actually, Tamzin is featuring in an ad campaign for us – we're super-excited of course! – and I wondered whether you wanted to come down for the filming tomorrow? I know you wouldn't normally expect to attend, but thought it would give you a better understanding of the brand?

I've also popped a few samples in the post – they should be with you today or tomorrow. I'd love to get some feedback!

Best,
Linda

Wonderful. A day with Tamzin Peters talking about urinary incontinence. Jessica opened her diary; she'd blocked out tomorrow to catch up with her smaller clients – important phone calls, new hooks for potential press coverage. That sort of thing.

But she didn't want to look as if she wasn't interested either. Because, while she wasn't completely sure about the product, Little Accidents was her biggest client yet.

To: linda@littleaccidents.com
From: jess@StarPR.com
Re: Re: Re: Press Release

Dear Linda,
Great to hear that you're filming the ad! I'd be delighted to attend! Let me know the time/location and I will make sure to be there.

Kind regards,
Jessica Bradley
CEO Star PR

She began to compile a list of outstanding calls she'd be unable to make and once again felt a warm glow of pride that she actually had people to help her keep things moving. The client list was growing, and she was becoming more widely known among journalists. It all helped.

When she got to the name 'Hugo' her hand wavered. Could she really pass him over to Natalie? She'd called and left a message, but hadn't spoken to him properly since penis-gate. She glanced at the clock: two thirty. If she tidied up here, she'd have time to pop into Hugo's studio before picking Anna up from school.

The phone rang and she almost jumped out of her skin.

'Hello, Star PR, Jessica speaking,' she said, feeling sure she was about to hear Hugo's voice.

'Hello, dear!'

Jessica's lips involuntarily stretched into a smile formation. 'Oh! Hello Mum!'

'Just wanted to make sure it was still OK for dinner Saturday?'

Shit.

'Um—'

'Lovely. Well, your father seems to be on the mend, so we'll definitely be there. Is seven still OK?'

'It's—'

'Lovely, well, I won't keep you. You sound awfully busy. Goodbye!'

The phone rang almost immediately as she placed it back on the desk.

'Hello, Star PR, Jessica speaking.'

'Hello, Jessica.' This time it *was* Hugo.

'Oh, hello. I was about to phone you, actually.'

'Sorry I didn't get back to you after your message. It's been a strange couple of days. I just ... well ...'

'Yes, I saw the story yesterday.' Jessica felt suddenly guilty. Hugo might not be a big money-spinner, but he was someone who'd had faith in her when she was a one-woman band just starting out. She should have gone to see him, tried a bit harder.

'Oh,' his voice was flat.

'Honestly, I don't think it was that bad. There's no such thing as bad publicity and all that.'

'You really think so?' His tone lifted with hope.

'Yes, I do,' she lied. 'Anyway, I wanted to pop by and see some of these oil paintings you've been talking about. And maybe the competition entry?'

'This afternoon?' His tone was suddenly guarded.

'Yes, if that's OK?'

'Yes. Yes of course. Will see you in a bit.' The call ended abruptly.

With an hour until she needed to set off, she picked up Robert's book again.

REMEMBERING RAINBOWS

ACTIVITY TWO
Muddy puddles

How do you feel when you look out of the window and discover it's been raining? Chances are, you're depressed by the puddles that pepper the pavement. Perhaps you'll choose to wear waterproof boots to work; take an umbrella in case there's another storm later.

Can you pinpoint a time in your life when rain started to symbolise doom and gloom for you? When you started to care if your hair got wet or your shoes started to leak?

Close your eyes for a second and try to think back to an earlier time – a time when rain meant puddles, and puddles meant fun! A time when you'd be begging your parents to let you into the garden in your wellingtons, or leaning your head back to feel the raindrops on your face.

The reason you find rain depressing is the (often adult) associations you've made about this type of weather. You're thinking about being damp and cold, looking messy at work, or having your hairstyle ruined.

But really, rain is just water. And water is the very essence of life.

Next time you open your curtains in the morning to damp weather, take a moment to remember how you used to feel as a child – excited at the new opportunities rain presented, eager to get outside and feel the sensation on your face, or jump in puddles until you were wet through.

Take a second to experience the rain again, and look at it in a new light. Then, when you have a moment, find somewhere you can go to rediscover the joy of this weather. A park, where you can jump in puddles, or run over the damp grass. Finding pleasure in something you've previously seen as negative is one of the steps to a happier, more positive you.

Was he right? Jessica wondered. Was it really that simple?

Walking to Hugo's studio a later, Jessica couldn't help but feel a little nervous. He was always on at her to visit his gallery 'where the magic happens.' So why the reluctance this time?

Puddles of rainwater from the earlier shower looked at her expectantly, but she was hardly going to start jumping in them like an idiot. Especially not in her new gold pumps.

Stopping briefly, she unlocked her phone and sent Dave a quick message. 'Great seeing you last night – time to talk? J X' then put her phone back into her bag.

Across the road was one of the play areas that were scattered around the city. A dad was there, pushing his daughter on a swing to her evident delight. Jessica looked away, suddenly overcome with a feeling of guilt. Why? It was hardly as if Anna would want to be pushed on a swing at her age.

The chip shop situated below Hugo's studio on the high street was frying and the smell of fat hung in the air. But the stairs to the studio were clean and had been recently swept. She walked up the narrow corridor and pushed open the door, which had been left on the latch.

She remembered the first time she'd entered this room. It had been in the early stages of renovation – dust sheets everywhere, easels, stands, paintings propped around.

The space had been light and airy, and had felt purposeful somehow.

Then the awful day when she'd come to see Hugo's 'new direction'. The walls had been painted black and she'd felt as if she was walking into some sort of horror-movie trap. Seeing lolling sculpture heads hadn't exactly helped her to relax. 'Darkness,' Hugo had told her solemnly, 'is the new light. By unleashing our inner darkness we find our real truth.'

She'd feigned an appointment and got out of there as soon as possible. Over time, she'd got used to the rather sombre studio, and felt pretty confident that Hugo almost definitely wasn't going to keep her prisoner or murder her or anything.

This time the studio had changed again. 'Oh,' she found herself gasping. Because the dark sculptures and black walls of her last visit had disappeared in favour of bright white walls and bare wood. An easel sat in the centre of the room, covered with a white sheet. Propped around the walls were several paintings in delicate watercolour or sketched in oil – all subtle portraits of women. And all absolutely breath-taking.

Hugo, who was washing his hands at the stainless-steel sink in the corner, turned around. 'What do you think?' he grinned. With a start, Jessica realised how much he'd changed too. Gone was the strange sliver of a beard that had run across his chin and instead he was clean-shaven. The piercing had been removed from his eyebrow and his hair was shorter – the small flecks of grey visible in its dark brown giving him natural highlights that set off his blue eyes. He looked about ten years younger, and several shades cleaner.

'Wow,' she said.

'Yeah,' he gestured flamboyantly around the room, 'bit different from the dark phase, yeah?'

'Yes. They're beautiful. And you're looking nice!'

'Oh this,' he ran his hand through his newly short hair. 'It's a disguise, I guess.'

'Disguise?'

'Oh, you know. People were stopping me a bit in the shops. Saying, you know. Penis stuff.'

'Oh.'

'Yeah.'

'Still, it looks great.'

'Thank you,' he smiled. Even his smile looked different – wider, more relaxed. More genuine.

Suddenly Jessica realised she had an artist she could promote. She imagined interviews in broadsheet weekend pull-outs. A chiselled shot, next to the best of his artwork. The studio itself looked raw – just right for a photo shoot. This could be good. This could be really good.

No more Mr Penis Guy.

'Can I see it?' she asked. 'The competition entry?'

'Do you really want to?'

'Yes, of course! I've been imagining what it might be like!'

'It's . . . I'm just not sure if it's impressive enough.'

'I'm sure it's great! Perhaps just a little peek?'

'Actually . . . um. Do you mind if you don't yet?' he said, raising his hand protectively to the cloth covering the easel; the awkwardness she'd heard on the phone back in his voice. 'Just . . . I'm just adding a couple of things.'

'Oh, but you said?' He'd known she was coming to the studio to see the painting, so why had he changed his mind?

Hugo flushed slightly. 'I'm sorry, I know I said . . . it's just . . . I'm not sure whether you're going to . . . It's just, it's not quite . . .' he trailed off, his eyes darting to the canvas.

For a moment she wondered whether she ought to just grab the corner of the sheet and whip it off before he realised what was happening, like a magician with a tablecloth.

But something stopped her.

'OK. Maybe next time?' she said.

Twenty minutes later, as she left the studio, she checked her phone to see if there were any messages. But nothing. She sent Dave another message. 'You know what I said yesterday? About not being ready to tell everyone yet? Well, Mum and Dad are coming for dinner. Could you come? Just this one time? You know what Mum is like. I've said you'll be there . . .

Seconds later, a vibration in her pocket. 'I'm sorry. Not sure I can lie to your folks.'

This from the guy who'd encouraged her to forget about a few kilos when recording her weight on the blog. The man who'd lied through his teeth to get out of work when they'd booked a last-minute mini-break. The man who used a special spray to disguise the tiny pink bald spot that had recently appeared on the back of his head.

He didn't mind lying when it suited him.

As she walked back to her car, her worries about the forthcoming dinner party faded as she thought again about the cloth-covered canvas. Something in Hugo's expression worried her – surely whatever he'd produced couldn't be worse than *Proud Man*? Couldn't be worse than the painting of a rotted corpse he'd given her to hang in her office?

It would be fine, she told herself. Whatever it was, it couldn't be that bad.

Chapter Eighteen

Jessica arrived home to find a parcel on the front step, complete with the Little Accidents umbrella logo. Gathering it in her arms, she turned the key in the lock to let herself and Anna into the house.

'Please, Mum!' Anna said as soon as they entered, picking up from where they left off in the car.

'No. Homework first.'

'Oh, but Mum!'

Anna stomped up to her room to complete her maths homework, after which Jess had promised to let her go online. Anna's smartphone had internet capabilities, but for now at least Jessica would only let Anna use it in the front room, in plain sight. She'd allowed her an Instagram account, which she followed and checked regularly. And supervised time on YouTube. But not WhatsApp or Messenger.

It made her very unpopular with her daughter, but meant that – for now, at least – Jessica could sleep at night.

Not for the first time, she felt annoyed at Grahame, who could swoop in once a fortnight, all permissive smiles and treats. He never had to be the bad cop – the miserable parent who said no to everything. Jessica knew, in the long term, Anna would probably appreciate everything she'd done, but it would be nice – just once – to have a little acknow-ledgement of it now.

'When you're a mother like me,' she often caught herself saying, 'you'll understand.'

Anna would look at her wearily with an expression which suggested that she would never end up in any way like her mother.

To be fair, Jessica had never imagined she'd be the kind of mother she'd turned out to be. Like most mums, she'd had great intentions at the start. But it turned out no matter how good her intentions had been, life and circumstances meant that her version of motherhood was a series of mistakes tied together with the odd moment where she'd inadvertently got something right.

The day she'd found out she was expecting, she'd resolved that she'd be one of the women who 'have it all'. Her start-up had been ticking over nicely, providing her with the part-time income she needed, so she'd have plenty of time for per-fect parenting. She'd yet to start following any supermums and yummy mummies online, so the only mums she had to compare herself to were the ones she saw in the supermarket clutching screaming toddlers under an arm and looking close to mental collapse.

Now, as well as the daily trolling over her menu choices, her social-media feed was peppered with smug mum-upman-ship – *Kelly and me, working on our craft projects together! Such fun!;* or *Sam baked oat muffins with Mummy – so deli-cious!*

She'd meant to give Anna a perfect childhood – but now look at her. A single mum, so preoccupied with work and the gym that she barely had time to iron the girl's school uniform and couldn't even manage to pick her up each day. The fact she also had to be the one who applied discipline and rules meant that she spent most of her time feeling pretty shit about her parenting abilities. And her own mum's interfering – albeit well meant – didn't help. Jessica had spent the first few years of single mumdom being showered with advice on the importance of a Stable Family Unit.

On the plus side, raising Anna had made her see her own parents in a much more favourable light. Mum's constant favouring of Stu; Dad's embarrassing school disco pick-ups; the time when Mum had bought her salmon-coloured trainers for PE and she spent six months being called shrimp feet . . . They'd been doing their best too, probably.

In the kitchen, Jessica put the box down on the table, quickly assembled a simple pasta-bake, shoved it in the oven on a low heat, and sat down heavily in a chair. With a sigh, she opened up the packaging to reveal the Little Accidents range. Sequinned, coloured, decorated. Lacy – where the paper had been cut into like a kind of doily – and a special 'wedding night' pair – white, and edged with artificial fur. She held one in her hand and was surprised how like a baby's nappy it felt. No attempt had been made to shape it more closely to the body, and the absorbency pad was thick enough to last a newborn for a month.

She grabbed the sequinned pair, which seemed to be the least offensive, and put them on in the downstairs toilet. The pants crackled as she slid them up over her thighs, the coarse paper grazing her skin. Once in situ, they were slightly more comfortable, but as she pulled her black trousers up over the top, Jessica found she could barely fasten them. Looking in the mirror, she grimaced – her bottom looked enormous, and her trousers were practically straining at the seams.

They might have been covered in sequins, but the effect certainly wasn't glamorous.

Half an hour later when the doorbell rang, Jess was half

asleep on the sofa, with her laptop balanced on her Little Accidents selection box. The trill of the electronic bell made her jump up, almost sending her laptop crashing to the ground.

Through the narrow window in the front door, Jessica could see the outline of a woman – her hair shimmering even through the frosted pane. Liz.

She was tempted for a moment to scuttle back into the living room and pretend she was out – the way her mother had used to when cold-callers had rung the bell when she was a child.

Jessica was a magnet for salespeople, charity clipboard wielders and anyone with a cause. She'd once bought twenty bunches of lucky heather from an old woman in the town centre, rather than admit that she wasn't interested. Once she engaged with people, she was trapped by her need to please.

Anna soon put paid to any notions of subterfuge. 'WHO IS IT, MUM?' she hollered down the stairs, just when Jess was considering a leap back onto the safety of the sofa.

'Just a friend,' she called up. Calling Liz a friend was stretching it a bit, obviously, but the glass wasn't sound-proof, and she didn't want to face the fallout. 'Mummy's friend,' she added, referring to herself in the third person in a way she'd always resolved she wouldn't.

'Hi,' she smiled, opening the door and feeling her jaw ache in the same way that it did after a phone call with her mother. 'What a surprise!'

'Hi,' Liz smiled. 'I know you're busy, but I was just passing and thought I might just pop in for a quick chat about how everything's going?

'How lovely!' Jessica was going to have to relax her smile a bit before she pulled a cheek muscle. 'Well, come in.'

For the first time she noticed that Liz was carrying a box. Which seemed rather ominous.

'So,' said Liz once she'd shed her coat and made it into the living room. 'This is where the magic happens, eh!'

'Magic?' Jessica looked around the room to see what had prompted Liz's description. A pile of magazines sat on the table, her laptop flickered where she'd left it on the couch. There were a couple of Hockney prints on the wall, alongside a tapestry she'd picked up in France with Grahame. Pretty, but hardly 'magical.'

'Oh you know . . .'

'I just think of you tapping away at the keyboard. Glass of wine. All Carrie Bradshaw. Except you're a lot more healthy, of course. Organic wine, then. And your lovely man to cuddle up to!' gabbled Liz.

She's nervous, realised Jessica.

'Was rather hoping I might meet the man himself,' Liz continued, looking around the room as if to verify that there was no muscle-bound hunk hiding behind the sofa. 'Not here tonight?'

'No. Gym.' Jessica said. Which, according to the law of averages, was probably true.

'Ah. And you didn't fancy it?' Liz asked.

It was just polite conversation, showing an interest. But it felt like an interrogation. Was her web of lies really so easily unpicked?

'Rest day,' said Jessica with an air of authority. 'Just as important.'

'Of course. Of course. Good for you,' Liz nodded, sitting down rather heavily on the sofa and causing Jessica's laptop to perform a little leap into the air.

Liz rested her cardboard box on her lap, her right hand

stroking its lid, as if calming a fractious cat. 'So, the quiz!' she said.

'Yes.' Jessica felt a bit like she had at school on the rare occasions that she hadn't completed her homework. A prickle of a blush started to climb up her neck.

'How's it all going? It's just, I know I'm probably seeming a bit, well, *pushy*. But I do keep reading your blog – of course I would anyway, it's so compelling – and I've not seen anything about the quiz yet.'

'No. It's scheduled for . . .' Jessica tried to sound in control. She'd actually hoped she could avoid referencing a local school quiz on her fitness blog. 'I'll have to check,' she finished with a grin. 'Sorry.'

'OK.' Liz eyed her suspiciously. 'I'm sorry if you feel it's a bit beneath you,' she said. 'I know it's only a stupid school quiz. Nothing in the grand scheme of things.'

It was like watching an advert for Save the Tiny Animals. Jessica could feel her guilt rising with every word. 'No! No, it's not that,' she said hastily. 'Far from it.'

'OK. As long as you're sure,' Liz continued, looking at her with eyes that appeared suddenly kitten-like. 'I'd hate to impose, but I just keep wondering how the teams will manage without a minibus soon.'

'Yes, of course.'

'And Dave will be helping, on the night?'

'Oh! Erm, I'm not sure.'

'Oh. I thought I mentioned it . . . I do hope he'll make an appearance; it's so nice to see fathers – or, um, stepfathers – getting their hands dirty, so to speak. Especially well . . . a local celebrity like your Dave.'

'I'll ask him.'

'So,' continued Liz, snapping brightly back to positive and pushy. 'The questions.' She opened the box to reveal rows of neatly stacked cards, all handwritten, and – evidently – colour-coded. 'I've just written a few – you know, to help. I'm sure you have hundreds of your own!'

The flush that had started as a prickle on Jessica's neck reached her cheeks. She opened her mouth to confess that she hadn't yet had time to think of any (in fact, she'd forgotten all about it for the last couple of days, what with the #penisguy incident).

'Oh! Are these them?' Liz asked suddenly, moving the laptop onto the table and picking up Jessica's box. 'Gosh, aren't we similar,' she said, with a grin. 'Both of us with our little boxes.'

'They're . . .'

As she opened the box, Liz's face turned ashen. 'Oh God,' she said. 'Jessica, I had *no idea*. I'm so, so sorry.' Her tone was grave, as if she was talking about a death.

'No, no!' Jess tried to laugh. 'They're for work. A promotional product.'

'Oh, how lovely. It must be nice to get things to try out. And . . . and so . . . *practical*.' Liz was almost hyperventilating.

'Well, they're not really to *wear*. I'm helping with the promotional side, so they thought I ought to see the . . . the *range*.'

'Of course. Of course,' Liz replied, nodding doubtfully, placing the box carefully on the sofa as if she thought it might explode. 'Anyway . . . do you have any questions? For the quiz I mean?'

'I'm so sorry,' Jess replied, feeling her cheeks flush again. 'I thought I'd do some later this evening . . .'

'Of course,' Liz's tone had gone from chirpy, to sympathetic, to that of a disappointed parent. 'Of course. You must have so much on. It was silly of me, really.'

'No. No, I really want to be involved. I was thrilled that you asked!'

'Really?' The kitten eyes were back.

'Yes, really. Let me take a look at those questions, add some of mine, and maybe we can meet early next week?'

'If you're sure?' Liz got to her feet, smoothing down her navy-coloured skirt. 'I must dash, actually; dinner won't cook itself! I tell you what, let's make an evening of it next time, shall we? Bottle of wi— water or something?'

'Yes, great.' Jessica stood up, hearing the sound of crinkling paper as she did so. Liz's eyes travelled to Jessica's pants-area, which was now quite obviously bulging. Jessica tried to smooth it down surreptitiously, but the sequins had clumped together underneath the fabric, meaning each quick flick with a hand made more obvious lumps appear.

In the end, she came clean. 'Thought I'd try one on,' she grinned. 'Just to see what it's like, you know!'

'Of course! Of course!' came the answer. Liz tapped the side of her nose as if to say *your secret is safe with me*. 'If anything, it's a relief to find out things aren't quite as perfect as they seem,' she said. 'Your blog posts make me so envious sometimes!'

'Yes, but as I said, I was just trying—'

'Oh, yes. Yes, of course! Well, see you soon!'

Jessica shut the door and leant against it for a moment, her head spinning. Then a burning smell alerted her to the fact that the pasta bake had been ready for half an hour. She grabbed it out of the oven with a tea towel and scraped away the blackened top with a fork. It would have to do.

Remembering her Instagram, she arranged the salad neatly in the bowl and set a large jar of ultra-virgin pure olive oil flavoured organic essence next to it, taking a snap on her phone. *Salad for dinner – so versatile!* She wrote. #goodfats #cleanliving #nutrition #thisisthelife.

Anna was going to Grahame's tomorrow; he'd agreed to babysit despite it being 'her weekend' and was picking her up shortly before Jessica's parents were due to arrive for dinner. When she'd first made the dinner plan, Anna had been due to join them, but this had been scuppered by the fact that Anna thought Dave was tucked up in a Premier Inn near Brighton and her parents thought he was laid up with stomach cramps at home. Jessica had made some excuse about needing some private time with her parents, which Grahame had swallowed but Anna had – quite rightly – found highly suspicious.

Jessica felt a sudden wave of exhaustion. Was it all worth it? This lying? And where would it all end? Of course, if Dave would only come back then everything could just go back to normal; they could pretend it had never happened at all.

She imagined him turning up on the doorstep, wearing his skinny jeans and that polo top that looked great against his skin. Suitcases, flowers and apologies. Green smoothies before bed; comparing their daily steps; snuggling on the sofa for a well-earned glass of alcohol-free wine.

'Mum?' said Anna as Jessica dished out the rather bloated pasta bake a few minutes later. 'What on earth is wrong with your trousers?'

Jessica blushed: 'I've no idea what you mean!' she said, sitting down abruptly and hearing the unmistakable sound of tearing.

Anna gave her a look which made it absolutely clear what she thought but Jess ignored it – her mind was on her impending blog post and just how much lying she could get away with.

Fit at 30

Five things that make a relationship tick

Now that Dave and I are settled, it's a great time to reflect on what has made our relationship so strong; especially as we've only been together for just over a year. And I've put together my top five for you to enjoy!

1. Have a shared passion

Dave and I bond over our time in the gym and enjoy supporting each other's goals. Being with Dave means I'm more likely to stick to my programme, and that we're more likely to spend evenings together, working up a sweat!

2. Eat together

Dave tends to get home from work later than I do – usually I collect A from school and finish work in my home office, and it would be tempting to start whipping up a vegan curry or steaming asparagus as soon as I get in the door. But we always make the time to eat together, meaning not only do we stay healthy together, we also spend time talking to each other rather than eating on the run.

3. Laugh together

Dave and I share a sense of humour – and even the moments that have seemed disastrous at the time have become private jokes in our relationship. Like the time I fell off the running machine and shaved the skin from my lower arm (ouch!), or the moment he posted the wrong selfie online and some of his followers laughed at his short shorts.

4. Build a family

For many years, it's just been me and A, so anyone who comes into our lives has to accept us as a pair. If Dave and A hadn't got on, or A was unhappy with Dave living with us, it'd have been game over. Thankfully, after a bit of initial awkwardness, they get on like a house on fire. A's father is very much part of her life, but Dave has become an honorary spare.

5. Work together

Now as Dave works in sales, and I run my own PR firm, you might think this last point is a little odd. But working on something together can be so healthy for a relationship! This is why Dave and I have decided to present the St Augustin's Academy parent–teacher quiz next week. We've been working on the questions and having such fun!

COMMENTS

Love Doctor
What about open communication? For more information on successful relationships visit www.lovemeforever.org

Mrs B
Glad to read that you and Dave are having so much fun together. Seems he's on the mend! Looking forward to scrummy dindins!

SB
Great post.

D
Confusing post, Jess???? Will call.

LH
Thank you!

Chapter Nineteen

As Jessica parked in the small bay usually reserved for residents but now marked 'Little Accidents', she felt a tiny bit excited about watching the ad being filmed. OK, so it wasn't the most glamorous of products, but this would be the first campaign that she'd worked on with proper national reach.

She climbed out of the car, brushing the crumbs from her morning cereal bar from her black trousers and looked over to the front of an ordinary-looking new build outside which the camera crew appeared to be gathering.

Her phone beeped with a message from Stu. 'Can't believe you're hanging out with Tamzin Peters!' it read. 'Fame and fortune at last. PS: give her my number (don't tell the wife).'

'Lol,' she replied. 'I'll put in a good word for you ☺.' Then she opened up Twitter quickly. 'So excited to be meeting @TamzinPeters from @Dagenham&Diamante' she wrote. '#LittleAccidents #goodtimes #thisisthelife #soexcited.'

She slipped her phone back into her pocket, still smiling.

The camera crew consisted of two men – one with a camera, the other with an enormous microphone on a pole – as well as several other people with clipboards. Jessica recognised Linda and gave a little wave. Linda spotted her and lifted her hand in recognition.

'I'm so glad you could come,' she enthused as Jessica

approached. 'Guys, this is Jessica – she's working on getting us some additional press coverage.'

'Hi, Jessica,' the team chorused, in the kind of bored voice reserved by children to welcome a teacher during school assembly. *Good morrrning Miss Bradley!*

'Hi,' she said, feeling a little overdressed when she realised that everyone except her seemed to be wearing jeans.

'Tamzin's just getting her make-up done inside,' Linda whispered, as if the fact that Tamzin wore anything to enhance her natural beauty was a carefully guarded secret. 'She'll be out in a minute.'

'Is there anything you'd like me to—'

'No, no! Just nice that you wanted to come. It'll give you a real feel for the campaign, you know?' Linda said. 'It's going to be a fun morning!'

Just then the front door of the house opened and a tall, slender woman wearing tight, white skinny jeans and a leopard-print top walked out. Her hair hung in loose chocolate-coloured ringlets down her back, her skin was her trademark orange and her lips had apparently been inflated to twice their natural size for the occasion.

Jessica was a bit embarrassed to feel a little frisson of excitement at seeing Tamzin – she'd skimmed through a few episodes of *Dagenham and Diamante* online last night in preparation, and as far as she could fathom, all Tamzin did on the show was work part-time in the hairdresser's, dress her two-year-old son in designer gear and maintain an on–off relationship with one of the popular male characters, Connor.

All the same, there was something weird about seeing someone step from screen to reality, and she felt herself blush.

'Oh *Tamzin*, you look great,' Linda gushed, stepping forward.

'Oh, fank you,' came the reply. Tamzin's lips moved briefly from their standard pout to something that might be construed as a smile. 'I ent sure about the animal stuff though.' She fingered her satin top uncertainly: 'It ain't real lion skin or nuffin', is it?'

'No, no, don't worry. It's just printed material, like the – you know – the jungle range we're bringing out.'

'Oh, awright.' This seemed to settle Tamzin, who flicked her hair over her shoulder and began to walk towards the crew.

A man stepped forward at this point. 'Hi,' he said, sticking his hand out. 'I'm Kenneth. I'm, er, the director.'

Tamzin looked at his hand, perplexed, before holding it briefly between two of her talon-ended fingers and wobbling it slightly. 'Awright, Kennef,' she said.

'So, are we about ready?' asked Linda, bringing up the rear.

'Yeah. But I ent sure about the pants.'

'Oh but they look great!' enthused Linda, waving vaguely at the white jeans.

'Nah, not these. The – you nah – the padded fings, knickers, whatever.'

'The . . . the product? The Little Accidents?'

'Yeah. Cos, you nah, I got white jeans on, innit? So I fort, I won't put um on. Cos you know, they show fru a bit.'

'Of course, of course! Don't worry! We're just trying to show customers how you can wear the product and still look sexy. Nobody will know what's under your jeans in the ad, so that's fine.' Linda smiled, unperturbed.

Jessica remembered the bulge beneath her own trousers

caused by the sequinned version. There was no way this product would work under white, skinny jeans.

'So,' continued Linda, 'if you want to take a seat over there for a moment, we'll just get things set up.'

'Sure.' Tamzin clacked over on her enormous heels and plonked herself in one of two foldable chairs near to where Jessica stood, caught her eye and smiled briefly. 'Awight? You ent sittin' 'ere, are ya?'

'No, no,' Jessica smiled.

Tamzin nodded, flicking a strand of glossy hair back in over her shoulder. 'It's good to get the weight off,' she said, pointing at her heels. 'Fuckin' shoes.'

'Yeah.' Jessica looked down at her own modest heels. She'd tried to wear higher ones occasionally but ended up stumbling around like a newborn gazelle.

'So,' she said, unable to help herself. 'Great product, yeah?'

'What? Oh, yeah,' came the reply.

'And do you . . .' Jessica thought of Tamzin's endorsement. 'Do you normally wear them? The Little Accidents, I mean?'

'Wear 'em? Nah. I don't need 'em really.'

'Oh, it's just you said . . . In the press release?'

'Oh yeah. Well, my agent said, you know, it would be good for publicity. You know, bein' a role model or whatever.'

'So you've never worn them?' Jessica pushed, feeling almost like a detective.

'Nah. Well, yeah. Sort of. After Rocky was born.'

Rocky was Tamzin's two-year-old.

'Ah, OK.'

'Yeah. I 'ad a few problems. But better nah.'

'Right.'

'And I tried 'em a few times. Not lots, no. They sent me some, wiv some baby stuff and I fort, you nah, why not!'

'Not, the . . . the sequinned ones?'

'Fuck no! Sorry. I mean, nah, not really my style. Nappies, innit!'

'So why . . .' Jessica began.

Linda interrupted. 'Kenneth's ready,' she trilled. 'If you could just come this way, Tamzin.'

Tamzin obediently rose and tottered towards the cameras.

While she'd never worked on such a large campaign, Jessica knew the fine line trodden by celebrity endorsers when it came to products they recommended. The careful language, which meant they didn't quite *lie* but didn't exactly tell the truth either. The fact that an endorsement from someone like Tamzin could send product sales through the roof.

Why did it bother her so much that Tamzin didn't really wear the product? That she was playing a bit fast and loose with the truth? That Tamzin wasn't even going to put on one of the pairs of 'designer knickers' for the advert?

Jessica began to chew her nail thoughtfully, something she hadn't done since she was about eleven. She tasted the bitter flavour of nail polish, and stopped.

Instead, she watched the action as the advert gradually took shape.

A row of male models appeared from nowhere, each smartly dressed and carrying a bunch of flowers. One by one they walked down the path, knocked at the door, which Tamzin would open wearing an outfit that reflected one of the Little Accidents styles: leopard-print, sequins, even fake fur. Each time, she'd give her 'date' a little twirl and wink elaborately at the camera as she passed, as if to say, 'They don't know my secret.'

The voice-over, which Tamzin would do later, was set to read: *'When it comes to dating, I like variety and it's the same with my underwear. No two days the same, but no nasty surprises.*

'*Like the surprises that come with bladder weakness.*

'*That's why I love the new range of Little Accidents disposable knickers. Sexy, stylish and – like all the best dates – you can chuck them away when you're finished.*'

The end of the advert saw a tousled Tamzin in a sequinned robe pushing her date out of the door in his boxers and winking.

'That's when the voice-over artist will say, "Treat yourself to a Little Accident every day",' Linda had explained.

'That's great,' Jessica had replied, uncertainly.

'I'm so glad you like it,' said Linda. 'I hope it'll give you lots of ideas for promotion,' she added. 'We're really hoping that a big name like Tamzin will help us appeal to a whole new demographic.'

No doubt it would, seeing as the advert would be suggesting that the bulging paper pants would disappear under tight clothing.

On the way back to the office, Jessica called Dave's phone from her car; his answerphone cut in after just one ring – obviously he was screening his calls.

'Hi, it's Dave. If you can't get me, I'm probably at the gym.'

'Hi, Dave,' she said, trying to inject a smile into her voice. 'Just a quick call. I know you said it wasn't . . . wasn't *honest*, but, well, Mum and Dad are still coming tomorrow. Anna won't be there, so it'll just be them. Could you . . .' she swallowed nervously. 'Could you maybe come over? Just this one time? It'd . . . it'd be good to see you anyway . . .' she heard her words trailing off. She sounded desperate.

Perhaps she was. But the thought of having to sit through the mixture of disbelief, pity and dismay that her parents would project at her over dinner if she had to come clean was too much to think about. Comparisons to Grahame and the wonderful Tabitha, Stu and his perfect relationship. And there she'd be – Little Miss Flawed.

As it was, Mum was sniffing around and dropping heavy-handed hints about weddings and rings and babies whenever Jessica saw her. 'So, when are you two lovebirds going to make it official?' she'd asked recently. And, in a surprisingly modern reference, she'd once asked Dave whether he ought to take some advice from Beyoncé and 'put a ring on it'.

It was hard enough dealing with her mum's continual disappointment that she wasn't remarrying and creating a whole new set of grandchildren, let alone telling her that Dave was now off the scene and she was back on the market like an outfit someone had tried on for size but returned to the shelf, complete with foundation stains and the smell of perfume.

Oh, Mum would be positive. She'd try to bolster her up. But every time she offered her well-meant advice, Jessica would be only too aware of the concern and disappoint-ment lurking underneath. 'Oh, don't worry. Lots of women are single these days . . . you'll find someone.' Or 'Be careful when you choose the new wallpaper, dear. Too many florals and no man will want to live here.' Mum was from a different generation – obviously. But it still hurt when her advice on Jessica's love life revealed the fact that she clearly didn't think that Jessica could manage on her own.

'I thought you were a feminist, Mum,' she'd said once. 'Women don't need men, you know. We can manage without.'

'But that was the seventies,' Mum had said, kindly. 'We paved the ground for your generation, so you could have it all, Jessica! Newsflash – we WON! And you know, you really could do with a nice man to look after you.'

Too late to get to the office, Jessica went straight to the school and waited outside for Anna. She was a little bit early, able to watch the children coming out – first the year sevens, then eights. Finally, year nine were released and walked towards the gates in small groups – talking and laughing.

Scanning for her daughter, Jessica looked across the playground and finally saw Anna walking on her own, her shoulders hunched, arms wrapped around her body. She looked, from this distance, as if she was weighed down with the cares of the world.

When she saw Jessica's car, she straightened up and waved.

'Everything all right love?' asked Jessica as her daughter clambered into the front seat.

'Yeah. Yeah, not too bad,' came the answer.

Later, she prepared a dinner of couscous salad, torn chicken pieces and parmesan and half-heartedly photographed it for her Instagram. '#DinnerWithMyDaughter #GirlsNightIn #HealthyFood #GoodTimes', she typed.

But even though they sat together chatting as normal, Jessica couldn't shake the image of her little girl, hunched over like someone five times her age, and looking utterly alone.

Fit at 30

Dinner for four

One of the challenges for those of us who take our diet seriously is inviting people around for dinner. It's hard not to appear fussy, or slip off the wagon and scoff a piece of chocolate fudge cake.

But there are ways around this for those of us serious about keeping in shape. Tonight, I'm cooking dinner for Dave and my parents. I love my parents, but their tastes are of the old-fashioned, stodgy kind when it comes to food. However, I reckon I've created a menu that would please even the blandest of palates – and without slipping from the low-cal, high-protein path.

The starter's going to be a salad – avocado (of course), with cucumber, feta cheese, olives and tomatoes, drizzled with olive oil.

The main: I'm going to get out the spiralizer and create courgette spaghetti, topped with steamed chicken and tomatoes.

Dessert? It's not impossible to create some mouth-watering desserts with a little imagination. I'm going for frozen raspberries and grapes with home-made, sugar-free sorbet.

I defy anyone's taste buds not to water with that on the menu!

#Healthy #DietFriendly #DinnerforFour

Comments have been turned off for this post.

Chapter Twenty

She uploaded the menu, feeling slightly guilty that most of the pictures had been stolen from her archives, or even – when it came to the salad – from someone else's Facebook post.

'Come on, Anna, Dad will be here in a minute!' she said, noticing the time.

'Coming!' yelled her daughter, who was already on her fourth outfit change.

Jessica sat on the stairs, wondering not for the first time why it was Grahame and Tabitha got to see the perfectly adorned, polite and enthusiastic Anna, whereas she had to live with the real-life stroppy version most of the week.

Jessica had spent the morning writing the blog, deciding to turn off the comments so even if Mum was confused about the fake menu, she couldn't let her know online. After lunch, she'd dragged Anna to the supermarket to buy ingredients; Anna had complained again about having to go to Grahame's, and in the end Jessica had compensated her with a new pair of headphones – probably Anna's intention the whole time.

When Anna emerged, finally, she was wearing a pair of pink jeans and a black cardigan. Her light-brown hair was pulled back into a plait and she appeared to be wearing lip gloss.

'Do I look OK?' she asked – and Jessica was surprised at how shy and uncertain her daughter seemed to be.

Anna had never seemed to notice how she looked at all until she was about eight, when suddenly she developed a penchant for anything with either glitter or unicorns – and preferably both. Four years on, she was starting to develop a personal sense of style, choosing her outfits carefully when she saw friends, and asking for things she'd seen on TV.

It was sweet, watching her daughter grow up. But sometimes Jessica longed for the scruffy-haired seven-year-old who hadn't cared whether her trousers were on the right way round, or if she had odd socks, as long as she was warm and dry.

'Of course, you look lovely!' she said. 'Come here.'

She opened her arms and Anna buried herself in them, nuzzling into her like a much younger child for a moment. 'Are you OK?' Jessica asked, breathing in her familiar scent – so typically Anna.

'Yeah. I just, you know . . .'

'No? What?'

'I just want Dad to be proud of me, I suppose.'

'Of course he's proud of you! Don't be silly.'

'It's just he's always telling me these stories about *his* boys at school, and how well they're doing. But he never mentions me.'

'Don't be silly. Your father probably tells Forest and River all about you when you're not there. He's so, so proud of you!' She squeezed her daughter a little tighter. 'And I am, too. You know that?'

'Yeah.' Anna shrugged. Clearly, Jessica's pride wasn't worth quite as much as the wonderful Grahame's. Jessica tried to swallow the jealousy down – this wasn't about one-upmanship. She'd talk to Grahame in the week, if she could catch him on the phone between meetings.

A sleek white Audi purred into the driveway and Anna

broke away instantly and charged to the door. 'It's him!' she exclaimed, as if Harry Styles had suddenly turned up on the doorstep. 'He's here!'

Grahame emerged from the car, looking as if he'd literally just left Gant in his new, completely crease-free clothes. His dark-blonde hair – what was left of it – was neatly brushed and as he approached, Jessica caught a whiff of Steam for Men before, by rights, she should have.

Back in the old days, Grahame had been a jeans and T-shirt man. Gradually she'd watch him morph into Tabitha's version of an ideal partner – his Levi's tossed aside for chinos, trainers replaced by faux leather footwear so highly polished she half-expected him to break into a tap dance on her doorstep. He'd had his hair highlighted at first, then, as it had receded, had started using 'product', as he called it, which as far as Jessica could see meant that he glued what was left of his fringe to his scalp using some sort of sticky oil.

'Daddy!' Anna cried, suddenly three years old again, and flung herself into his arms. As he enveloped her in a bear-hug, it was hard for Jess not to feel a pang of regret that they couldn't have tried a little harder to keep things together for their daughter. Had she been too unforgiving? Could they have worked something out? Or was it her destiny to always pick guys who disappeared the moment things got a little rocky?

Jessica smiled – fakely – for probably the tenth time that day and opened the door up a little wider. 'Coffee?' she asked, confident that her invitation would be refused – which would be a relief seeing as she had about an hour and a half to whip up some sort of dinner for her parents.

'OK, why not!' he replied cheerily and she felt a frisson of annoyance. She'd been asking this question every other week since they split, and this was practically first time he'd decided to take her up on the offer.

'Great!' she lied, opening the door a little wider. 'Well, come on in.'

'I can't stay long, I'm afraid,' he said, unzipping his jacket but leaving it on. 'Tabitha is making vegan paella.'

Jessica was tempted to ask whether this meant she was whipping up plate of boiled rice, but managed to hold her tongue. 'Ooh, lovely,' she said instead. 'I don't suppose you could take a pic of it, could you? Might be able to use it on the blog at some point.'

'Yeah?' Grahame looked doubtful. 'OK, why not.'

Jessica quickly loaded two espresso pods into the coffee machine and deposited the result into two small cups. 'Oh, sorry,' she said, handing it to him. 'I should have asked whether you wanted a cappuccino or something. I've got soy milk.'

'No, this is fine,' he said, grimacing a little at the bitter taste. He'd always hated espresso – and this was a double.

'Anna, do you want to nip to the loo before you go?' asked Jessica.

'OK,' her daughter moaned, rolling her eyes in the way she did when she saw through a grown-up 'ploy'. 'Hurry up talking about me, though.' She trudged pointedly out of the room and closed the door with a click.

'Everything OK?' Grahame asked when their daughter had gone.

'Yeah, look – thanks for taking her tonight. I know it's not strictly your weekend.'

'Don't be silly – any time!'

'Thanks – you might regret saying that!' she joked. 'Anyway, look . . . I just wanted to say, well, Anna mentioned that you were really proud of the boys.'

'Yeah? Well, that's OK, right?'

'Sure, sure, of course. I didn't mean *that*! It's just I think she's got the impression that you're not very proud of *her*.'

'What?'

'Yeah, I know. I told her that you were, of course, but maybe a couple of compliments over the weekend . . .'

'Sure.' Grahame drooped over his tiny cup. 'You try and try, don't you? To get it right. And you still end up getting it wrong.'

'That,' said Jessica, in a rare moment of utter honesty, 'is the story of my life.'

'Really? You seem as if you've got it all together.' Grahame gestured around the kitchen, which was – it had to be said – unusually tidy, but it was still only a flatpack self-assembly she'd bought on sale at the local DIY store.

'Yeah, I suppose.' She shrugged. Clearly he had no idea. But then, why would he? Even her daughter didn't know the mess her life seemed to be in – and she only shared edited highlights online. Maybe if she'd been more honest, she'd have had more support.

'Honestly, I don't know how you do it. Anna's always going on about how great things are here – and how you're so successful now, and stuff. Me and Tabby spend the whole week getting ready for her to come round just so we can compete!'

'Really?' Jessica was astounded. 'All I hear is Dad and Tabitha this, the twins that . . .'

Grahame shook his head. 'We love having her, it just never seems as if she enjoys herself much. I think she misses you, to be honest.'

Their eyes met briefly and Jessica felt herself having to look away. What was it about Grahame? Something about the age at which they met, perhaps. Something about having grown up together? The fact he still knew more about her than anyone else?

She'd used to love watching him holding Anna, the way he'd sing 'Twinkle, Twinkle Little Star' quietly in their daughter's ear to make her go to sleep. Carrying her on his back in that ridiculous baby carrier they'd bought. Yes, Tabitha might be the perfect woman, but she'd never understand what had made him walk away from his tiny daughter.

'Oh,' she said, after a pause.

'Yeah . . . and . . .'

But Anna burst in the room at that point. 'Finished talking about me?' she said, glaring at them. 'I heard my name as I was coming downstairs.'

'Don't be silly,' said Jess, reaching over to rub her daughter's head, but choosing at the last minute to pat her on the shoulder, remembering the hard-won hairstyle choice.

'Ready, sweetie?' Grahame said, putting his arm around his daughter. Jessica would never get away with calling Anna something so *babyish* but Anna smiled at her father and leaned into him as they walked out of the door.

'Hang on!' Jessica said suddenly, running after them and planting a huge kiss on Anna's cheek. 'Miss you,' she said.

'Mum!' Anna said, but she was smiling. 'You're so embarrassing!'

Jessica looked up, caught Grahame's look and grinned. 'I know,' she said. 'But it's worth it.'

'Come on, let's leave your mother in peace,' Grahame said, nodding his goodbye.

Jessica watched the car drive away: she might sometimes look forward to her 'nights off' when Anna was with her father, or the evenings when her parents took over to give her a break, but when push came to shove her life was always a little bit greyer when Anna wasn't in it.

147

It struck her suddenly, too, that a lot of what she'd been jealous of when it came to Grahame and his perfect life had been a fabrication – partly created by Anna, partly by her own imagination. Like her, Grahame didn't feel as if he had it all together, despite appearances.

Noticing the time, she realised this really wasn't the moment to sit and ponder. She had a meal for four (or three) to cook. And a whole elaborate fabrication to plan.

Because her parents were expecting Dave. And they were going to get him.

Chapter Twenty-One

Catching up with my parents over a family meal!
#GoodTimes

'Hello, darling!'

Jessica opened the front door to her mum and dad. Mum in front, as always, clouding the air with lavishly applied Chanel No. 5, Dad loitering in the background, like a reluctant teenager being dragged to a family do. Mum was wearing a garishly floral blouse and had clearly spent some time blow-drying her blonde hair into a kind of candy-floss puff. Dad was sporting a dishevelled-looking white shirt, creased jeans and a pair of brogues. His hair, as always, was practically non-existent.

'Hi, Mum, Dad.' Jessica smiled, opening the door to let them in. It was seven o'clock, but the gathering cloud made it seem much darker than usual.

After the rigmarole of hanging up their coats, thanking them for the wine, accepting profiteroles; giving Dad a hug, breathing in his familiar smell of paper and ink and forbidden ciggies, and kissing the air near to her mother's cheek, Jessica waited for the inevitable question.

'Where's Dave?' her mother asked, as she settled herself onto the leather sofa. 'Is he cooking?'

'No. Actually, he's still a bit *under the weather*,' Jessica replied. 'He thought he was fine, until about half an hour ago. But he's had to go to bed, I'm afraid.'

'To bed?'

'Yes. He's taken a turn for the worse.'

'Poor chap,' said her father, probably secretly relieved that he wouldn't be expected to talk about muscle mass all evening. 'You should have told us not to come.'

'Well, it was very, uh, last minute,' Jessica replied, with a wry grin that she hoped communicated to her father that she *would* have cancelled had she been able to get past her mum.

'Didn't I see a picture of him from the gym earlier?' piped Jessica's mum, frowning. 'Something about a new target being met or something? He was wearing some sort of spandex, I think. Rather fetching, actually. Reminded me of your father in his heyday.'

'Um, yes . . . I think . . .' Jessica said quickly. 'Actually, I think that might have been what did it,' she added, realising she might be on to a winning argument. 'You were right, Mum. All that gym isn't good for him, especially when he's been poorly.'

This seemed to settle her mother. 'Well,' she said, shifting slightly in her chair. 'Well, I do always say, less is more when it comes to exercise.'

'Yes,' nodded Jessica, pouring a generous serving of her mother's favourite sweet wine. 'You're so right.'

'And you know, I read recently that too much of that,' her mum lowered her voice, '*testosterone* stuff these fitness fanatics have, the worse their little swimmers are.'

'I think that must have been an article about steroids, Mum. Dave doesn't take anything like that.'

'No, no. It's testosterone, I'm sure of it. And, whether you like it or not, that man is full of it. You know, you haven't got long if you want to give that poor child a sister or brother.'

Across the room, her father gave her a barely perceptible wink.

'Would you rather we headed off?' he asked. 'I'm sure Dave could do with the peace and quiet. You know . . . to replenish his testosterone levels . . .' His eyes met hers and they both looked away abruptly before giggles set in.

'Oh, don't be silly!' Jessica smiled. It was better to get on with it, especially as she'd have to come up with another excuse if they wanted to rearrange. 'I've done all the cooking now anyway.'

It was sort of true. Jessica seemed, in fact, to have lost her cooking mojo. She'd been to the local deli and bought some pumpkin soup for a starter, fallen back on a simple salmon with pesto crust for main, and given in to the fact that, whatever she made, they'd end up having profiteroles for dessert.

What was it about feeling a bit down? It seemed to suck all the energy out of her; she'd lost impetus – with the campaign, with her cooking; she'd kept up her social-media presence, but her heart wasn't in it.

Too heartbroken? Or was it like missing the gym – once you ducked out of that world it was hard to get motivated again. Hard to find the will within yourself to even take a picture of your dinner, let alone post it for your followers. And you could forget hashtags.

'Are you sure Dave doesn't want to come down for a bit of soup?' pressed her mother as they sat down at the glass topped dining table. 'I'd have thought it would do him some good.'

'Oh no.'

'Are you sure? It's actually quite tasty!' continued her

mother, clearly astounded by the fact that anything Jessica had (purportedly) cooked could taste good. 'Better than that cabbage stuff last time. And, I must say, better than the recipe you put on your blog earlier. Not that I . . . I mean, not it didn't sound simply *delicious*,' she corrected quickly. 'Just, well, this is rather special. Let me take him a bit up, poor boy.'

'Yes, last-minute change of plan on the recipe front . . . no, um, well the avocados were . . .' she stammered. 'But I really think Dave is . . .'

'It's actually great, Jessica,' interrupted her father. 'Nice to know you're eating properly now.'

'What do you mean?'

'Well, all that diet stuff. There didn't seem to be much, well, substance to it,' he said, stirring his pumpkin soup thoughtfully. 'You're skinny enough as it is.'

'I don't know about that,' Jessica replied looking pointedly at her midriff and grimacing.

Her dad gave her a grin. 'Call that a belly . . . ?' he said, reaching towards his shirt. 'THIS is a b—'

'Clive! Not at the table!' snapped her mother. Her father's shirt dropped down like a heavy curtain. 'Anyway, dear, I do think I should go up. It's important he keeps up his strength.'

'No. I mean, ah, I'll save some for him for later,' Jessica said hurriedly. 'He's, well, he's not keeping much *down* at the moment.'

She saw her father's eyes travel down to the orange, slightly chunky liquid on his spoon at the thought of Dave vomiting upstairs.

'Sorry, Dad.'

'No problem,' he said, tearing off a bit of bread and chewing at it doggedly.

'I think I might have to pop up and see if he's all right?' persisted her mother. 'It sounds like he might have something nasty.' She shovelled pumpkin soup into her mouth, parting her lips widely to avoid smudging her magenta lipstick, and clearly unaffected by the thought of Dave's emissions.

'That's so nice of you, Mum. But I wouldn't want you to pick up the same bug.'

'Nonsense. I told you about these immune-system boosting thingies. Over fifties, they're called. We're right as rain, aren't we Clive?'

Her father emitted a defeated cough.

'Well,' Jessica felt her mind begin to race. Once her mother got the bit between her teeth, it was almost impossible to stop her. Which would be endearing if Dave really was upstairs heaving. But completely alarming in the current situation. 'Perhaps a little later.'

'No, don't be silly. He'll probably be sleeping later. I just think someone else ought to check his pallor – you know, I used to be a school nurse?'

'Of course I know, Mum, Just—'

'Well, that's settled then,' her mother placed her spoon into her empty bowl – she had an amazing capacity to be able to dominate the conversation and demolish her food simultaneously.

'Wait!' cried Jessica as her mother scraped her chair back from the table. 'I mean, let me just go up to check that he's . . . he's *decent*.'

This, at last, stopped her mother in her tracks. 'OK,' she relented. 'Tell him I'll pop up in a mo.'

Sweaty and breathless, Jessica arrived at the top of the stairs and burst into her bedroom. It was a mess of cast-off clothes and discarded teacups. Seeing it for the first time through her mother's eyes made her prickle like a defensive teenager.

But the mess wasn't her first concern. There wasn't time. Instead of tackling that issue, she got two pillows and arranged them under the covers in a man-shaped hump. She put a couple of the cups on the floor by the bed, and kicked some of the other debris out of sight. Then she closed the curtains and switched the low light in the en suite on to give the room a dull glow.

Hearing her mother's footsteps on the stairs, she realised it would have to do. Stepping out of the door, she raised her finger to her lips. 'He's asleep,' she whispered. 'I think we ought to leave him.'

She pushed the door open a fraction to reveal the humped figure in the bed, hoping to God that her mother would at last be put off.

'Oh dear, poor chap,' she said, peering into the darkness. 'Do you think I ought to go and see if he has a temperature?'

'Oh, no. I checked his forehead. He seems to be over the worst,' said Jessica, hastily. 'And I'd hate to wake him up.'

'And,' Jessica's mum lowered her voice, in case the sleeping Dave heard. 'He has *flushed*, I suppose?'

'Yes. Yes. All clean and tidy in the bathroom.'

Her mother nodded. 'Good. It doesn't do to let these bugs hang around. The last thing you need is to catch something like this, what with your business doing so well.'

Jessica started slightly at that. It was the first time her mother had actually acknowledged that her *little enterprise* was a business. Let alone that it was doing well.

'Good point,' she said. 'Thanks, Mum.'

'Well, it wouldn't be *Star PR* without its star, now would it?' Her mother rubbed her arm in a rare moment of physical affection.

Was it possible that her mother was actually proud of her? Jessica felt herself begin to blush.

'And of course, with the two of you *trying* now.'

'We're not, we haven't . . .'

Her mum winked elaborately. 'Oh, I *know*,' she said. 'It's all very private, I'm sure.'

'Shall we . . . ? Perhaps we should . . . ?' Jessica gestured to the stairs.

'Right. Well, perhaps I'll pop up after dessert, just to make sure he's not taken a turn for the worse,' her mother continued – not realising the shockwaves her casual comment about her daughter's business had caused.

'Yes, that's a great idea,' Jessica replied, hoping a couple more generous servings of wine would help her mother to forget about the sleeping pillows in her daughter's room.

As they walked down the stairs, they could hear the low tones of Jessica's father, mumbling away on his own in the kitchen. Jessica stopped to listen.

'Is Dad all right?' Jessica asked. She'd heard Dad singing on occasion when he thought no one could hear, or shouting at the TV, but never talking to himself.

'Silly man,' came the response. 'I caught him talking to the kettle the other day. Telling it to hurry up and boil, or something. He's probably talking to the oven.'

But it wasn't funny, was it? Jessica thought about the new wrinkles she'd noticed recently; the fact he seemed to be more forgetful than he used to be. Yes, he was getting older, but even so, talking to himself was a new, worrying development.

Strangely, though, as they approached the kitchen, it was clear that not only was her father talking to someone, but that someone was answering.

It was only when they pushed open the door that Jessica

realised the 'real' situation she'd unleashed on herself. Because, standing in a crisp white shirt, hair styled, carrying a bottle of wine, stood a fragrant and definitely not vomiting Dave.

#OhShit

Chapter Twenty-Two

To: jess@StarPR.com
From: hugo@freemail.com
Re: Studio

Hi Jess,
I've made a few changes to the studio – to do with the new
focus – and thought it might be a good idea if you have time
to pop in and see the new work after the weekend? Think I'm
ready to show you the competition entry too.

H

To: hugo@freemail.com
From: jess@StarPR.com
Re: re: studio

Sure, I'd love to. Will give you a call to arrange.

To: jessica@StarPR.com
From: claudia@dailynews.com
Re: Interview

Dear Jessica,
I came across your blog when a friend of mine tweeted your
'tips' for a good relationship. I loved reading it! I see you've
also been featured in *New Woman* mag recently.

I'm putting together a piece for the website featuring couples who have a shared interest, and I'd love to feature you and Dave in the piece.

You'd need to attend a photo shoot together and answer a few questions on your relationship to take part. And I'd be able to pay you each £150 as a thank you.

Drop me a line and let me know what you think.

Best wishes,
Claudia Hibbert
Daily News

Sitting in her home office, catching up on her backlog, Jessica was tempted to hit her head against the desk. Was her life getting more complicated, or was she just getting more incompetent when it came to managing it? This was the kind of opportunity she'd have jumped at a few weeks ago when her life had bordered on normal.

Last night, she'd spent an hour and a half lying to her parents about why her boyfriend, who was meant to be curled up either in bed or over the toilet bowl upstairs, was magically standing in her kitchen brandishing a bottle of wine and smelling strongly of Blue Sheen.

Her mother had gone pale when they'd entered the kitchen and Dave had turned to greet her with a smile. 'Hello, Jean!' he'd cried, leaning towards her for a peck on the cheek.

She'd recoiled as if she'd seen a ghost. 'Dave!' she'd screeched. 'What are you doing here?'

'I live here,' he'd lied.

'Erm, Mum,' Jessica had said, her brain whirring like a fruit machine trying to find a plausible excuse and gently pushing her mother back into her chair. 'I can explain.'

She'd shot Dave a look which was designed to say: For

God's sake don't say anything! This is a VERY COMPLICATED SITUATION – quite a feat for her eyebrows.

'Are you all right?' he'd asked, looking at her with concern. 'Your eyes have gone all strange.'

'Yes. I'm fine,' she'd hissed. 'Mum, Dad. I'm sorry that told you Dave was SICK IN BED,' she'd continued, slowly and clearly in the hope that she could help Dave to catch up at the same time as somehow getting herself out of the mess she was suddenly plunged into without looking like a downright liar and fraud or (of course) revealing that she and Dave had split. 'It was ... um ... well ... we wanted to, er, surprise you!'

'Well, you've certainly done that,' her dad had said, softly, almost to himself. 'I think your mother is about to have some sort of breakdown.'

Jessica had glanced at Mum, who had slumped into her chair and was gripping the stem of her wine glass so tightly that her knuckles had turned white.

'Sorry,' Jessica had continued, with a grimace. 'Um, we thought, well, it was meant to be a bit of fun!' she'd tried to smile and felt the muscles around her mouth ache.

'I'm not quite—' Dave had begun.

'Not NOW, Dave,' she'd hissed. 'Look, Mum and Dad ... Dave ... I mean we ... wanted to surprise you ... because, erm. Because ... well ...' she glanced the bottle in Dave's hand. Prosecco. Perfect.

Suddenly, like the sun breaking through persistent cloud, her brain had come up with what could only be described as a Perfect Plan. Three cherries lined up in the fruit machine of her mind.

'Well,' she'd snatched the bottle from Dave's hand. 'Well, we've just, erm ... Truth is, we're engaged!' She'd stepped lightly towards Dave and made sure his toe was under her

159

heel. Applying pressure, she'd continued. 'I'd . . . um, I'd told you that Dave was sick earlier in the week . . . and, well, we were cooking the, ah . . . the pumpkin soup together, when he, well, he asked me to marry him,' she'd looked at Dave, desperately. Luckily, he'd been speechless.

'Then, well, we thought we'd buy some bubbly,' she'd said, waving the bottle precariously close to her mother's head. 'And . . . and, so I made an excuse. I, I didn't want to tell you – you see – why Dave wasn't here. So, I said he was in bed . . .'

'But—' her mother had begun weakly.

'But when you asked to see him, I . . . I panicked' (this, at least, was true). 'So I rushed up and, you know, put the pillows on the bed . . .'

'So, you're not sick?' her dad had asked Dave, as if piecing together a very complicated puzzle.

'No?' Dave had replied, although the upward inflexion of his voice made it sound as if he was starting to think he might be.

'No, no!' Jess had continued, beaming. 'No! It was just part of the . . . the surprise!' she'd waved the bottle again, noticing that it was marked '£2 off' on the back. She'd put it down, heavily on the table, feeling slightly knock-kneed.

'So, you mean to tell us, Jessica. Are you and Dave engaged?' her mother had asked, brow furrowed.

'Yes! Yes we are!'

Dave had stayed silent. But suddenly Jessica had felt his arm wrap around her back and pull her to him. She'd felt almost weak with relief – he wasn't going to blow her cover.

'Well, congratulations!' The pair of them were up then, shaking hands, hugging, clapping on the back.

'I can't pretend to quite understand what just happened,' her mum had said, after giving her a squeeze. 'But I am *so pleased* for you!' She'd lowered her voice to an all-too-audible whisper. *'And remember what I said about testosterone,'* she'd added. *'Your father never had a drop of the stuff, and we always conceived very easily.'*

'You know, your mum's always wondering if you're going to settle down again,' her dad had told her, in a low voice when she'd hugged him. 'Now she can move on to her next victim!'

Dave had stood there, looking bemused, but was thankfully silent as he'd endured a clap on the back from her father that almost sent him crashing into the half-eaten soup bowls, and a kiss from her mother that had left a cartoon-style lipstick print on his cheek.

'We'll talk later,' Jessica had hissed in his ear when her parents had settled back down for the next course, glasses overfilled with Prosecco in the hope that nerves would be calmed and they'd all make it through the next hour or so unscathed.

Later, her dad had pulled her aside in the kitchen when he was helping to clear the table. 'Congratulations again,' he'd said quietly. 'As long as you're sure?'

'Sure?'

'I'm your dad; it's my job to disapprove of your boy-friends,' he'd said. 'But, I don't know . . . *Dave?* You're sure?'

'Why?' she'd said. 'What's wrong with him?' She'd spent the last year on cloud nine, assuming that everyone thought she'd won the love lottery.

'I don't know, nothing, I suppose,' her dad had shrugged. 'It's just, well, you two seem so different. I . . .'

Then Dave had come through with a pile of plates and the conversation had abruptly turned to the benefits of coconut oil.

What had she been thinking? This was the absolute

opposite of a Perfect Plan! This was so much worse than omitting to tell her parents about a break-up. She had a fake engagement she had to wriggle out of.

Plus, this email from the *Daily News* meant she was either going to have to turn down what was a pretty good chance to plug Little Accidents, her blog and her business, or somehow convince Dave that it was worth his while to come on board and wax lyrical about their non-existent relationship and – God help them – *engagement*.

Unless she was missing something. She'd never really got to the bottom of why Dave had decided to do a U-turn on his decision to miss dinner. And he'd stood there, mute, while she'd told her parents they were engaged. Perhaps he had taken pity on her and decided to help her out. But was it possible he was regretting their split?

After they'd waved her parents off and she'd thanked him, he'd left her with a 'no problem' before she'd had time to properly talk things through. At the time, she'd been too exhausted and relieved to care. But now, she wished she'd taken the chance to speak to him.

Could he possibly want her back?

'No,' she said aloud, dismissing the thought.

One thing was sure though – they hadn't had time to talk the night before, but they surely had to now.

When she dialled his number she nearly hung up immediately. But then, of course, she'd probably get the answerphone and could just leave a message or something.

'Hello?' He answered immediately.

'Oh, eh, hi. It's . . . Jess,' she said.

'Yes, I know. Caller ID.' Was he smiling? He sounded as if he was smiling. That, at least, was a good thing. Wasn't it?

'Ah. Yes. Look, I just wanted to say, sorry about last night.'

'Don't worry about it.'

'Seriously? You don't mind that my parents now think you're their future,' she lowered her voice to a whisper, '*son-in-law*?'

'I don't think your parents quite knew what was going on.'

'No. I'm not sure any of us did. Thanks for not giving the game away.'

'That's OK. I know what your mum's like . . .' At one time she would have taken issue with his insulting her mother – it was OK for Jessica to say things about her mum, but she'd defend her to the death if anyone else started. But, in the circumstances, she let it go.

'Yeah . . . Look, Dave, I've got a favour to ask.'

'What, besides *making an honest woman of you*?' he laughed.

'I'm not sure that's possible,' she joked, weakly. 'But look, the *Daily News* have asked whether they can interview me, well, *us*, actually. After that blog post about doing things together? There's a fee. You can have mine, too, if you want. It'd be so good for the business, and maybe I can plug Little Accidents . . .'

'Little what?'

'Don't worry,' she realised that she'd barely spoken to him about the contract. 'I just wanted to ask whether you'd be OK with, you know . . . Keeping things going a little longer? Just long enough to do the piece, and maybe for a bit after? The . . . the *engagement* and everything?'

'OK. Why not?' Considering his attitude to lying even about the dinner, this was surprisingly nonchalant.

'You know it'll mean everyone thinking we are actually *tying the knot*? Your mates? Your parents?'

'I haven't told anyone we're over yet,' he replied in a tone that suggested it was no big deal. 'Kevin just thinks I'm stopping over at his for a bit to give you some time with Anna.'

'What?'

'I don't know.' He paused. 'I suppose maybe I was a bit hasty to, you know, leave that note. You just seemed so wrapped up in yourself; never really noticed me. I suppose . . .' he stopped for a moment. 'I suppose I wanted to see if you really cared about me.'

'Oh Dave. Of course I care about you. Of course I . . .'

'I should have told you how I felt, I suppose.'

'Yeah. Well, it's not always easy to be upfront about things.' She, if anyone, knew that to be a fact. 'Anyway, so you're OK to do the interview?' She tried to keep her voice calm and casual, as if it was no big deal. Inside, she was screaming. What did this mean? He'd left the note to punish her? He'd left her to make a point? Were they together or not? And did she want to be?

She'd wait until after the interview to find out. Just in case.

'Yeah, why not.' He said.

'And . . . and a photo shoot?'

'No probs – just let me know. Try and sort it on a Saturday.'

'Wow. Well, thank you.'

'So . . .' he said, his voice suddenly different. 'I suppose we'd better be getting you a ring?'

'What?'

'You know. *For our engagement*,' he said, meaningfully.

'Good idea.' He was making this too easy! She'd have to get something from eBay – a bit of cubic zirconia would be bling enough for the *Daily News*. 'Do you want me to sort that out?'

'Don't be silly – that's my job surely?'

'OK, thank you.'

164

'So, call me?'

'Yes, as soon as I hear.'

'Thanks. And Jess?'

'Yes?'

'It was good to talk to you — fiancée!'

Jessica hung up the phone feeling more discombobulated than she would have had he lost his temper at her. He'd simply handed her everything she needed on a plate.

Perhaps it was guilt. Or perhaps something else. What if he really did want her back?

She thought about the Instagram numbers, which had fallen slightly already. And her PR clients. The article in the *Daily News*. And being able to work out next to Dave at the gym again.

It was probably the shock of it all, or something about not wanting to get her hopes up, but she didn't feel as happy as she thought she should at the idea.

A text message suddenly flashed onto her phone. Bea. *Can we meet up? Need to talk* 😞

She'd reply later, she thought, when she had things straight in her head.

Then, still reeling from it all, she left the house to pick up Anna.

Chapter Twenty-Three

Having a rest while catching up on #work. Stomach crunches later! @Fitat30

'Good quiz questions.'

'100 quiz questions.'

'Best pub quiz.'

Jessica sat on the sofa, frantically googling. Liz had been right, writing quiz questions wasn't child's play. She'd spent most of the journey home from Grahame's trying to think of ideas, but had found that her general knowledge was even worse than she'd thought. All the questions she could think of had sounded like the kind doctors ask in hospital when someone suffers a head injury. *'Who is the current prime minister?' 'What year is it?' 'Do you know your own name?'*

She supposed she ought to write a few celebrity-based questions, but whenever she thought of Tamzin or any of the other D-listers she'd supported over the years, all she could think of was the Little Accidents advert and the sequinned nappy she'd squeezed herself into.

Thank goodness for Google.

'What are you doing?' Anna said from the other sofa where she'd been sitting, reading her tablet since they'd got back. 'Blogging or something?'

'No, just looking up some info,' she replied. 'Why?'

'Oh, nothing. Just wondered.'

'Anna . . . Have you read my blog?' Jessica asked, feeling suddenly self-conscious.

'A bit.' Anna blushed slightly.

For some reason, Jessica felt a bit uncomfortable. It was OK to share her body hang-ups and waxing comments with an unknown audience, but it was far too private for her twelve-year-old to read.

But it's online. Why hadn't it crossed her mind that Anna might look at it too?

'Oh! Well, it's all a bit, you know, I mean, what you read isn't necessarily—'

'Yeah, but you have like thousands of followers, Mum! I mean, that's amazing!'

Jessica felt herself blush slightly. 'Well thanks, but . . .' She didn't know how to tell her child that most of the thoughts and experiences on her blog were doctored to sound much better than they really were. And that the followers were following someone who didn't exist.

'I've got, like, four or something,' Anna continued, her brow furrowed.

'What? You're blogging?'

'No, I mean on Instagram.'

'Oh, right. Should you be on Instagram?'

'You said it was OK, remember? As long as I only followed people I knew. So I follow you, and Dave, and, like, a couple of kids from school.'

'OK.'

'But, well. Dave's stuff is a bit weird, isn't it?'

'It's just gym pics.'

'I know, but . . .' Anna went red.

Jessica thought about this morning's post-shower towel pose.

'And is he back from his work thing?' added Anna. 'Because the gym in his picture today looked like his normal one.'

Jessica felt her stomach somersault. She hadn't mentioned Dave since she'd made the excuse to Anna about his whereabouts. 'Yes,' she said, slowly. 'He's just ... um ... staying with his friend for a while.'

'Oh.' Anna's eyes looked directly her way. 'Mum, has he like gone for ever?'

Looking back, Jessica realised that this had been the moment she'd had a window of opportunity to do the right thing. Then again, what *was* the right thing? Admitting a lie was good, but involving Anna in her deception was the opposite. Far better to leave her ignorant of it all until she'd worked out what to do.

'Mum?'

'Um. No. No, Anna. He'll be back.' It was sort of true after all; he still had some clothes to pick up. Her stomach churned in protest. Lying to your kids was OK when it came to Santa or the tooth fairy. But lying about this? She had a feeling she'd be blasted off the internet if anyone found out.

She found a site and copied and pasted a bunch of geographical and historical questions, as well as some celebrity-focused ones and hoped that they would do. After all, it was only a local quiz – hardly *Mastermind* or *University Challenge* (which, she reflected, looking at the questions, was probably a good thing).

Then she picked up Robert's book again.

ACTIVITY THREE

Let's get physical! Next time you pass a park, take a look at the children playing there. Children tend to smile when they run, climb and jump.

Now look at an adult jogging along the road. They often look far from happy! But why? Exercise fills us with endorphins and keeps us fit – so why are we so miserable?

It's a case of feeling we *have* to do something, rather than doing something because we *want* to. It's hard to get a child to run if they're not feeling like it! Equally, when the urge takes them it's almost impossible to stop them.

The answer is to get in tune with our bodies. Of course, this doesn't mean we should always sit on the sofa, and it certainly doesn't mean being lazy. It's about taking our exercise as and when we feel like it – breaking into a run during a walk to work; jumping up and down by our desk in the workplace.

Next time you feel a bit restless, try a little jog on the spot or a few star jumps. Soon you'll find yourself incorporating exercise into your everyday activities without even trying.

And guess what – you'll be smiling!

Was he right? she wondered. She certainly couldn't remember ever smiling at the gym, except when posing for a pic. There was also something engaging about his tone; it made her want to try.

She was about to ask Anna if she'd fancied doing some exercises together, when her phone started to ring.

'Hello, Jessica speaking?'

'Hi, Jessica,' the voice was warm and friendly, but she couldn't place it. 'How are you?'

'Hi, erm . . .'

'It's April from Channel 6! We got your press release about the *Remembering Rainbows* book.'

'Oh yes?' Jessica asked feeling slightly nervous.

'Yes. And thank you for that. Sorry we didn't get back to you sooner, but you know . . .'

Jessica knew. They received thousands of press releases every day. And it had been a long shot to see if they'd feature her unknown author. She'd worked with them before a few years ago with a stylist she was promoting – they'd featured her on a debate for and against bigger eyebrows. The stylist had ended up having her own column in a beauty magazine as a result of her performance. Exposing clients to this kind of audience could be pure gold. 'Sure,' she said.

'Anyway, I'm not sure how Dr Haydn is fixed tomorrow, but we've had a bit of a disaster this end. We're building a feature about childhood happiness, on the back of that survey about computer games and stress last week? But Dr Marylin – you know, our usual psychologist, has come down with that sickness bug that's going round, and we need to find someone else, sharpish.'

'Oh right?'

'And obviously, with *Remembering Rainbows* being about happiness, we immediately thought of Dr Haydn.'

Jessica glanced at her watch. It was 7 p.m. on a Sunday evening. She was willing to bet that Robert's name was towards the bottom of a very long list. That said, she knew how it worked – and definitely knew better than to pass up an opportunity like this. 'Wonderful – he'll do it!' she said.

'You don't need to check?'

'No, no,' Jessica lied. 'He's definitely free tomorrow.'

Because I'll make sure he is, she thought. She knew that if she didn't get him confirmed, they'd ditch him at the drop of a hat if someone better came along.

'That's great! Well, I'll send all the details through to your email in that case.'

'Brilliant.'

The phone went dead.

Jessica felt almost rooted to the spot. She'd sent the press release out, but hadn't really expected a bite. The programme usually only featured people with contentious opinions, or those who'd been on *Love Island*. Her fairly innocuous psychologist was not controversial enough and – to her knowledge – wasn't a love rat, had never been arrested, slept with a celebrity, had plastic surgery go terribly wrong, or bared all on a naked quiz show.

This was the kind of opportunity that could take Robert's book from a small print run to something stocked in all the high-street and online outlets, if he could play his cards right.

Ignoring Anna, who was trying to show her something on her tablet, she picked up her mobile and dialled.

'Robert, speaking.'

'Hi, Robert, it's Jessica from Star PR.'

'Oh hi. How are you?' he sounded almost too pleased to hear from her.

'Great thanks. Look, sorry to ring you on a Sunday evening, but what are you doing tomorrow?'

'Not much. I've got a few copies of the book to sign for the publishers, but I can do that any time.'

'Right, in that case you're going to appear on the *Wakey Wakey!* sofa with Paul and Hannah.'

'What?'

'Yes, I've just had a call and they'd like you to appear as an expert tomorrow morning!' she said. 'Hello? Hello?'

'Yes. I'm still here,' he said, after a pause. 'It's just, I'm not sure I can do that.'

'What? It's a great opportunity!' In her wildest dreams, she hadn't expected him to have any reservations about appearing. Nerves, maybe. Excitement, definitely. But not reluctance.

'I know. It's just. Well, I don't really *feel* like an expert.'

She chose her words carefully. 'But Robert, you're a trained psychologist. And you've written a book on happiness. Have you seen the programme? You're probably the most qualified interviewee they'll ever have.'

There was a long pause in which she wondered, again, whether he'd hung up.

'OK,' he said, at last. 'It's just ... I'm not sure whether speaking on TV will be my thing.'

'Don't be silly,' she said, sensing victory. 'Hearing you talk about your book was wonderful the other day – really inspiring.'

'You really think so?'

'Definitely.'

'OK. OK.' There was a pause. Then, 'Well, email me the directions,' he said at last.

'They'll send a car. I'll forward the details to you.'

A pause.

'Jessica?'

'Yes?'

'Is there any chance ... do you think you could come with me at all?'

Jessica flicked up her diary and checked. She was booked for most of the day, including the lunch with Bea. But then, this was a once-in-a-lifetime opportunity for someone like Robert. 'Um, you know, I'm not sure I could—'

'Because, if you can't. I'm not sure I can ...'

'What about someone from the publishers?'

'It's not that! I mean, I know I could do that, but it's ... it's *you.*'

'Me?'

'Yes. I know it seems daft, but when I was talking to you about the book, I felt so, well, confident about it all. I just feel like if I'm going to do this thing, it'll be better if I know you're there.'

It was flattering to find that someone she'd only just met had this much confidence in her. 'Right. Well, let me see what I can do.' It would be fun, she supposed, going to the studios. She'd been there a couple of times in the past, but not since the refurb.

'Then, I'll do it!' he said.

'Great. I'll send the details over.' She pressed red and watched the call disappear, before looking up at Anna. 'Sorry, sweetheart, were you going to say something?'

'No. No, it doesn't matter.'

Chapter Twenty-Four

'A text cancelling lunch? No surprises there, then.' The message from Bea arrived when Jessica was putting on her shoes. Bea had obviously not been sleeping, it was practically the middle of the night. Perhaps Lewis was having one of his nightmare phases.

'Sorry, something just came up. TV.' She typed quickly. 'Another time though?'

'I'll have to check my hectic schedule.' No emoticon to tell her whether this was a friendly sarcastic comment rather than a snub.

Great, now she'd upset her best friend. OK, Bea wanted to talk about something, but surely this was an understandable reason to cancel? Jessica thought back to the other two times she'd put the lunch off – once to go to the gym, the other time because she needed to have a spray tan before she took some new shots of herself in some freebie gym gear she'd been given. Both pretty flimsy reasons.

She was the girl who cried wolf and her poor sheep were doomed.

'Sorry, I'm a crap friend,' she typed back. She added an emoticon of a little poo, crying yellow tears, for good measure.

No response.

GIF of a woman sobbing.

Nothing.

Jessica hadn't banked on the car arriving at four in the morning. Although, of course, it made sense when she thought about it. It was the first time she'd left Anna in the house alone, but after ringing Jenny's mum yesterday evening to arrange a lift to school, she had decided four hours wasn't really very long. Anna would probably enjoy the peace and quiet!

After getting dressed, Jessica softly slipped into her daughter's room for a moment. Anna was completely surrendered to sleep, lying on her back with arms and legs flung wide. Her blue pyjamas were getting too small, Anna noticed, the legs and arms a few inches higher than they ought to have been.

Her long hair was tangled on the pillow and, as Jessica watched, Anna gave a snort-like snore, which from Dave or Grahame would be absolutely disgusting, but in her daughter was almost overwhelmingly adorable.

'Sorry,' Jessica whispered to her suddenly. 'Sorry I'm always making such a mess of things.' She pulled the duvet back over her daughter, who snuggled gratefully into its warmth but didn't wake.

After leaving a note to say goodbye, Jessica stood on the front doorstep in the early morning chill. The road was empty, and most of the houses remained dark, save for a couple of upstairs lights at one of the cottages over the road.

A car purred up the street – nothing flash, more of a people carrier, but shiny and sleek – and she stepped forward. The back door opened and she saw Robert, dressed in a blue suit, clean-shaven but looking as if he hadn't slept. His hair was nicely styled, though; he'd used some sort of product in it and it was behaving itself.

'Hi,' she said, climbing in beside him. And 'hi,' again to the driver, who nodded in acknowledgement.

'So,' she continued, once the car had pulled away. 'All ready for the big interview?'

Robert was clutching two copies of *Remembering Rainbows* tightly to his chest; his jaw was set. 'I think so,' he said, his voice sounding far less confident than it had when they'd first met. 'It's s–such an important t–topic.'

Had he had a stutter before?

'Do you want to run anything past me, while we've got time?'

'Maybe . . . w–what do you think they're going to ask me?'

'Well, about happiness and where you think it comes from,' she said, suddenly drawn in by the intensity of his gaze. 'And, how to, ah, find happiness.'

'Right.' He reached and grabbed her hand and she nearly pulled it away. Until she realised that it was more of a child-ish need for reassurance than a come-on. She squeezed his fingers slightly.

'So,' she said, trying to mimic the tone of the interviewer. 'Dr Haydn, may I call you, Robert?'

'Yes of course! You always have!'

'I'm being,' she said, 'the interviewer on the TV.'

'Oh right. Right. Yes of course you may.'

'Robert, what are your thoughts on happiness? Is it real-istic to try to be happy all of the time?'

'I don't know.'

She rolled her spare hand at him, encouraging him to say more.

'I don't know. I mean, yes, I do. Perhaps not all the time, b–but most of the time,' he said, hurriedly.

'And how do you advise viewers go about this?'

'Erm, well, just being like a child.'

The hand roll again.

'You know . . . trying to, er, be like a child because, you know. Children . . .' he trailed off, his cheeks bright red. 'Children are happy, well, not *all* children, obviously, but naturally they're quite happy. Sometimes. I mean, kids, you know?'

Oh God. He was going to have to do better than this.

'See,' she lied. 'You're a natural.' This time she was confident that the truth wouldn't help either of them.

'Really?'

'Actually,' she said, 'you know, I get pretty nervous at things like this.'

'You're kidding?'

'Yes . . . I mean, not when I'm supporting a client. But if I have to speak in public, I'm a wreck inside. I used to be shy – and it's kind of still there, deep inside – the lack of confidence I suppose.'

'Honestly, you'd never know.'

'Thank you.' She blushed, not quite knowing why she'd admitted her inner angst to a man she'd only just met. It wouldn't exactly fill him with confidence about her PR skills.

There were still holding hands, she realised. She gently extricated herself and they grinned at each other briefly.

When the car pulled up outside the studio, Jessica felt a strange sense of familiarity, the feeling you get when you drive past a house you've once lived in, or walk into your old school. She quickly took a selfie outside the building and tweeted her whereabouts.

#funtimes #soexcited #RememberingRainbows @Channel6 @WakeyWakey! #EarlyStart 😊

On entry they were whisked past the reception and into the green room they were to share with the other *WakeyWakey!* guests: a comedian called Steve who'd won a TV talent contest last year; a rather severe-looking psychologist called Meredith, whose eyes flicked briefly from her book when they walked in, then returned to the page; and a singer called Poppy whose recent hit 'Selfie Stream' had reached no. 2 in the download charts last week.

A screen in the corner of the room revealed that the programme hasn't started yet, but the presenting duo were in situ, having the last shine dusted from their skin with big brushes and having microphones adjusted while reading through their notes.

'Jess,' Rob whispered, 'I'm not sure I can do this!'

'Don't be silly,' she hissed, feeling a rising panic.

'But—'

Aw, is that *Catching a Rainbow*? asked Poppy, leaning towards Robert with a smile and touching the dust jacket of one of his books.

'Yes.' Robert flushed and showed her the cover so she could see it properly. 'Well, *Remembering Rainbows*, actually. I can't believe you've heard of the book!' he said.

'Are you kidding? I read about it online the other day. Might just be what I need after breaking up with Shane.' She grinned and shuffled closer to Rob. 'Did you write it?'

'Well, yeah.'

There was a snort from Meredith's direction, but she kept her eyes firmly on her book and continued to read.

'That's amazing,' Poppy said, looking genuinely impressed. 'I can't believe I get to meet you. Can I take a picture?' she asked, lifting up her phone.

Jessica hurriedly retrieved her own phone from the bottom of her bag too and took a snap of the pair of them in conversation. This ought to do well on Instagram. @DrRobHaydn and @PoppyT at @WakeyWakey, with @StarPR.

A runner turned up, all acne and clipboard. 'Robert?' he asked and Robert leapt to his feet as if he was in a court of law.

'Here.'

'Meredith?'

'Yes?' Meredith closed her book and slipped it into her bag.

'OK, if you'd like to come with me.'

'Can...' Robert said, a flush rapidly rising on his face. 'Would it be OK if my... if Jessica...' he indicated Jessica weakly.

'If you could wait here, ma'am,' the runner said, looking at Jessica.

Great. She'd been ma'am-zoned.

'I think he wants...' she said.

'Could she possibly come with?' asked Robert. 'It's just...' he looked at the teenager pleadingly.

'Sorry, mate. But don't worry, we'll look after your wife,' said the runner.

'She's not—'

The runner glanced briefly at Jessica. 'Sorry, we'll take care of your... mum,' he said.

He led a defeated Robert from the room to meet his fate. Meredith followed them.

'That man is *gorgeous*,' Poppy whispered, the minute they'd left the room. 'How do you keep your hands to yourself?'

'He's...' Was Robert gorgeous? Sweet, perhaps. But nothing like Dave.

Before Jessica could come up with a suitable answer, the

screen in the corner flared into life and the familiar credits of one of her favourite morning shows began to run.

Ten minutes later, it was time for Robert to make his appearance.

'Now all week, we've been looking at happiness. Is it something we can learn, or are some of us just born happy?' the male presenter, Paul, began. 'We'll be speaking to Robert Haydn, author of *Remembering Rainbows*, who believes that happiness lies in embracing our inner child, as well as psychologist Meredith Hornchurch who believes that rather than seeking happiness, we ought to aim for contentment at best.'

The camera panned out to show Robert sitting next to Meredith, who looked even more severe on screen than she had in the flesh. She glared at the camera, her mouth set in a straight line.

'So,' said Hannah, the female presenter, 'Should we aim to be happy, or is the quest for happiness itself making us miserable?'

In the green room, Poppy was looking at the camera transfixed. Steve was picking his nose, ostentatiously, and rolling the result between his fingers.

'Dr Haydn, Robert – can I start with you? What do you believe to be the secret of happiness?' asked Hannah, flashing her trademark smile.

'Well, Hannah,' Robert smiled. 'As I say in my book, *Remembering Rainbows*, it's all about letting go of the inhibitions that we have as adults. Children are much freer; they live from moment to moment without worrying about the consequences or getting bogged down in what other people think.'

Next to him, Meredith snorted contemptuously. Robert flushed.

'I see, so how would you suggest viewers go about revisiting their childhood?'

'Well, I–I'd . . . I mean, what did *you* like doing when you were a kid. Say when you were five years old?'

'Um. Well, I suppose I liked skipping.'

Robert nodded, as if he had expected this answer all along. 'And do you skip now?'

'Er, no.'

'Because, what I've found is that when we engage with the things we were naturally drawn to as a child – when we were unencumbered by adult concerns, it can really help us to feel happy again,' Robert explained.

'Wow, that sounds amazing!' Hannah smiled. 'So all I have to do is skip, and I'll feel like I did when I was five?'

Robert smiled. 'Well, not quite. But it's a step in the right direction.'

Meredith shifted forward on the sofa. 'I'm sorry,' she said. 'But I can't see how *skipping*,' she uttered the word as if it was somehow dirty, 'can make a grown woman happy.'

'Well, OK. What did you like to do when you were a child, Meredith?' Hannah smiled.

The question seemed to throw her. 'A child?' she asked, as if she'd never been one. Jessica had a sudden vision of her being born as a fully-fledged and utterly joyless adult. 'Well, I suppose I had a few toys . . .' Meredith looked wistful for a moment. 'But I fail to see how—'

'Well, we've got a selection of kids' favourite activities in the studio today,' said Paul, finger to earpiece, 'so perhaps we could see this theory in action?'

Meredith tutted loudly and Robert squirmed.

The camera panned out again to reveal a small area in front of the sofa. Two floor mats were laid out with a selection of children's toys, a small plastic slide and a football.

'Go on, Hannah,' coaxed Paul. 'Let's see some skipping.'

With feigned reluctance, Hannah stood and picked up the skipping rope. She held the wooden handles and began to skip, tripping slightly over the rope after five turns and starting again. Gradually a grin spread over her face. 'Do you know what?' she said. 'I actually *do* feel better.'

'I'm sorry,' said Meredith. 'But we all know that exercise makes us feel better – momentarily, at least. I can't see that this is an example of Hannah embracing her inner child. Simply releasing a few endorphins!'

'Fair point,' said Paul. 'But let's give Dr Haydn's idea a go before we talk about your theories. Is there anything you used to enjoy doing as a child?'

'Reading, I suppose. And Mummy used to let me polish her jewellery sometimes.'

'It needs to be something more authentically child-like,' interrupted Robert, finding his voice again. 'Rather than an activity that can be equally enjoyed by an adult or child.'

'OK.' Meredith appeared to be thinking hard. 'Well, I suppose I did have a dolly – I mean, what girl didn't? My mother took it from me when I was about five years old, I think. And quite right too. Utter nonsense.'

'Your mother took your doll away when you were five?' asked Hannah, her expression disproportionately horrified.

'Yes, and of course I was upset. But the strength it gave me—'

Hannah picked up a doll from one of the boxes. 'So, according to Robert, re-engaging with that inner child, the one who liked the dolly, should help you to feel happy,' she said. 'May I?' She offered the doll to Meredith with a sympathetic smile; Meredith snatched at it rather impatiently.

'Yes, but I really don't *see*,' she began. Then something in her demeanour changed. 'I suppose she is rather a pretty little doll,' she said, cradling the tiny plastic baby in her arms. 'Rather sweet.'

'And do you feel anything? Any reconnection with your past?' Paul prompted.

'No, of course not.' Meredith replied with a curt nod. 'Of course I can appreciate the dolly, but . . . Actually, I remember my doll's name now. Rosie. Rosie Pie.' She studied the doll closely and raised it to her shoulder, like a mother holding a baby. 'Rather similar to this little dear.'

'So you are engaging a little with your inner child?' Robert prompted. 'Embracing that part of yourself can lead to—'

'Ridiculous!' Meredith snapped. 'I provoked a memory, obviously, but that's all.' Her hand continued to pat the doll's padded back.

'OK, well we've looked at Robert's theory, and I think there is some truth in it. But tell us about your theory, Meredith,' Hannah smiled, taking a seat and reaching out for the doll. 'Contentment at best. Is that really all we have to hope for?'

Meredith snatched the doll from Hannah's outstretched fingers.

'Sorry, I'll just take this so you can introduce your book,' Hannah smiled, reaching again.

'No, she's mine!' Meredith snapped.

Hannah laughed. 'Ha. Well, it looks like you've engaged a little with your childhood, Meredith! But tell me about your book, *Who Needs Happiness*?' She held out a copy of a book and smiled anxiously.

'No! Rosie mine!' Meredith continued, wild-eyed. 'She my dolly NOT YOURS!' she clutched the plastic infant to her chest desperately. 'Stop it, Mummy! Stop it!' she stood up and stumbled towards Hannah, brandishing the newly reincarnated 'Rosie Pie'.

'Well, it's time for a break now,' said Paul, the camera

zooming close to his face to avoid the fight that was starting in the studio. 'But we'll be back, talking about bladder weakness and whether a new device could signal the end of problems for thousands.'

The credits cut in.

In the green room, all three of them sat in stunned silence.

Chapter Twenty-Five

Had a great time @WakeyWakey!
#RememberingRainbows was a real hit. @DrRobHaydn
@StarPR #PRLife #GoodTImes

'So, you think it went well?' Robert grimaced at her in the back of the car, and she wondered whether he was joking.

'Well, you certainly outlined your points very well,' Jessica replied. 'It's a shame obviously about the other expert...'

'Do you think she'll be OK?'

'I'm sure she will.' She leant over slightly and patted his arm, thinking of the moment when Meredith had been led sobbing from the studio, still clutching 'Rosie Pie'.

She'd already had a look on Twitter. *Remembering Rainbows* was trending. Only it seemed that many of the Tweeters had thought that Meredith – who'd been unable to promote her own work – was part of a collaboration with Robert.

Can't believe what I'm watching on @ WakeyWakey!
Some freaky scientist having a breakdown over a doll
#RememberingRainbows

Wow, @WakeyWakey! If that's embracing happiness, I'd rather
be miserable #*Remembering Rainbows*

Great.

Jessica tried to remind herself that no publicity is bad publicity and that two of her clients had been trending on Twitter in the last couple of weeks. But somehow it didn't seem like a success.

Loved watching @DrRobHaydn on @WakeyWakey! Embrace your inner child! #RememberingRainbows

she tweeted half-heartedly.

Her phone beeped with a text from her brother: 'Watched your programme – never laughed so hard in my life!'

'Yeah, thanks for the support, bro.'

'Seriously, what do they say – no publicity is bad publicity!'

Why did people always say that? 'Let's hope so ☺' she replied.

As the car turned into familiar streets she began to long to get home, sling off her work shoes and make the most of an 'at home' lunch break. But as they neared the high street, Robert's hand suddenly gripped her arm. 'Ask the driver to stop!' he said, excitedly.

Jessica looked out of the window but couldn't see anything particularly worth stopping for. A newsagent's, a fish and chip shop with steamed-up windows, and a charity bookshop. But she avoided suggesting he actually ask the driver himself and leaned forward. 'Would it be OK to stop here?' she asked.

Two minutes later they were standing on the pavement, watching the sleek black car drive away. Home for Jessica was still a good fifteen minutes' walk and as they clearly hadn't been important enough for the driver to wait for, he'd headed back to the studio, or wherever his next assignment was.

'What is it?' she said, turning to Robert and trying to smile. In truth, she was pretty knackered and just wanted to get back for a forbidden full-strength coffee.

'I just want to show you something,' he said, gesturing to a small alleyway.

Robert didn't seem the sort that would want to show her something dodgy in an alleyway, so she persevered, 'Yes, but show me what?'

'What I mean by embracing your inner child.'

Oh gawd.

She followed him along the alleyway, dodging around the obligatory fag-ends, broken bottles and dog shit that seem to collect between buildings, and emerged into a small park.

In the corner of the grassed area, there was a tiny fenced-off playground. A man stood at the bottom of the slide, arms wide ready to catch a small boy. Two women sat on a bench, close to where two toddlers were scaling a slightly rickety-looking climbing frame. Both women were on their mobile phones, eyes fixed to their screens. Jessica felt a pang of recognition.

'Great, it's not busy!' said Robert, seeming more enthusiastic than he had in the studio when promoting his book. He grabbed her hand and began to run. Rather than slap it away, she was so taken by surprise she found herself tottering by his side, her heels sinking slightly into the fudge-like mud.

When they reached the small area, Robert flung the gate open with such force that all three children squealed. Unperturbed, he dragged Jessica to the swings. 'Sit!' he said and, feeling a bit self-conscious, she perched on the edge of one of the plastic seat and gripped the chains. She'd assumed he was going to sit on the swing next to her and start to rock back and forth, but instead he hopped behind her and began to push.

Whoosh! His hands thumped into the small of her back and she found herself thrust forward. Back again, and again the hands pushed her. Faster and faster until something actually did change inside. She began to stretch and bend her legs, encouraging the swing to go higher and higher. The hands on her back reminded her of being a child, her dad's powerful pushes sending her high enough to 'bump the moon', as they'd used to joke.

She watched the horizon stretch and fall away as the swing moved; the landscape became a blur of indiscriminate colour – blue, green, brown – the red brick of the wall; then up again. A feeling of excitement – adrenalin – began to pump through her and her heart began to pound. When had she last sat on a swing? Probably sometime in the nineties before she'd become a teenager and far too cool for that sort of thing. She'd pushed Anna on them when she was younger, of course, but never sat on one herself.

She realised she was smiling. Genuinely smiling. And she began to think that maybe there was something in this reconnection theory. 'Wow,' she said as she whooshed forward. 'This is . . . this is . . .'

'See!' Robert called from behind her. 'See what happens when you let go!'

'What?'

'LET GO!' he yelled.

Something about the fact he yelled so forcefully made her respond to his request on autopilot. She loosened her grip on the chains and flew off the swing at top speed, crashing to the ground with enough force to knock the wind out of her.

'Jessica!' Robert cried, running forward.

The other adults regarded the pair of them with silent, judging eyes.

'I'm fine, I'm fine,' she said hurriedly, getting to her feet and feeling her knees scream in protest. Tears stung the back of her eyes. *Don't cry, don't cry*, she told herself. Her cheeks were burning.

'I'm so sorry. So sorry!' Robert said, gratifyingly concerned about her. 'I didn't mean . . . I meant, you know, metaphorically . . .'

'I know. I know! It's my fault.' She had gravel wedged in the skin of her palms and rubbed her hands together to remove it.

'Look,' he said helping her up. 'My car's parked at my flat — just round the corner. Do you want me to give you a lift home?'

Minutes later, they were in Robert's small hatchback heading for Jessica's place. 'Thank you for today,' he said. 'I mean, I'm not being completely blind about . . . about *what happened* in the studio. And I didn't mention it, but I checked my phone and there's been a bit of tweeting going on about it.'

'Yep, a bit,' she said, with a grimace of sympathy.

'Oh. Well, I just try to look at the positive side of things when I can,' he said. 'For me, I managed to go on a live TV show, I didn't mess up my lines and I definitely didn't look like a fool compared to, well, you know.'

It was true, and hearing him describe it like this made her feel better. 'You're right,' she said.

'You know, it's more than nerves for me — I have a bit of a, well, phobia I suppose, of public speaking.'

'But . . .'

'But you – something about your encouragement – helped me to overcome it somehow.'

'Oh!'

'I'm sorry about the swing though.'

'It's not . . . don't worry about it,' she said. 'I mean, I understood what you meant for a minute, before, you know.'

'Yeah.' They grinned at each other suddenly. It had been pretty ridiculous. And now that her knees had stopped stinging, the whole thing seemed hilarious.

'Next time, I'll choose my words more carefully,' he smiled, pulling up outside her house. 'Number ten, right?'

'Yep. That's me.' She looked fondly at the red-brick semi that had been her home for over a decade.

'Listen, thanks. Especially, you know, for coming with me. Because I realise that you have a lot of other stuff on. And you didn't have to come.'

'Pleasure.' And actually, she realised, in many ways it had been. They looked at each other for a while.

'Well, I'd better . . .' she said, nodding at her house.

'Yeah.'

He leaned forward and she leant towards him, aiming to kiss the air next to his cheek. There was a moment where they both changed sides, then changed again, to try to line up cheek to mouth and mouth to cheek.

And misjudged it. Before either of them had a chance to pull away, their lips collided in a clumsy kiss.

'Oh!' he said, pulling away. 'I'm sorry! I didn't—'

'I know, don't worry.' She felt her face get hot. 'It's well . . . these things happen.' For some reason, her lips ached to lean into him again. It had been a while since she'd been kissed. She grabbed her bag and gave him a quick nod before she could give in to the urge.

Exiting the car with a quick goodbye, she looked towards her front door and saw a tall, slender woman standing there: her hair glittering in the sunlight, her eyes fixed firmly on Robert's car.

Chapter Twenty-Six

Jessica tried not to think too much about Liz's face as she
drove the short journey to Hugo's studio. That raised eyebrow, slightly inhibited by Botox, the knowing look on her
face. 'Everything all right, Jessica?' Liz had said as Jessica
walked up to her. 'Just came to drop a few ideas off, but had
no idea you'd be here!' She'd held a white envelope out and
Jessica had taken it, mutely.

'I've used some of the questions you provided – and thank
you for that; and added a few, you know, *extras* just to keep
everybody happy!' she'd added with a smile.

'Thank you.'

'So . . .' Liz had continued, seemingly unable to help herself. 'Who was that handsome chap?' she'd nodded towards
the space where Robert's car had been. 'Couldn't help but
notice he gave you rather a large peck.'

In fact, it had been a full on-the-lips smacker, which they
both evidently knew. 'Oh, Robert?' Jessica had replied in
what she'd hoped was a light-hearted tone. 'He's just a client.'

'Wow, do all your clients thank you so . . . so *enthusiastically?*' Liz had followed this question up with a light-hearted
titter, but her pointed look had revealed real interest.

'No, of course not,' Jessica had snapped, trying to keep

her cool. 'He's, well, he's a *writer*,' she'd explained with a *what can you do?* eye roll and shrug combo.

'Ah OK. Artistic.'

'Exactly.'

There had been a pause as the two women regarded each other. She wants me to invite her in, Jessica realised. 'Look, I'd love to ask you in, but I'm just off to a meeting. Well, a viewing, really.'

'Oh?'

'Yes, one of my clients has finished a competition entry, and I promised I'd swing by'

'Sounds exciting. Well, I'd better . . .' Liz had gestured to the road.

'Sure. But look, we must get together for a proper chat,' Jessica had added, automatically.

Which of course had been immediately scheduled into Liz's smartphone rather than left vague.

As Jessica swung into the car park near to Hugo's studio, she almost took the bumper off a car that someone had parked awkwardly by the entrance. 'Shit.'

She paid her parking after the fourth attempt using the text-and-pay number then walked the short distance to the chip shop. The door to Hugo's studio room was slightly ajar, but she knocked anyway. Just in case.

'Jessica!' said Hugo, leaning his head and shoulders over the bannister. 'Come up!' he was grinning broadly. He'd maintained his clean-shaven look, she noticed, but a slight shadow suggested that he might be entertaining the idea of a moustache.

She trotted up the stairs and followed Hugo into his studio.

The room looked pretty much the same as it had last time: the same subtle paintings on the walls, a new one half-finished by the window, and what she assumed was the competition entry in the centre, hidden under a cream-coloured cloth.

'So,' she said, smiling. 'The big reveal.'

'Indeed.' He suddenly seemed less sure of himself as he stood there, rocking slightly from foot to foot. He was wearing jeans so immaculate that they had to be brand new, and a floral shirt that still had the creases from being folded in the shop. He looked dressed up for the occasion, but why?

'So . . . ?' she prompted.

'So,' he replied. 'Look, Jessica, I'm not sure what you might think about this.'

Which didn't bode well.

'Have you . . . have you changed your entry?' she asked, wondering whether his 'dark phase' had had a resurgence.

'No, it's not that. It's . . . well. You know, you've been such a support, such an inspiration to me, really . . .'

'I have?'

'Yes! You were the one who believed in me when no one else did! You were the one who supported me when I changed my work – I'd never have continued with *Drowning Man on Fire* or *Proud Man* if it hadn't been for your positive feedback.'

'Right . . .'

'Anyway, so when I thought about the competition, I wanted to reflect that. How . . . how we're only as good as the people we rely on . . .'

'Yes?' She had no idea what was coming.

'So . . .' He pulled the cloth and it flopped lightly to the floor. Jessica looked up at the picture and gasped.

Before her was a self-portrait of Hugo, standing at his easel. Painted in minute detail, the skin was luminous and every hair, every tiny feature was immaculately formed on the canvas. There was no doubt that Hugo was a brilliant artist. The second figure in the painting was Jessica – depicted in almost photographic detail. In the composition she was his subject, reclining on a chaise longue while also talking on a mobile phone. She also appeared, in miniature, on the tiny canvas the painted Hugo was working on.

As far as her – fairly untrained – eye could make out, this piece of work was as good as any she'd seen in the National Portrait Gallery.

But that wasn't why she'd gasped.

She'd gasped because in the painting both she and Hugo were entirely and graphically naked.

'Ta dah!' Hugo said, looking at her expectantly.

'Oh!'

'You don't like it?'

'It's not that . . .' she paused trying to find the right words. 'It's, well, We're . . . we're not wearing anything!'

'Ah, the *nude* element,' Hugo said, as if he hadn't been sure whether she'd notice. 'It's meant to demonstrate the fact that when we're stripped back our real characters shine through,' he explained. 'At the core, I'm an artist, you're an inspiration and support. You see,' he pointed to her hand on the phone in the picture, 'how you're simultaneously inspiring me and showing that you're far more than just a muse – a working woman who inspires both with the flesh and the mind . . .'

He smiled slightly, seemingly not getting the point.

'Yes, well, but I mean . . . We're . . . we're not actually wearing anything.'

'No.'

'You can see my . . . there aren't any clothes,' she continued, helpfully.

'Yes.'

'And this is going in the gallery?'

'Yes.'

'Where . . . where people I know . . . where my mum will see it?'

'Yes.' Catching her tone at last, Hugo looked crestfallen. 'I thought you'd be . . .'

'What?'

'I don't know. Proud, maybe? Flattered.'

'Oh. Well, I guess I'm flattered.' Looking at Hugo's depiction of her naked form, she could see that his idea of what she might look like under her clothes was pretty amazing. Clearly, he'd never seen a woman with stretchmarks and a post-baby tummy droop. 'It's just . . .'

But what could she do? Ask him to enter *Drowning Man on Fire*? Ask him to blur her features and possibly wreck the picture? The picture was brilliant. And if she was truly on his side she ought to support him.

'It's great,' she said, at last. 'I was surprised, that's all.'

'And you don't mind me entering it?'

'No. No! of course not,' she smiled. 'It's a winner, I'm sure of it.'

'Really?'

'Yes.'

Was that a good lie? she wondered on the way home. Saying she was OK with it? Her intentions had certainly been good. All she'd have to do is keep her mother away from the gallery for a week or two. Surely that couldn't be too hard?

She wouldn't let herself think about what might happen if he won – for now, at least.

Waiting outside school for Anna – and early for once – she checked her phone and discovered an answerphone message: 'Hi, Jessica. It's Robert. Look . . . I wanted to. I wanted to say sorry. You know with the, well, the kiss thing.'

Ought she to be upset? It had been such an odd day, what with the *Wakey Wakey!* experience, flying off a swing and skinning her knees for the first time in a couple of decades and then being shown a piece of artwork destined for public display in which her entire (albeit flatteringly imagined) body was on view, that in all honesty she'd almost forgotten about their embarrassing cheek-kiss fail.

She dialled Robert's number and prayed for an answerphone so that she could put the whole thing to bed without having to relive it with her client.

Bad luck; he answered.

'Hello? Jessica?'

'Hi, Robert. I got your message – don't worry about it. Just one of those things!'

'Oh, phew. I mean, it was . . . I just didn't want you to think—'

'Don't worry, honestly.'

'Although,' he paused. 'I always . . . I try to be honest about things. The kiss was accidental, but I started to wonder. You know, whether there'd been a part of me that did it on purpose.'

'On purpose?'

'Yeah. I mean, it sounds silly. It's just . . . I have thought about it. Kissing you, I mean.'

'Oh.' He'd thought about her in that way? She'd spent so much of her time obsessing over her weight gain recently that she'd thought herself completely invisible to the opposite sex.

'It's . . . it's OK,' she said at last.

'So . . . I got an email through from Mindhack Publications,' he continued clearing his throat and changing the subject. They've had a lot of enquiries – people ringing up, emailing . . .'

'That's brilliant!'

'Yes, apparently one of the clips has gone viral.'

'Oh wow – fab news!' It was hard to get her mind off the kiss, now he'd admitted how he'd felt. Well, it had been nice. 'So,' she continued, trying to sound professional and on the ball, despite the fact that her heart had started to race. 'Your publisher is keen that you do a few book signings, maybe a reading? Would you like me to put out some feelers?'

'Sure, yes.'

'OK. Well, I'll get onto it and we can discuss the details.'

'Brilliant. Thanks, Jess.'

'Welcome. See you soon.'

Hanging up her phone, she saw that pupils were now starting to stream out of the gate. Anna was walking with a group of girls she didn't recognise. When she saw the car, she said something and ran over.

'You OK?' Jessica said, as her daughter got into the car.

'Yeah.'

'All right this morning?'

'Yeah.'

'Sorry I didn't ring.'

A shrug.

'I really did mean to.'

'I know.' Anna looked at her then, her eyes bright. 'But you're busy – I get it.'

'Never too busy,' Jessica said, rubbing her daughter's leg slightly before starting the engine. 'I'll do better, I promise.'

She was about to suggest that they popped out for something to eat as a treat later, when, as they pulled up outside the house, she realised yet again someone was standing on the doorstep. This time it was Dave, with a bunch of lilies. Her favourites.

'What's this?' she asked as she got out of the car.

'Just saw these, and you know . . .' he said. 'We are engaged after all!' He winked.

'You're what?' Anna asked.

'Engaged . . . but,' Jessica said, with a smile that felt more like a grimace.

'When were you going to tell me?' Anna's face visibly paled.

'Well, we hadn't really—'

'Your mother thought I should come round and we could tell you together,' Dave said, nudging Jessica slightly. 'We thought you'd like to hear it from both of us.'

'But I thought you'd . . . Hadn't you split up or something?'

'We'd . . .' Jessica unlocked the door and tried to put an arm around her daughter.

But Anna had had enough. Silently, she walked into the house and disappeared upstairs, her feet thudding with insolence.

'Poor kid,' Jessica said, feeling the familiar guilt rush through her system. 'Perhaps this wasn't a good idea.'

'Sorry,' he replied. 'Kids, eh!'

It wasn't 'kids' though, was it? Anna was reacting as anyone would in her confusing situation. And Dave had made it worse. Had he not even considered how Anna might feel?

'Yeah,' she said, doubtfully.

'I wanted to come over to say we ought to start discussing ideas. But I'd better let you sort that out first.'

That? Did he mean Anna? His theoretical stepdaughter-to-be?

'Ideas?' she said.

'Yeah. Flowers. Venues. Lots to do.'

'Yes, *of course*,' she said, in what she hoped was a deliberately sarcastic tone.

He kissed her then, a big, familiar but non-sexual smacker, right on the lips.

'Goodbye, bride-to-be. And sorry, you know, for the upset.'

She waved and smiled as he drove off, but couldn't shake a nagging concern, as she dropped the elaborate bouquet on the hall chair and padded up the stairs to console Anna with more lies and half-truths.

Did Dave actually think this engagement was real?

Chapter Twenty-Seven

> Just dropped my entry off to the @ArtisArt competition. So
> excited! #ampainting #penisguy @StarPR

Hugo's Tweet was accompanied by a large photograph of the piece of artwork in question. And so far had received 1.2k retweets. He was clearly embracing his penis-guy identity as far as social media went.

She didn't click to read any of the 126 comments that the tweet had received, but *liked* it and hoped against hope that Candice wouldn't notice that her boss was the subject of the painting. She might not even look that closely, surely? And the online thumbnail was pretty small unless you clicked on it.

Before she could think about it too much, the phone rang on her desk. An unknown number. 'Star PR, Jessica speaking!'

'Hi, Jessica.' It was one of those callers who expected Jessica to know their voice without actually introducing themselves.

'Oh hi! How are you?' she asked, desperately flicking through her in-brain database of potentials.

'Yeah. Yeah all right.'

'Great.'

There was a pause in which Jessica could actually feel her heart hammer against her rib cage.

'So,' the caller continued. 'I was finking about my career and that.'

'OK?'

'An' I fought maybe I need a better team on the case, you know?'

'Right.' So a potential new client, hopefully? Either that or she was being sacked.

'Yeah, I mean, it's good to get some adverts an' that, but you know them nappy fings, they're not exactly me, not really.'

Tamzin Peters. Jessica's heartbeat slowed now she'd identified the voice. 'Right.'

'So, I fort maybe, I dunno, you could 'elp?'

'Yes. Yes of course.' Jessica straightened herself in her chair. 'Well, obviously we'd love to work with you, if you're looking for new representation.'

'Yeah? Well, I fort maybe I could come in or somefink?'

'Yes, no problem at all.' Jessica began to scroll through her online diary. 'How's tomorrow sound?'

'Actually, I fort I might pop in in a minute,' Tamzin said, sounding a bit put out. 'You naw, get on wiv it an' that?'

'Oh . . .' Jessica paused for a minute, looking at her schedule. She could shift some things around. 'OK, sure of course!' Business was business after all.

After giving Tamzin directions, she hung up the phone and asked Candice to set up the meeting room: a small, glass-fronted affair in the office, which boasted four royal-blue plastic chairs, a small table and a plastic pot-plant with dusty leaves.

Jessica cleared the empty cups from her desk and tucked her hair back behind her ears.

Minutes later, Tamzin appeared in the doorway. Candice – a big fan of *Dagenham and Diamante* – virtually fell over herself in her haste to greet her. 'Hello, Tamzin!' she said, sticking out a manicured hand. 'I'm Candice, Jessica's, ah, *assistant*! Let me show you to the room.'

'Aw, ain't it cute!' Tamzin exclaimed on seeing the tiny meeting room. 'Really dinky, innit!'

'Yeah, we're a boutique firm – we prefer to keep things smaller and intimate,' Candice said, delivering the well-rehearsed line.

'Thanks, Candice,' Jessica smiled, appearing in the doorway looking – she hoped – efficient and welcoming. 'Hi again, Tamzin.' She stuck out her hand, but Tamzin had other ideas.

'Hi, babe!' she exclaimed, planting an elaborate kiss on each of Jessica's cheeks, one of which was coated in cover-up where a spot had appeared overnight.

They sat opposite each other, Tamzin wiping her mouth on the back of her sleeve as she did so.

'So, you're thinking of . . .' Jessica began. But before she could go on, she saw Tamzin's face change.

''Ere, who's that?' she asked, pointing at the glass panel behind Jessica.

Jessica turned and nearly jumped out of her skin. Dave was standing there, his face practically pressed up against the glass, clutching a huge bouquet of flowers.

#BadTiming

'Oh hang on,' she said trying to maintain her carefully crafted calm and business-like exterior. 'I'll just have a word.'

She opened the door and stuck her head out. 'Hi, Dave, I'm sorry, it's not a great . . .'

But he interrupted her.

'You're too good to be true,' he said.

'What?'

'Can't take my eyes off of you . . .'

'Look, seriously, Dave, what are you talking about?' Couldn't he see she was busy?

But it got worse. He began to croon, in a surprisingly high, almost girlish voice. 'You feel like heaven to tooouuucchhhh.' He pushed the flowers into her hand and picked a microphone out of his inside jacket pocket. Candice, over at her desk, reached down and soon the screech of feedback emitted from a speaker concealed under her desk. She was also holding Dave's phone, Jessica realised. Filming.

'I wanna hold you so muuuuccchhhhh.'

'Dave, this really isn't . . .' Jessica wondered, briefly, whether Dave had completely lost the plot.

She glanced back over her shoulder and saw that Tamzin had now started filming everything on her mobile phone too.

At least it couldn't get any worse, Jessica thought. But like most thoughts of this nature, this was almost immediately proven wrong.

Four men, at least one of whom she recognised from the gym, marched in, wearing tuxedos as music suddenly burst out in the background. They began to dance, elaborately, and picked Dave up, placing him in the centre of their group just in front of Jessica. 'I love you, babbbyyy, and if it's quite all right, I need you babbbyyy,' they chorused.

She began to feel a little bit faint. Perhaps this wasn't really happening? Perhaps she was ill? That was it. She was ill, in bed and hallucinating.

Before she had time to react, hands suddenly grabbed her and she was held aloft by the four men. They spun her round like a doll, setting her down in front of Dave just as he . . . Just as he . . . Just as he began to kneel down.

'Let me love youuuu, baby, let me love youuuuuu!' he finished, putting down the microphone and opening a ring box which he brought out of his pocket with a flourish.

She looked up. The four men looked at her expectantly. In the background, Candice was watching, entranced. Natalie was standing by the doorway, practically giggling with delight. And, of course, Tamzin's phone continued to record the whole bizarre spectacle, no doubt for the world (or at least her several million Twitter followers) to see.

It wasn't the right time to ask him to sit and talk to her; to work out how they felt. To ask him to cool it, or suggest that they go on a few dates. Or find out whether he really thought they could make it work in the long term or whether he was really committed to making a family with Anna. That sort of thing would really bore their audience.

So, really, she had no choice.

'Oh Dave!' she gushed. 'I'd love to marry you!'

He pushed the ring onto her finger, stood up and planted an enormous kiss on the lips. His friends grinned, then everyone burst into spontaneous applause. As proposals go, it was pretty bloody perfect.

Except, of course, it was completely and utterly fake. At least, she thought, it must be. Then again, surely even Dave wouldn't have gone to so much trouble just to get a few hits on social media?

With a sudden lurch, she looked up at the face of the man she'd just publicly promised to marry and saw that his cheeks were flushed, his eyes were bright. And the smile upon his face was completely and utterly genuine.

Chapter Twenty-Eight

It was later than usual when Jessica left the office and headed to her car. Candice and Natalie had left at 5.30, but with Anna out at Jenny's tonight, she'd stayed an extra hour to clean up her inbox, sort through the pile of paperwork that had been gathering in her in-tray and attempt to recover from Dave's unexpected serenade and proposal.

As usual, her car was parked in one of the bays marked out for their shared office space, and as she walked towards it, she saw some movement. A small figure with dark, curly hair was standing next to the passenger side, facing away from her. 'Bea?' she said, as she approached, wondering what on earth her friend was doing at Star PR's offices, the other side of town from the hospital where she worked.

'You didn't answer your phone earlier,' her friend said, without turning around properly.

'No, sorry, I was going to—'

'Does it ever occur to you,' Bea continued, turning and staring at Jessica with eyes so puffy and sore from crying that she was barely recognisable, 'that other people have things going on their lives too?'

'Bea! What's happened!'

Her friend barked out a short, dry laugh. 'What am I even doing here?' she asked.

'Don't be silly,' Jessica raced round the car and wrapped an arm around her friend's stiff shoulders. 'I'm glad you've come here. I should have returned the call, I shouldn't have cancelled on you. I should have . . .' she trailed off, realising the list of should-haves would probably take about an hour if she recited them all. When had she become such an awful friend?

Bea made a move as if to shrug the arm off, but then something changed within her and she collapsed against Jessica, her chest heaving with sobs. Jessica dropped her bag and wrapped both arms tightly around her, feeling her face, hot against her shoulder like a sick child's. 'Shhh,' she said, not knowing how else to react at seeing Bea – the strongest person she knew – in such a state. 'Shhh, it's OK.'

Minutes later, they drove out of the car park, Bea staring silently out of the passenger window. 'Bea,' Jessica said again, softly. 'What's happened? You have to tell me.'

'I don't even know where to start.'

'Try though,' Jessica glanced across. 'Please.'

So Bea tried. She told Jessica how she and Mark had been trying for another baby since two years after the twins were born. 'I didn't tell anyone,' she said. 'It's just, I suppose, I wanted to have a girl. You know, silly really,' she wiped a hand across her face, smearing make-up, tears and snot across her skin.

'So, nine years?'

'Yeah,' Bea glanced over. 'You feel daft at the start, you know, trying for another baby after you've had twins. Then you feel embarrassed that's nothing happening.'

'But it's normal, you of all people must know that!'

'That's the thing with infertility though,' Bea said. 'It's one thing knowing all the stats and the facts, it's totally another when it's happening to you. After a while, I even began to get jealous of some of the new mums – can you imagine! A midwife cooing over your new baby and wishing it was hers!'

'But that must have been torture for you!' Jessica said, pulling on the handbrake and unclipping her seatbelt as she stopped the car in front of her house. 'Come on. Come in.'

Over a coffee, Bea told her how she'd had all the tests four years ago, when it had become really apparent that something was up. But nothing could be found. 'We have what's called unexplained secondary infertility,' Bea told her, wryly. 'Which is pretty much the same as the doctors saying they don't have a clue why you're not banged up by now.'

Jessica set a plate of biscuits – ginger ones, coated in dark chocolate – on the table. 'So, did you try any treatment or anything?'

Again, the short, clipped laugh. 'Oh, only for about three years,' Bea said. 'Let's see. Clomid.' She counted on her finger. 'That's a lovely tablet that makes your hormones go into overdrive so you fire eggs out at a rate of knots,' she explained. 'Then IUI, where they stick needles into your stomach and then you go into a clinic where a doctor shoots a syringe of your hubby's sperm up your baby tunnel,' she said, raising a second finger. 'Then the joys of IVF. Three times, two failures – each felt as if someone was reaching in and ripping my heart out, not to mention draining our bank balance.'

'So, you've been going through all these years of hell and you haven't let on at all?' Jessica felt a tiny, inappropriate surge of anger. 'Why didn't you confide in me?' After all, she'd been crap recently, but some of this had happened years ago.

'I know,' Bea was silent for a second, then looked up. 'When we started trying, I thought it would be easy. I wanted to surprise everyone with our happy announcement!'

'Oh.'

'Then time went on, things got more serious. And I suppose there was never the right time to say anything. Then the IVF, well, that was more recent . . .'

'Right.'

They sat and sipped their coffee silently for a moment before Jessica said: 'Hang on, you said three IVFs . . .'

'That's right . . .'

'And two failures? Does that mean . . . are you?'

Her friend's eyes told her all she needed to know.

'Not any more,' she said, grimly. 'I was, briefly. Eight weeks. Then the early scan the other day and . . . no heartbeat.' Tears began to silently slip down her cheek and splash onto the wooden counter. 'God, I'm so *angry* at myself! The way I've chirpily told women not to worry about an early miscarriage, that it wasn't even a baby yet, or that they can try again in a few months.'

'But . . .'

'But it *was* a baby, Jessica. To me. All the embryos we produced, all those tiny collections of cells. All babies.'

'What are you going to do?' Jessica asked, after a pause.

'I don't know. Nothing, I think. Mark wants to stop, and he's right. We've barely a credit card that isn't maxed out; it's going to take us years to pay off our misery.'

'Oh . . .' Jessica wished there was something she could say. 'Oh Bea.'

'And that's another problem,' Bea said, meeting her eyes again. 'Work sent me home today. Said to take some personal time. But I'm not sure I can ever go back to that job again.'

'But you're so good at it!'

'So I've lost everything,' Bea said, ignoring her. 'My profession, my . . . my baby. Mark and I are barely clinging together. And I've just been called into the school because

209

Lewis and Lucas have been messing about in class. And I don't blame them. Because for most of their lives their mother has been preoccupied with something else.'

'Hey,' Jessica reached her hand out. 'Don't be so hard on yourself.'

'Thanks. But it's true. I've been a crap mother.'

'Well, on that front, welcome to the club,' Jessica said with a tiny, brief grin. 'There are plenty crap mothers about, believe me!'

Bea grinned a little through the tears. 'Not to mention crap friends.'

'Or friends that go through awful, life-changing treatment and don't even mention it to their so-called best friends . . .'

'I know. I'm sorry.'

Jessica thought for a moment. 'Hang on,' she said. 'When we met at the pub, didn't you have an enormous glass of red?'

'Blackcurrant. I wasn't ready to say anything yet . . . couldn't face the whole "why aren't you drinking?" convo. Sorry. What an idiot, eh.'

'Don't be silly,' Jessica said, walking around the breakfast bar and grabbing her friend in a bear hug. 'You've got nothing to be sorry for.'

Fit at 30

I'll be honest. We all like a treat from time to time. And I'm no different from the rest. A bit of hummus with carrot sticks is a great way to refuel. And I'm no stranger to a handful of sunflower seeds.

So when I was sent some Nutty Nut Bars, I wasn't really in the market for another snack option. But, on reading the details, I was blown away. Nutty Nut Bars have fewer calories than a celery stick, with twice the protein of a chicken breast! What's not to love!

Super excited, too, to be working with the lovely Tamzin from *Dagenham and Diamante* – a real inspiration to anyone who wants to know how to raise their butt cheeks to the next level. She's already shared her secret crunch exercise with me, which I'll reveal next time.

Love to you all,
Jessica

Chapter Twenty-Nine

'Of course I'm coming to the quiz – we're engaged, after all,' Dave chortled on the phone, making Jessica grip the receiver even more tightly. How could she actually ask him whether the engagement was fake?

If it wasn't, she might blow the whole thing; if it was, then he might worry that she was entertaining false hope about their relationship.

'Yeah, ha ha,' she replied, feeling her cheeks redden and putting up a hand to hide her face from the others in the office. 'Well, thanks. I mean, I really appreciate it.'

She hadn't meant to tell him about the quiz at all – trying to keep her guard up among all those parents with Liz there, would be hard enough. But that was the problem with blogging – anyone could read about your life. Even your fake fiancé.

Given the chance, she'd have given it a miss and gone to see Bea. She might have smiled a little before she left yesterday, but Jessica could see that it was going to take a long time for her friend to get over what she'd been through, to move on.

But Bea was having a family night, cooking a meal for Mark and the boys. She'd promised she'd be fine. 'Besides,' she'd said on the phone, sounding a little like her old self again. 'I know how much you're looking forward to doing that quiz. What sort of friend would I be if I made you miss such a wonderful evening?'

'Well, it starts at seven – shall I meet you there?' Jess said now, uncertainly, to Dave.

'Sure, I can get in a quick session after work then I'll get over there. Don't suppose you want to join me at the gym?'

'Um . . . not this time, if that's OK?'

'Right, but I meant what I said. We're going to have to get you back on track.' Another laugh. Another ambiguous moment.

'Thanks,' she said. She'd worry about it all after the quiz.

It was kind of exciting being *engaged* now that she had a ring on – an expensive one too, probably. She gazed at it now – at least a carat, set on a white gold band. But a carat of what? Cubic zirconia, or diamond? One of them was meant to reflect a range of colours in the light. The other wasn't. But which was which? Perhaps she'd look it up.

Not that she was particularly fussed – it was a beautiful ring. But if he'd spent a couple of months' salary on it, then it would give her a clue about whether the engagement was real or not.

She hadn't really thought much about any long-term possibilities. Like whether or not she actually wanted to get married to Dave. It was too difficult to contemplate. What if she realised she really did want to spend the rest of her life with the man, then found out this engagement was all an invention? What if she realised she didn't want to be with him but ended up so invested in the wedding that she went through it anyway? And when had her life become so complicated?

And, even if it was a real engagement, was Dave actually interested in her, or just *the* Jessica Bradley, fitness fanatic, he'd first dated at the gym? Because while she wouldn't mind toning up a little again, the whole strict diet, gym-bunny thing just wasn't her. Not long-term.

'OK, bride-to-be,' more laughter.

She laughed too, nervously.

'But, look, I won't come back after. Not yet, if that's OK?' he added.

'OK?' Not yet?

'Yeah, I thought maybe we should tell everyone we're waiting until after the wedding, or something. Before I move back.'

'OK?'

'And maybe wait until Anna's a bit more sure about the idea.'

'Yeah, good point.' Anna hadn't yet warmed to the idea of the potentially fake, potentially real wedding. Probably as Jessica had barely mentioned it – not knowing what to say.

'But was he giving her excuses to use on others to keep the lie believable? Or was this really what he wanted to do? Her ring sparkled on, teasingly.

Once she'd hung up, she found she had two hundred alerts on her Twitter app. Clicking on it, she found that Tamzin had tweeted the video proposal and tagged her in. Her notification list was full of congratulations. She shut it down with a groan.

'Saw you on Twitter getting engaged!' her phone beeped with Bea's message. 'Call me?' Jessica put the phone on her desk; she'd do it later, when she knew what she wanted to say.

After an afternoon of clearing her inbox of 176 emails – only three of which showed any promise whatsoever – she left Candice with a list of clients to call for updates and went to pick up Anna.

214

'I don't see why I can't stay at home on my own,' Anna said almost immediately when she heard she was going to her father's for the night yet again.

'I'm fine, thanks. How are you?' Jessica replied sarcastically.

'Well, you left me at home the other day!' Anna continued, ignoring her.

'What? When?'

'You know, when you went to do *Wakey Wakey!* or whatever.'

'Oh Anna, that was for a couple of hours at in the morning and Jenny's mum picked you up for school. Leaving you alone for an evening is completely different.'

'But I'm—'

'I know you're twelve. But one day you'll realise that really isn't so very old,' she said, trying not to smile at Anna's indignant face. 'Anyway, Grahame, I mean, *Dad*, is looking forward to having an evening with you. He's going to stream a movie or something.'

'Great. Another one of *Dad's* movies.' It was the first time that Anna had spoken negatively about Grahame to Jessica in months. She tried to push down an ungenerous bit of pleasure at hearing that Anna wasn't as in thrall of her other family as she'd thought.

'Oh, come on, Anna. It'll be fun,' she said, giving her a nudge.

An hour later, Jessica was cramming herself into her smartest black trousers, a grey silk blouse, a small pair of heels. Her hair, which was still in desperate need of a decent cut, was tucked back behind her ears and tamed with wax. She added a pair of diamond earrings to match her (possibly) diamond ring and stood back to admire the result.

Staring back at her was a reasonably slim, professional-looking woman. Neither a dynamic, calorie-obsessed, muscle-honed inspiration nor an overweight couch potato. Just Jessica.

On the way to the quiz, an envelope of questions skidding around the passenger seat, she began to feel a bit nervous. She might be able to chat away in her professional role, but when it came to just being herself, things like this could feel a bit nerve-racking. Liz had mentioned a microphone and – worse – a stage. The idea of standing on display, reading quiz questions to a bunch of folk from the PTA, didn't fill her with delight.

Seeing Dave waiting outside was quite a relief; it made her realise how much she'd missed having him around these past couple of weeks. Just having someone who was definitely on your side, who would come along to things like this was great (even if that person thought you'd piled on rather too many pounds recently).

'Ready?' he said, giving her an ambiguous peck on the cheek. Who knew so many things could be ambiguous?

'Just about,' she replied with a grin.

'You look nice,' he said. 'That blouse really hides your spare tyre.' He smiled at her, clearly expecting her to react to his flattery.

'Thanks,' she said. He meant it as a compliment, she told herself. He meant it as a compliment.

Inside, Liz – her mane so glossy that at one point Jessica had to look away or risk blindness – met them with a smile. 'I've got to pop off to a thing in a bit,' she said, vaguely. 'But I thought I'd just come and see that you have everything you need.'

Hang on a minute, thought Jessica. I thought this was a

joint enterprise? That I was just providing and reading out a few of the questions. Not running the whole thing!

'There's quite a good turnout,' Liz grinned. 'But don't worry, the ladies will take all the money at the door,' she gestured to a group of rather harassed-looking women poring over a cash box. 'Hi there, ladies!' she trilled as she passed them.

'Hi.'

'Oh, hi Liz!'

They basked in her brief attention before returning to the collection of 20p coins they seemed to be arranging into piles.

'And this is you,' said Liz as they entered the school hall. On the stage at the end was a microphone next to a table that held two glasses of water.

'Up there?'

'Yes! Gives everyone the best view, and you can keep an eye out for anyone with a mobile phone,' came the reply. 'You know,' Liz said, lowering her voice conspiratorially, 'there's one cheater every year, I find. Don't make a fuss, just make sure that table doesn't win and – if necessary – give them your best glare.'

'Right.'

Dave poked the small of Jessica's back lightly as they walked, which she took to mean that he was finding the whole thing hilarious in some way (or perhaps he was seeing how many inches she needed to lose).

'So, that's me!' said Liz, checking her watch. 'I'll be back at the end to help get things packed away. Susan and Dan are in charge of the drinks – just make sure it's no more than two bottles of wine per table, if poss? Toilets are at the back – I'd use the staff ones if I were you. Any questions?'

'No, no, I think you've covered everything.'

'Sorry, I didn't introduce myself properly,' Liz said, as if finally noticing Dave's presence. 'I'm Liz, of course. And you must be the lovely Dave! Jessica's . . . er boyfriend!'

'Fiancé, actually.'

'Wow, congratulations!' Liz said, her eyes darting down to look at Jessica's ring finger. 'And what a fabulous diamond! You'll have to tell me all about it later, Jessica. Goodness, you do have an exciting life!'

And with that, she was off, her long black coat billowing out – witch-like – behind her.

'So that's Liz!' Dave said.

'Yes!' Jessica replied, treating him to a grimace.

Various people started filing into the hall and setting themselves up around some of the tables and the room gradually filled with noise.

After about ten minutes, one of the cash-box ladies came to the back of the hall and shut the doors. She gave a nod to Jessica, which seemed to indicate that it was time to start.

'Ladies and gentlemen,' Jessica said into the microphone. 'Welcome to the quiz. Funds for tonight will be going to the St Augustus Academy minibus fund.'

There was polite applause.

'If you could choose your team names and just write them clearly at the top of the paper to start,' she continued, reading from the script that Liz had given her.

There was a pause while teams discussed which whimsical name would suit them best. Jessica turned to Dave and clicked off the mic. 'All right?' she asked.

'Yes,' he grinned. 'You look good tonight, by the way. Have I told you that?'

'Yes,' she replied, suddenly unable to stop herself

responding to his earlier comment. 'Well, we fat girls can scrub up all right when we want to! Spare tyres and all!'

'Oh don't be like that,' he seemed genuinely put out. 'You're not *that* fat.'

'Don't be like what?'

'You know. All defensive. I thought you'd thank me for pointing it out. You know, it's a slippery slope once you start to let things go.'

'Well,' she began to feel a little indignant. 'I'm sorry I don't live up to your idea of perfection! Ten pounds I put on, at best, and you walk out the door!'

'Come on, I've explained all that.' He put his arm out as if to tuck it behind her back, but she was suddenly, inexplicably, angry. 'I didn't want you to affect my regime. I've been working on my body for months! I dunno. I felt betrayed, I suppose.'

Betrayed? 'Well, plenty of people like me just the way I am,' she snapped, pulling out the first stack of cards and sorting out the questions into piles.

'What's that supposed to mean?'

'I'm just saying, I've got options.'

'Oh really? Like who?' He seemed genuinely jealous, and she didn't know whether to be secretly flattered or whether to twist the knife a little more.

'I don't know. Maybe an author I'm working with?' she thought of Robert and the kiss in the car. The little stomach somersault that had accompanied it.

'What, that little rat-faced man who I saw on the TV?'

'Hey, he's a great guy!'

'Right.'

'I'm just saying,' she said, walking back to the little table and switching off the mic. 'You might not want to shag me at the moment, but there are plenty of people who would love to get into my knickers.'

The hall that had been rumbling with the low tones of conversation suddenly fell silent. Each and every participant turned their face to look directly at her.

And with a rising feel of panic, Jessica realised that she hadn't turned the mic off.

She'd turned it on.

Fit at 30

Keeping up the regime

People often ask me how I manage to get everything done. Being a mother and running my own business, it would be easy to let the gym slide. But it's so important to keep up a routine, or you'll easily slip back into bad habits.

Sometimes it can feel like there aren't enough hours in the day – from volunteering to run a quiz at my daughter's school, to catching up with clients, it can be hard to imagine hitting the treadmill or lapping the pool on top of a busy schedule.

But schedule is the key. Get out your diary and mark in where you have a spare hour, or even half an hour, for fitness. Planning your week in advance means you'll definitely find the moment you need to keep yourself in shape.

And ring in the changes too – this week I'm trying a new venue for my workout in the hope it will improve my motivation. Wish me luck!

#FitforLife

COMMENTS

Sally
You are such an inspiration.

Victoria
Good for you!

Chapter Thirty

'You have one message,' Jessica's mobile phone answering service informed her as she walked to her car. She clicked '1' as prompted and hoped to God that she wasn't about to hear anything more about the quiz last night.

After the initial silence that had followed her microphone faux-pas, the room had erupted with noise. Some tables had descended into heated conversation, others had roared with laughter. Jessica, standing there in her most professional-looking get-up, had blushed to her roots.

'Sorry about that, ladies and gentlemen,' she'd said. 'I hadn't meant to turn it on. Turn on the microphone, I mean,' she'd added for clarity.

It hadn't helped much.

She'd limped through the quiz with the help of Dave, who veered between chuckling to himself at the fact his fake or real fiancée had embarrassed herself in front of a room of parents and teachers, and sulking at what she'd said. When Liz had breezed in at the end and thanked them for their help, Jessica had accepted the praise graciously and slunk off into the dark car park as soon as humanly possible.

Mind you, Anna had given her a kiss this morning. 'Thanks, Mum,' she'd said.

'What for?'

'You know, the quiz.'

'Of course!' Jessica had said, surprised (and hoping that

none of the details would reach her daughter's ear at school).
She'd started to tweet: *Feeling great after . . .* then stopped.
No, this was just for her.

Last night in the car park, Dave had given her a quick
peck on the cheek. 'Well, that was eventful,' he'd said.

She'd been filled with sudden remorse. If she really was
engaged to this man, hinting that there might be someone
else was a horrible thing to have done. 'Are you sure you
don't want to pop back to mine for a coffee?' she said,
instantly regretting her choice of proffered beverage.

Why had coffee become a euphemism for sex? Should
she have offered tea, just to be absolutely clear about her
intentions.

Dave had raised his eyebrows. 'Perhaps not right now,' he
said. 'Let's just say, I'm not really thirsty.'

Which had meant what? That he didn't fancy her? That
he was still annoyed after her exhibition? Or that he didn't
want a caffeinated drink at quarter to eleven in the evening?

She'd driven home, wondering what on earth she should
be hoping for. Did she want to be engaged to Dave? She
missed him, definitely. Loved him, maybe. But surely true
love shouldn't hinge on whether she was a size ten or a fourteen? Surely her tiny muffin top shouldn't be a deal-breaker?
And did she even want to marry someone who didn't love
her completely for who she really was?

She looked at the ring again, and this time it didn't seem
to glitter as brightly as it had before.

Whatever the answer, it seemed her life would be easier
if she just went back to who she'd been before.

To:	manager@gofigure.com
From:	jess@StarPR.com
Re:	Gym Membership

I'd like to book a fitness assessment with one of your personal trainers, please. I have a wedding coming up and it's really important that I look my best. I was hoping you might be able to fit me in early next week?

Regards,
Jessica Bradley
CEO Star PR

To:	jess@StarPR.com
From:	nelly@gofigure.com
Re:	re: Gym Membership

Hi Jessica!
I'm Nelly, one of the trainers here at Go Figure! Stacey, the manager, passed this email to me as I have a suitable spot this evening, if you can make it at short notice? One of my clients has had a prolapse.

So – great news! There's a free slot at 7! Let me know if you can make it.

Cheers,
Nelly

Tonight. That seemed almost ridiculously soon.

To:	nelly@gofigure.com
From:	jess@StarPR.com
Re:	re: re: Gym Membership

Hi Nelly,
That's great. I'll be there at 7.

Best wishes,
Jessica.

She drummed her fingers on the table, then pressed 'send.' She'd always resolved that she'd be her own woman in relationships, that she wouldn't do anything to herself to please a man. Especially as a single mother bringing up a girl – it was her duty to set a good example, right?

But was it really Dave driving this change of heart on the exercise front? Going to the gym, eating healthily. They were all things she ought to be doing anyway. And surely if she tried to become the person she'd been at the start of her blogging journey, she'd no longer be lying.

And maybe, even if this engagement wasn't the real deal, perhaps Dave would fall in love with her all over again; they could get back together. It might not be the stuff of dreams, but she'd at least have caught up with her own fiction.

Fit at 30

Second time lucky!

As I type this blog post, I'm looking at one of the most beautiful engagement rings I've ever seen. And it's on my finger.

That's right. Dave has finally popped the question. And I have to say the man has style. Not only did he surprise me in my office (where I was having a meeting with the gorgeous Tamzin Peters of *Dagenham and Diamante*) but he roped in some of the guys from the gym to perform a dance number in my honour.

It was the kind of surprise that many women dream of – the whole choreographed romantic proposal to the classic 'Can't Take My Eyes Off You.' Not many women could resist such a romantic gesture.

So, I'm about to become a blushing bride. And I think that means it's time to step up the fitness routine! I'm going to be working with trainers at Go Figure! who've kindly agreed to get me in shape for the big day. And I'll be hoping to feature some fabulous designer dresses in the weeks to come. Once I've toned up a little bit more.

I hope you'll be coming with me on this amazing journey. 😊

COMMENTS

KD
Congratulations! Saw the proposal on my Twitter feed. So lucky!

CR
Marriage is over-rated if you ask me.

D
Dave sounds like a great guy. Check him out! @MuscleDave

To: Midwife35@monkeymail.com
From: jess@StarPR.com
Re: You

Hi Bea
Hope you're OK.

Thinking of you.
J x

Chapter Thirty-One

'Feeling awful, can you come?' The message came through just as Jessica was packing her bag for the gym. Bea.

It had been hard to get the appointment with Go Figure! And she'd blogged about it now. She picked up her phone to say that she could pop by on the way to her session, or maybe come around afterwards. Then stopped herself.

Would the world really end if she cancelled an arrangement (even one that felt overdue)?

'On my way,' she typed instead, leaving her gym bag half-packed on the bed.

In the car, she played a variety of scenarios through her head. Was Bea feeling depressed, desperate even? Was it something to do with Bea's work? Had Bea and Mark had an argument?

She pulled up in a space a few doors down from her best friend's house – the street was overrun with cars, parked haphazardly here and there where people had managed to fit them in. Bea lived on a new estate and it always amazed Jessica that builders were so keen to fit in that one extra property that they made constant compromises on the kind of space that was needed. Garages too small for cars. No driveways. Roads so thin people tipped their cars onto pavements to get them out of the way.

The door opened as she walked through the small gate on

the front garden and Bea was there, tear-stained and wearing a dressing gown.

'Oh Bea,' Jessica said, leaning in for a hug.

'I know,' said her friend. 'It's just . . .'

'I know. Where's Mark and the boys?'

'He's taken them to football. He said just to have a bath and relax, but I sat there thinking about everything and just driving myself mad.'

'Oh Bea.'

'Hey, less of the "oh Bea's",' her friend said, with a look that broke through her fragile exterior. 'I didn't invite you to placate me. I just thought we could have a cup of tea or something and put the world to rights.'

'But you're depress—'

'I know. I'm depressed. But the last thing I want to do is wallow.'

'But we could talk about it.'

'Seriously,' Bea said, as she flicked on the kettle. 'I really feel as if I'm all talked out. There is no solution. And I've got a counsellor to help me with that, a bit. Your job is to cheer me up – tell me something good. Or regale me with stories of your chaotic life. Or tell me how Anna's doing. Normal stuff.'

'Normal stuff.' Jessica repeated, wondering if there was anything in her life that could be considered normal.

'Well, you know,' Bea said, dropping teabags into enormous mugs. 'Normal for *you*.'

'Hey!' but it was nice to be teased. Nice to see the real Bea fighting back. 'OK,' Jessica continued as they both slipped into their places at the kitchen table. 'Well, if it's a laugh you want then I pimped myself out to half of the PTA at the school quiz for starters.'

'What?' Bea narrowly avoided spraying her with tea.

'Yep,' she said. 'And, let's see, if Liz is the gossip I think she is, then half the school now think I've got a terrible incontinence problem and wear nappies.'

'You what?'

Jessica grinned. It was funny, viewed from the outside. 'Oh, and what else? Oh yes, oh, and I have my first celebrity client.'

'I read that on your blog – that Tamzin woman. What's she like in real life – as vacuous as she seems on TV?'

'Actually, I think she might be quite bright.'

'Now you really have surprised me,' Bea grinned. 'Go on then, tell me everything.'

'Thanks,' Bea said a bit later, as Jessica scrambled in her bag for her car keys. 'I really needed that.'

'Me too.' Jessica grinned. 'It's good to have a proper catch-up.'

Although she felt a bit guilty that she hadn't mentioned her engagement worries, or anything about Robert and the kiss – things she'd have probably confided in Bea once.

'No, but I really needed it,' Bea said, all seriousness now. 'And you came, didn't you – straight away.'

'Well, yes.'

'And didn't you have the gym booked?'

'It'll keep.'

'Thank you,' Bea said again, as she watched Jessica walk to her car. 'See you soon.'

Chapter Thirty-Two

To: Jess@StarPR.com
From: Mum
Re: Re: Re: Re: Re: FW: Hello

Jessica,

I was very shocked to receive this note from Wendy.
Apparently there's some sort of naked picture of you displayed
in the gallery near the Town Hall! I know you like to be honest
and revealing in your blog, but may I say there is a level of
dignity a woman should stick to and you have gone too far
this time, Jessica!

How I'm going to hold my head up at the club I'll never
know. I feel utterly ashamed!

Anyway, give my love to Anna!

Toodle-pip!
Mum

>>>>> Begin forwarded message
Dearest Jean,
I'm so sorry to do this to you, but I thought you ought to
know what I've seen today in the gallery. Well, you know
I like to visit all the new exhibitions of course, and when I
found that there was some sort of competition going on for
artists, I had to go and see what the entries were like.

I have to say I was rather shocked when I saw a painting
by an artist called Hugo Henderson. It appears to feature your
Jessica completely in the nude! At first I thought it must just
be a girl with the same likeness (of face, you understand), but
when I read the information on the painting she is actually
NAMED!

It's not that I object to nude modelling in art – in fact, I'm
very open-minded when it comes to that sort of thing, despite
what Sheila may have told you. But I think you'll agree that
the picture shows Jessica in a very undignified position.

I have attached a picture so you can see for yourself.

Sorry to be the bearer of bad news.
Wendy.

Attached was a close up of Jessica's part in Hugo's picture. Languishing on a sofa, legs akimbo, chatting on the phone.

'Jessica!' Candice said, walking over to her desk. 'Visitor!'

Jessica hastily brought her email screen up to protect her dignity.

'Who?' she asked, her mind scrolling through possibilities: Dave? Mum? Roger the pig farmer?

'That Dr Haydn chap. I've buzzed him up. Shall I show him to the meeting room?'

'Yes, please,' Jessica said, suddenly conscious that her hair was in complete and utter disarray thanks to the combination of light, misty rain outside and the fact that she'd forgotten a brush today. 'I'll, I'll just pop to the loo first.'

'Right.'

Inside the small cubicle, Jessica looked at herself in the mirror. She ran her fingers through her hair in an attempt to comb it, but it kinked and curled and seemed determined to resist any attempt to tame it. She ran some water over her fingers and patted it onto the ends, before pulling the top portion back into a half-ponytail. It wasn't great, but at least it was in place.

Pulling a tinted lip balm from her bag and scraping off the crumbs and clay that had attached themselves to the tiny pot, she smeared a little onto her lips. Then she smoothed out the make-up that had settled into her under-eye creases and inspected the result. It would have to do.

Before she left the loos, she sent a quick 'How are you?' and heart emoji to Bea and received an almost immediate 'OK' and blowing-kiss emoji in response.

'I've got him a coffee,' Natalie said, as she passed her on the way to the meeting room. 'Do you want me to get you a tea?'

'Yes, please,' Jess replied. 'Um. Actually, no. I'll have a coffee too, I think.'

'Bean-free?'

'No, real please.'

'Oh!' said Natalie, surprised. 'I thought your limit was one a day? You mentioned in your blog—'

'I know,' Jessica said, trying to smile. 'But it's important to try to make clients feel at ease, don't you think?' Besides which, she needed coffee.

'Great tip!' winked Natalie. 'Thanks, Jessica.'

When Jessica arrived at the small meeting room they shared with other start-ups in the building, Robert was sitting back in his chair and staring out of the window, lost in thought.

'Hi, Robert,' she said, sticking her hand out for a shake. 'What can I do for you?'

'Um,' he said. 'Actually, I wanted to see if I could do something for *you*?'

'For me?' Was he asking her out?

234

'Yes,' he grinned. 'I, well, the team at the publishers are so excited about the TV thing – did I tell you that sales tripled after that hashtag?'

She flushed – embarrassed that she'd assumed he was after a date. Surely turning up at her office and meeting her in the official meeting room should have given her a clue that this was a professional visit.

'Even after the . . . doll incident?' she said.

'Yep. It didn't matter, apparently. It got into people's heads. People remember the name, you know? And then they're in the bookshop, wondering what to buy . . .' He pushed his glasses back up onto his nose self-consciously. 'Anyway, suddenly the guys at MindHack publications are wondering whether they might have an . . . erm . . . bestseller on their hands.' He flushed at the thought of himself as a bestselling author.

'That's brilliant!' she replied, still not quite sure what he wanted from her.

'Well,' he said. 'MindHack asked me for your details – I'd told them, of course, that I'd engaged outside PR at my own expense. And I think they're going to give you a call about representing some of their other writers. Their PR department is very small, well, non-existent really . . .'

'That's wonderful.'

'I just wanted to check that it's OK with you for me to pass your details on?'

'Of course.' She was a bit confused by this; surely he should know that she was all over the internet? Her contact details weren't exactly a secret. 'Thank you,' she added.

'Sure!' Then: 'Oh!' he said suddenly, on getting up – as if it was an afterthought. 'I also wondered, well, if you'd mind me taking you out for a coffee, or smoothie or whatever, to, you know, celebrate the success?'

'I'm not sure . . .' Perhaps she'd been right after all?

'No parks, I promise.'

She looked at him, his smiling face open and hopeful.

'Don't worry,' he said. 'I know you're with someone. But I'd like to be your friend, if that's OK? As well as a client?'

It was nice, his frank honesty. He wasn't afraid to say what he thought; wasn't obsessed with being liked or rejected.

'OK,' she said. 'Why not?'

Chapter Thirty-Three

Hitting the gym @GoFigure! #FitforLife #Energy!

That evening, as she pulled into the car park and grabbed her gym bag out of the boot, she was flooded with fatigue. Tempted to jump back in and head for the sofa, she forced herself to climb the six concrete stairs that led to the innocuous metal door.

When she'd rung Nancy the previous evening before popping to Bea's she'd been really understanding. 'Don't worry,' she'd said. 'It happens that I have another appointment free at seven tomorrow too!'

Which – while being very convenient – had made Jessica slightly suspicious that Nancy seemed to have so much free time.

She'd enjoyed her afternoon chatting with Robert – Dave or no Dave, there was nothing wrong with being friends. He'd told her about his children – Bobby and Alice – and how they'd struggled during the divorce. And how he'd tried the gym once but pulled a muscle in his groin. And how he'd tried to go on a writing retreat to finish his book, but thought the holiday cottage he'd booked might have been haunted.

"I had to sleep with the light on," he admitted. "I'm practically 40, for God's sake!"

She couldn't remember the last time she'd laughed so much.

'What shall I get you?' he'd said, when she'd arrived. 'Carrot cake? Cappuccino? Coke?'

'I'll just have a glass of water please,' she'd replied, her stomach growling with longing at the array of cakes on display.

'Really?' he'd said. 'Why not treat yourself?'

It seemed an alien concept. 'Oh no,' she'd said. 'Too many calories – I'm at the gym later!'

'Is it worth it?' he'd asked her when her unappealing glass of water was plonked down by the waitress.

'Is what worth it? The water?'

'No, not the water. I mean, the diet. I know we probably shouldn't eat cake – but seriously, do you really feel so great on your diet that you daren't stray from it?' he'd asked. 'Not even, say, once a week?'

Feeling great wasn't really something she'd considered. If anything she spent much of her time feeling tired and often hangry. 'It's more about looking the part,' she'd replied. 'And I've been a bit, well, naughty lately. Got to get back on track.' It wasn't a full confession, but it was the closest she'd come.

'But how do you feel?'

'I don't know . . . overweight?'

'But Jessica,' he'd said, 'that's not a feeling. It's a medical condition. And one that you definitely *don't* suffer from!'

'You don't think so?'

'Seriously. You look great. You must know that.'

'OK, well, I feel . . . I feel . . . ?' she didn't know, she'd realised. She didn't even know how she really felt.

'I don't want to be the devil on your shoulder,' he'd said. 'But why not just let yourself have a piece of carrot cake? In the great scheme of things, wouldn't you rather relax a little bit more, listen to your inner child?'

'My inner child,' Jessica had replied, 'is a greedy pig.' She'd smiled, hoping he'd realise she was half-joking.

'OK,' he'd said, sticking his fork into a piece of chocolate fudge cake he'd ordered. 'But, you know. Self-denial is not always the best route. Moderation, sure. But whenever I start something new, I think about whether it's realistic long-term. Going to the gym every night, eating like a saint – nobody can keep that up for ever.'

'I think . . .' He was right though. She'd stuck to the diet for ages – but had come to resent how it dominated her life.

'I just think,' he'd continued, 'you're setting yourself up to fail. Stretching yourself. And who for? Do you think Anna cares if you're a size eight or ten?'

'No, of course not.'

'And Dave loves you for who you are; you're engaged after all. For richer, poorer – all that.'

'Uh huh.'

'And do *you* care?' he'd asked, looking at her intensely. 'Really?'

She felt herself blushing. 'Well, a bit, I suppose.' Did she? she'd wondered.

'I have to ask then,' he'd said. 'Is it worth it?' He'd broken his chocolate fudge cake in two, removed his teacup from its saucer, placed the larger piece on it and slid it across the table. 'Go on,' he'd said. 'I won't tell if you don't.'

The cake had been frickin' delicious.

She'd enjoyed herself, she'd realised, and not just the cake. It had been opening up – at least slightly. Unburdening. Having the closest thing to a frank and honest conversation she'd had in months. And something else – feeling good in

Robert's company. Somehow, when she was with him, she felt better about everything.

In fact, she'd lost track of time and had had to ring Jenny's mum, Sylvia, and ask her to pick Anna up for her.

'She can have tea here, if she likes,' Sylvia had said. 'I think the girls are working on some sort of project anyway.'

'That would be great.'

Once she'd climbed the concrete steps to the gym, Jessica pushed the final door open and was confronted by noise, heat and light. Women clad in tight Lycra trotted on running machines; men spotted each other by the weights bench. Through a door to her left she could see the movement of an aerobics class.

She felt a little nervous – she'd grown used to her old gym, but there was no way she was going to be returning until she was back in shape – everyone there knew who she was; knew her usual routine. This was a smaller place – more anonymous; plus, it promised results.

There was a desk set slightly to the side, at which a woman wearing leggings and a sweatshirt was rifling through a drawer full of paperwork. As Jessica approached, the woman straightened, her blonde hair falling gently over her shoulder.

'Hi, are you Jessica?' the woman said, holding out a confident hand for a shake.

'Yeah,' Jessica smiled.

'Fab. I'm Nelly. Hey, thanks for reaching out to us for personal training.'

'Erm, that's fine.'

Why did she feel nervous? Perhaps because Nelly was ten years younger, with the sort of figure she'd only achieve after extensive plastic surgery and by eating nothing but celery for a month.

'Right, do you want to come through?' Nelly guided

240

Jessica to a little office behind the front desk with a couple of white chairs, a table and a clipboard of questions.

'So, let me see . . .' Nelly began. 'What would you say your fitness goals are at the moment?'

'Well, I'm getting married—'

'Oh, congratulations!'

'And I'm hoping to – you know – slim down for the big day.'

'What are you aiming for, size-wise?'

'I don't know. Just toning up really? Sticking to a size ten?'

Nelly's face said it all.

'Or,' Jessica continued, sensing Nelly's disappointment and overcome with her usual need to please, 'a size eight?'

This got a better response. 'Right.' Smiling with approval, Nelly wrote 8 down on the form. 'And shall we take a few measurements now? You know,' Nelly continued, reaching for a box marked 'fat assessment'. 'You look really familiar. Have you come here before?'

'No, never.'

After Jessica had been weighed, measured and pinched with something that looked like a pair of salad tongs, she was led to the main gym and asked to get on the treadmill.

A month ago she'd been able to run for an hour with ease. But this time as the treadmill whirred into action, her legs felt heavy and clumsy. She began to sweat, first a few beads appearing on her forehead and then more profusely as the programme spread up. After fifteen minutes when she was finally asked to stop, she could feel her heart hammering against her ribs, and seemed to have pulled a muscle in her bum. If there was one there to be pulled. A couple of gym-goers glanced at her as she doubled over to catch her breath.

'Don't forget your stretches!' Nelly chirped, with an

annoying smile pulling a perfectly toned leg up behind her. 'Nice and slow, and hold . . . That's right! Well done!'

Jessica wobbled, sweat streaming. But at least it was over.

'And now a bit of kettlebell work.'

Jessica followed Nelly to the mats like a reluctant school-girl. She'd never used a kettlebell before. She'd picked one up once, in her previous gym, but had felt a bit stupid and stuck to her usual free weights.

Nelly, all toned limbs and blonde hair, picked up a hot-pink version and gripped it between her fingers. 'The trick is to use your body to create momentum,' she said. 'And one!' she sang, swinging her own kettlebell down between her legs and up again in a swooshing movement. 'Two!'

'Come on, Jess,' Jessica thought to herself. 'Four weeks ago, you'd have done this in your sleep.' She lifted the kettle-bell into the starting position, then bent down, swinging the weight between her legs, and up again, just as Nelly had demonstrated.

Her shoulders screamed in protest, but she was deter-mined. Surely she couldn't have lost so much fitness so quickly? It was just a case of mind over matter. She bent her knees and the let the kettlebell swing down again, then, feeling every sinew in her body protest, she lifted it up.

On the third swing, she felt a sudden blast of cold air from behind. Was the air-conditioning unit nearby? Was it blowing directly onto her arse?

Then she heard a slight gasp and turned to look, stagger-ing and dropping her kettle ball.

She caught a glimpse of herself in the mirror.

She'd split the back of her leggings, and her bottom – like a sun-deprived, pasty-skinned prisoner fleeing from a dark cell – had rushed forward into the light.

Chapter Thirty-Four

Dave was late to the station, and she began to worry that he wasn't going to make it at all. She pulled Robert's book from her bag to distract herself and began to read:

REMEMBERING RAINBOWS

The best policy?

Honestly, how honest are you? When you were a child, you probably didn't worry too much about how people might feel when you said something. But over time, you learned to doctor your truth to make it more palatable to others.

Sometimes, this can be a good thing – if a friend's bottom really does look big in her jeans, there are tactful alternatives to telling her outright when she asks! But it can also mean that we hide complicated or difficult feelings, both from others and even from ourselves.

Try opening up the door to a more authentic you by being truthful. If someone asks you how you are, tell them honestly. If someone asks for your opinion, give it.

This doesn't mean shedding the adult sensibilities you have – it's not about hurting anyone's feelings or telling your boss that you hate your job. It's about gradually allowing a bit more of yourself to shine through – to trust yourself to be more open.

You will find, in return, that others open up to you more.

'What's that?' said a familiar voice at her shoulder.

She jumped slightly. 'Oh! Dave! You made it!'

'Course I did – did you think I was going to leave you stranded at the *Daily News*?'

'No, of course not,' she lied. 'Look, thanks for giving your Saturday up for this.'

Two minutes later, the train to London arrived. She slipped Robert's book into her bag as they boarded.

'I'm not sure about this,' she said for the twentieth time as they rode the tube to Kensington High Street. 'I just don't feel like having my picture taken.'

They'd caught the seven o'clock from Hatfield to King's Cross, grabbed a black coffee and banana and then taken the tube. The interview was at 9.30, and they were running a little late.

'But you love photos! What about all those selfies you posted last night?' he replied. 'You looked OK in those.'

'Yeah. Filters. Anyway, it's not really my face, it's, well, you know. My body.' Jessica gestured down at her tiny belly, which seemed to balloon over the top of her skinny jeans. She should have worn the more forgiving pair. But they had looked OK when she'd squeezed into them in front of the mirror this morning. Bloody gravity.

Dave looked at the muffin top as if seeing it for the first time. A brief expression of horror flitted across his face.

This was the point at which a loving fiancé ought to provide supportive feedback.

'Oh God! I see what you mean!,' he paused, apparently to

get his breathing back under control. 'But, hey!', he said, with a weak smile. 'Ask them to Photoshop it. Or maybe just suck in or something? It's amazing what the right pose can do too. But don't let them,' he said, leaning in for a whisper, 'photograph your bottom. Not right now, at least.' He nodded, as if he'd just imparted a sage piece of advice.

She resisted the urge to hit him square in the jaw. Or in his chiselled, *I didn't quit the gym and still go every day* six-pack. Although she'd probably have broken her hand.

Ironically, one of the things that had attracted her to him in the first place was his enthusiasm to work out, to better himself. And, admittedly, seeing him take off his shirt for the first time had been quite a moment. She wasn't made of stone after all. It was catching, too, his quest for perfection. She'd changed in the first months of their relationship; she knew she had.

As her muscle-to-fat ratio had improved, so had her confidence. The inner introvert she had to quiet in order to do her job had disappeared. She'd felt great.

But somehow that world of extreme fitness that had sucked her in looked different to her now. Yes, she'd like to have a perfect body. But was it worth pounding treadmills in a gym, deprived of natural daylight and surrounded by sweaty strangers every night? Did she really want to eat a diet of seeds and organic vegetables, with her every move constrained by the fact she had to eat at certain times and photograph it too, rather than just opting for some beans on toast or a bowl of cornflakes on days when she didn't have the energy? And was it really necessary to achieve perfection in order to harness her inner confidence? Surely, projecting an image of a perfect life was just another way of shielding herself from reality.

Was it toned thighs she wanted or the confidence they'd given her?

'Thanks,' she said, at last. It wouldn't do to upset him before the interview. Especially if they weren't really engaged and this was just some bizarre overblown favour on his part.

Claudia, the journalist who was be conducting the interview, met them in reception with a smile. 'Hi,' she said, grinning broadly. 'We're all set up in the other room. We've laid out a few outfits, and hair and make-up people are on hand, if you want to go through and take a look.'

'Thanks!' Jessica said, feeling nervous. She'd brought a bag of her own stuff, but it seemed that even the *Daily News* liked a bit of fakery.

Two hours later, they grabbed a quick decaff coffee in a small café down a backstreet. Black, of course. With a flapjack that was so low in fat that it might as well have been a pile of birdseed. Still, she ate it hungrily.

'So, what did you think?' he asked.

'About the shoot? It was OK, I suppose.' She tried not to think of the generic wrap dress they'd made her wear. With the obligatory 'nude courts'. And the fitness shots hadn't been quite what she'd expected – lots of Lycra, and posing together. In one shot, they'd asked Dave to bench-press her. He'd been able to do that once. But this time he'd turned red with the effort and she'd tumbled down on top of him.

'I hope they don't use that weightlifting shot,' he said, as if reading her mind. 'Don't want people to think I can't manage to lift my own girlfriend up.'

'That's your concern? What about me? That all-in-one running thing didn't leave much to the imagination. I mean, who wears a Lycra onesie to the . . . I mean,' she continued, remembering some of Dave's more daring gym outfits, 'who wants to be photographed in Lycra?'

'Yeah, but you sucked in, right?' He seemed genuinely concerned. 'I mean, even I sucked in, and I don't really, you know, *need* to.'

'Yeah.' She'd barely breathed from one shot to the next. Still, the fact that the camera had flashed almost constantly made her feel a little uneasy. She hoped it was going to be the positive feature they'd promised.

'Come on, smile!' the photographer had urged. 'Look like you're enjoying it!' But she hadn't been able to force a grin when fighting for air and tensing her stomach muscles. And as they made her perform press-ups for the shot, adopt a plank pose and run on the spot, she'd become sweaty and out of breath. Have I ever enjoyed myself at the gym? she wondered.

She remembered the park, then. The rush of air on her face as the swing had rocked back and forth. Perhaps she'd be better off doing something outside rather than being stuck in the machine?

Claudia had then taken each of them aside and asked them questions about their relationship – how often they had sex, what daily life was like. How the gym helped bring them closer. She'd even mentioned the quiz; clearly she'd been reading the blog. 'So, how did it *go*?' she'd gushed.

'Oh, pretty well,' Jessica had answered, blushing at the memory. She really should have prepped Dave first. He'd probably roll that one out as an amusing anecdote.

During the interview, Jessica had felt like one half of a couple suspected of having a sham marriage. Would Dave's answers match hers? She tried to remember what life had been like when things had been better. Preparing food together, setting off for the gym. Buying sports kit. What else had they done together? There hadn't been much time for anything else, what with their jobs and Anna and shopping for obscure vegetables.

Just when she'd thought it was over, Claudia had leaned in, her eyebrows set to 'sympathetic' and asked, 'I hope you don't mind me asking – but how do you feel about the gym pictures posted to your Twitter?'

'Gym pictures?'

'Yes. You haven't seen them? Someone posted them to your account earlier – I had a look just now and . . .' Claudia had looked genuinely flustered. She'd handed over her phone. On the screen was a picture of Jessica on a treadmill, everything paused in mid-wobble. Some idiot had tweeted a picture of her at the gym yesterday. At least it wasn't . . . well, it could have been worse. 'And there's this one,' Claudia had continued, leaning over and scrolling down. And there it was, Jessica's bottom, exposed to the world through a split in her Lycra.

Underneath, the hashtag #notsofit.

Jessica had mumbled something about camera angles, Photoshop and how she'd changed her regime a little recently. 'Perhaps the new exercises haven't quite . . . kicked in,' she'd said, handing the phone back to Claudia, who'd nodded her understanding.

'Of course. And camera angles can be a bitch, right?' Claudia had smiled.

'Did she show you any . . . pictures?' Jessica asked Dave now, removing a seed from between her teeth with a finger-nail.

'No? Why?' he smiled innocently.

'Oh nothing.' Probably better to wait and see. There was a chance he might not see them at all. She tried to remind herself that no publicity was bad publicity. But she couldn't put a positive angle on the picture of her bottom straining through her leggings.

There was no positive angle.

Her phone beeped with a message from Robert. 'Free for a coffee and chat – with or without chocolate fudge cake?'

'Sure,' she texted back. 'Monday?'

'Are you all right?' Dave asked, after a brief silence.

'Yeah, just thinking about the article. I hope that it's OK, you know?'

'Look, don't worry.' He reached hand across the table to grab hers. 'It doesn't matter if you look a bit bigger than usual.'

'It doesn't?' she asked, looking into his chocolate-brown eyes and holding his hand in return. 'I mean, you don't mind if I look a bit different from . . . you know. What I used to? Because you said . . . you know, the weight . . .' Perhaps Robert had been right. If Dave wanted to marry her, it was because of who she was, not what she looked like. Had she been wrong about him all along?

'No, the important thing is you're *back on track*.'

'Back on track?' She felt the hairs on the back of her neck stand up in protest.

'Yes. You're working out again; you'll be back to normal soon. We can put it all behind us. *Thank God*.' He wiped the back of his hand dramatically across his brow in mock relief.

'Right.' He was speaking as if she'd been ill or had an affair, not put on a dress-size.

He smiled benignly, pleased with himself. 'I'll have my Jessica back,' he said. 'We can be like we used to be, maybe?' It seemed like a question rather than a statement.

She looked at the ring. Suddenly it looked like glass.

'But what if you didn't? Does it really matter if I don't have the perfect body? Are you really saying that if I don't lose the weight it's a deal-breaker?' She remembered that she wasn't sure if they were actually together and that there was a deal to break. 'I mean, that you won't find me attractive any more unless I shed the pounds?'

'None of that matters,' he said, reaching out his hand.

'It doesn't?' She felt a surge of hope. Was this the point at which Dave would apologise for being cruel about her weight gain? Admit that he was a bit obsessed? Declare his unconditional love for her over a flapjack?

'Yeah, because you're going to lose the weight. So what does it matter what I'd feel if you didn't?' He smiled again, completely unaware that he had his size-ten stuffed firmly in his mouth, metaphorically speaking. And that if he wasn't careful, Jessica's very literal size-six was going to join it.

Fit at 30

I've been thinking a lot about filters, Photoshop and how, these days, we can alter an image until it's almost unrecognisable. I post a lot of selfies and most of the time I try to avoid the temptation to edit out a spot or slim down my thighs – I'm all about keeping it real.

Some of you may have seen some rather cruel pictures of me from my recent workout, where I admit I wasn't looking my best.

But in a way they've done me a favour. Seeing my bottom in all its glory helped me to realise that I've still got some way to go when it comes to being as toned as I'd like.

When it comes to eating well and exercising, we can sometimes hit a plateau. And that's why I've decided to step it up. Doing the same old moves, eating the same foods – however healthy – can sometimes mean we fall into a bit of a rut.

This is one of the reasons I was at the 'Go Figure!' gym in the first place. Wanting to rethink my routine and get back to my best.

So maybe I'm a bit angry at some of the comments, but I'll just pound it out on the treadmill. Stand by for a better bottom shot in the future!

#Determined #Toningup

COMMENTS

S
Good for you!

TS
Was that really you then? I'd assumed it was a hoax?

JK
Real girls have bottoms. You're an inspiration! So brave.

HKL
Ban #cellulite with our @miraclesmoother. Visit www.lumpylegs.com

Chapter Thirty-Five

After a few rings, Tamzin answered. In the background, Jessica could hear the hum of a road and the buzz of people talking.

'Hi, Tamzin.'

'Oh, hi.'

'So, great news!' Jessica said. 'I've been in touch with my contact at *Proximity* magazine and they'd like to do a little piece with you. You know, a day-in-the-life sort of interview with hopefully a reference to the Little Accidents range?'

'Yeah, brilliant, go on then. Oh, and fanks.'

'That's OK.'

Jessica put down the phone and ticked the item from her 'to do' list. The email, arriving in her inbox just five minutes ago, had been a great boost for a Monday morning. Just the right target market for Little Accidents and a readership with plenty of *Diamante* fans.

If Tamzin seemed a little underwhelmed, it was probably just because she was used to doing magazine interviews. Jessica's clients to date had had barely any followers online, so she'd had to work hard to get them any mention in the media. It was no surprise that things were different with someone who was used to a bit more attention.

She checked her messages. Some spam to delete after she'd neglected her inbox over the weekend. One possible lead from a freelancer wanting to interview Hugo for the arts section of a broadsheet. *A line-up with all the front runners in the art competition*. Front runners? Jessica thought of the picture again; imagined it spread out across her parents' breakfast table. Brilliant news for Hugo; not so good for her dignity.

'That's great,' she wrote back at last. 'We'll get something set up.'

She should really have been the one setting Hugo up for interviews, rather than being approached out of the blue. Had she been holding back because of the picture? If it had been of anything else, she'd have been shouting from the rooftops.

She'd barely checked her emails yesterday – usually Sundays were spent tidying up her inbox, but having been out with Dave all day on Saturday she'd wanted to spend some time with Anna. After she'd blogged and attempted a yoga DVD, they'd watched a movie together. It had been nice to stop for a moment.

But it wasn't taking an afternoon off that had put her off her game. It was the situation with Dave, she realised. She found it hard to think about anything else when she was sitting at her desk; and it was showing in her work.

Plus, starting back at the gym had been more punishing than she'd expected – come three o'clock in the afternoon she could barely keep her eyes open, and walking up the stairs, she could feel the muscles stretching on the back of her legs like overworked elastic in a too-tight pair of knickers.

'Just stepping outside!' she trilled suddenly to the quiet office, picked up her mobile and made her way to the car park. Inside the safety of her car, she dialled the number of one of the few people she could actually rely on.

'Hello?'

'Hi, Stu.'

'Hello, stranger!' her brother's voice on the phone was warm and welcoming and, as with every other time she rang him, she inwardly chastised herself for not calling more often.

'Yeah, sorry I haven't been in touch. Can you talk?'

'Yeah, don't worry. It's good to have an excuse to avoid work. Although I probably shouldn't be talking to you full-stop.'

'What? Why?'

'Well, I was a bit put out that you didn't mention your engagement to me. Mum told me!'

'Oh! Sorry about that . . .'

'It's OK. Saved me sending Erica out to buy you a card.'

'Hey! It's not too late!' But she was smiling. 'Actually, Stu, it's kind of about the engagement that I'm calling you.'

'Yeah? Please tell me you're not going to ask me to be a bridesmaid?'

'Ha! It's just that, well, I'm not sure whether I'm actually engaged or not!' She let out a slight laugh as if this was a relatively normal, albeit confusing, situation to be in.

'What?' his tone, as it might well have been, was incredulous. 'Isn't the fact that your boyfriend proposed and you're sporting a ring that even Mum was impressed by, well, a clue?'

She explained the situation. That Dave had walked out because he thought she was jeopardising his gym routine by eating biscuits. Stu snorted at that, but said nothing. Then she told him about the engagement. About how it had happened as a result of her asking Dave to stand in as her boyfriend for a bit but how now he seemed serious – as long as she lost the weight that had stood in their way in the first place.

When she finished, he was silent for a moment.

'Stu?'

'Yeah, yeah. Still here.'

'And?'

'And what do I think?' he said, sounding bemused.

'No, *and* will you help?' she replied. 'Please?'

'How on earth can I do that?'

She was ready for this particular question. 'I just thought, you know, prospective brother-in-law. You could take him out for a drink or something, suss him out a bit.'

'Seriously?'

'Yeah, why not?'

'I'm meant to ask the idiot who thinks it's OK to walk out one morning on my sister and my niece whether he's serious about marrying you? I should be punching him in the mouth, surely? And he called you fat? And you're OK with that?'

She hadn't really thought about it that way. 'Well, not OK, as such. But I guess I have let myself go a bit.'

'So what, you're going to write it into the marriage vows? *In sickness and in health, but not if she puts on a few pounds*?'

Jessica was silent. It didn't sound very romantic when you put it like that.

'You want to marry this guy? I mean, Grahame was bad enough. But at least he could talk about something other than how many weights he can bench press. Turned out to be a bastard in the end, obviously. But before that you two were . . . well, I used to be jealous of how you two were.'

'Really?'

'Of course! Mr Chronically Single vs Mr and Mrs Perfectly Happy. Course I was.'

'Why didn't you say? I always assumed . . . I was quite jealous of you – all young, free and single.'

'All lonely you mean?'

'Oh, Stu...'

'Crying myself to sleep and watching *Love Actually* on repeat every night the phone back'

'Aww you poor lickle baby...'

'Seriously, though, it was a bit of a shit time.'

Why hadn't she known? 'But you always looked so happy on Facebook.'

'Of course! Because everyone's completely honest online, right?' He laughed.

'Good point,' she said. 'Sorry.'

'S'all right. Ages ago now.'

'I do want to marry Dave, you know?' she said, getting back to the subject. 'Or at least, I think I do. It's just, until I know whether it's real, it's impossible to really know *how* I feel about it.'

'Well, that makes sense. A bit. What does Anna think?'

What did Anna think? She had no idea. 'I've... I mean, I've not really spoken to her much about it.'

Stuart was silent.

'I should have, shouldn't I,' she admitted, feeling a pang of guilt in her chest.

'Well, I've only got a toddler, so not quite in your parenting league, but I think you probably should have.'

'But you'll help?' she prompted.

'I suppose so. But I can't promise not to accidentally sneeze into his vodka and lime.'

'That's OK. I've been tempted to myself recently,' she grinned.

'And you'd better be there for me the next time I get engaged and am not sure whether things are real or not...' There was a smile in his voice again and she felt herself relax.

'Count me in.'

'You're an idiot, you know that, right?'

'I'm beginning to realise, yep . . .' She hung the phone up, smiling. Despite his tendency to drop the odd, painful truth bomb, she was lucky to have Stu as a brother.

Half an hour later she had a text saying he'd rung Dave and they were going to meet in a couple of days. *If I end up drinking some sort of health shake at the bar, you're going to owe me big time!* he'd added.

To distract herself from thinking about what Stu might discover, Jessica began to read some of the analytics from her blog. She hadn't posted a new recipe for a while; it was time to get back on the wagon – for better or for worse.

She scrolled through the recipe options that Candice had flagged up for her, and chose a vegan fry-up with sea-foam garnish. It looked both insubstantial and so healthy that it ought to satisfy both her trainer and her followers, if not her stomach.

Later, having popped to the grocery store en route and stocked up on as many of the ingredients as she could identify, she shoved the lot into the boot of the car and went to pick up Anna.

This time, she was a little bit late, and Anna was leaning against the wall at the front of the school, her face a carefully crafted frown.

'Are you OK?'

'Yep.'

'Sorry I'm late.'

Anna shrugged. 'It's all right.'

'Sure you're all right?'

'Yep.'

'Listen, Anna . . .' Jessica lifted her hand from the steering wheel for a minute and touched her daughter's arm. 'I wanted to say I'm sorry. I haven't really asked you how you feel about everything.'

'What, the Twitter stuff?'

'What Twitter stuff?'

'That picture of you at the gym, you know . . .' Anna's cheeks reddened. 'Someone sent it to me on my phone.'

'Oh, Anna. I'm sorry,' she thought again of her bottom straining at the hole in her leggings. 'I mean, it was an accident, obviously. And I'm pretty embarrassed . . .'

'It's OK. I guess it's not as if you're in the *Daily News* or anything,' said her daughter, shaking her head. 'And it's not like you're naked or anything.'

'No,' agreed Jessica, her mind hovering around the interview she'd just taken part in that was yet to go into print, and the picture of her imagined naked form reclining in Hugo's competition entry. 'Neither of those things.'

'I guess it's a bit embarrassing.'

'Yeah.' They sat in silence for a while, until Jessica remembered she was trying to talk to Anna about Dave, not about her bottom bursting through her leggings. It was hard to concentrate once confronted with a mental image of that magnitude.

'Actually, darling, it was the thing with Dave I wanted to talk to you about.'

'What thing?'

'Well, you know. The wedding. How you feel . . .'

Anna shrugged. 'It's OK.'

'You like him?'

'He's OK.' She paused. 'I'm not going to have to call him Dad or anything, am I?'

'No, not if you don't want to.'

'And you're not going to have a baby, are you?' Anna screwed her nose up with distaste at the very idea.

'No, no, I don't think so.'

There was silence for a mile or so. Then, 'Do you love him, Mum?'

'What a funny question!' Although it wasn't really. Maybe a little surprising. But quite a reasonable, adult question. 'Of course!' she answered brightly, wondering if it was true.

'OK.'

This seemed to satisfy Anna, so she left it at that.

An hour later, once she'd chopped vegetables, taken a selfie, arranged food on the plates, taken a selfie, set the table, taken a selfie, Jessica called Anna down for dinner.

'What's this?' her daughter said, suspiciously.

'It's a vegan fry-up,' she answered. 'I've got some quiche in the fridge if you'd rather.'

'No, this looks good, kind of,' said Anna, sitting down and picking up a fork.

She cleared her plate within a few minutes.

'Wow, did you enjoy that?'

'Yeah,' her daughter shrugged. 'It was OK. I just held my breath so I couldn't taste the leafy bits.'

'Do you want any pudding? I've got some dark chocolate mousse if you want.'

'Nah. I'll get some crisps or something.'

'OK.'

'Mum?'

'Yes?'

'Did you take a picture of the food?'

'Yes, of course!' Otherwise nobody would know she'd eaten something so healthy – what would be the point of that?

'Can you send it to me on my phone . . . uh, I want to show my friend.'

'OK.' She wondered if the friend was Grahame's wife

Tabitha. She couldn't help but hope so. 'Let me know if she wants the recipe!' she said, pushing send.

'Will do.' Anna went to leave the room.

'Hang on a sec,' Jessica said, and standing up, pulled her daughter in for a quick squeeze.

'What's that for?' Anna eyed her suspiciously.

'Just proud of you.'

'What, for sending a photo?'

'No, just, well, you're getting so grown up.'

'Thanks,' said Anna, smiling bashfully.

Jessica smiled back, but as she watched her daughter climb the stairs she could see Anna's expression change from smile to worried frown.

Chapter Thirty-Six

Alfresco meeting in the park with @DrRobHaydn #PRLife
#sunnydays #lovemyjob @StarPR

'You don't mind meeting here?' Robert asked for the forty-fifth time.

'No, it's fine,' she said. Although in truth she wished she'd worn a warmer jacket to the park. The lake shimmered in the afternoon sunlight, but there was a chill in the air.

Sitting at a picnic table by the water, she laid out her armoury – notebook, laptop, phone, pen – and smiled. 'So, how's it going?'

'I just feel so much more inspired in the open air, you know?' he continued, as if she hadn't spoken. 'Especially when it's sunny.'

'Yeah,' she agreed, mostly to move the conversation on. 'It's really nice.' It actually *was* nice to get out of the artificial light of her office. She breathed deeply. 'Relaxing.'

She grabbed her phone, the way she always did when something seemed worth recording, in order to take a selfie of them both together at the bench. But he reached a hand out and put it over hers.

'What are you ... ?' she started, then realised he was stopping her from picking up her phone. 'Oh. I can put some filters on it if you like,' she said, assuming it was something to do with his fine lines being on show in the bright day-light. She got it.

'No, it's not that. It's just, well, I hate selfies.'

'You what?' It was as if he'd said he hated babies. Or puppies. Or baby puppies.

'I just hate the way it looks, you know. So vain! Like writing, *I spent an hour taking pics of my own face, and this one's the best! Please compliment me below . . .*'

'Oh.'

'And then all your friends, they can't exactly say you look awful can they? So they play along – *wow, you look great! Your hair looks good! Brilliant pic!*' he said.

It was true. 'I suppose it does seem a bit pointless when you put it like that.'

'It's not just pointless, though, at least, not in my book. I think it's sort of damaging.'

'Damaging?'

'I guess . . . well, you know. Our childhood memories. We've got them all up here, haven't we?' he tapped the side of his head. 'We don't need to look back through the photos, we remember most of the important stuff.'

'But . . .'

'And even when we do dig out old family albums they're not all edited and filtered and false. They're funny and ugly and messy – real life; real memories.'

'Oh.'

'And when our kids look at the photos we've taken in the future it'll seem like every moment was happy and beautiful and impossibly perfect.'

'Yes.' He was right, she realised.

'And they'll look at their lives and compare them to these childhood moments. And they'll feel they don't measure up. Because they'll be comparing reality with a lie.'

'You're right,' she said her stomach sinking. 'They'll feel like failures.'

'And even when they do have authentic memories,' he continued. 'All they're going to remember is that their parents were flashing a phone in their face, or liking someone else's picture, rather than being really *there*, you know?'

'But there are no kids here . . . ? And . . .' she said, still not understanding his reluctance to snap a pic of this moment.

'I know.' He grinned. 'Call me old-fashioned, but I've made a pledge to myself that I'm not going to be in any more selfies.'

'Ah.' She took a snap of her laptop instead. #outdoor-working, she tweeted. #goodtimes.

'Why do you do it?' he said then.

'Do what?'

'You know. Photograph everything.'

'Well, I suppose it's just what you do isn't it? Got to keep your social media up to date, or the followers soon drop off.'

He was silent for a moment. 'Would it really matter if they did?' he asked.

'Well, kind of. In PR, you have to get yourself out there. Otherwise no one will think you can promote them properly.' She felt suddenly anxious, as if at any moment he was going to ask her to turn her phone off.

'I guess.' He looked out over the lake, the sun highlighting his face, the crinkles around his eyes, the early-morning stubble forming on his chin. 'I sometimes wonder where it's all going to end.'

'What do you mean?'

'Well,' he continued, 'it's like everyone's riding high on this big bubble of likes and retweets or whatever. And we, like, forget everything that's really around us, you know?

And did you know,' he leant forward conspiratorially, 'most of these accounts are fake.'

She raised her eyebrows and tried to look surprised. 'Really? Fake?'

'Well, not fake as in one of those robot accounts you hear about, but people lying, or only saying the good stuff when there's other stuff to say.'

'Yeah.' She flushed slightly.

'And I worry, you know. It's probably the psychologist in me, but it seems to me that if you're making friends with people who only know a false version of you, then they're not really friends at all.'

'No.' Jessica felt her knee begin to jiggle under the table – a nervous habit. 'I know what you mean,' she said. 'I think there's an element of that in everything.'

'Oh I didn't mean *you*!' he said, hastily. 'It's only really a problem when people begin to define themselves, their success, their value in "likes" that it becomes an issue.'

'Right,' she said, turning her phone over to face the wood of the table and realising almost instantly that she felt a little lighter when she did so. As if she was shutting the door on a room full of noise and chatter.

'Anyway, we're not here to talk about my philosophy on modern social media, or the fact that I'm a dinosaur and don't take selfies,' he said, with a self-deprecating grin. 'Sorry.'

'That's OK,' she smiled, moving her laptop to angle the screen away from the light. 'So tell me about this new project.'

'Yeah, they've asked me to write another book!'

'That's fantastic! Do you know what you're going to write about?'

'It's early days. Maybe relationships. Maybe more on happiness.' He stopped for a second, his gaze fixed on a little boy with red wellington boots, splashing in a puddle at the side of the lake. The boy's mother stood and watched, arms folded. 'Sorry about the park thing,' Robert said at last.

'Park thing?'

'You know, your spectacular swing dive.'

She blushed. 'Oh yes. That. It's OK. I've had worse things happen.'

'Puddles are another one, you know.'

'What?'

'Puddles. Splashing in puddles. Look there, at that kid,' he gestured to the little boy, still intent on soaking his trousers as much as possible.

'Aw, cute. I remember when Anna was that age.'

'Yes, there's something reckless about it, isn't there? He's totally in the moment.'

'Yeah.'

'But his mum,' Robert continued, lowering his voice as if the woman could potentially hear him from across the park. 'She's just standing there.'

'What do you expect her to do?'

'Well, wouldn't it be great if, as parents, we just joined in? And why don't we? Fear of judgement; fear of getting our precious clothes wet.' He grabbed her hand. 'Come on!'

'Wait, Robert. No, seriously,' but she allowed herself to be pulled along to another of the puddles on the edge of the grassy mound their picnic bench was perched on.

'What do you reckon?' he said, his eyes sparkling. 'Fancy jumping in, so to speak?'

She looked at her shoes – red leather boots, small, modest heel. Her favourites. 'I can't,' she said.

'Oh go on,' he said.

'Seriously, another time. Maybe in trainers?'

'Suit yourself.' Then, bending his legs in an exaggerated

fashion, he leapt in the air, landing in the puddle with an enormous splash and sending large droplets of muddy water onto her trousers.

'Robert!' she said, her voice coming out in a shriek.

'What are you going to do about it?' he grinned.

She wondered for a moment whether he'd lost his mind. Then, deciding that his expression was silly rather than psychotic, she leant down and scooped some water in her hands, sending it flying towards his face.

'That's more like it!' he said, kicking more water in her direction.

Then she found herself running after him, intent on pushing him over in the mud. She ran as fast as she could, pumping her arms, her heart hammering in her chest.

In the end, they both collapsed on the grass, panting and laughing and drawing strange looks from passers-by.

'I know you're a client, so I have to be polite,' she grinned. 'But you're a complete idiot, aren't you?'

'Gawd, what would you have said if I *wasn't* a client?' he asked.

'You don't want to know.'

He glanced at his wrist. 'That's about a thousand steps, right there,' he said.

'What?'

'Yeah, look,' he lifted his sleeve for her to inspect. 'Trying a fitness tracker.'

'A thousand steps, eh?'

'Yeah, and I bet you worked harder than you do plodding on the treadmill at the gym.'

'Yeah.' It hadn't actually felt like exercise.

'And I bet,' he said again, 'you don't laugh this much at the gym.'

No. No she didn't.

He stood up, and held out a hand to pull her to her feet. 'Can't laze around all day,' he smiled. Their eyes met for a moment and something about his gaze made her wonder whether he was going to kiss her. She leaned forward slightly.

He didn't.

They packed up shortly afterwards and she nipped home to get changed before going to the office. They hadn't achieved much at the meeting – nothing concrete, anyway. But she was beginning to suspect that Robert hadn't intended to discuss book sales or potential markets.

He'd wanted to show her something.

Fit at 30

There's nothing like working outdoors to get your vitamin-D levels up. Yesterday, I had a meeting in the park with one of my clients, Dr Robert Haydn, author of *Remembering Rainbows*. It was great fun sitting in the sun with my new laptop from LaptopsRUS – which is by far the lightest and most portable laptop I've ever owned!

It got me thinking about getting outside more for my workouts – a bit of running in the park, maybe some al fresco push-ups using some of the play equipment. I've spoken to Nancy at @GoFigure! who's going to help me to devise a great new workout for all of you who fancy doing it in public!

Then back for a well-earned nettle tea – great for recharging those batteries!

Jessica

COMMENTS

IP
How do you make nettle tea? I tried the other day and stung my tongue ☹ Recipe?

Cally
Nettles are actually relaxing rather than recharging. Try a shot of bean-free coffee-substitute with added avocado essence instead.

Chapter Thirty-Seven

#TuesdayThoughts working on my new account today!
#exciting! @TamzinPeters @StarPR #exciting #lovemyjob

The phone rang a few times before it was answered.

'Hello?'

'Hi, Bea.'

'Oh, it's you again!' her friend joked.

'Yep – just checking in to see how you are!'

'I'm getting there.'

'You know I'm here, right? Never too busy, whatever it might look like online.'

'What, you're saying you'd ditch the gym again for me again if I needed you?' Bea sounded a little more like herself.

'I wouldn't necessarily go *that* far!' Jessica joked. Then, 'Of course,' she said, just in case there was any misunderstanding. 'I've been a rubbish friend, but I'm starting to, I don't know, realise what's important, I suppose.'

'Which is me, obviously,' Bea replied.

'Exactly, you are my whole world!'

'You idiot.'

'Yep!'

'OK, how's next Saturday sound?'

'Perfect – and, you know, ring me if things get tough – promise?' Jessica added.

'I promise.'

Almost immediately after she hung up, the phone began to ring again. Grahame. She almost didn't answer.

'Hello?'

'Hi, it's me. Grahame.' No matter how much she reminded him that his number was programmed into her phone, therefore she always knew it was him, he started calls in the same way.

'Oh hi, Grahame!' she said, as if surprised. 'How are you?'

'Yeah. Yeah, fine thanks.' He paused, and she suddenly felt a bit anxious about what he might be calling about. Everything had been so strange recently, she wouldn't have been surprised if he'd left Mrs Perfect Second Wife and was ringing to beg her to come back, flaws and all.

'So . . . ?' she said, trying not to sound as impatient as she felt.

'So I hear congratulations are in order. Well done,' he said, rather awkwardly.

'Thanks.' Well done?

'Yeah. Dave seems like, well, he's a nice guy.'

'Yep.' Surely he hadn't just been calling to wish her the best with her nuptials? 'So, everything all right with you?' she ventured.

'I'm actually calling about Anna.'

'OK, let me check my diary,' she said, bringing it up on her desktop. 'I think you're on next weekend.'

'No, no, not arrangements, I've got those written down for once. No, I suppose I'm just a bit worried about her.'

'Worried?'

'Maybe it's nothing, but we chatted on the phone the other night and she seemed kind of . . . down.'

'Down? In what way?'

'Well, just a bit monosyllabic, I suppose.'

'Oh. Maybe she was tired.'

272

'Has she seemed OK to you?'

Jessica thought about the bowed shoulders and the drooping posture that she'd witnessed in the playground. The solitary figure standing by the school gates. 'I suppose. I mean, maybe a bit down at times. It's probably just her age, though. And the monosyllabic bit too – probably entering the dreaded teenage years,' she said, with a laugh that sounded false even to her. Because something at the back of her mind was telling her that Grahame was right.

'Anyway,' he cleared his throat as if about to make an announcement. 'Anyway, I asked her if everything was all right, and she said yeah, that it was just something to do with her friends.'

'Really? She hasn't mentioned anything!' Jessica remembered her own schooldays. Girls could be a complete nightmare: best friends one day, mortal enemies the next. Anna had a modest group of girlfriends – at least those she mentioned – but they always seemed to rub along well together.

'Yeah, and she wouldn't say anything else.'

'Oh.'

'I mean, it's probably nothing. And I know you see her all the time, so you're bound to notice if anything was really happening. I don't know, bullying or whatever.'

'Yes, well . . .'

'But I haven't been able to get it out of my mind. The tone of her voice, it was different – sad, somehow.'

'Poor Anna.' Jessica felt a jolt of anxiety.

'Yes.'

'Well, thank you. I'll talk to her.'

'Thank you. I'd feel a lot better. Like I say, it's probably just me. I've been up half the night with the boys – chicken-pox.'

'Oop. Don't envy you,' she smiled. Although she did, a bit. Not the night-time waking, but the fact that he had a family; that he was in the thick of being a parent. And, if she was completely honest, a bit jealous of the fact that, despite all of that, he'd noticed something about Anna that she really hadn't.

'No. No, it's not much fun,' he conceded. 'Look, you'll ring me, won't you, if anything's wrong?'

'Of course! You're her dad.'

'Thank you.'

'That's OK – thanks for calling.'

The end of their conversations were always awkward – all the missing 'I love yous' that had used to finish their phone calls when they were together (at least in the beginning) somehow conspicuous in their absence. Once she'd actually said 'I love you' to him out of habit when she was talking to him and watching *EastEnders* at the same time. Not her finest hour.

She sat staring at her inbox, drumming her fingers on the desk. Had she really not noticed that something was wrong with her daughter? Was it the wedding? She wondered. Or the idea of having a stepdad? Or perhaps it was nothing – just Grahame overreacting.

She ignored a message marked 'urgent – pelvic floor stuff' from Tamzin and shut her computer down early for the day.

'I'm going to finish up at home, Candice,' she said as she left. 'Got something to sort out.'

'Sure, no problem,' came the reply – as if Candice was granting her permission.

'Thanks.'

At four o'clock, she was parked outside the school – the first parent to arrive. Anna was visibly shocked when she saw her mum at the head of the car queue.

The journey home was almost silent – the radio filling the space where the conversation ought to have been. Jessica didn't want to jump on the girl as soon as she got out of school, so she was biding her time. But her innocuous questions about how the day had been, or what Anna had had for lunch, seemed to be falling on stony ground.

'Everything all right?' Jessica ventured at last.

'Yep. Fine,' came the reply.

It was just teenage stuff. Probably.

'You would tell me if something was bothering you – wouldn't you?' she asked again as they pulled up in front of the house.

'It's just . . .'

But Jessica's attention was drawn to the front doorstep, on which sat a dishevelled-looking Robert. 'Goodness, what happened?' she asked, cranking on the handbrake and climbing out of the car.

He grinned, embarrassed. 'You don't want to know.'

Were his trousers actually wet? 'I think I do,' Jessica said, trying not to laugh.

'Well, I haven't peed myself, if that's what you're worried about,' he joked, pulling at his trousers, which were almost completely soaked through.

'Right, I'm going to my room,' Anna interrupted, pushing past them and into the house.

'OK, I'll call you when dinner's ready!' Jessica said, turning her attention back to a dripping Robert. She'd talk to Anna later.

'Let's just say it was an experiment that went wrong,' he said as they walked through to the kitchen.

'What *kind* of experiment?'

'Well, book research. I thought why not try one of the pedal boats at the lake.'

The pedal boats were a new addition to the attractions offered by the local council at the lake in the park close to Jessica's house. A small area had been cordoned off, and a few white pedal boats had been purchased. Tiny pedal boats.

'Aren't they for kids?' she asked.

'So I realised . . .' Robert replied. 'The guy gave me a funny look when I said I wanted to book one. But I thought that I can't recommend this kind of thing to readers if I haven't tried it myself!' He shook his trouser leg slightly, spraying droplets onto her kitchen floor. 'Sorry,' he said.

'Don't worry about it.'

'So, I got into the boat and of course, I'm immediately tipped into the lake. Which is freezing cold, by the way. And up to my thighs.'

'Oh dear,' she tried to suppress a giggle, but it was hard.

'And then I got my shoe tangled up in a reed, so the guy had to wade in and drag me out.'

'Whoops.'

'Let's just say he wasn't exactly over the moon.'

'I can imagine,' she found herself laughing again, and this time he joined her.

'I'm an idiot, basically,' he said.

'Yes, yes you are!' she smiled. 'But somehow you get away with it.'

'Thanks . . . I think.'

'Look, do you want me to dry those trousers? You can't stay in those.'

'Would you mind?' I was walking home, then realised yours was closer and wondered, well, I thought you'd be back from the school run around now. And people were looking, laughing a bit.'

'Of course. I can get you a pair of Dave's joggers or something?'

276

'No. No, look, I've got boxers on – still dry. They're practically shorts. I'd rather not, erm, borrow anything.'

'Ok then, hand them over.' She held out her hand and he peeled the wet trousers off, revealing boxer shorts adorned with a picture of Mr Happy.

'Seriously?' she said, taking the wet trousers and nodding at his choice of underwear then feeling embarrassed that she'd acknowledged his pants at all.

'Yeah. Well. Didn't expect to have to take my trousers off in front of anyone today,' he said. 'Besides, they're my lucky ones.'

'Or, perhaps not.'

'Good point.'

'Well, look, I'll get these in the dryer – you finish making the tea,' she said. Their eyes locked for a moment as he passed the soggy trousers to her and she felt a shiver of something she hadn't felt for years. The combination of excitement and a feeling of being utterly safe: at home.

He smiled, self-consciously. 'It's not often that a woman gets to dry my soggy trousers, you know.'

'Yes, I feel very honoured,' she grinned. It was somehow both the least and the most romantic moment she'd had in a long while. If they'd been stars of a rom-com, they'd have begun kissing passionately, or dancing in the kitchen. Or he'd have told her that he was just a boy, standing in front of a girl, asking her to dry his kecks.

As it was, she held the sodden trousers at arms' length and walked through, dripping, into the utility room. Who needs romance?

She was shoving the wet trousers into the dryer and setting it to 'rapid' when she heard the doorbell ring. 'Just a minute!' she shouted, out of habit.

'Don't worry!' Robert called. 'I'll get it.'

Was he seriously going to answer her door in his pants? Jessica straightened up and raced through to the kitchen, to find it empty – a pool of water the only evidence that Robert had been there at all. She was reminded of the scene at the end of *The Snowman* – had it all been a dream?

He probably wishes it had, she thought when, walking through to the hallway she found the him standing next to a Lycra-shorted, grim-faced Dave.

'What on earth is going on?' Dave asked, his voice a Phil Mitchell growl.

'Nothing!' she and Robert said in unison.

'Nothing,' Jess repeated, despite a sinking feeling in her stomach. 'Robert just, well, popped over. He'd had an accident and—'

'So you're inviting so-called clients back out of hours now?' Dave stormed. 'And they're hanging around half-naked while your daughter's upstairs? And,' he eyed Robert suspiciously, 'what *kind* of accident?'

'Honestly, mate, you're overreacting.' Robert interjected. 'It really isn't what it looks like.'

Dave looked at him. 'So you're telling me there's nothing going on with you and Jess?'

In front of the stocky, built-up Dave, Robert looked like a flimsy schoolboy. 'Well, no. I mean, I suppose she's told you about the kiss, and—'

'What kiss?'

'It was nothing!' Jessica said, a smile still fixed on her face. 'Honestly. I didn't tell you because, well . . .'

'Seriously, I would never have kissed her on *purpose*,' Robert added, helpfully.

'So you're saying you don't find my fiancée attractive?' Dave continued, his features clouded with rage.

'No. I mean, yes. I mean, she's very attractive. She's great.'

Robert began, not doing himself any favours. 'But I know she's engaged, mate. With the kiss, well, I guess I hoped, but...'

'So you *do* find her attractive?' Dave raged, making it very hard for Robert – or anyone else – to understand exactly what he wanted him to say.

'Seriously, Dave. This is all about nothing!' Jessica interjected.

'A kiss?' Dave said. 'And this clown saying that he thinks you're unattractive? You're OK with that?'

'It was nothing!' she insisted.

'It wasn't nothing,' Robert said, suddenly. 'I do, I mean, I really do like you, Jessica. Of course I find you attractive. Very attractive, if I'm honest.'

'What?' Why now? If there was ever a time to tell a lie, this was it!

'But I'm not going to mess with your happiness,' he said. 'That's if you *are* happy,' he added, darkly.

Jessica closed her eyes. Robert was a good two inches shorter than Dave. And a good 50 per cent less musclebound.

'Look, do you want to take this outside, mate?' Dave said, squaring his shoulders in a way that Jessica recognised.

'Don't be ridiculous!' she said, putting a hand on Dave's arm. 'Look, Robert fell in the lake at the park, OK? I'm drying his trousers and he's having a cup of tea, and that is *it*.'

'Because I'm not going to let anyone make me look like a mug,' Dave went on, ignoring her. 'We've told people we're engaged, and if you're hooking up with clients left, right and centre...'

'What?' And what did he mean about 'telling people'? Was it his image rather than his heart he was concerned with? 'Hooking up with clients?' she was angry now. 'Perhaps you'd better go if you think so little of me.'

'No, no. I'll go,' said Robert, picking up his shoes and opening the front door.

'But your trousers!'

'Don't worry, you can keep them. Or whatever.'

'Good idea,' Dave said, darkly. 'Mr Happy.'

Robert stopped, his shoulders tense, but seemed to work through whatever retort had come to him and let it go. 'OK. Bye, Jessica. And sorry,' he said, without turning round.

As the door closed, Jessica stood in front of Dave – his face still red from the confrontation. 'Thanks a lot, Dave. If you must know, Robert is one of my most successful clients. And now I doubt he'll be coming back.'

'Look, Jessica – client or no client. He doesn't have the right to kiss you—'

'He knows that. The kiss was ages ago. It was a goodbye kiss that went wrong.'

'And you didn't think to tell me?'

'I don't think we were even together!'

'Look,' Dave said again, his voice a little calmer. 'I brought some stuff with me. I was going to talk about maybe moving in again. But perhaps it's not the right time.' He turned his back, spinning expertly on the balls of his feet like a dancer.

'Seriously? But—'

The door had closed behind him. Moments later, she heard his car fire up in the drive and screech away.

Chapter Thirty-Eight

Meeting with @TamzinPeters from @Dagenham&
Diamante for an interview with Proximity Magazine!
#FunTimes #LovemyJob #realitystar

'Fanks so much for comin' wiv me,' Tamzin said again, managing to plug her seatbelt in after a battle caused by her acrylic nails – each of which was pierced with a small ring. 'I 'ate these interview fings.'

'It's no problem,' Jessica smiled, as their taxi pulled away from King's Cross. Although in truth it was a bit of a problem. Because she'd had to leave early again. And cancel a meeting. And even bin a call from Dave when he'd finally rung shortly before she needed to catch the train, after a morning of missed calls and silence.

'So, you really hate interviews?' It was hard to believe somehow.

'Yeah.' Tamzin stared down at her shoes, each of which had a heel so high and thin that Jessica wondered how she managed to keep up with Rocky without them snapping. She'd switched to flats when Anna was born and had only just worked her way up to her three-inch maximum twelve years on. 'I loike bein' on TV n' that, but some of the journos, they just make me look stupid all the time. You know. Loike they want me to get it wrong or whatever,' continued Tamzin.

Which was probably true. Jessica looked at her with new sympathy. She'd always thought Tamzin was oblivious to the way she was portrayed. 'I get it,' she said, at last. 'Trying to trip you up, that sort of thing.'

'Yeah. Sometimes I fink I should start a blog. You know? To write the troof – loike your one. Keepin' it real.'

'Yeah.'

They arrived at the hotel where they were due to meet the journalist. The small café area with its leather club chairs and oak tables was almost empty. In the corner, a man was talking on a mobile phone. An elderly woman sat with a book and half an orange juice. A tall woman in her thirties, sitting with a laptop, got up as they came in.

'Hi, Tamzin!' she gushed, holding out her hand and wincing slightly when Tamzin grabbed it with her talons. 'I'm Suzy. How you doing?'

'Yeah. Fine fanks.'

'And you are . . . ?' Suzy said, looking Jessica up and down quizzically.

'I'm Jessica Bradley – Tamzin's PR. I'll be sitting in on this, if that's OK.'

'Sure,' came the response, although Jessica felt the atmosphere freeze up slightly. She understood. Suzy had wanted free rein with Tamzin. Well, Jessica was on the case now and no one was portraying her client as an idiot. Hopefully. 'You look awfully familiar,' Suzy said to her as she took a seat. 'Have we met before?'

'I don't think so. I've been in the *Daily News* recently, though – so maybe from that? And I do a bit of blogging.'

'Oh right . . . yeah. I think I might have seen that,' came the answer. 'One of those clean-eaters, right? I suppose you're going to put us to shame now with an herbal tea?' Her tone was slightly challenging.

Damn. 'Well, green tea and mint, hopefully,' smiled Jessica, inspecting the menu and wishing that she could plump for a croissant as well but deciding against it.

'It's hot chocolate for me,' smiled Suzy, gesturing at the waitress who was putting fresh oranges into the plastic tube leading to the juicer. 'With extra cream,' she added, her eyes meeting Jessica's with a challenging look, 'and sprinkles! Tamzin?'

'Water,' Tamzin said. 'Bottled,' eyeing Suzy suspiciously, as if she might be slipping something into her drink, or trying to paint her in a certain light depending on what she ordered.

'Sure.' Suzy smiled at the waitress and reeled off the order quickly, before bringing out her phone and opening up a voice-recording programme. 'You don't mind me recording, do you?' she asked. 'My shorthand is terrible.'

'No problem,' said Jessica quickly, after Tamzin looked at her for a response.

After a few generic questions to put Tamzin at her ease, Suzy came to the Little Accidents campaign. 'So, lots of mums are interested in your bladder problems,' she smiled. 'I wondered how everything's going. And whether you're benefiting from these products you're endorsing.'

Tamzin paused, as if wrestling with something, then said, 'Actually, I don't need 'em now.'

What? The whole point of the interview from Jessica's perspective had been to promote Little Accidents and her new client in one fell swoop – a double whammy.

'Really?'

'Yeah. I mean, they were good when I'd just 'ad Rocky, you know? But I did me exercises and fings have got better.'

'I see.'

'What Tamzin means,' interjected Jess, 'is that the Little

Accidents range have helped her to feel better, even when things *do* go wrong.'

'Nah, that's not it!' Tamzin retorted, ignoring the nudge that Jessica gave her under the table. 'I don't piss meself, awright?'

'So you're not endorsing the range any more?'

The penny dropped. 'Oh. Yeah. Well, I fink they're great, you know. If you need 'em. And . . .' she looked at Jessica pleadingly.

'Yes,' Jessica said, stepping in automatically. 'And as a mother, I really rely on them, like lots of women do.'

'You do?' Suzy's eyes lit up. 'How about in the gym? Do you find that they help there?'

Surely she was meant to be interviewing Tamzin? 'Yeah, I mean, of course,' Jessica lied.

'Right.' Suzy scribbled something on a pad. 'So, Tamzin, you're now saying you no longer use or need Little Accidents?'

Tamzin flushed. Under the table her leg had begun to wobble slightly with the stress.

'What Tamzin wants to say,' said Jessica, 'is that although she enjoys wearing the range, and although she still does suffer from time to time, her pelvic floor is much stronger now. Little Accidents are a good – and attractive – fail-safe.'

'Yeah, what she said,' nodded Tamzin.

'Right.' Suzy's tone was notably more clipped. 'So Tamzin's not able to say that for herself.'

Tamzin flushed. 'Look—' she began.

'Let's move on, shall we?' Jessica interrupted.

'OK,' Suzy said. She picked up her phone and swiped onto the net. 'Tamzin: I want to ask a bit about *Dagenham and Diamante* and your possible relationship with Connor. But

before I do . . . Jessica, your blog is *Fit at 30*, is that right?'
She held up her phone, revealing Jessica's blog homepage.

'Yep, that's me.'

'OK. Do you mind if I quote you, perhaps for another piece? Just a bit about sportswomen and urinary incontinence?'

'Yeah, OK.' Jessica flushed. 'But—'

'That's great. Thank you.'

The interview concluded with a few probing questions about Connor and his suspected 'other woman' on the reality show, questions Tamzin answered quite admirably.

'How do you fink it went?' Tamzin asked as they walked into the fresh air.

'Oh, pretty good,' Jessica said, still a little uneasy about what she might have agreed to personally. It wasn't as if *she* was being paid anything to endorse Little Accidents, after all. She was just meant to be getting them coverage, not to *be* the coverage.

The taxi arrived and Tamzin stepped in. 'Fanks again,' she smiled, lifting her long legs into the back of the cab. 'D'ya want a lift or anyfink?'

'No, it's fine. I have to make a few calls,' Jess said, waving her mobile phone.

'OK, call me tomorrow?'

'Yep, no problem,' she smiled.

As the cab drew off, Jessica looked at her phone. She had another missed call from Dave – no message. She debated whether to leave it after his behaviour yesterday, but decided to be grown up about it.

'Hi, Dave,' she said when he answered. 'You called?'

'Oh, yeah.' A silence. 'Look, I just wanted to say that I'm sorry about yesterday, you know? It was a bit of a shock to find a bloke at your house walking around in his pants.'

'Yeah, I suppose. But you know *me*, Dave. You should trust me.'

'I know. Sorry,' he said again, sounding genuinely crest-fallen. 'Look, I think we ought to get back on track, don't you? Things have been a bit . . . weird. You know, what with me leaving you, and the whole pretending I hadn't thing.'

'Yeah,' she said.

'And, well, you . . . you quitting the *gym*,' he said, his voice breaking slightly with trauma.

'Not quitting, exactly . . .'

'Anyway, now we've said we're engaged,' he continued. 'I thought maybe we could go out for dinner or something? There's a new vegan restaurant in town I want to try – it's French cuisine, thought you might like it. You know, keeping on track with the diet and everything. And reconnecting a bit?'

'OK. Sounds good.'

'Tomorrow night?'

'Yep, why not?' She felt a bit resigned about it: was it the food or was it Dave that was putting her off?

'Great, it's a date!' He rang off without saying goodbye.

On the train, she began to plan what to wear. Maybe her almost too-tight black jeans? With something looser on top? Or might her navy dress fit again? She googled the restaurant's website to see whether it was fancy or more casual. All she could find was a picture of an enormous onion, sporting a handlebar moustache and a chef's hat and winking conspiratorially. 'We put the veg into vegan!' was the restaurant's inspiring slogan.

The site also went on to claim the restaurant was the 'only Hertfordshire-based vegan restaurant to be featured in *Plant Yourself Here* – a guide to the best vegan dinners'. And that 'all meals are calorie-counted and contain no flavours'.

She assumed (and hoped) this was meant to read 'artificial flavours'.

After half an hour, the train pulled into St Albans station and instantly the scent of coffee and baked cookies entered her nostrils. She wondered what the vegan onion would make of that? *Mon dieu! C'est terrible! Il y a trop de sucre!*

The kiosk on the platform continued to pump out some powerful fumes – no doubt crafted in a lab somewhere to tempt passing customers – but highly effective.

She was just going to treat herself to a low-fat latte – the middle ground between indulgence and sticking to the straight and narrow – when she saw a familiar figure sitting at one of the tables.

'Robert!' she said, noticing that he was reading his own book while munching on some kind of chocolate-filled muffin.

He looked up, clocked her and smiled. He had a smudge of chocolate on his cheek and she longed to wipe it off for him. (Which made her what? His mother?)

'Nice to see you haven't wet your trousers today!' Jessica quipped, a little too loudly. A woman in front of her in the queue turned and looked at Robert with interest.

'No, no nasty surprises today!' he said, with a wink at the woman, whose ears went red as she turned back to make her order. 'Sit down,' he added, pushing the seat in front of him out with his foot.

'Thanks,' she said. 'I was just, well, I've been to London and—'

'Really? I'm off there in a minute. Just psyching myself up for the train. Can't stand being squashed. And I have to take the tube too, after. Why does everything have to be based in London?'

'What are you doing?'

'Just meeting a friend. Well, my sister, actually,' he said, as if divulging a state secret. 'She's a lawyer. Older. Used to scare me when I was a kid. Still does, in fact. Somehow, she's roped me in to watch a play about the Middle Ages ... or being middle-aged – I'm not sure. One of her friends wrote it.' He passed Jessica a leaflet, featuring a scowling woman wearing a black hat. 'Perhaps I should have gone for a double-chocolate muffin.'

'It looks great,' Jessica said, with a wink, and they both laughed.

'So you don't want to join us?'

'Think I'll give it a miss,' she grinned, passing back the depressing-looking flyer. 'Have fun though!'

'You really would be welcome, you know.'

'Thank you,' she said, genuinely pleased. 'I'm just completely exhausted – couldn't bear the train again today. And have to get home for Anna.'

'Course, course,' he said. 'Still, at least you would have made the evening more fun.'

'Oh! Thanks!' she said, surprised by his directness, by the compliment.

'Sorry about ... the trousers thing,' he added.

'Nothing to be sorry for. Sorry about Dave – he, well, he can get a bit jealous sometimes.'

'I just ...' he said, his eyes serious for a moment. 'Well, I wanted to say, I hope Dave isn't always so ... so, well, aggressive.'

'No, no! Of course not! Just not used to strange men in the house.'

'Yeah. OK. But look, Jessica, I've got to go in a sec. And I don't want to make things awkward, but something about you, him. Maybe it's just my view of things. But you don't

288

get to be an expert on happiness without being able to notice whether people actually are . . . happy, that is.'

'And?'

'And, I know I've said it before. But you don't seem happy. Not really happy.'

'But—'

'And don't you think someone newly engaged ought to at least be a little bit happy?'

She knew he was right, but something about him just coming out with it made her feel annoyed. 'Well, I am. Happy, that is. Very Happy. Thank you,' she said. 'I am.'

'OK.' He got up, wiping chocolate from his fingers and leaving his napkin in a little ball on the plate. 'Anyway, better go. Train'll be here in a sec.'

'Hang on,' she said. 'I mean. It's nice that you . . . it's nice you care about it. And I suppose I'm . . .'

'It's fine,' he said, smiling tightly. 'I'm glad. If you're happy, I'm glad.'

And with that, he picked up his jacket from the back of the chair and walked towards the staircase leading to the opposite platform. 'See you, Jessica,' he said, waving his hand briefly.

'Bye.'

Watching him go, she felt slightly sick.

As she walked back across the car park to collect her car, she noticed how the rainwater from the night before had pooled in the potholes, dips and rivets that covered the tarmac surface. Glancing around to make sure nobody was looking, she gently trod in one of the shallower puddles to test her shoe's waterproof credentials.

Then, feeling both reckless and ridiculous but somehow unable to stop herself, she put her feet together, leapt into the air and jumped into the shallow pool of water; feeling the spray speckle her thin cotton trousers and watching as the water displaced around her feet.

In for a penny, she thought, looking at her ruined clothing and jumped again. This time, more water rose and sloshed into her shoe. The cold, muddy wetness on her skin was like a slap to the face – breaking the mood and bringing back her normal level of self-consciousness. Across the car park, she saw a man, key in his car door, looking at her.

But instead of rushing to her car with embarrassment, she caught the man's eye and grinned. To her surprise, he grinned back, shook his head in mock judgement, and gave her a little wave before disappearing into the driver's seat of a small Renault.

As she soggily continued her way back to her car, she found she couldn't stop smiling.

Chapter Thirty-Nine

#DateNight with my fiancé @MuscleDave @VeganPantry #delicious!

'Mum! Dave's here!' called Anna from the living room.

'Just a minute!' Jessica applied the straighteners to the last bit of her hair and studied the result. It would have to do, she decided.

Her new black jeans highlighted the fact that she'd begun to get her figure back. Her black top, edged with diamante, sparkled. Her ring – zirconia? diamond? – glittered on her finger. Her hair had grown a little and had been tamed into place with a thirty-minute blowdry. In fact, it almost looked glossy.

'Welcome back,' she whispered to herself, recognising the woman from her blog. 'It's *the* Jessica Bradley.'

In the hallway downstairs, Dave stood on the doormat and whistled as Jessica appeared on the stairs. 'Hey! Looking good, Jess!' he said, beaming. 'I might even be able to take a picture together tonight, you know, one I'm not embarrassed to share on Instagram!'

Jessica tried to grin. It was almost definitely a joke.

'You do look really great, Mum,' Anna echoed from the living-room doorway.

'Do you really think so?'

'Yeah!' her daughter nodded approvingly.

'And you're sure you'll be OK?' She was trying to give Anna more room; trying to stop 'over-mothering', as Anna had put it.

'Mum!' the teenage eye roll again. 'You know I'm practically thirteen now! I'll be allowed to babysit soon! I can look after myself.'

Jessica smiled. 'Well, we won't be long anyway,' she said, brushing her daughter's hair out of her eyes as Dave slipped a proprietary hand around her waist.

'So, I've been looking at venues,' Dave began as they started the short drive to the centre of town in his two-seater.

'Venues?'

'Yeah! I mean, I know it's going to be our choice together as a couple, but I thought it wouldn't hurt if I got a few ideas.'

Venues. 'Oh, right?'

'Yeah, and you have to book some of them up way in advance.'

'Oh.'

'But some you can get in sooner – maybe if there's been a cancellation or something. I thought maybe we could choose a couple and go and see them?'

'Sure,' she glanced at the ring on her finger. Perhaps it was a diamond after all?

'Because I wanted to say, babe. You seem more like yourself – like *my* Jessica now. You're looking like yourself again.'

'Thanks.'

'So, maybe we should go for it.'

It occurred to Jessica that if Dave hadn't been fully serious in the past, then this was her proposal. A sort of reclaiming of lost baggage. Not one for the Instagram feed then. #truelove

Her phone beeped, and she instinctively pulled it out

of her bag. A message from an unknown number read: 'So excited about tonight! I'll be there from 8 — look forward to seeing you! H.'

She nearly deleted it thinking it must be a mistake, but at the last minute felt a prickle of realisation. H. Hugo. The competition.

She glanced at the date. Shit. 'Um, Dave?'

'Yep?' He glanced briefly from the road to look at her face. 'What's up?'

'I've made a mistake.'

'What do you mean?' He looked at her defensively, as if expecting to be dumped.

'I forgot a work thing. An artist — remember Hugo?'

'What, the penis guy?'

'Dave! He's a serious artist! But yes, the penis guy.'

'What about him?'

'Well, he's entered a . . . um . . . a new work in a competition at the gallery. And I forgot totally that there's an open evening before the prizes are announced. There's this whole wine-drinking soirée thing I'm meant to be going to.'

'So no dinner tonight then?'

'Do you mind?'

'Nah, it's OK. Restaurant's not going anywhere!'

Jessica smiled. She'd forgotten how relaxed and easy-going Dave could be when he wasn't at the gym. 'Do you think you could drop me there?'

'Drop you there? I'm coming with you!' he said.

This was unexpected. 'Really? I didn't think you liked mixing with "arty types",' Jessica said, remembering one heated argument they'd had when she'd convinced him to skip the gym to go to an after-party at the Grand.

'But I won't have to mix with anyone talented or accomplished,' he smiled. 'I'll have you to talk to!'

'Of course!' she said. 'I'd love to have you there—'

Before she could finish her sentence, an image of the painting flashed through her mind. Surely he'd already seen it online? Someone must have told him, mustn't they? He'd be OK with it? She took a sideways glance at his face: it wore the unmistakable smile of someone blissfully ignorant that he was going to a soirée celebrating – among other things – a pretty graphic picture of his fiancée reclining on a chaise longue.

'Actually,' she said, thinking better of it. 'Actually, maybe you ought to go to the gym. I mean, you're making good progress at the moment. You could really benefit from an extra workout.'

'No,' he said after a pause. 'I mean, yeah, you're right, but you always said you wanted me to be more involved, so I guess that I ought to make more of an effort.'

She felt guilty then, because he was being genuinely nice, and she was being misleading for all the wrong reasons.

'OK, thanks,' she said at last, wondering whether she ought to fake a headache and get out of the thing altogether.

But then, he'd see it in the end anyway, wouldn't he? Or hear about it on the grapevine (if there's such a thing as a grapevine in the world of fine, but pornographic, art).

'Dave,' she said as they pulled into the car park and he reversed the car with such ease into a tiny space that she developed a whole new respect for him. 'You should know . . . about Hugo's work . . .'

'Yes?' he said, distractedly.

'Well, it . . . it might be a bit . . . surprising.'

'More surprising than a three-metre penis?'

'Depends on the circumstances.'

He laughed: 'I'll cope!'

'It's just—'

294

But he had climbed out of the car and was already around her side, opening the passenger door for her. She wasn't sure whether she was meant to be offended as a feminist at this level of chivalry, but something about the gesture made her heart melt. What did Robert know about how she felt? She was happy with Dave. And he was clearly going to make sure he ironed out all the creases in their relationship before the big day.

The art gallery was bustling with life. As they entered, a girl with a tray offered them both a glass of sparkling wine. Couples and small groups milled around the twelve unique artworks displayed in the foyer. A landscape in oil, depicting a local scene in intricate dots of colour, a portrait of a woman – just her eyes and the top of her nose, a tear running down; one of those random splashes of colour type paintings that everyone pretends to appreciate and understand. Hugo's work was thankfully tucked away at the back somewhere, rather than being evident straight away.

'God, it's packed,' Dave said, a little too loudly, spilling a little of his wine. 'Didn't think there'd be so many people here.'

'I know . . .' Jessica began, but then . . .

'Helllooo!' said a rather excited voice, and suddenly Hugo was there, obviously a couple of wines down already, looking a little flushed but surprisingly dapper in his well-ironed chinos. 'Jessica, I am so glad you came,' he said, then added a little more quietly. 'I'm totally shitting myself.'

'Hugo, you remember Dave?' she said.

'Oh yes, hi,' he said, somehow shaking hands with Dave without breaking eye contact with Jessica. 'Look, there's a photographer here – from one of the broadsheets, could you believe? And he wanted a picture of me with my . . . my painting. But then I saw you come in and said, well, even better, you could have me with my muse!'

'Your . . .' Jessica trailed off, realising exactly what Hugo meant. 'Oh.'

'What, Jessica's your muse?' Dave said, his mouth slightly turned down at the corners.

'Yeah. Oh, not like *that*,' Hugo added, catching Dave's meaning. 'Purely in a professional sense, you know. The painting's about how women – well, not all women, but certainly this one – can juggle so many things so professionally and yet appear so . . . effortlessly beautiful.'

'Right,' Dave clearly wasn't sure whether to be reassured or not by this. Which didn't bode well when Jessica considered what was coming next. 'What's a muse?'

'So, he's waiting!' Hugo trilled almost manically, and Jessica found herself being led by the hand towards a display at the back.

'Here she is!' Hugo said to a bearded man with an enormous camera. 'The woman behind it all!'

Jessica could feel her cheeks begin to redden. Dave trotted at her heels like an obedient puppy, with no idea what horrors lay ahead.

'Now, if you could stand this side, and Hugo that. That's right. Now smile!' said the ridiculously youthful photographer. He stopped and inspected his work. 'Right,' he said. 'Shall we go for one more – perhaps of you two together – and the painting on your right. Excellent, excellent. And how about a kiss?'

Jessica leaned in for a professional peck on the cheek, only to find herself swooping towards the ground, in Hugo's arms. He planted a smacker on her surprised mouth, as the camera flashed.

'Sorry about that,' he said as she righted herself. 'Always get a bit carried away at photos.'

'But . . .' she began.

Then noticed Dave.

Whether he'd even noticed the kiss at all was unclear. What he had definitely noticed was the painting. He stood, wine glass in hand, motionless, the colour draining out of his face, his neck muscles tensed – hackles up like a dog, eyes fixed on the canvas.

'Dave, it's not—'

'What,' he said, 'the fuck is that?'

'It's, well, I told you it would be a bit—'

'That is not a *bit* anything! That's a picture of my wife, bits on show, for the whole world to see!'

'It's not what you think, it's—'

'Look, I'm not sure what kind of PR firm you're running,' he said, his voice growing louder as a hush fell over the room, 'but it seems to me that you're going above and beyond for more than one of your clients. And, by above and beyond,' he informed bystanders, loud and clearly, for clarity, 'I mean she's offering herself up on a plate for them to enjoy.'

'Dave!' Jessica gasped. A camera flashed.

'Seriously. You think I want to marry a woman who hasn't even got a shred of modesty?' he said, gesturing again at the picture; spilling more wine. 'For God's sake! Look at that picture! You look *fat*!'

'Fat? But . . .' Surely, looking at that picture, something else stood out a little more than the size of her thighs . . .

'Look, mate,' Hugo said. He was one of those people who should never use words like 'mate'; the word sounded forced, desperate. 'Look, mate, it's not what you think.'

'Oh really?'

'She didn't pose for me. She didn't even know. I just . . .

it's my imagination, is all,' he said with a 'what can you do?' kind of shrug.

His lip trembling, Dave turned on his heels and walked out, shoulders hunched like an ape's.

Realising he was out of imminent danger, Hugo rushed to Jessica's side. 'Oh, I am so sorry,' he said. 'I had no idea!'

'No, how could you? It's fine,' she replied through gritted teeth.

A camera flashed.

Notebooks were scribbled in.

People watched. The room was quiet.

Then, gradually, a murmur of conversation broke out again. People returned to discussing the art. Normality resumed.

'Oh, there you are!' came a voice.

Jessica started. Crossing the room were her parents, with Stuart trailing in their wake.

I WEAR NAPPIES TO THE GYM, FITNESS BLOGGER ADMITS

A fitness blogger whose popular site 'Fit at 30' draws over 75,000 hits per month, has admitted to wearing nappy-like protection during her gym workouts.

Jessica Bradley, 36, from Hertfordshire, who also runs a small PR firm, was left suffering from the embarrassing problem of urinary incontinence after giving birth to son, Arthur, now 11.

'I don't think women should feel ashamed about this problem,' the glamorous blonde argued. 'And the Little Accidents range ensures no embarrassing leakage when on the treadmill.'

Ms Bradley, who drew criticism from some followers recently after a candid shot of her splitting her leggings during a workout revealed what one Twitter user termed 'blancmange buttocks', believes that the range of disposable pants produced by the Little Accidents brand can 'fit in on any occasion'.

But former band ambassador Tamzin Peters, of hit reality series *Dagenham and Diamante*, who was sacked from her role as a result of negative comments about the paper underwear, has claimed that the range of protective products are 'no better than nappies' and 'made her bum look big'.

'I may have worn the product shortly after giving birth

to Rocky,' the part-time model and actress claimed, 'but I believe that a solution to incontinence is far more effective than just soaking up the problem.'

It has emerged that Peters is currently in talks with Snapped Shut!, a range of apps claiming to help women strengthen their pelvic floor after childbirth.

A spokesperson for Little Accidents admitted that Peters was no longer working with their brand due to 'creative differences,' but confirmed that mum-of-one Bradley was an 'avid fan' of the product.

Ms Bradley was unavailable for further comment.

THE TALK OF THE TOWN!

An award-winning work by local artist Hugo Henderson has divided opinion.

The Hertfordshire Art Association has hit back at comments that one of the finalists for the 'Art is Art' Bursary was chosen simply to attract media attention.

The work, entitled 'Naked Ambition' by Henderson, 43, has divided opinion due to its depiction of a voluptuous woman reclining naked on a chaise longue, together with a self-portrait of the artist, also naked, at an easel.

'The work is hard-hitting, definitely,' agreed Cuthbert Crinkbottom, patron of the H.A.A., 'but no more so than, say, some of the nudity depicted in works by Picasso or Renoir.'

'It's disgusting,' said local resident Jean Bradley, 65. 'The artist should be ashamed of himself.'

However, others disagreed, commenting on the fine level of detail in the painting. 'Of course, it's a controversial work,' explained Sally Smith, one of the four judges, 'but the painting itself is exquisite. The artist has captured every detail of the woman's body – from the delicate hairs on her upper thighs, to the roundness of her stomach.'

The woman who posed for Henderson, is thought to be local fitness blogger Jessica Bradley, who was there to support the artist on the evening itself in her role as his agent. 'He's such a fabulous artist,' Ms Bradley gushed. 'I think he has a great future ahead of him.'

TAMZIN PETERS WOWS AT GALA EVENT

Popular model Tamzin Peters from hit reality series Dagenham and Diamante stunned fans in a revealing diamante gown, with matching clutch.

The model and actress, 23, from Essex refused to comment on the recent controversy sparked by her rejection of feminine hygiene range Little Accidents, but did confirm that she would be leaving her role in her reality show in an upcoming episode.

'I feel like I've given so much of my life to the series,' Peters explained. 'It's time to try something new.'

Chapter Forty

To: jessica@StarPR.com
From: rob@easymail.com
Re: Award!

Dear Jessica,

Just a quick note to say that I saw you in the paper this morning. You must be thrilled about Hugo Henderson's award! Well done.

   Got a few ideas for the new book – will be in touch soon 😊

Best wishes,
Robert

To: Stu1981@internet.com
From: jessica@StarPR.com
Re: Help

Dear Stu,

What shall I do about last night! What an absolute nightmare!!!

   Help!

Jess

To: jessica@StarPR.com
From: Stu1981@internet.com
Re: Help

Sorry, sis, but looks like you've made your chaise longue and you're going to have to recline on it! I'll remember the expression on Dad's face until the day I die! What on earth possessed you to invite them to the awards thing? Nice painting, though. If a bit graphic! 😊

If it's any consolation, it won't be long until you're back being Mum's golden child again.

Have a glass of wine and forget about it. I know I'm trying to . . .
Stu x

To: Stu1981@internet.com
From: jessica@StarPR.com
Re: Help

Golden child? You're kidding, right?

Mum constantly criticises me – whereas you can do no wrong!!

Good idea about the wine. And have you seen <u>this article in the Daily News</u>? 🙁

To: jessica@StarPR.com
From: Stu1981@internet.com
Re: Help

Did you seriously have to send me that picture of your bare arse at the gym? Haven't I suffered enough?!

Honestly, don't worry – tomorrow's chip wrappings . . . no such thing as bad publicity – all the usual platitudes.

Careful what you wish for eh! Fame and fortune come at a price! Xxx

By the way, do think about what I said last night. xx

To: Stu1981@internet.com
From: jessica@StarPR.com
Re: Help

Careful what I wish for? Seriously, I didn't wish for any of this! The blog was never meant to go viral.

And yes, I am honestly.

To: jessica@StarPR.com
From: Stu1981@internet.com
Re: Help

Then seriously, sis, why do you do it? It doesn't seem to be making you very happy.

Here if you need to talk.

S x

Last night, when Stuart had sidled up to her and given her a squeeze, she'd almost burst into tears.

'Hey, hey,' he'd said, 'it's OK, Jess.'

'I know, I know.'

'And you know, Mum and Dad will forget about it pretty soon.'

'I know.'

'And I'll be able to get some therapy or hypnosis or something . . .'

'Hey!' she'd said, feeling the hint of a smile. 'It's not *that* bad.'

'No,' he'd said, taking an exaggerated sip of his wine. 'The painting itself is pretty much a masterpiece, actually.'

'Thank you.'

'It just might have done irreparable damage to my subconscious. Scarred me for life, and all that.'

'Hey!'

'Seriously, Jess. Would you like to see me reclining on a sofa, all my bits and pieces on display?'

'No, I think I could probably do *without* that.'

'Exactly.' Another sip of wine. 'Anyway, where's Dave?'

'Gone.'

'Gone? Without you?' Stuart's brow had furrowed with concern. 'I just assumed he hadn't wanted to come.'

'No. Before you got here, he kind of kicked off.'

'About the painting?'

'About the painting. Apparently I look fat in it.'

Stuart had bitten his lip for a moment. 'Look, I can't do it,' he'd said. 'I want to be supportive and everything, but I can't do it. That man . . .'

'What?'

'Well, you know. We went for that drink, yesterday.'

'Yeah. You said you couldn't get much out of him in the text?'

'That wasn't strictly true.'

'What?'

'Well, I mean, I didn't get much out of him about the engagement. Whether it was real or whatever. He was going on about it, but it was hard to know whether it was part of the "ruse".'

'Yeah?'

'But Jess, the way he spoke about you!'

'What do you mean?'

'I can't really put my finger on it – it's not like I can pick out a phrase and say *he said this! Or he told me that!*'

'Right?'

'But . . . he talked about you as if you were a prize he'd won. How you look – how you're going to look. That sort of thing.'

306

'Oh.'

'And I mean, that's OK – I mean it's OK that he likes the way you look. But there should be more to it than that, shouldn't there?'

'Yes . . . of course . . . I mean, there is, isn't there?'

'Maybe. I tried to talk about Anna, though, and he didn't have much to say.'

'OK?'

'And . . . it's more the impression he gave me. I'll be honest, sis. I'm not his biggest fan.'

'Oh, but Dave is lovely,' she'd said, uncertainly. 'He's—'

'Is he though? Making a scene at an important work do? Calling you fat?'

'He was just upset . . . he—'

'OK. Just – well. I'll support you all the way, but just be careful.'

Before she'd had time to answer, Hugo had skipped up. 'Sorry about all that,' he'd said. 'Hope I haven't messed things up for you at home?'

'Don't be silly,' she'd smiled. 'He's . . . Dave was just . . . Well, you know.'

'Of course,' Hugo had replied, only half listening. 'Look, I probably shouldn't say anything, but I overheard someone talking about my painting in glowing terms. Turns out it was Bernard!'

'Bernard!'

'Only Bernard Cribbins! The art critic from the Herald!' he'd said, excitedly.

'That's fantastic.'

'Yes! Ooh, just a second, must dash.' And with that, Hugo had left her side and disappeared into the crowd after a woman who seemed to be trying her best to dive into the loos before she was apprehended.

'I don't know how you do it,' Stu had said, then. 'He's quite the character!'

'Oh, I get by,' she'd smiled, drinking a sip of wine. 'Somehow, I cope.'

'We're Ok, right? You didn't mind me saying?'

'Not at all. It's, well, I know it mustn't have been easy. I don't necessarily agree . . .'

'That's your call.'

And they'd chatted then about Mum's birthday and Dad's forgetfulness – normal things – until it had been time to go home.

All the same, when she'd stepped in a taxi and sunk into the seat to head home, she'd felt on the verge of tears.

Fit at 30

Losing motivation

When things are going well, it's no trouble going to the gym. But things aren't always so smooth – and when I'm stressed or under pressure it's harder to maintain a routine. So I hope you don't mind if I admit to you that I'm not always as brilliant at sticking to the plan as I'd like to be.

And a little treat now and then doesn't hurt! Even a bit of chocolate once a week if you really fancy it.

Many scientists agree that it's what we do most of the time that makes the difference, so maybe relaxing once in a while is a good thing?

COMMENTS

MB
Traitor – I read this blog for inspiration, not so that I feel better about FAILING!

SW
Thanks for your honesty.

RF
Is it honest though? She's never mentioned her bladder problems on this – and have you seen this? www.dailynews.co /I-wear-nappies-to-the-gym

MD
Oh great, that's really helpful. Unfollowing.

Chapter Forty-One

Feeling a familiar adrenalin rush after reading her latest comments page, and realising she'd lost over a hundred followers, Jessica left her desk and dialled Bea's number from the car park. She needed an injection of normality, and Bea would be the best person to deliver it. Her friend was back at work part-time, but on lates, so she should be at home.

'Hello?'

'Hi, Bea.'

'Hi, you.'

'You OK?'

'Yeah. You know, I'm feeling much better. Helps being back at work. They're phasing me in, as if I'm a new government strategy, or a reduced speed limit.'

'Oh, I'm glad it's going OK!' Jessica tried to keep the doubt out of her tone.

'Don't worry, I'm not completely deluded. I'm still pretty depressed, all said and told.'

'Glad to hear it.'

'But you know. Slowly and surely. Like a tortoise.'

'Good. That's really good, Bea. And, you know, everyone likes tortoises.'

'Ha! So . . . why were you calling?'

Suddenly the idea of telling Bea that she was losing followers or getting negative comments on her fitness blog seemed utterly ridiculous. 'Oh, nothing. Just seeing how you are.'

'Really, because I've seen the article. Ouch. Are you OK?'

'Yeah. It's not just that though,' Jessica sighed. 'I tried, well, the blog, the Instagram, it's getting a bit . . . pressured.'

'So, don't do it!'

'Yeah. I thought that.'

'And . . . ? Don't tell me, you're addicted to the attention.'

'No, well, yeah, kind of, but it's not that. It's, well, I lost some followers today just because I admitted to eating some chips.'

'Oh no!' Bea's tone was mocking. 'What on earth should we do?'

Jess grinned slightly. It was nice to speak with Bea, even if she did perpetually take the piss. 'I know, it seems stupid. But most of my clients discovered me because I'm an influencer, or whatever. They rely on my social-media presence.'

'Right. So I guess you keep blogging. Surely it can't be that difficult writing about your fabulous life!' There was an edge of frustration to Bea's voice. 'I'm sorry, Jess. It's just – you know . . .'

'I'm sorry, Bea.'

There was a pause.

'I know. And it doesn't mean your problems aren't important. It's just, well, perspective, I suppose.'

'Definitely. Look, Bea, can we meet up for that lunch still? I need to talk about something else, something private.'

'Sounds serious. You're not having an affair with that artist bloke, are you?'

'As if!'

'Had to ask. He looked quite fit in the photo. As did you, I must say.'

'Thanks.'

'Look, I do sympathise, Jess. And I want to help. It's just . . .'

'Yeah, I know. I'm crap.'

'You said it,' but there was a laugh in Bea's voice.

They hung up after making a lunch date for the next day. Jessica put it into her online diary and set herself several reminders. Because she was absolutely, definitely not going to let her friend down.

To: rob@easymail.com
From: jessica@StarPR.com
Re:

Dear Robert

Thanks – it's all very exciting! And I'm sorry about what I said – things have been a bit up and down recently; it's hard to know how to react.

Let's meet up soon for a debrief.

Jess

To: jessica@StarPR.com
From: rob@easymail.com
Re:

Sure.

I wanted to say – I'm sorry if I came on a bit strong. I realise you're my PR, I'm your client, primarily. And that you're happy with Dave. I think I got my wires crossed.

From now on, it's strictly business (and maybe a bit of coffee).

Speak soon,
Robert

It was eminently sensible.

But somehow, also disappointing.

Chapter Forty-Two

When the doorbell rang at 7.30 a.m., she assumed it was a delivery. She'd been promised a sample of the new Christmas range of Little Accidents. 'They're just lovely!' Linda had gushed on the phone. 'There's a fur-trimmed pair, one with a button that plays "Winter Wonderland", one with ribbons – you know, like a present – and the best one can be pulled apart: when you take it off it bangs like a cracker!'

'They sound wonderful,' Jessica had replied, doubtfully, wondering whether the paper pants also contained a couple of lame jokes and a party hat. 'Can't wait to see them.'

Instead of a box of festive drawers, she found her father, his hair still dishevelled from sleep, standing on her doorstep with his coat on over what appeared to be a pair of pyjamas. Scenarios flashed through her mind – had Mum kicked him out? Had there been a fire? Was he losing his mind?

'Dad!' she exclaimed.

'Hi, Jessica,' he said. 'Not too early?'

'Of course not,' she said, backing away so that he could come in. 'What's the matter?'

'Anna around?'

'Still asleep.'

'Oh good.'

This was an unexpected response; the first thing he usually did when he came over was seek his granddaughter out for a hug. Something must be wrong.

'So what's up?' she asked again as they sat down in the kitchen. 'Is Mum OK?'

'She's fine. Well, she's the same as ever,' he said with a slight grin. 'It's nothing like that.'

'No?'

'No. Actually I wanted to talk about Anna. I couldn't sleep, so . . .'

'Anna?'

'Yes. I hope you don't mind me saying. But she didn't quite seem herself when she came over the other night. Quiet. Your mother said she was probably tired, and that you oughtn't let her watch that awful soap where everyone's blond, but I think it might be more than that.'

'Really?'

'Yeah. I mean, I could be wrong. And she won't talk to me about anything, of course. But I woke up early and just didn't feel right not mentioning it.'

'Thanks, Dad,' she said, grabbing his hand and giving it a squeeze.

'That's all right, it's what I'm here for.' He looked around. 'Dave not here?'

'Er, no. We're going to move in after . . . after the wedding.'

'Very traditional,' he nodded his approval. 'But, hang on, I thought he already lived here?'

'Um, well, kind of,' she felt her cheeks flush. Without mentioning the break-up, it was hard to explain. But this was her *dad*! He'd accept her whatever, so why was she lying? 'We just thought, you know, it would be romantic.'

'Right.' He nodded again, a bit more uncertainly this time. 'And you're OK still?'

'Yes, of course! Why?'

'I don't know. Obviously I don't know the chap as well as you do. But all I've ever heard him talk about is food, the

315

gym and the different muscle groups. I've probably seen more of his naked body than I have of your mother's recently.'

'Oh!'

'Sorry. Sorry. That was too much. I mean – good for him. It's a different world. It's just, well, his outburst at the art thing. Stuart said he'd been . . . quite aggressive, and well, *mean.*'

'I know he seemed that way, Dad,' she said, almost bursting with the desire to confide in him, but keeping her feelings inside. How would she even start to explain? 'He's not, he's a good bloke – honest.'

When Dad had left, trapping a bit of his coat into the car door that flapped wildly as he drove off, Jessica sat stirring the remainder of her coffee and listening to Anna padding about upstairs.

Was something wrong with her daughter? Two people had now mentioned her seeming down, but Jessica hadn't noticed anything unusual. She resolved to find out the truth.

SOMETHING FOR THE LADIES!

All the latest celebrity gossip, fashion talk and beauty buzz – because that's what women love best!

KEEPING LOVE ALIVE
We speak to three loved-up couples about what makes their relationship tick.

WE FIT TOGETHER
Jessica Bradley, 36, from St Albans, believes shared gym sessions with muscle-bound Dave Brown, 37, is what helps to keep their love alive.

When I first met Dave, I was beginning a new fitness regime. He'd been going to the gym for four years and offered to show me the ropes.

Since then, we've bonded over our shared love of fitness – and Dave's been inspirational in helping me to achieve physical perfection.

Evenings together involve a two-hour workout, followed by a healthy shake at the gym café. And when we're not working out, we're snuggling on the sofa watching Rocky movies or planning recipes for the week.

Having a shared interest is what binds us together – without the gym we'd really have very little in common.

Dave says:
Jessica was overweight when we met, but I've helped to

get her on the right track. She's put on a bit of weight again recently, but we're determined to tackle the problem together.

COMMENTS

Misty74
Wow – look at his pecs! Almost worth going to the gym to meet a gorgeous guy like that.

> **Newshound**
> Seems like a lot of work to me – and she doesn't exactly look as fit as she seems to think she is.

> **Misty74**
> Oh and I suppose *you're* so fit yourself.

> **Newshound**
> No, but then I don't parade myself in Lycra in a revealing photo shoot.

> **Misty74**
> Well, I think she looks great.

Green Goddess
I love this couple! You go guys!

Sal
Seems like a lot of work to me – and do they really have anything in common?

Caren1

That's what I was thinking. And I'd hate a guy to tell me I needed to lose weight – what a cheek!

Sal

I know – and does anyone really watch *Rocky* these days?

Caren1

I know! What is this? 1990! :D :D :D

Dave1

This comment has been removed by moderators.

Chapter Forty-Three

Lunch with my #BFF Heathy meals. #Fitat30 #stayingconnected

The restaurant was buzzing with life, but Jessica headed to the back where things were quieter. Things at work had been manic – they'd lost a client and Candice had convinced her to take the 'honest' post off her blog. 'People don't want to see the person they rely on for inspiration losing faith in things,' she'd said. 'Anyway, I don't believe you ever eat chips, really, do you?'

Dave still wouldn't answer her calls. Anna had been moody and silent that morning, but wouldn't say why. Jessica suspected that the fact the *Proximity* article had gained traction on Twitter probably wasn't helping.

At least *Proximity* had described her as having a son called Arthur rather than a daughter called Anna. Hopefully that would minimise the number of people who would make the connection at school next week.

Jessica was ten minutes early for once, so ordered a small white wine and took a tentative sip. It was bitter and cold from the fridge, but hit the back of her throat in exactly the way she needed it to.

When Bea arrived, her curls escaping from a minuscule ponytail, make-up smudged, she was twenty minutes late. 'Sorry,' she said, giving Jessica a quick peck on the cheek.

'I'm not making a point, honest. I overslept. We had a bit of an emergency in the delivery suite yesterday and I ended up working until 4 a.m.'

'Gawd, what happened?'

'Oh the usual. Not enough beds, too many babies. Not enough midwives. Just takes a crisis and everything goes to shite.'

'Makes my whole PR crisis thing seem pretty inconsequential,' Jessica said, taking another sip of her wine. She reached across the table and gave her friend's hand a squeeze. 'How are you coping being back at work?'

'It's all right,' Bea grinned, starting to seem more like her usual self. 'Besides, I know things are going to pot in my life, and with my work, but as soon as I walked in here all I could think about was the state of my bloody hair. How come yours is always so damned neat?' She attempted, in vain, to smooth down her curls.

'Is it really?' Jessica persisted. 'All right? Your life I mean.'

'Yeah,' Bea said, nodding. 'I mean, it'll take time. But work keeps me going.'

'That's good. And you're great at it, you know!'

'Thanks.' Bea took a sip of her drink to mark the end of the conversation.

'So how are your lot?' Jessica continued.

'Oh, don't do that.'

'What?'

'No offence, but we both know you want to talk about your problem. I'll fill you in on the boys' exploits afterwards. Besides, you said it was a crisis, right?' And you're drinking wine at lunchtime, which is pretty worrying, even if it is Saturday.'

'Thanks, Bea.'

'That's what friends are for. Is Anna at Grahame's this weekend?'

'No, she's at home. We're going out later, hopefully.'

'Ah, OK. She's doing all right?'

'Yes. Yes, I think so.'

'Good.'

'It's just,' said Jessica, taking a gulp of her wine for good measure. 'I know this sounds completely inconsequential when compared to everything you've been through, and I wouldn't normally bother you ... but it's just ...'

'Just what?'

'Just ...'

'Yes?' Bea leaned forward, her brow furrowed. 'Go on, you can tell me, Jess.'

'I think my whole life might be a lie.'

'So you're telling me,' Bea said, after listening intently for half an hour, not without a couple of giggles, 'you're being forced to go to the gym to live up to the ideals of the person on your blog, who used to be you but is no longer. You're engaged to a man you're not sure you want to marry, but equally aren't sure he wants to marry you anyway. You have a client who has some sort of obsession with nudity and possibly enormous penises. And the reason your skin looks so damn good is you've had it massaged with bull semen. Am I up to speed?'

'Yep.' It would be funny, if it wasn't her life. 'I've no idea how I got here.'

'No.'

'Or how to get out of it.'

'Oh, that part's easy!' Bea replied, putting her glass down on the table with a confident clink. 'Just end the blog. Stop lying online, and your real friends will gradually realise you're back to being a little more normal than you've seemed for a while.'

'But—'

'And with Dave, start out by deciding whether you want to marry him or not. And if not, break it to him gently in case he really thinks you're heading down the aisle. And if you do want to go ahead, have a conversation with him. Because if you can't be honest with each other . . .'

'But—'

'Seriously, I can sort of see where you're coming from, but surely you're just making life unnecessarily hard for yourself,' her friend said in her matter-of-fact way. But Bea's life existed here in the world of flesh and blood, not on the confusing world of Snapchat and snap judgements.

'It's not that easy, Bea. If I come clean online, I'll lose like a zillion followers. Some of them are very critical as it is.'

'So? I'll never understand this obsession with followers. Who cares if some random person in cyberspace doesn't want to copy your dinner?'

'No, but the thing is I lost loads when I suggested that I might fancy chips once in a while. What would happen if I did this? Most of my clients came to me because I'm popular.'

'Are you sure?'

'At least some of them, yes.'

Bea was silent for a moment, contemplating the ice floating on top of her Diet Coke. 'Sorry, Jess. But I still think you should come clean. Because what's the alternative? Great business, but your whole life is a lie? What's the point?'

Bea was right, Jessica thought as she waited for her Uber. But then Bea had what her mother called 'a trade'. She was properly qualified. Besides experience, Jessica had nothing to back herself up. No qualifications, nothing. Then the blog had come along. And Instagram. Suddenly thousands of people were offering their approval – coming to her for advice. If she wasn't 'the' Jessica Bradley, then who was she?

The house was quiet when she let herself in, although Anna was evidently home. 'Anna!' Jessica called up the stairs. 'I'm back! Everything OK?'

'Yeah,' came a muffled voice from her daughter's room. 'Yeah, fine Mum.'

'Want to come down for a cup of tea or something?'

'No, thanks.'

'Did you eat the cookies I left for you?'

'Yeah, thanks.'

'OK.'

Jessica stood at the foot of the stairs, wondering whether she ought to go up and check on her daughter, but her visit wouldn't be welcomed. Anna had been working on some sort of project recently; she was always hunched over her laptop. Somehow both laptop and phone had quietly made it into Anna's bedroom despite Jessica's rule. Jessica decided against calling her out on it. She'd take her shopping later, maybe. Have a chat. Something mum-and-daughter-ish.

Half an hour later, there was a creak on the stairs followed by the sound of a tap running in the kitchen. She got up and poked her head around the door. 'OK, Anna?'

'Yep.' Anna's back was to her as she filled a glass with water at the sink, her light brown hair – when had it got so long? – hanging softly against her back.

Something about the way she was standing didn't look quite right. Jessica padded up behind her in her sock-clad feet and slipped an arm around her daughter's waist. 'Are you sure?'

When she finally saw Anna's face, her heart did a somersault. It was red from crying, eyes pink and swollen, a streak of mascara on her unmarked skin.

A million ghastly scenarios rushed through her head. 'Anna, what's happened? What's wrong?' she said.

A shrug. 'Nothing.'

'Don't be ridiculous, look at you!' she turned her daughter gently to face her. 'You look like you've been crying for hours! Is it because I was out again? Am I leaving you alone too much?'

'No, it's all right.' Anna's eyes didn't meet hers.

'Well, is it the engagement? You're not comfortable with it?'

'No, it's nothing.'

'Something at school?'

'No!'

'You don't feel well? You're worried about, erm, changes to your body?'

'Mum! No!' Anna's face reddened as it always did when Jessica tried to talk about puberty or periods. 'If you must know, it's because I'm totally unpopular! No one likes me. OK?'

Jessica held her daughter to her, before leaning away and looking into her eyes. 'If that's true – which I doubt – then there's something wrong with those so-called friends of yours. If they can't see what a wonderful—'

'No, I don't mean at school, Mum!' Anna replied with exasperation. 'I've got "schoolfriends"!' she held her fingers up, framing the word in an air quote, as if her real life friends were ridiculously unimportant. 'It's my blog, OK?'

'Your what?'

325

'I started a blog, OK? A kind of diary thing.'

'Oh.'

'Yeah. So. You're not the only one who knows about the internet, OK? I'm not copying you or anything!' Anna flushed again; this time with indignation.

'Anna, I wouldn't care if you *were*!'

'Well, I'm not!'

'Right. So what's the problem?'

'I've got like . . . like . . . twenty followers! And most of them are just my friends.'

'But that's really good! It's great to be writing and—'

'You would say that. What have you got, thirty thousand or something?'

'But that stuff doesn't matter, Anna! They're just . . . just cyber-people, not real people. It's real people who are important. Real people who matter.' This is what Bea must have felt like earlier, she realised, as she gathered her poor, confused daughter into her arms.

But once she'd calmed Anna, who'd disappeared upstairs after promising she was OK, Jessica noticed that her followers had grown again by fifty or so. And try as she might, she couldn't help feeling a little bit pleased about that.

Then, thinking of Anna's tear-stained face, she felt a familiar feeling of nausea. She'd told Anna it wasn't important; that it didn't matter. Was she lying to Anna now, too?

The electronic ting of a text message interrupted her. It was from Dave.

'Sorry,' it read. 'Just a shock seeing you like that. Forgiven?'

'OK.' It wasn't really though, was it? But what else could she say? That he'd embarrassed her in front of everyone? That his concern with her weight over the nakedness in the picture was insulting? It would be easier to just let it go.

'My place tomorrow? Seven-ish?'

'OK, see you then.'

#DateNight

Chapter Forty-Four

Robert was late, and when he rushed into the café he looked a little red-faced.

Jessica got up and waved – the high-street location had seemed like a good idea, but the place was rammed with customers and she'd only just managed to find a table, closer to the door of the toilets than she'd prefer.

'Hi, I'm so sorry,' he said once he'd made his way between tables, almost tripping over someone's shopping. 'I was walking Hamish.'

'Hamish?'

'Labrador. Me and Susie – the ex – share custody and it was my turn this week. I wanted to give him a quick run in the park before handing him back.'

'Aw. Sorry. I hope I didn't cut your time short?' Jessica had never had a pet, but she imagined the pain of handing a loved animal back to be similar to waving Anna off when she went to stay at Grahame's. That horrible ache and sense of guilt that she couldn't have created a better home.

'No, no,' he said, plonking himself down in the seat and removing his jacket. 'It was my fault. I had a quick sit on the swing and Hamish ran off into the lake and began trying to chase the ducks.'

'What is it with you and swings?' Jessica grinned.

'I know.'

'And water?' she said, checking his trousers.

'Dry as a bone this time,' he said. 'I called him and he lolloped out. He knew he was in the wrong.'

'Bless.'

They sat there awkwardly for a moment. 'Shall I grab you something?' Jessica asked. 'Tea?'

'Tea would be lovely,' he said. 'Not green.'

'No problem.' She went and queued for a second time at the counter, returning with a cup of water and a teabag on a string.

'Thanks,' he said. 'Not having anything yourself?'

She'd already had two coffees while waiting for him – any more and she might burst. But it would be mean to highlight his lateness. 'No,' she lied. 'I'm fine at the moment.'

'So, Anna?' he said, after a messy couple of minutes dunking the bag until the colour flooded out, then adding milk from a tiny plastic pot on his saucer. The teabag was now on the table, set on a serviette, which was gradually turning from white to orange.

'Yeah,' she felt awkward suddenly. 'Look, thanks for meeting me on a Sunday. It's just . . . I'm worried about her. She seems – she's not herself.'

'Eating OK?' he asked.

'Seems to be.'

'Good. Any problems with friends that you know about?'

'I don't think so. She's got a best friend – Jenny – and they seem to be spending as much time together as usual. And school seems to be going OK.'

He sat for a moment, thoughtfully looking into his tea. 'What about at home?' he asked. 'Is there anything that might be upsetting her there?'

Jessica thought about the ups and downs with Dave. The fact that her business had been even busier than usual and that perhaps she hadn't been around as much as she'd like.

'Maybe,' she said, feeling herself blush. 'I mean, things haven't been that... settled recently, I suppose.'

'And what does Dave think of it all?'

'Pardon?'

'Does Dave have any theories about Anna? Does she talk to him?'

'I haven't... I mean. We don't really talk much about Anna.' Hearing the words said aloud made Jessica feel slightly alarmed. Her future husband, Anna's future step-father; and they barely spoke about Anna at all. Barely did any real parenting.

'Oh.' He looked surprised and began to stir his tea un-necessarily. 'Well, OK. Um...'

'Yeah,' she said, wishing she'd bought another drink after all – something to focus on.

'Well, maybe...' He said at last. 'Maybe it's something to do with that. I feel... it's difficult to give advice because, well, you know how I feel about you.'

She felt herself go red. 'But...'

'You know. I like you Jessica. I'm not going to act on it, of course. I wouldn't – I know you're in love with Dave and the last thing I want to do is upset a happy home.'

She almost snorted with laughter at his description of her home life then realised how unfunny it was.

'But maybe,' he continued, 'maybe it's time to get Anna and Dave to bond a bit. Maybe that would help her to feel more grounded.'

He was right. Dave and Anna had never spent much time together, except when they were dragging Anna out with them, or they were eating at the table together. And the odd times when Dave had used to do the school run. But neither Dave nor Anna had ever expressed an interest in hanging out, she thought. And it just hadn't crossed her mind.

'Thank you,' she said. 'I mean, it's a bit embarrassing to have someone point that out. I'm her mother after all.'

'Sometimes,' he said, looking at her so directly that she felt herself shiver. 'Sometimes it takes someone on the outside to see things a little more clearly.'

'You're right.'

Once they'd said goodbye – this time with a more appropriate cheek kiss – the day had gone quickly. She'd taken Anna shopping and treated her to some new tops, then spent the rest of the time planning for next week.

All the time, though, her mind had kept flitting throughout to the conversation she'd had with Anna the night before. Where she'd told her daughter that nobody cared about the number of followers she had. That it didn't matter. 'It's real people who matter – me, Dad, Uncle Stu, Granny, Granddad,' she'd said. 'Not some random strangers online.'

'Then why do *you* do it Mum?' her daughter had asked, genuinely confused. 'You're always going on about followers or whatever.'

'It's different for grown-ups,' Jessica had said uncertainly. 'It's a work thing.' But was it?

This afternoon, she'd rung Dave and told him she was bringing Anna with her that evening – Jessica couldn't bear the thought of leaving her alone. Dave had replied 'the more the merrier', which had made her feel quite positive about things, about their making a success of becoming a blended family, or whatever the current buzzword was.

And maybe tonight there would be time for a heart-to-heart. She wasn't about to admit that she'd thought their engagement might be fake at first, an overblown PR stunt. But perhaps she could start to suggest that she might not spend quite so much time at the gym as before, even if she did get 'back on track'. Just to test the water. A bit like the story of the princess and the pea; she needed to slip a little test into proceedings to discover whether Dave was the real deal (albeit, hopefully not a real princess).

All in all, she was feeling quite positive as she drove towards the house owned by Dave's gym-buddy Kevin, despite Anna's sombre presence in the passenger seat. They spent most of the short journey in silence, listening to radio discussion on whether fried chicken shops should be situated so close to schools.

The house was silent when they arrived, and no lights were visible as she pulled up outside. Jessica wondered whether she'd got it wrong. Was Dave waiting at hers? His car was parked outside, but he might have decided to jog over. She glanced quickly at the screen on her phone – no message.

'Hope he's in!' she said to a silent Anna as they walked up to the door and she rang the bell. When she heard the tap of footsteps in response she was relieved. The last thing she'd needed was yet another case of crossed wires with her possible fiancé.

'Hi, baby!' Dave flung the door wide, treating them both to a whiff of heady aftershave. 'You look gorgeous!'

'Thanks,' Jessica said, ignoring Anna's contemptuous snort. She allowed herself to be swept up into a bear hug.

'And you too, Anna banana!' Anna banana was not a nickname he'd used before and evidently didn't go down well.

'Yeah.' Anna said. Then, 'Can I use your computer?'

'Sure, in a minute,' he said, slightly subdued by the rebuff. 'Just . . . I just want to show you guys something first.'

He stepped back, and they entered the hall, hanging their coats on the bannister. Then he paused by the living-room door. 'It's been a weird few weeks,' he said. 'And I know we've had a few ups and downs.'

'Uh huh.'

'But I want this night to be the start of things – of a special new time for us. Getting our lives back, you know? Working out together, living together, being happy as a family.' He gave a nod in Anna's direction. 'Just like old times. Only better.'

And with that, he flung the door wide and snapped on the light.

The room was full of people, glasses in hands, grinning at their own subterfuge. 'Surprise!' came the cry, and Jessica nearly jumped out of her skin. So much for the quiet evening she'd had in mind.

'Wow!' she said, baring her teeth in what she hoped was a happy fashion. 'This is amazing!'

'Yeah. I mean, our engagement was kind of, uh, un-expected,' he said. 'But now things are, sort of, on track, so to speak, I thought it was about time we celebrated, you know, properly.'

She looked at her ring, involuntarily. 'Oh,' she said. 'Brilliant.'

Feeling slightly sick, and wondering why Dave hadn't warned her to wear something other than her jeans and trainers, Jessica took a proffered 'virgin cocktail' and walked into the room, Dave's arm resting gently on her back. Anna trailed behind.

Someone started up a playlist, and a few of the people crowded in the living room – nonc of whom looked that familiar, but all of whom seemed to be toned and coiffed to the max – began to sway slightly to the beat.

Across the room was a table laden with vegetable sticks, hummus, crackers and a few (naughty!) cheeses. Another

333

table in the corner bore a large cake, three tiered, complete with bride and groom. 'You bought a wedding cake?' Jessica whispered to Dave. 'For our engagement?'

'I just wanted to make a statement,' he said quietly. 'Don't worry, I won't let you eat any just when you're starting to make progress!'

Because obviously that's what she'd been worried about.

Thirty minutes later, she wondered how much longer she could last. Jessica was far from an alcoholic, but without a little wine to blur the edges, the party seemed formal and the conversation stilted. After failing to commandeer Dave's laptop, Anna had disappeared to the kitchen and was sitting silently with her mobile phone, sullenly scowling.

It didn't help that as far as Jessica could see, Dave had invited all of his friends and not one of hers. 'Did you ask Bea to come?' she whispered at one point. 'Or Stu?'

He went red. 'Um. Well, I was going to . . .'

'Don't worry.'

She wandered rather lost through the groups of minglers, occasionally proffering her ring for inspection and smiling her acceptance at comments on how beautiful and 'sparkly' her diamond/cubic zirconia chunk was. She began to nod in benign deference when they lifted her hand for inspection – and for a little while felt more like the Pope than she'd ever have thought possible.

Dave soon disappeared but she could hear his laughter from time to time as he threw himself into what seemed to be ostensibly a party celebrating him.

Then, after what seemed like hours (but was actually fifty-one minutes and twenty-three seconds according to her watch), the kitchen door opened, and Anna slunk in – reluctantly – followed by Dave, who'd obviously gone to get her. Then he tapped the side of his glass.

Obediently, the room fell silent.

Dave, puffed with self-importance, stood beside the cake. A camera flashed. 'I just wanted to start by thanking everyone for coming,' he began.

Jessica felt her cheeks begin to redden.

'As you know, this lovely lady and I have had our ups and downs...'

They knew? Who knew?

'In life,' he gestured to Jessica. 'And on the scales.' He paused for laughter and a couple of people tittered obediently.

'Anyway, over the past few months I've come to realise more than ever that my life wouldn't be complete without this little, or perhaps medium-sized, lady.'

Murmurs of 'ahh'.

Jessica smiled and raised her glass awkwardly. *Yes, that's me. The little fat wife.*

'And I'm proud too at how hard she's working to get back in shape for the wedding day!' he went on. 'She's had a slip but we're all here to support you, Jess, in your journey back to being your True Self.'

'Hear hear.'

'Which is why we're not going to offer her any of this delicious cake!'

Laughter.

'And I'd like to raise a toast,' he finished. 'To my perfect, fit future wife and her soon-to-be-toned bottom!'

'To her bottom!' everyone chorused, as if it was a completely normal toast. Jessica felt her shoulders stiffen.

'Actually, I'd like to say a few words,' she said before the silence disappeared again under a hum of conversation. 'If you don't mind.'

'Sure!' said Dave, all permissive smiles. He clinked the

spoon against his glass unnecessarily – the room was already quiet.

'All my life,' began Jessica, 'I've wanted someone who loves me for who I am.'

Choruses of 'ahhh'.

'And this man,' she said, indicating a smiling Dave, 'has stuck with me through thick and thin. Although he's made it pretty clear he prefers the thin.'

Laughter – this time just from Dave, still blissfully misreading her tone.

'But seeing as we're all family now,' she continued, 'there's something you ought to know about me. That I might talk a good talk. But maybe I'm not quite as perfect as everyone thinks!'

She walked over to the cake, carefully removed the bride and groom then plunged her hand into the soft sponge, pulling up a fistful and stuffing it into her mouth, feeling chunks of icing gathering at the corners of her lips and dribbling down her chin. Then another, and another.

'That's right,' she said spraying crumbs. 'I love cake. I eat cake! And I guess I don't care as much as some of you if that shows on my thighs.'

She paused, seeing the horrified look on Anna's face, but couldn't seem to stop. 'I'm a fraud. The whole health and fitness thing. It's not me at all. My whole life is a lie. And I'm not even sure what's real any more,' she said, her voice faltering in the stunned silence.

A large blob of butter icing dropped softly onto the carpet from her chin. She wiped the back of her hand across her face self-consciously and brought it away, covered with crumbs, chocolate and other cake debris.

She looked around the room, registering the silence, the shocked faces, Anna's appalled expression. 'Come on, Anna,' she said shaking chunks of cake and icing from her T-shirt and grabbing her daughter's hand. 'Let's go.'

Anna followed her silently to the car. As the door closed behind them, Jessica could hear the rumble of talking in the room, soon drowned out by the sound of her revving engine.

Chapter Forty-Five

The great thing about being your own boss?
#WorkingFromHome in your PJs when you fancy it!
@StarPR #WinningatLife

'Hi, Candice, I'm going to work at home today if that's OK?'
Jessica instantly cursed herself for asking rather than telling
Candice what she was going to do. After all, she was the
boss.

'OK. Everything all right?'

'Yes. Just want to spend a bit of time catching up,' she
lied. In actual fact, she felt exhausted. Flashbacks from yesterday evening – without the excuse or memory-suppressing
power of alcohol – had tormented her all night. She'd veered
between anger, embarrassment and calorie-counting into the
small hours of the morning. Anna had hardly spoken to her
in the car on the way to school. She didn't blame her.

'Sure. Oh, and Hugo called.'

'OK, I'll get back to him later.'

Just as she was about to hit her emails and study her
blog analytics, the phone rang. She almost ignored it, but
glancing at the screen she saw the call was from Anna's
school.

'Hello? Jessica Bradley speaking.'

'Hello, Mrs Bradley. It's Stephanie, the secretary at St
Augustus Academy.'

There was a silence in which Jessica suddenly started to become afraid. 'Um... is everything OK? Is Anna OK?'

'I'm afraid we're having a bit of an issue this end,' continued Stephanie carefully. 'Anna didn't turn up for her science lesson first period.'

'What?'

'Yes, now please don't panic. She was there for registration. And it may be, well, occasionally children do absent themselves. You know, hide in the loos or something, when perhaps there's a subject they're not so keen on.'

'Right...' Jessica's heart was hammering hard enough to break through her ribcage.

'But an initial search has proved unsuccessful.'

'Oh my God! So what are you doing? Have the police been called?'

'That's the next step. We just wanted to inform you and to double-check that she hadn't contacted you, or turned up at home.'

'No! No, she's not here; she hasn't called. I can call her, she's got her mobile.'

'OK, and can you call us back please?'

'Of course.'

Jessica ended the call abruptly, her fingers almost shaking too much to scroll through her contacts list. Luckily, Anna's name was at the top, and she pressed the green button, feeling sick.

An answerphone cut in almost straight away.

She tried again.

Answerphone. 'Anna!' she said this time. 'Please call me. I need to know you're OK. You're not in trouble.' She imagined suddenly herself on the TV, like those families of missing children, begging her daughter to get in contact. What had happened? She'd left Anna safely at school this morning;

339

her daughter had seemed OK, if a little sulky after Jessica's embarrassing display the night before.

Grahame. She quickly found his number and called. 'Hello?' he said.

'Grahame, is Anna with you?'

'No, I mean, it's ... why? What's happened?'

'She's disappeared. From school. She might be hiding. I don't know. I don't know,' Jessica said, barely able to breathe.

'OK, OK, calm down. I'm coming right now,' said Grahame. 'Where are you?'

'Just at home. Oh Grahame, where is she?'

'Sit tight,' he said before the line went dead.

Jessica picked up the phone again to call the school and inform the police; anyone who might be able to help. Before she could dial, though, it began to ring. Anna's name flashed on the screen.

'Anna!' she said, answering it immediately. 'Anna, are you OK?'

'Yes.'

'Where are you?' She began to feel anger bubbling up where fear had been.

Silence.

'Anna, are you OK? Are you with anyone?'

'No, I'm just ... I just needed to get away.'

'I'll come and get you. I'll come right now.'

'No, Mum, I just need to be by myself.'

'Anna, we can give you space here. Where you're safe. Whatever's going on, I'm here to help.'

Silence.

'Anna, please ...'

'OK, OK,' Anna replied, sounding more like herself. 'I'm at the train station, OK?'

'Oh my God, Anna, do not get on a train, OK? I'm coming right now.'

Sending a quick text to Grahame to tell him Anna was safe, and asking him to ring the school, Jessica raced to her car to pick up her daughter.

Chapter Forty-Six

'Do you know how worried we were!' Grahame said, pacing back and forth in front of the sofa.

'Grahame, she's here. She's OK,' said Jessica, putting her arm around her daughter. 'Let's calm down a bit.'

'But you could have been—'

'So?' Anna said suddenly. 'None of you would have missed me, so it doesn't matter, does it?'

'What?' they said, almost in unison.

'Well, you've got your perfect family,' she said, gesturing towards Grahame. 'And now Mum getting married, or whatever.'

'I don't think . . .' Jessica began, thinking back to last night and feeling her cheeks flush. 'We're not exactly . . .'

'But you always make up!' Anna said. 'You row, then you make up. And the whole time I have to watch you, and you don't notice me at all.'

'But—'

'And it's OK, I know you just want to be happy or whatever. But I just don't fit anywhere.'

'Oh, Anna!' Jessica pulled her daughter to her. 'Don't be silly. Neither of us . . . you can't really think we'd . . .'

'Anna,' Grahame said, his voice softer now. 'Anna, you're just as important to me as the boys, you must know that.'

'Yeah, but I'm not part of your family, not really,' she replied. 'And then Mum will have a new family – or a new husband or whatever. And I won't really belong with them either.'

'Of course you do . . . you always will . . .'

'Jenny said,' Anna said, with a shrug. 'Her mum got married again, then had a baby. Then it was all about the new kid – *their* kid. And she was just . . . extra.'

'That sounds horrible for Jenny . . . but it doesn't mean—'

'And then, you know. You're so busy already. And if Dave comes to live here again, you'll be at the gym all the time. Dad'll be with his new family. I'll just be nowhere. No one's.'

'Look, I'm sorry if we've made you feel like that,' Jessica said, her mind racing back to the times recently when she'd cut Anna short or not listened. 'But that's something we're going to have to work on, because believe me, darling, my life – our lives – without you just wouldn't work.'

'And you won't let me go on WhatsApp!' her daughter added.

'What?' it seemed a complete change of subject. 'What's that got to do with it?' Jessica blurted out.

'I knew you'd say that! You just don't understand what it's like!'

'What do you mean?' Grahame asked. 'Your mum is all over the internet – she knows exactly what it's like. That's why she makes the rules she does.'

It was nice to be stood up for, for once.

'Yes, but you don't get it, Mum. Not what it's like for me.'

'OK,' Jessica said, sitting down and trying to sound understanding. 'What is it like, Anna?'

'All my friends, they're all on WhatsApp. They have a group. And they chat together – all evening, weekends. They make arrangements. Then they forget to ask me, because it's a whole other thing – a text or an email. And they make jokes I don't understand. They . . . I just don't feel part of things there either. Me and Jenny – we're like outcasts.'

'Oh Anna.' Jessica thought back to her own school days. How her mother hadn't understood that unless she watched *Neighbours* she'd be left out of pretty much every conversation in the playground. 'You just don't get it, Mum!' she'd yelled.

For them it had been a different world. And now Anna was living in a new kind of 'different world'.

Later, when Anna had gone to her room for an enforced rest, Jessica and Grahame sat together on the sofa, wired from the shock of it all. 'We're going to have to get better at this,' Jessica said.

'You're right there. Maybe . . . maybe we need to do more things together. We get on OK, right? Maybe I could come round sometimes, so she's got us both? Maybe . . . maybe talk more often, to each other, I mean. Once a week or something?'

'That sounds good.'

'For what it's worth, I think you're doing a good job,' Grahame said, getting to his feet. 'I, well, Tabitha and me just about cope and there's two of us there all the time . . . I can't imagine.'

'Thank you.'

'It's true.'

'We'd better find a way of helping her with this WhatsApp thing. I don't really like it, but . . .'

'I know,' he said.

They smiled at each other.

'Did you ever think,' he said. 'All this could be so complicated?'

'Not in a million years.'

After watching him drive off, Jessica did something that

she hadn't done for several years. She switched off her mobile phone.

Instantly, she was hit by a surge of anxiety – what if she missed something important? What if something happened at work? What if Dave finally ended the silence and contacted her after last night?

She couldn't think of yesterday evening without her cheeks feeling warm. Had she really stuffed the top tier of a wedding cake into her mouth? She'd woken in the morning sticky and ashamed, her hair spattered with icing, crumbs on her pillow.

Stirring her coffee, she watched the light reflecting from its black surface and inhaled its comforting aroma. Despite her overconsumption of the drink, she wasn't that keen on the taste. But the smell took her back to breakfasts at home with her father – he'd always knocked back a couple of strong ones before a day at the office. Back to a time when she'd felt safe and lived in a world where grown-ups had all the answers, and nothing was a mystery.

Jessica had never been one for making an exhibition of herself. Maybe once or twice when she was in her teens – a memorable traffic-cone-on-the-head incident at uni – but usually she liked to keep herself out of the limelight. Then the blog had come along and suddenly she'd been on show in a way she never could have imagined. But it was different, somehow, online. It didn't really feel like her.

Then the lies that she'd become trapped in. The build-up. It was inevitable that it had come to a head. It was just a shame that it had happened in the middle of a party. Where at least one of the guests had filmed the incident on their phone and uploaded it to the masses. Nothing was private any more.

She resisted logging in to her laptop to see how many comments and retweets the footage had now. It could wait.

A couple of hours later, when Anna was occupied with the *Hollyoaks* omnibus, Jessica finally gave in to the urge to switch her phone back on. As it leapt into life, flashing and beeping with missed messages and calls, her sense of panic returned.

'You have two new messages,' said the robotic voice of the answering service. 'And twenty-six missed calls.'

Twenty-six?

'Message one,' continued the robot, unaware of the effect it was having on her blood pressure.

It was Hugo. 'Jessica! I've just heard! I've been awarded the Bursary!'

In spite of herself Jessica felt a warm glow that Hugo seemed finally have had his talent recognised (the art kind, rather than the penis kind).

'Message two.'

Candice. 'Hi, Jess, are you OK? We've been sent something at work that you probably need to see. Could you call, when you have time?' Her voice was uncharacteristically soft, as if talking to someone very vulnerable, old or borderline insane.

No call from Dave, she realised, opening her messages folder. But two text messages from him she hadn't noticed before. The first, sent last night:

COME BACK? WHERE HAVE YOU GONE?

The second, this morning.

I CAN'T BELIEVE YOU EMBARRASSED ME IN FRONT OF ALL MY FRIENDS. WHAT ON EARTH GOT INTO YOU LAST NIGHT? ☹

Great.

She began to reply, her thumb moving at lightning speed, then stopped. Because writing was what had got her into this mess in the first place. With her heart in her mouth, she dialled his number instead.

'Jessica?' he said, his tone unreadable.

'Dave,' she said. 'About last night.'

'Yes?'

But she wasn't sure what to say. 'I'm sorry,' she began.

'What happened to you?'

'No, wait,' she continued. 'I'm sorry for the way I behaved, but, but I'm not sorry for feeling the way I do.'

'What do you mean?'

'Well, it seems to me that you only love me if I fit a certain mould. A . . . a . . . cake-dodging mould,' she said, feeling suddenly indignant. 'It's hardly unconditional love if it won't allow for a couple more inches on my thighs!'

He was silent for a moment. 'Is that what you think?' he asked at last.

'What am I supposed to think? Your comments on that picture of me? Wanting me to get back on track? That whole "thick and thin" comment?!'

'I thought that's what you wanted.'

'Oh.'

'I read everything you write, Jessica. You're always on about fitness; some of our best nights out have been at the gym. I wanted to encourage you, I suppose.'

'Oh.'

'But you're right in a way – I mean, "Gym Jessica", she's the girl I fell for. The woman I met, I mean. It's like – it's what we have in common, isn't it? We're driven; goal-orientated. We're on the same page. And it's a page without,' he said, his voice suddenly trembling with emotion, 'cake, carbs and . . . and . . . mashed potato!'

What was this obsession with mashed potato?

347

'I know, but that isn't me. It *was* me for a while. It's part of me. But it isn't everything, Dave.'

'Yeah, I know that now. You know after . . . the cake?'

There was a silence.

'So where do we go from here?' he asked at last.

'I'm not sure,' she replied.

'Maybe we need to talk about it?'

'OK. But not yet. I have to think . . .'

They hung up shortly afterwards. Jessica looked at the ambiguous ring on her finger and removed it, putting it into a little dish where she kept her car keys, hairgrips and the odd stray earring. It might go back on. But only when she'd worked out who she was. And discovered whether that someone loved Dave. And whether Dave loved that someone back.

On a roll, she dialled the office.

'Hi, Candice,' she said, as her PA answered. 'You called?' She tried to keep her tone light.

'Yeah, it's just there's this . . . this . . . Someone's tweeted some, er, footage to our feed and I thought you ought to know.'

'Let me guess. Cake?'

'Yep.' There was a silence. 'What shall I do? Emergency blog post? Tweet back?'

'Take it down.'

'The footage? It's already been retweeted.'

'No. The blog. The Twitter feed.'

'You're kidding, right?'

'No. I mean, just for now. Just until I've decided what to do going forward.'

'Are you all right?'

'Yes,' she replied, feeling suddenly lighter. 'Actually, everything is fine.'

Chapter Forty-Seven

'Darlings,' her mum gushed, opening her arms and sweeping Anna into them. 'How are you? How are you *feeling*?'

'Mum,' Jessica admonished, following her daughter into the house. 'I said subtle.'

'Sorry, sorry,' her mum replied, sounding anything but. 'But honestly, Anna darling, what were you doing at the train station yesterday? Where were you going? You know you could always come here, don't you? If you're struggling!'

Anna grunted and walked through to the living room, her cheeks bright red.

'Mum,' Jessica said, softly, in the hallway, 'honestly, I think it's better not to talk about it too much right now.'

Yesterday, once Anna had had her fill of *Hollyoaks*, Jessica had made them both a late lunch – spag bol, one of Anna's favourites – and they'd talked through how Anna had been feeling. How she'd enjoyed the time without Dave being there: 'I don't mind Dave,' she'd said. 'It's just, well, I felt kind of on the outside sometimes, that's all. Then when you said he was coming back forever, and Jenny told me that thing about her mum . . .'

'I know, darling,' Jessica had said, reaching and squeezing her daughter's hand briefly. 'I've been a bit . . . preoccupied, haven't I? And Dave, well, I suppose we did spend a lot of time at the gym when he used to live here, right? I thought you quite liked the time at granny's or Jenny's.'

'I did, I do,' Anna had said. 'But it was kind of nice, you know, when I didn't have to do that any more.'

'OK.'

After extracting faithful promises that Anna would never run away again and always talk to her, and promising that next time Anna asked to talk she would make sure she listened – no matter who turned up on the doorstep with wet trousers – Jessica had rung Mum, who'd instantly invited them for what she called a 'high tea', her way of fixing almost any trauma. 'I'll do choc fudge cake,' she'd said. 'Anna's favourite. You can come straight after school tomorrow.'

'But are *you* OK? It must have been a shock,' her mum said quietly once Anna was out of earshot.

'To be honest, Mum, I'm not sure whether I'm coming or going. How could I have got it so wrong?'

'Wrong?'

'Yes, my daughter ran away. If I hadn't got hold of her, who knows what might have happened? And I had no idea she was upset!'

'Don't be daft,' her mum said, wrapping an arm around Jessica's back. 'You're a great mum! Don't think your father and I always got it right, will you. Because you'd be wrong. Once you even packed your bags when you were about seven . . . moved out to the playhouse in the garden.'

'Still, not the train station.'

'Well, perhaps Anna's just a bit more resourceful!'

'Thanks.'

'Seriously, though,' said her mum, lowering her voice even further in a rare moment of discretion. 'As soon as I heard, I thought, Jessica is bound to be beating herself up about this.'

'Did you?'

'Yes, you've always been such a perfectionist.'

'Oh.'

'And you've got to realise, sweetheart, that being a mum is an impossible job. You try to do the right thing, but put your foot in it.'

'You haven't—'

'Don't be silly, I know I have. And it's OK. Believe me, once Anna's pushing thirty, you'll realise that doing your best is all you've got. It doesn't get any easier when they grow up, you know. If anything, it's harder.'

'Oh.'

'And with your wedding on the way, and who knows what else . . .' her mum added, looking pointedly at Jessica's womb area, 'it doesn't do to get too stressed.'

'There's not—' she started.

'Hello, love,' she heard her dad say to Anna in the next room. 'You daft thing.'

'Granddad!'

'Let me take your bag and coat,' her mum said then, as if Jessica was a child herself. Something about the gesture made Jessica feel like crying.

She passed over her bag, the zip open and overstuffed content exposed.

As she went to hang it up, her mother glanced into its depths, and her expression changed. 'Jessica,' she said. 'I'm, well, I'm speechless.'

'What is it?' said Jessica, confused.

'Perhaps this isn't the best time to bring it up. But does this mean? Well, you know!'

'Mum?'

Mum pulled Jessica's dried clay work from the leather depths and brandishing it like a trophy. 'Is this . . . ?'

'Oh God,' Jessica said. Because the forgotten piece of clay had been dried and smoothed and pounded in the bottom of

351

her bag and now, grasped in her mother's firm grip, looked to all intents and purposes like a penis.

What was it with her life and artificial penises? Was it the universe's way of hinting she might as well give up on netting herself a real one with a decent man attached?

'It's not...' she began.

'Oh, Jessica. A fertility symbol!' Her mum smiled, still brandishing the penis. 'I suppose this means that congratulations are in order? Or soon will be?'

'It's not, um...'

'Oh, you don't have to tell me. When your father and I were trying, I became obsessed with phallic symbols.' Her mother stroked the penis thoughtfully. 'I've got quite a few in a drawer somewhere.'

'It's not – I mean – it's just... I was trying to find true happiness!' Jessica gabbled.

'I completely understand,' her mum replied, seriously, slipping the 'penis' back into her daughter's bag and giving her an elaborate wink. 'Your secret is safe with me.'

'What I don't understand,' her mum said a little later once they'd all been given their cups of overly milky tea and been forced to load their plates with scones and cake from an elaborate three-tier cake stand, 'is why you didn't talk to us, Anna?'

'Mum, leave it,' Jessica warned.

'I don't know, Gran,' Anna said, sadly. 'Maybe the whole engagement party thing...'

'Engagement party?'

'Don't ask,' said Jessica. 'It wasn't exactly the best experience of either of our lives.'

'Yes, but why did your father and I not get an invite?' her mum sniffed, setting her cup back into its saucer.

'It was a surprise party, Mum. Dave arranged it,' Jessica explained.

'Well, I'll be having words with that young man.'

'Honestly, Gran, you didn't miss anything,' Anna interrupted. 'Except Mum being embarrassing.'

'Anna! Don't talk about your mother like that,' Jessica's dad butted in.

'Actually,' Jessica told him, 'she's right.' She told him about the cake incident and they both looked horrified.

'You're telling me,' her mother said, focusing on an entirely unexpected part of the anecdote, 'that Dave doesn't think you should eat *cake*!' Her face wore a look of horror.

'I know, Mum.'

'Well, I never did!'

'I know.'

'And you really stuck your hand into the cake in front of everyone,' her dad chuckled.

'Yep!' Jessica grimaced. 'I can't believe it either!'

'Well, good for you, love.'

'Really?'

'Yes, you're always so worried what people think. It's nice to see you standing up for yourself for once.'

'Oh.' This was unexpected.

'And,' her dad cleared his throat and looked at his wife as if for consent to speak. She gave him an almost indiscernible nod. 'Um, we wanted to say sorry, you know, for our lack of enthusiasm at the exhibition the other night. It was quite, well, your mum had seen the picture, I know. But seeing it in the flesh, so to speak. Well, it was quite . . .'

'I know, maybe I shouldn't have invited you.'

'Don't be silly! Your mum and I love to see what you're up to! Can't say I always understand this PR stuff, but it seems that you're doing really well.'

'Thank you.'

'Just, well, the painting . . . you know.'

'Yes, I know.'

'What painting?' Anna asked.

'I'll tell you later,' Jessica replied.

Fit at 30

Sorry to anyone who's been wondering why the blog disappeared for a bit. I wanted to write a post to update you all before I take it down again.

This blog's been quite an adventure. I started it in the hope of getting fit, and in the end, I got so much more. I lost weight but gained followers – even a tiny bit of fame. And it's been wonderful.

But I've decided it's time to stop. While I want to be fit and healthy, I'm not as committed to being superfit as I once was – I've relaxed, and I think that's probably a good thing.

As for my relationship with Dave – although we had some great times, we also had our ups and downs. Nothing is perfect and maybe we shouldn't expect it to be. Who knows what the future holds?

I wanted to thank everyone who's come on this journey with me – I've appreciated your comments, your connections, your motivation.

But for now.

That's it.

Jessica.

COMMENTS

Linda87
Oh no! Where am I going to get my motivation?

Paulie
I think it's awful that some people think it's OK to tout a message out on the internet when it suits them – and turn out to be a fraud.

Stu
Good for you.

RW
Want to follow someone who really knows what they're talking about? Check out this blog! www.cleanforlife.org

Comments have been turned off for this post.

Chapter Forty-Eight

'Hi, Jessica,' Candice smiled as she entered the office the following day. 'How are you?'

'Yes. Yes, I'm fine thanks,' Jessica said. Because that sort of lie was OK, wasn't it? That was the sort of lie that everyone allowed themselves from time to time.

'Good. Um, we read your blog post,' Candice said, glancing at Natalie for support.

'Oh, yeah. Sorry about that,' Jessica grimaced. Seeing as she'd brought the blog, the strategising of key terms, and hashtags into the office, she probably should have consulted the girls before she'd written something so final.

'No, no, that's OK,' Candice soothed, still eyeing her rather cautiously. 'I just wondered. What with Twitter down, and the blog down, you're not, I mean, you're not closing the firm down, are you?'

'Not at all,' Jessica smiled, genuinely. 'Sort of starting over.'

'Yeah?'

'Yes. Taking the Jessica out of Star PR. Letting our expertise stand for itself, that sort of thing.'

'OK...'

'And I'd like you to perhaps start a blog.'

'Me?' said Candice, looking amazed.

'Yeah. Not a health-focused thing, but maybe a showbiz

blog, with profiles and news about our clients, that sort of thing?'

'You really think I can do that?'

'Of course you can – you were practically writing mine for me by the end.'

Candice flushed a little. 'Thank you!' she said.

'And a new Twitter feed too – one for the company, not a personal one. For now.'

'OK!'

'Let's face it, I'm a dinosaur when it comes to that sort of thing.' But this dinosaur was determined not to become extinct.

'Aren't you worried it's going to affect the business?' piped Natalie from the other side of the office. 'There's been some pretty negative comments on the blog. I just thought . . .'

'Yeah. I am. I am a bit,' said Jessica. 'But we've got quite a few clients on board. I think we'll be OK. Who knows, maybe some people are put off by the whole blog thing?'

Natalie nodded. 'True. And that Hugo has won his award, hasn't he?'

'Yep.'

'And he's one of the clients you've had for ages – way before all the blog stuff.'

It was true. Maybe she was more than a fitness blogger after all.

FITSPO? OH NO! FITNESS BLOGGER DUMPS THE DIET

Fitness blogger Jessica Bradley, 36, today shocked her followers by admitting that much of her recent diet and fitness blog content has been false and that she no longer subscribes to her own fitness message.

Ms Bradley, who gained notoriety when her recipe for pomegranate surprise went viral last year, was unavailable to comment.

Clients have taken to Twitter, accusing the mother of one of misleading them from the outset. Recent pictures taken at the gym revealed that Ms Bradley, a PR executive, was clearly not the avid gym-goer her blog suggested.

Ms Bradley, who lives in a £325,000 three-bedroom house in St Albans, is also the agent for Hugo Henderson, the artist known to his followers as Penis Guy after a theft of an artwork earlier this year.

Kelly McCarthy, fitness blogger and part-time model who writes the blog Clean and Green, commented: 'It just goes to show that there are a lot of people out there who aren't true to their own message. I applaud Jessica's honesty in her final blog post but would urge all bloggers to realise that if we aren't true to ourselves and our readers, ultimately we all lose out.'

Follow Kelly McCartney at www.ilovesalad.com

Chapter Forty-Nine

'Jessica,' said Candice, covering the mouthpiece, 'it's some guy from the radio or something? He wants to know if you'll go on at four o'clock?'

'What about?'

'The whole blogging backlash, he says.'

Blogging backlash.

'Tell him I'm busy,' she said at last.

It was time to take a step back.

To: jess@StarPR.com
From: rob@easymail.com
Re: Are you OK?

Hi Jessica,
Sorry to contact you on a personal note, but I read your blog post. And heard all that stuff on the radio. Things have gone mad – are you OK? Do you still want to meet up?

Love
Robert

To: rob@easymail.com
From: jess@StarPR.com
Re: re: Are you OK?

Hi Robert,
Thanks – yes, I'm OK. Just going in a new direction. Quite

surprised at the reaction to it – I mean, I knew I had a lot of followers, but didn't know they were so 'dedicated'!

Sorry about the silence. A few things have happened. It would be nice to meet up and have a chat. I've got some questions about, well, parenting, life ... the usual stuff. If you don't mind, that is?

Best wishes,
Jessica

Chapter Fifty

'Here you go,' she said, putting the small rectangular package on Anna's lap. Her daughter looked at it suspiciously and put down her phone – on which Jessica had now installed WhatsApp on the understanding she might sometimes take a peek to check everything was OK.

'What's this for?'

'Oh, just for you.'

Anna pulled the paper off, still glancing suspiciously at her mother from time to time. Eventually she pulled out the beautiful, silk-covered book. 'It's pretty,' she said. 'What's it for?'

'It's a diary,' Jessica said, opening it to show Anna the golden embossed letters and thick cream-coloured paper.

'Oh.'

'You can write down how you feel, you know. That kind of diary.'

'I know. But I normally keep all that on my computer. You know, on my blog.'

'I know,' Jessica said, walking to the bookshelf and picking up her own new diary to show Anna. 'Me too. But I've started to wonder whether that's a good idea.'

'Too much screen time?'

'Well, yes. But more too much scrutiny.'

'What?'

'Too many people looking, the pressure to try to please other people.'

'I thought it was good to please other people? You said—'

'Oh it is!' Jessica said. 'Being nice, working hard, that kind of thing. But I mean the kind of . . . seeking approval, I suppose.'

'I don't do that though.'

'Have you ever,' Jessica said, sitting down next to her daughter, 'left something out of your blog because you thought people might not like what you've done or what you've thought?'

'Well, yeah.'

'And would you put private stuff, like, I don't know – a boy you fancy!'

'Mum!' Anna blushed. 'Of course not.'

'Then it's not a diary. Not really.'

'But what's the point?' Anna said after a moment's silence.

'What do you mean?'

'Well, no one sees it, so what's the point?'

'I suppose,' Jessica said, 'I've thought about it and I suppose that the point is that *we're* important too. How we feel, our private feelings.'

'Right?' Anna eyed her suspiciously.

'Look, just try it. I promise I'll never read it. You can lock it – look – if you're worried.'

'Ok. Thank you.'

That afternoon after Anna had gone to the cinema with Grahame to watch *Girls Go Shopping III* as a special treat (Jessica had booked the film and *forgotten* to tell Grahame the title until she'd handed over the tickets), Jessica walked to the Bridge Café to meet Robert.

It was a warmish afternoon, so she set off on foot, making her way through the park, but resisting the temptation to dive onto the roundabout (which in any case was covered in small children). She paused out of habit to take a selfie by the lake, which was shimmering in the sunlight, but instead chose to turn her phone around and take a picture of the scenery without her face gurning in the foreground.

She arrived at the café five minutes early, beating her power-walking target, and felt quite pleased with herself as she settled down at the only free table – Saturday afternoon was clearly peak café time.

The café bustled with life, families squeezing round tables and drinking milkshakes. Couples chatting over cappuccinos. There was a hum of noise and energy that felt infectious.

'Can I get you anything?' a young boy in a black shirt arrived at her side.

'Just a green . . . No. A cappuccino please,' she said, giving in to her inner child for once (although to be fair, she wasn't sure many children craved caffeine fixes).

'Anything else?' he asked.

'No, thank you.'

The waiter nodded and turned away.

'Actually,' she called after him. 'Actually, yes.'

Hearing her, he spun on his heel. 'Yes?'

'Yeah, sorry. Um, flapjack please,' she said. Which was a compromise, after all. Oats for health; butter for the inner child; sugar, well, it had never done her father any harm!

'Of course.' He turned towards the kitchen, scribbling in his notebook.

'With chocolate,' she added.

He turned again, gave her a nod and scuttled off as quickly as he could without running, before she could change her mind again.

Minutes later, she was biting into an enormous slab of buttery biscuit when she heard the words 'Jessica Bradley!'

in an unfamiliar voice. 'What *are* you eating?' She turned her head and was relieved to find Robert standing behind her, wagging a finger and putting on the voice of a critical parent.

'Sorry, *Mum*,' she said, grinning. 'My inner child was hungry.'

'I bet,' he replied, sitting down. 'You've been starving that poor little mite for years!'

'Thanks for meeting me,' she said, after he'd given his order. 'Especially after, well, you know.'

'Don't be silly,' he said. 'I want to help, if I can. Anna seems like a nice girl, I hate to think of her struggling.'

'Well, I appreciate it,' she said.

She told him about the train station, Anna's feelings of being lost, that she didn't fit in. The fact that Jessica had now reluctantly allowed her on WhatsApp. That she and Grahame had decided to work more closely together with the co-parenting. 'The thing is,' she said, 'I don't know whether I'm doing the right thing? It all seems . . . I don't know . . . such a mess.'

'So a normal childhood then?' Robert suggested.

'What?'

'How many of us had what we'd describe as a conventional, normal childhood?' he said. 'Once you start talking to people, you realise just how different our childhoods are. And I don't think anyone has one they see as perfect. Because life isn't perfect, and I suppose one of the lessons of childhood is accepting that.'

'Right? But there's a big gap between perfect and where I seem to be.'

'OK, maybe you've had your eye off the ball once or twice recently,' he said. 'And it's great that you and . . . and

Grahame are meeting up more and trying to work together. But you know, you're not doing such a bad job of it.'

'You think?'

'Absolutely. For a start, you care about it. You care whether you're doing a good job or not. Do you realise that you're already ahead of the game just by feeling like that?'

'Oh.'

'And Anna talks to you. Most of the time she tells you things. She trusts you.'

It was true. She always thought that she and Anna were quite open with each other. Until recently, of course.

'What about the chatroom stuff? I'm just . . . well, you read all these things about the bad effects. I said I'd never ever let her on WhatsApp, and yet here I am.'

'Yes,' he said. 'You listened. You weighed up the pros and cons and you made a decision. And you know that I'm no big fan of social media, but I think it was the right one.'

'Really?'

'Yes. This is the world Anna is growing up in. I suppose, it's the modern equivalent of letting her go out to play with her friends. It's limiting the time, I think, that's important. And I . . . I know I sometimes seem like I've got all the answers. But honestly, with my lot it's really, really hard. And then my ex, well, she has totally different rules from me. We clash a bit, I suppose. I feel like whatever I say gets ignored most of the time anyway.'

'Oh, Robert.'

'Yes. Not exactly finding the rainbows in my own life at the moment – with or without roundabouts and puddles,' he said. 'I'm sorry – we're meant to be talking about you. It's just . . . you're so easy to talk to. I've never really spoken about this before.'

'It's OK. I wish I could help.'

'You are, you know? Just by listening. By sharing your own stuff.'

'Thank you. And thanks for the advice. I feel so much better,' she said, taking a rather too-large bite of flapjack and feeling the oats tickle the back of her throat. She suppressed a cough, tears building in her eyes as she held herself back.

'Honestly, don't thank me. I'm not here to make you feel better – it might seem that way. But I would never mislead you when it comes to this stuff – it's too important. I'm saying this because I think it's true.'

She nodded, still trying not to choke and spray him with oats. Tears of effort gathered in her eyes.

'Hey,' he said. 'Don't cry.'

'It's the flapjack,' she tried to say. Too late, opening her mouth was the final release her throat needed and she coughed, raining fragments of oat and chocolate onto the table in front of her and flicking his face and shirt with half-chewed crumbs.

'Thank you very much,' he said, wiping a crumb from the corner of his eye and grinning. 'I was going to ask you if I could have a taste.'

'Oh! I'm so sorry, Rob!'

But he was smiling.

As their eyes locked she saw the whole thing from his perspective. Not horrible. Not embarrassing. Funny.

They began to laugh – the uninhibited, infectious giggles of childhood.

Chapter Fifty-One

'And you'll call me, won't you, if there's anything?' Jessica said for the fourth time, as she walked to the door.

'Of course,' Grahame answered.

'OK,' she said, steeling herself. It had been hard to leave Anna since the incident, but she had to let things get back to normal. Or, not exactly normal, but new and improved normal.

It had been the first time she'd set foot properly in Grahame's house. Thinking about it now, walking to her car, she felt quite embarrassed. He'd lived with Tabitha for almost a decade, been married to her for six. And of course it was difficult seeing her replacement and the babies that could have been hers. But the space between their two families had left a gap into which her daughter had fallen. And she wasn't going to let her pride damage Anna any longer.

She'd sat with Grahame and Tabitha while the twins played with Anna on the rug, giggling and chortling as their big sister zoomed their toy cars around and enjoyed taking the lead. It had been awkward. But not unbearable. And with time, it would get easier. Hopefully.

When she'd said goodbye and left Anna with her second family for the evening, her daughter had whispered a heartfelt thank you. 'I know that wasn't easy, Mum,' she'd said, sounding older than her years.

The journey to Bea's was only a couple of minutes, but

it took her at least five to park the car in one of the minuscule spaces left on the crowded street. Once she was fairly confident she'd got close enough to the kerb to avoid being rammed by a passing van, she locked the car and went to knock.

Bea answered the door. 'Right on time,' she grinned. 'I'm impressed.'

'And with chocolate,' Jessica grinned, waving the brightly coloured box as she walked into the house.

'Thanks, I think,' said Bea. 'Although I'm actually on a diet. Sort of.'

'What? Really?'

'Don't get too excited. I'm not going to start blogging about it or anything—'

'Hey!'

'And I'm definitely not going to be asking you for one of your seaweed and salad recipes.'

'Fair enough.'

'But I want to shed the few pounds of . . . of baby weight,' Bea said, her voice faltering slightly. 'From the boys. I never really . . . I suppose I never really addressed it because I always thought there'd be another . . .'

'Oh, Bea . . .'

'Don't,' said her friend. 'It's OK. It's got to be OK, hasn't it? I'm so much luckier than so many people.'

'Well, maybe we can do something together? No, no, don't look at me like that! I don't mean anything extreme.'

'Extreme, like going to the gym?'

'Yes, if you'd rather not. How about something outside? Walking, maybe?'

Bea looked at her midriff. 'Would take a LOT of walking to shift this.'

'You'd be surprised.'

'OK, we can always try.'

They grinned at each other for a moment. 'But no selfies,' Bea added. 'And definitely no tweeting.'

'No.'

'Or blogging.'

'Nope.'

'Just walking.'

'Just walking.'

'Anyway, you look great, baby weight or no baby weight,' Jessica said, perching on one of Bea's kitchen stools. It was true – Bea was wearing a red top with a sequinned neckline, and a slick of matching lipstick. She'd had her nails done and was wearing black, fitted trousers and red heels.

'You think?' Bea said, shifting slightly at the praise. 'I always feel a bit idiotic with lipstick.'

'Well, you shouldn't. It looks great. He's a lucky guy.'

'Oh am I?' said a voice behind her. Jessica turned to see Mark standing there in a blue checked shirt. He grinned at her.

'Hi, Mark,' she said. 'Yes, I think you know you are!'

'Well, I've escaped from twin story-time unscathed, so I suppose that's pretty lucky!' he joked.

'Oi!' Bea said, chucking a tea towel in his direction. It hit him in the face.

'Oh, that's nice, that is,' he said, chucking it back.

Bea giggled. 'Idiot.'

'Right back at you.'

The pair of them grinned at each other and Jessica suddenly felt a combination of jealousy and awkwardness. 'Anyway, I'll handle it from here,' she said. 'What time's lights out?'

'About nine-thirty, but don't worry if they can't settle. They've been a nightmare recently. Let them play for a bit.'

'Right-o.'

'And thanks, Jessica.'

'Don't be silly,' she smiled. In fact, she felt guilty that she hadn't babysat the twins for a while. She'd used to offer fairly frequently, despite the fact it could be hard work. But recently, Bea hadn't asked, and she hadn't offered.

'And look,' Bea said as she and Mark put on their coats to leave. 'How about getting together for a drink later in the week?'

'Yeah? Sounds good.'

'Come here – Mark can take the boys bowling so we can talk about wombs and vaginas and ovaries without any of them dying of embarrassment.'

'Do I get any say in this?' Mark quipped.

'Not a bit.'

She watched them walk towards their car, Mark's hand hovering by the small of Bea's back protectively, and felt suddenly alone. Bea and Mark had had their ups and downs, and more downs than seemed fair sometimes, but they'd made it through.

What had they got that she hadn't got?

Letting the curtain fall into place after giving them a final wave, she turned towards the stairs and went up to see the boys.

Chapter Fifty-Two

She knocked on the door and waited for him to answer. She'd checked, so she knew he'd be in this morning; she'd wanted to surprise him.

He answered the door and grinned. 'Hello, trouble,' he said. 'To what do I owe this honour?'

'I come bearing gifts,' she said, holding up the small rectangle she'd carried with her. 'And hopefully you've got time for a coffee?'

'None of that alternative stuff?'

'No, I'm keeping it real these days; at least when it comes to coffee!'

'So what's this for?' said Stuart as they walked through to the living room and she handed him the package wrapped in silver paper.

'I suppose it's a thank you. Or an apology,' she shrugged.

'Sounds like you should have got two presents,' he grinned, tearing off the paper to find the PS4 game he'd been lusting after but had been banned from buying by Erica. 'Wow, thank you!' he said. 'Although you'll get me in trouble with the Management.'

'I won't tell if you won't.'

'Ah, Miss Duplicitous strikes again.'

'Thank you.'

'Anyway, seriously. Apologising for what?' he said, as he sank into the sofa, making exactly the same groaning noise their father did, Jessica realised. Josh was there, crashing two cars together with his fists and laughing uproariously. Erica was at her mum's.

'Being a crap sister? Being jealous, I suppose? And thanking you for helping out with the whole Dave situation.' Jessica leaned forward and grabbed her nephew around the waist. He allowed her to lift him onto her lap, and snuggled against her, still clutching the cars.

'Jealous?'

'Yeah, you know. You did everything right. You were the one Mum and Dad always favoured. But it wasn't your fault.'

'Favoured me?' Stuart looked genuinely surprised. 'I always thought you were the one they were proudest of. *Oh, Jessica's business is doing SO well!*' he said, in a voice that sounded too much like their mother's for comfort. '*Oh, isn't Anna a lovely young girl! I don't know how she does it all by herself. AND her house is always spotless.*'

'You're kidding, Mum says that? She's always giving me advice on my love life, or implying that I need to have another baby. And telling me how great you are. And she's saying that to you?'

He nodded. 'Do you know,' he said, 'when that Henderson bloke won the award . . .'

'Hugo?'

'Yeah, the artist guy. Mum was going to buy a print of that picture of his, and frame it on their living-room wall. Me and Dad had to gang up on her to talk her out of it.'

'Oh God. Thank you, Stu.'

'Oh, no worries. Honestly. I did it for me. I'd never be able to eat one of Mum's muffins again with your, well, you know, staring at me.'

'Don't even joke about it.'

'But don't you think,' he said, more earnest now, 'that she

must have been really proud of you to want to display that? To not even think about . . . all the consequences?'

'I suppose . . .'

'There's no suppose about it. And you know, when he was in the *Guardian* on Saturday, she rang us up at six in the morning to tell us.'

'Oops. Sorry.'

'Not your fault.' He grinned. 'The point is, sis, I think you've probably been looking at things from the wrong angle.'

Maybe he was right, she thought as she drove home. Maybe she'd not recognised the good in her own life.

She reflected on the events of the last fortnight. She'd survived her honest blog post . . . just. It was early days, but after the initial online eruption, the internet had moved on to its next hero and victim.

Other than a couple of smaller clients expressing concern, her agency had remained largely unaffected. While her infamy might have encouraged clients to look her up, it certainly wasn't a condition of their staying. Besides, Linda at Little Accidents seemed delighted with the coverage they'd received so far. 'After all,' Linda had gushed on the phone, 'there's no such thing as bad publicity.'

Maybe not, Jessica had thought, but there is such thing as a bad product. She had decided to bite the bullet and part ways with the nappies in disguise, even though her revenue might take a hit.

She'd started to speak to a few fledgling non-fiction writers through MindHack publications and was beginning to look at new ways of promoting them. And Candice's blog, while only just up and running, would soon get noticed.

She'd even opened a new Twitter and Instagram – 'Just Jess.' Today she'd tweeted a positive mantra: *Open your heart*

and the rest will follow. #TrustYourself #BeStill @Jess-BB
@DrRobHaydn. She'd tagged Robert in to make sure he saw
it, after all, his book had been a big part of her journey.

'Oh no,' Bea had said when she'd told her, 'you're not
starting all over again, are you?'

'No,' she'd smiled. 'I'm hoping just to use them as a normal
person, just as myself.'

'Bit of an oversell, though!' Bea had replied.

'What is?'

'Describing yourself as normal!'

'Bea!'

When she'd met up with Dave the previous week and told
him that things just weren't going to work out, she'd felt
such a sense of relief. As if she could finally relax. He'd taken
it well, although had asked whether he could still tag her in
some of his Instagram posts.

She still had a couple of sessions booked with Nelly; after
all, it wasn't the gym that had made her unhappy, but the
need to sculpt her body into almost impossible perfection.
She still wanted to keep as much distance as possible between her arse and the floor.

She pulled up outside the office and saw that Robert's
car was already there, waiting. But before getting out, she
checked her mobile phone quickly to see if there were any
updates – then froze.

Her mantra, picked up by Robert's followers, had been
retweeted over two thousand times.

Acknowledgements

Thank you to Victoria, Alex and Olivia at Orion for their help and guidance – and for believing in me as a writer. And to my agent Ger Nichol of the Book Bureau for her encouragement and support.

Thanks to Natalie Trice for her PR insight.

Thank you, too, to Ray for putting up with my ups and downs and for being willing to read drafts whenever required. And to Lily, Joe, Tim, Evie and Robbie for only bursting through my office door occasionally when I was scribbling away.

Finally, thanks to Eve, Ema and Judith from my little writers' group, who lifted me up and kept me writing through difficult times.

Credits

Gillian Harvey and Orion Fiction would like to thank everyone at Orion who worked on the publication of *Everything is Fine* in the UK.

Editorial
Victoria Oundjian
Olivia Barber

Copy editor
Justine Taylor

Proof reader
John Garth

Audio
Paul Stark
Amber Bates

Contracts
Anne Goddard
Paul Bulos
Jake Alderson

Design
Debbie Holmes
Joanna Ridley

Editorial Management
Charlie Panayiotou
Jane Hughes
Alice Davis

Finance
Jasdip Nanra
Afeera Ahmed
Elizabeth Beaumont
Sue Baker

Production
Ruth Sharvell

Marketing
Tanjiah Islam

Publicity
Alex Layt

Rights
Susan Howe

Krystyna Kujawinska
Jessica Purdue
Richard King
Louise Henderson

Sales
Jen Wilson
Esther Waters
Victoria Laws
Rachael Hum

Ellie Kyrke-Smith
Frances Doyle
Georgina Cutler

Operations
Jo Jacobs
Sharon Willis
Lisa Pryde
Lucy Brem